Princess Sarah

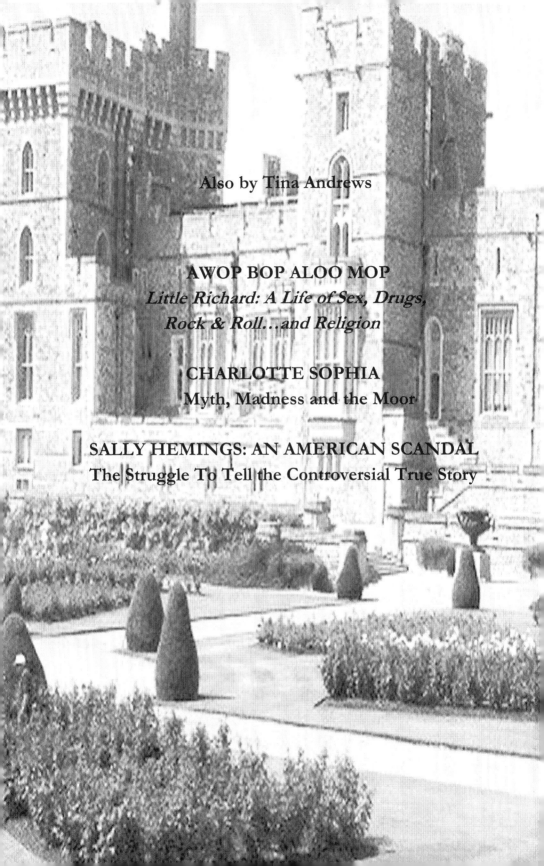

Also by Tina Andrews

AWOP BOP ALOO MOP
Little Richard: A Life of Sex, Drugs,
Rock & Roll…and Religion

CHARLOTTE SOPHIA
Myth, Madness and the Moor

SALLY HEMINGS: AN AMERICAN SCANDAL
The Struggle To Tell the Controversial True Story

Princess Sarah

QUEEN VICTORIA'S AFRICAN GODDAUGHTER

a novel

TINA ANDREWS

THE MALIBU PRESS
New York Los Angeles London

Rights inquiries should be made to:
Rights Manager, The Malibu Press,
954 Lexington Ave., Suite 505
New York, NY 10021
info@themalibupress.com

The Malibu Press logo and colophon are registered
trademarks of The Malibu Press, a division of
The Malibu Press Publishing Group, LLC

ISBN 10: 099822605X
ISBN 13: 9780998226057

Library of Congress Cataloging-in-Publication Data has been applied for.

Limited Special First Edition

Printed in the United States of America

[Preceding pages: Windsor Castle, circa 1840]

For

Donald, Beverly,
Rachel, Kim & Neal

The great joys of my life

Aina (Sarah Forbes Bonetta) a child

Contents

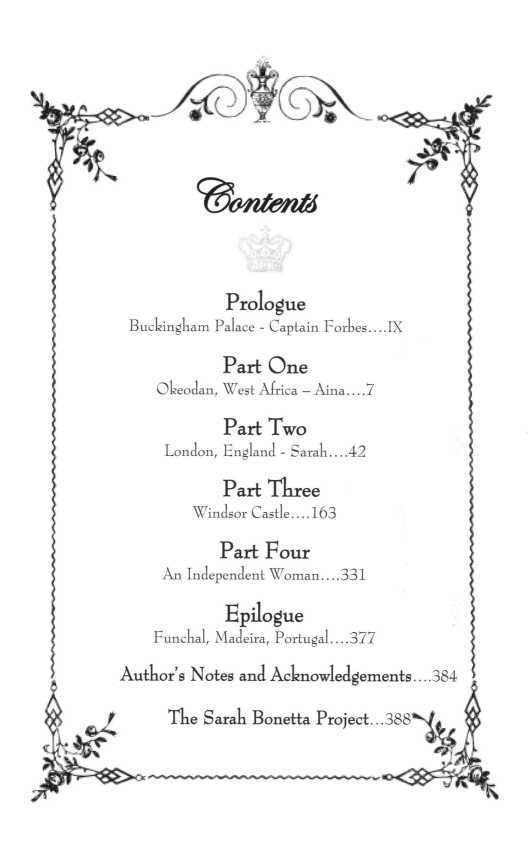

African slavers transporting slaves to Whydah Port,
West Africa

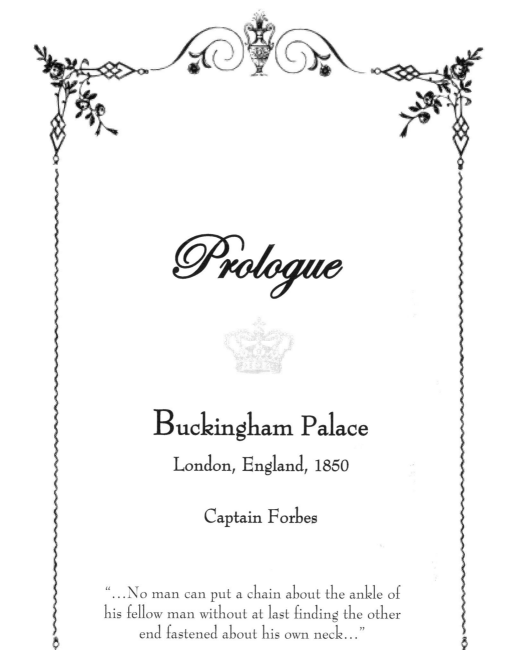

Prologue

Buckingham Palace

London, England, 1850

Captain Forbes

"…No man can put a chain about the ankle of
his fellow man without at last finding the other
end fastened about his own neck…"

Frederick Douglass

Sarah Forbes Bonetta (circa 1860)

er unsteady hand lifted the pen and dipped it into her favorite silver inkpot given to her by the man she had loved. As its nib anxiously scratched against the smooth parchment paper which lay before her, she stopped a moment to assess her life. A slight smile crossed her face as she gazed upon all of her books. Hundreds of them, which she had collected over the last twenty years, were arranged on beautifully built bookcases near her hospital bed in Funchal, brought in by her husband. They gave her so much joy just to see them.

She nodded, then drew in a deep breath. But a coughing fit took her over for a few moments leaving her weak. After sipping some water, she steadied herself for she had to finish these entries into her journal—the only thing left for her to do in this world. And she had to do it before it was too late.

8 January 1880
Funchal, Madeira, Portugal

My dearest daughter Victoria,

There is a proverb the ancestors say—'If you speak the words of your life aloud, you gain a new perspective on the truth of it—even if no one ever hears your words.' These are my truths.

I was born Princess Aina Okonjo of Okeodan, West Africa. I am an Egbado Omobo. Yoruba royalty. My perspective on the experiences which have shaped my existence are naturally heightened as I lay here in Madeira awaiting my ultimate demise. But I pray that you will come to understand my mystifying yet deferential relationship with your namesake, and know my whole story, from my deepest heart, before I close my eyes and meet the maker of all things...

On a rainy, chilly April day, one ever so typical in London, a horse-drawn carriage pulled in front of what had become, by 1850, one of the most iconic royal residences in the world. Buckingham Palace. Four British Grenadier Guards in full-dress red tunics, wearing tall, black, bearskin hats, stood at the entrance. The flag was flying which indicated the British sovereign was in residence, and an air of regal sobriety permeated.

Inside the carriage driven by his longtime employee, Mr. Nelson, was Captain Frederick E. Forbes, a handsome, thirty-nine-year-old British naval officer. Forbes eyed the guards a moment in both awe and terror. He needed to steady his nerves as he had been summoned to the palace by one of the most powerful sovereigns in the world, Alexandrina Victoria, Queen of England, and he wondered why he was asked, as he was neither a royal nor a member of the aristocracy.

As he gazed upon the limestone edifice of Buckingham, he removed a polished silver flask given to him by his wife from his inside pocket. He took a swig of rum to fortify himself as a footman opened his carriage door. He nervously swallowed and began tugging at his blue military jacket hoping he looked serious and respectful for her Majesty.
Then Captain Forbes found his comportment and confidently strode into the palace.

Once inside, he was immediately met by Buckingham's stern-looking Lord Chamberlain, John Campbell, the 2nd Marquess of Breadlebane. Lord John had been a friend of Victoria's since 1840, three years after she became Queen, and his wife, Lady Elizabeth Campbell, was the Queen's Lady of the Bedchamber. They were two of Victoria's favorites.

Lord John took Forbes up the winding stairs to the red parlor for his audience with the Queen. Forbes already knew the proper protocol for meeting a sovereign. You waited for him or her to extend their hand, bowed from the neck down, then went to her or him, bowed again and shook their hand, or if a female, kissed her hand.

"Your Majesty, Captain Frederick Forbes." Lord John announced.

As Forbes listened to the beating of his heart he looked the Queen in the eye—something one was not supposed to do—but he could not help it. She was diminutive, barely five feet tall, and not a raving beauty. But at thirty-eight years old there was something about her that was uniquely authoritative and appealing, and when she smiled she could light up a room with the warmth of a thousand suns. He knew she had been a neglected teenager born Alexandrina Victoria Hanover but deeply disliked her given name. Thus, upon becoming Queen at age 18, she insisted on using her second name by which she was universally renown.

After dismissing Lord John, Victoria held out her hand. Forbes bowed, went over, bowed again, then kissed it. "Your Majesty."

"Captain. How is your family? Well I hope?" Victoria smiled brightly allowing her teeth to show which was not something she did often. It made Forbes' heart leap.

"All very well, ma'am. My wife, Mary sends her regards."

"How nice." The Queen indicated that he sit across from her on the light blue tufted settee.

"Then I shall get to the point. You are Chief Commander of my West African Squadron. As such, at the behest of Parliament, I have selected you for a mission regarding the suppression of the slave trade. This year, since Louis-Napoleon made France a Republic, and declared himself Emperor, he has rightfully re-abolished not only slavery but the slave trade on French soil. Now, they are determined to keep the Africans from selling their own people to other countries as slaves. This is quite a noble cause. But I shall not allow France to supersede England on a point of morality. Thus, we must exert our influence within our West African territories to stop the people there from selling one another into the trade."

So, Forbes thought, this audience with her Majesty was about her own sense of self-importance. Making sure Britain stayed ahead of France as a world power and leader of social and racial equity. Yes, it was noble indeed—on the face of it at least.

"Well, if I may, Majesty, the King of Dahomey does not see himself as 'selling their own.' He engages in intertribal wars and sells their 'prisoners' as slaves." Forbes then cleared his throat. "The Trade accounts for 80% of West Africa's economy. The money slavers make outweighs any concern they may have for the freedom of their enemies—especially when there is so much money in the production of sugar, cotton and tobacco for them *not* to sell slaves."

"Quite right," Victoria nodded. "Such insights are why I am sending you to the Kingdom of Dahomey."

The moment he heard the word *Dahomey*, Forbes' heart sank. He hated Dahomey, its people, and most especially its king, all barbarians and heathens to him. But he said nothing to the Queen.

"Since you are experienced with the Dahomeans, I want you to go to King Gezo's court and have him sign a treaty we've drawn up."

Forbes tried to keep his face serious and frozen neutral lest he give away his complete disgust for the place—and her request. But his brow betrayed his disdain by furling into a frown. Yes, he did indeed know those particular West Africans—especially the ones in Dahomey whose cruelty to one another was unmatched. His trip there in 1848 was enough to poison his good opinion of the entire continent forever. He saw for himself how, on orders from a sadistic and beastly king, the soldiers and Amazon warrior women captured natives of their own race, pillaged and decimated their villages, then sold the prisoners to white slavers from any country in need of free labor who had money. And, if the prisoners protested, they would be exterminated in the most heinous and merciless way.

"If I may, ma'am," he started, speaking slowly so not to reveal how much this task abhorred him. "Would not Lord Palmerston be better equipped for this task—he being the Foreign Secretary who used secret service funds to authorize the navy to board Brazilian slave ships, and destroy the property of slave traders?"

"He *illegally* boarded those Brazilian ships, Captain. So, if I had wanted Lord Palmerston I would have commissioned Lord Palmerston," Victoria snipped. "Besides, he's far too rude and impudent. He lacks your sense of diplomacy and, dare I say it, well-bred English decorum. Palmerston would start a war in Dahomey we can ill afford. No, it shall be you."

"But why would King Gezo's people agree to it?" wondered Forbes aloud. "And what is in it for us? England abolished the Trade in your grandfather's day?"

The Queen was growing weary of Forbes' resistance. "Contained in the treaty is a clause. If Gezo signs, England shall, for six years, control all the palm oil their land makes. They would make a tidy sum. So, I need you to encourage them to accept this money, not blood money."

Forbes frowned slightly. "What are the French offering?"

"That is what you must find out. Hopefully, Gezo will agree to our terms, sign the treaty, and make the world a better place."

"And if he does not?"

"One is hopeful."

Hope was all they really had, thought Forbes as he considered what his Queen was asking of him.

"On one condition," he heard himself say.

The Queen's congenial face now dropped in indignation. It was apparent Forbes was disinterested in this mission.

"One has 'conditions', sir?" she asked coolly.

"Yes. Lieutenant David Brandon must come to assist me."

Victoria brightened again. "Granted. Sir Charles Phipps will take care of your seafaring needs…" she smiled despite herself and stood, "…Which I understand involves a good deal of rum?"

Forbes smiled and stood as well. Victoria rang for Lord John indicating his audience was over. Forbes bowed, and backed from the room.

Later that week, Lt. David Brandon, a forty-year-old, Scottish navy officer with auburn hair, was clutching his crucifix praying on the docks of Gravesend Port of London. The ship he was assigned to was docked just behind him proudly bearing the insignia: 'HMS BONETTA.'

Seconds later, his prayers were interrupted by Lt. Peter Gibson, a ruggedly handsome blond officer assigned to the same ship who looked far older than his thirty-eight years.

"You'll need more than God where we're going, Brandon," said Gibson as he pulled a flask of rum from his uniform. "These savages require rum. And lots of it." He took a swig, then handed the flask to Brandon who also took a swig—then another one.

Soon they heard: "Gibson, Brandon!"

The men turned to find Forbes grinning. "I should have known I'd find you two drinking on the job before we set sail." They all hugged as Forbes snatched the flask from Brandon and had his own swig of the rum. "Thank God for reinforcements."

"Aye, Captain," laughed Brandon. "She sent 100 kegs."

Forbes nodded. Now he finally felt the mission was worthwhile. "You have to love Her Majesty. She truly understands men."

And war, he thought.

Part One

KINGDOM OF DAHOMEY
WEST AFRICA, 1848

Aina

*"…She shall be a gift from the King of the Blacks,
to the Queen of the Whites."*

King Gezo of Dahomey, West Africa

*King Gezo's men capturing Yoruba slaves in Okeodan,
Dahomey, West Africa*

One

Oh, how well I remember it. It was late summer in the year of our Lord, 1848. The day my life inextricably changed forever. It had been a beautiful, cloudless morning, not unlike many in my life in Okeodan. Warm, with a gentle breeze just licking across the densely forested terrain, slightly cooling our idyllic village.

I loved days like this—and this day in particular, for it was my commitment day. My Kwanjula. Everyone was preparing for the ceremony to be held later, and gifts of cowries, cloth, and beads had been presented to me and my family all morning.

Just outside our large, luxurious hut children played, my grandmother Kiriki was crushing maize with her withered fingers, and women were gossiping. My younger brother Nadir, age 7, and my older brother, Kenge, who at 13 was four years older than me, were playing a wicked game of Qudon. It was a kind of Cricket which had migrated from South Africa, and was played with a long, paddle-shaped stick you smashed against a ball made from a gourd stuffed with mud and feathers, covered in leather held together with shaved reeds. A game which had migrated from South Africa. I loved hearing their laughter as they played against the other boys in our village. The Egbado Yorubas were a peaceful people.

That afternoon, there was great commotion and celebration. Okeodan men were pounding Djembe drums—fingers in frenetic, sweaty syncopation and everyone was dressed in colorful clothing, dancing the Ya Moto Dance *around a large fire. I was dancing too—with Kua, my fiancé, who was fourteen, tall and muscular. I loved watching him move—seeing his confident, sinewy body pulsate to the rhythms and give in to the beat as it drove him. He was something to watch.*

We loved dancing and each other. Kua had been 'assigned' to me at birth. As the son of the Bouhula—the medicine man, and second highest, most important advisor in our village—Kua was to marry the daughter of the Chief, which was my father, Prince Derefaka. We had grown up together knowing our day of Kwanjula was already arranged. So even as small children we were always together.

I liked Kua. He was fun, considerate, and protective. A true knight. He had leadership abilities and was learning how to cure—like his father and be the next Bouhula. I learned many healing techniques from him.

So when our day of Kwanjula arrived, I was more than ready to be Kua's 'Kwanjulli'—his wife, and later bear him the children we both wanted. In the meantime, we would dance, and thank the Gods for true love. Yes, we were very young, but the ceremony was always, for the woman, in her ninth or tenth moon.

As we danced around the fire, I saw my mother, Akinyi, dancing with Father, who, at thirty-five was the most handsome man in Okeodan. Kua was sheepishly grinning at me, and then stole a kiss. I gasped because no touching was allowed between the would-be spouses the day of the wedding until they had been carried across the threshold into their new hut. But I will admit I did like it, and I loved his tenderness. I was happy. I would marry the boy I loved. All in my world was good, and as the drums beat I could see a future which lay brightly before me.

Unbeknownst to Aina, a few well-toned Africans were furtively crawling through the bushes toward the Okeodan village. They were armed with swords, machetes, and some had scimitars between their teeth. Finally, they encircled several huts, and the dancing villagers. A cock crowed, setting off an echoing chorus—and the face of a Dahomean warrior became visible. Vicious, dark, and muscular, the whites of his eyes, yellow and sinister, he made a war cry prompting hundreds of fellow warriors to stand up and cry out. Suddenly they attacked. Among them were the ferocious Amazon women warriors who fought hard and were as deadly as the men.

With weapons and eyes on fire, they began killing mercilessly, severing heads from the bodies of innocent, defenseless villagers frightened out of their minds. Huts were set on fire, and pandemonium ensued.

Aina clutched Kua, scared to death. Kua, trying to be a brave warrior, grabbed a sword from a dead villager wanting to defend his fiancée and her family. But Aina gasped when she saw a machete blade rise up...

...then slice down on Kua's neck and in an instant, the love of her young life was dead—his blood having splashed on her body.

Aina screamed and began running for her life. Her heart pumping, her body hurtling through the low brush like a fast racehorse. There was no time to grieve as Dahomean warriors chased her through the rugged jungle terrain.

But though Aina was fast and had been known for her speed against all the other boys in her village, she was no match for the Dahomean warriors pursuing her. A net was thrown, and the Princess of Okeodan was caught in it. Kicking and screaming nine-year-old Aina was dragged back to the other warriors where she saw the continuing warfare and violence. Through the night, families attempting to flee were silenced by death one by one. Desperate howling and crying echoed through the darkness, and Aina choked on her tears as hope for her own life drained from her body.

And then she saw it—and cried out. There amongst a pile of dead villagers were the bodies of her mother, father, brothers—and Kua before the Dahomean warriors set fire to them and next, her village.

The following morning as the sun ascended from the far reaches of the ocean, the chants of glory could be heard from the warriors as their captives including Aina—walked shackled together, pulled along through their destroyed huts and villages, and down the long red clay road toward Abomey, the capital of Dahomey. She and the others trodded five meters in silence afraid to look up for fear the taker of all things, death, would brutally come. By the time they reached King Gezo's palace in Abomey late that afternoon, Aina's feet were swollen and her wrists bloody from the metal manacles cutting into her flesh. She realized that despite being a royal, she was now a slave prisoner.

A select group of prisoners were pulled up the steps of the market place in the center of town just behind Simbodji Palace, Gezo's palatial compound where Aina, who was among them, could see Amazon women dancing vigorously in bright colors and head gear. The Dahomean warriors surrounded the perimeter of the arena space and monitored all things as spectators circled the barricaded palace to see how victorious they had been.

On the platform arena, called an *Ah-toh*, was a section of seats, one of them larger than the others, all outfitted with large umbrellas to shield against the harsh sun. This was for King Gezo, and the smaller seats for his Chiefs, advisors and cronies. Aina and the other Okeodan captives were pushed toward the back of the staging area, whipped into submission and ordered to sit.

Soon Gezo's wives, who were all tall, deadly Amazons, came out and circled the throne area. Next emerged five chiefs, two advisors, three elders who sat, a medicine man…

…And then, finally, King Gezo himself appeared.

As he strode out and stood before his subjects thunderous cheering and chants rose from the crowd of onlookers. He grinned at his reception and held his arms up as they continued lionizing him.

At forty-eight, King Gezo was tall, muscular, sinister looking, and commanding. Tribal scars adorned his blue-black face and his large eyes, yellow from a malarial jaundice, lit fire as he announced to the crowd in native Fon language: "The Yorubas are ours in Okeodan!"

The crowd yelled and stomped. Warriors roared their approval. Chiefs nodded and raised their hands in the air in endorsement.

"Two hundred years ago, King Gangnihessou received power from the Great Creator-Mother, Goddess Mawuh, by slitting the belly of a captured Prince and burying his body beneath this very palace," Gezo continued. "It is how our Kingdom got its name—Dahomey. So, in honor of Gangnihessou and to continue our power, I, Gezo, dada and ninth King of Dahomey, announce the *Seh que ah ee*—the watering of the graves, will COMMENCE TOMORROW!"

Chanting was deafening from all in the area. So much so that it frightened Aina. The natives screamed "Gezo the King!" over and over. Then the music and dance began again and lasted all through the night.

At one in the morning, several captives were pushed into a holding room just past the palace with bars on the windows. Gezo's guards surrounded the room. Strong looking Okeodan men were kneeling on the ground, praying, helpless. Women were crying.

> "…It was into this room I was thrown. As I focused on where I was and what my fate may be, I witnessed a white Portuguese slave dealer negotiating with King Gezo in what must have been their usual routine. It was all in Fon and the exchange was almost humorous.
>
> "8,500 cowries for the lot," Gezo insisted.
>
> "7,000 is my final offer," countered the slave dealer.
>
> "You rob your best customer? 8,000."
>
> "7,500 cowries it is, then."
>
> Gezo grinned. "Thief!" then motioned to his chief negotiator to complete the transaction with the slave dealer while Gezo moved to inspect his prisoners. Many of us were being stripped of our clothing. Some of us were chosen to be covered in white cloth. I was one of these. Some of the prisoners

were petrified, and some cried. Gezo soon came over to me and looked me over menacingly. I was numb. I could neither cry nor pray. But when Gezo saw the tribal scars on my shoulder he became curious—and spoke to me in Fon.

"So, you are the Princess of Okeodan?"

"Yes," I answered flatly.

He grinned with ominous relish and nodded to an aide to unlock my manacles. I rubbed the raw, scraped area of my wrist as Gezo's eyes narrowed, "'Then you will give your most precious gift to my people." His gaze on me suddenly became deadly. "Your life."

But I, being a proud, outspoken girl, showed no sign of fear even though my insides shook violently. "This I do gladly," I said in Fon. Then I spit at him. Before he could hit me, there came a knock followed by a servant who entered with a letter and prostrated himself before Gezo. "Her Majesty Victoria, the Queen of England has written, Honorable one," he began, then handed Gezo the letter. "Her representative, Captain Forbes, arrives in the morning. She wants an audience with you for him." Gezo smirked.

"Yes, yes. "Stop slavery," "free slaves." "Stop the Trade." She's a tiresome white Queen who wants the Trade to end. But England, France, Spain—they all began the Trade. It made them rich and fat. Now they say they want no more and to stop it. But Gezo wants more. Send the new interpreter to meet them."

The servant nodded and left. Then Gezo looked back at me and narrowed his eyes. "Yes, you will satisfy the Gods well, royal one. And I will keep you here to remind me I have the greatest prize. the Princess of Okeodan."

King Gezo held me captive for two years. I never knew when I was going to die…until the year the British Queen sent Captain Frederick E. Forbes back to Dahomey…

King Gezo of Dahomey, West Africa, 1850

Two

The new day dawned with a sweltering, humid morning as Captain Forbes stood on deck of the HMS Bonetta looking at the approaching landmass. Whydah Port in the Kingdom of Dahomey on the West African gold coast was dead ahead, but its dread had occupied his mind for a month. Only for the Queen, who, like the rest of England, he adored, would he even return to this horrid place.

The last time he was in Africa proved so displeasurable, he told his wife Mary upon his return that he was considering resigning from the Anti slave trade squadron to which the Queen had personally assigned him.

Twice he was almost killed by rebel soldiers and Amazon warrior women, and twice he had come down with raving dysentery. He simply hated Africa. He hated slavery too, but the idea that Africans would capture and sell their own into it or subject their victims to such heinous torture, was too sickening to overcome. Dahomey alone was exporting the largest number of Africans in the Atlantic slave trade with more than 5 million men, women, and children sold into slavery.

Now here he was, 2 years later, coming back to the same godforsaken place and he had no idea what he'd face this time. When he had come in 1848, he was summoned to Abomey, the capital of Dahomey, where he found himself in the center of town—a place known for its fiercely militaristic society hellbent on conquest by the vilest king Forbes had ever encountered—King Gezo. Gezo's soldiers struck fear into their enemies all along the Slave Coast because he had ascended the throne after overthrowing his equally cruel brother, King Adandozan, in a coup d'état. It was Gezo's ambition to show off the finest fighting unit in his army to his European guests… his Amazon warrior women.

The Dahomean soldiers were already a fearsome sight, barefoot and bristling with clubs and knives. Some, known as Reapers, were armed with gleaming three-foot-long straight razors, and each was capable of two-handedly slicing a man clean in two.

But it was the Amazon warrior women who inspired awe. These women knew how to stealthily advance in silence and overcome any obstacle—including the protection walls around most of the cities, which were over ten feet with huge piles of acacia branches bristling with needle-sharp thorns, forming a barricade stretching almost 440 yards.

The Amazons would rush it, furiously ignoring the wounds that the two-inch-long thorns inflicted on them, and after scrambling to the top, began hand-to-hand combat with defenders, then storm a group of huts dragging the cringing "prisoners" to Gezo's location miles away.

Forbes had seen the bravest Amazons awarded by Gezo with belts made from acacia thorns. Proud to show themselves impervious to pain, the women warriors would strap their trophies around their waists. Forbes had also remembered meeting the Amazon general who led the assault and found her captivating. She was slender but shapely and had a proud bearing with no affectation. She wasn't tall or excessively muscular. But then, the general was a woman, as were all her troops.

Now it was 1850 and King Gezo had expanded the number of women soldiers to 6,000 – roughly half of his fighting forces. When, or why he recruited female soldiers was not clear in Forbes' mind. But one theory traced their origins to becoming palace guards who were formed from among King Gezo's "third class" wives—the ones he considered too ugly to share his bed who had not borne him children.

Nonetheless, Forbes considered them extremists and was not anxious to cross paths with them, nor their king. All he wanted was a meeting with Gezo to discuss the treaty, for Gezo to sign it, and he'd go home to London. With that, all would be well in his world.

Now, after a long thirty-five-day journey from Gravesend port of London, stopping at three ports along Africa's Gold Coast for supplies and fresh water, the HMS Bonetta finally moored at Whydah port on a Tuesday morning. Forbes noted in his ship's log that he'd landed safely with Lt. Brandon and a crew of fifty, and that they would immediately go to Abomey and get the business at hand taken care of.

The way Whydah port was situated required a ship to be moored over a mile from shore as there were no natural deep-water ports along the West African coast. Transportation to and from ship was by means of a surfboat or canoes called *'Kroo canoes'*. It meant loading and discharging of all goods, including slaves, took place off open beaches sometimes buffeted by strong surf varying in depth, tides and currents. Thus, getting from the ship to shore could be dangerous and bad weather could cause delays. Plus, there was always the possibility of loss of cargo. Many a slave drowned on the way to a slave ship when their Kroo canoes toppled over due to strong currents.

As Forbes and Brandon came onto shore from their canoe wet and tired, a thin, cheery-faced African, Emeka Dikeledi, had tied off three camels on the dock. He rushed frantically to the military-dressed white men he saw disembarking from the canoes on shore. "Captain Forbes...?" inquired the African curiously.

"Yes," said Forbes, who then pointed to Brandon. "And this is my first—Lt. Brandon."

"Me, Emeka, the King's emmi, uh, emmi..." he couldn't remember the translation and was embarrassed that his English was so poor.

"Emissary," Forbes offered.

"Yes. Emissary. Get here safe?"

But before Forbes could respond, Brandon rudely interjected, "Aye...since we are here."

Understanding English far better than he spoke it, Emeka glared at Brandon, before gesturing the men toward the camels. "Come. Ride to Abomey."

Brandon grunted, then protesting loudly he leaned into Forbes, "Please tell me we're not riding camels 25 meters to Dahomey's capital?"

But Forbes answered by mounting a camel forcing Brandon to grumble in frustration.

When finally the Englishmen and Emeka reached Abomey, their ultimate destination was in fact a large grass and mud hut. It was all Brandon could do not to scream in dissatisfaction as the three men dismounted their camels. "What did you expect?" Forbes smirked to his cohort, "The Rose and Crown Inn?"

Guards were watching the hut as Emeka showed the Englishmen in. "Come. Sleep here, eat here," – which was an undesirable invitation to which Brandon grumbled, "Time for a drink," and he took a swig of rum from the flask in his pocket.

Worn out from travel, the men wandered about the hut filled with Dahomean delicacies of fruit, food and drink. Brandon said nothing for fear he'd be killed for his insolence as Forbes turned to Emeka who was sneaking food. "So, when do we meet his Majesty?" he asked, anxious to get negotiations started and leave this godforsaken place.

Less concerned with Forbes' frustration, than hiding his culinary cache, Emeka replied, "Celebration with the, er, gods first."

"So...when do we meet *His Majesty*?" Forbes repeated.

"Seh que ah ee, first. Water graves!"

Forbes had no clue what "water graves" nor the Fon language term Emeka used meant. But he forced himself to maintain what the Queen had called his "Well-bred English decorum."

"But when is that? Today? Tomorrow?"

Emeka patronized Forbes with a non-answer, "Yes, yes."

Now Forbes was as frustrated with Emeka as Brandon, and the two Englishmen looked at each other trying to stay calm.

"Please thank his Majesty for us," motioned the Captain of her Majesty's ship Bonetta, and he escorted Emeka to the door. Brandon gave the African a patronizing wave goodbye then looked around the hut once Emeka was gone.

"25 fucking miles smelling camel shit, an idiot interpreter, and now dirt floors. Who did I kill in my last life!" he lamented.

Forbes responded by pulling out his own flask, taking a long dose of rum, then dipping a finger in the lamb stew. "'Water Graves' must be a metaphor, and not us watering actual graves."

Brandon grabbed some water from a wooden bowl and sipped it. He disgustedly spit it out. "What the hell is this?"

Forbes, needing to stay focused on their mission, found himself scolding his friend. "David, please."

Brandon heeded his superior's request, "Okay, what is our plan?"

"I don't bloody know," lamented Forbes. "How do we get Gezo to sell Britain Palm Oil when he earns £50,000 a year selling slaves to the world?"

Hearing that, Brandon spit out the stew. "Hell, *I* should sell slaves."

As sunset descended on Simbodji Palace, many Dahomeans dressed in ceremonial robes were celebrating. Male soldiers and Amazon female warriors danced to drummers.

In the center of the marketplace was a platform enclosed by colorful cloth, surmounted by tents with skulls, tobacco, cowries and cloth.

A wooden ladder jutted from the platform to the ground. On the edge of the platform were a few prisoners dressed in white cloth. Aina and others were in small, canoe-like baskets carried by muscular Dahomeans, as Amazons danced onto the platform.

Forbes and Brandon, escorted by soldiers and Emeka, walked through, and climbed the ladder onto the platform just as King Gezo appeared, surrounded by his chiefs. Gezo was greeted with celebratory traditional shouts as he gestured for Forbes and Brandon to sit. Emeka stood by to interpret.

Three hours of celebrating had passed as Forbes, Brandon and three chiefs remained with Gezo, and Emeka continued to interpret. Then finally, Forbes was able to state his case.

"We suggest instead of selling your prisoners—make them better your own country. Make them cultivate the soil and plant things. In turn, sign this treaty and England will purchase your Palm oil exclusively."

He passed the treaty to Gezo. But the king was no dummy and said in his native Fon, "The slave trade is the source of our wealth and power." He then gestured to Emeka to make sure this was relayed in English with the right emphasis. It was. Then Forbes tried an additional tact. "If you sign the treaty, Her Majesty will send you a financial present for the first six years."

Suddenly Gezo stopped speaking in Fon and held his hand up for Emeka to stop interpreting. He turned to Forbes and looked at the Captain incredulously. Then he spoke in perfect English.

"Captain, Palm oil is not as lucrative as humans. Palm oil will not process sugar nor cotton, nor tobacco," Gezo informed. "Your King lady seems serious. But so am I. Whydah port must stay open to my ships—or bad things happen."

Forbes could not contain his shock that the king was bilingual and had understood English all this time. He stared at Brandon who was just as surprised.

Upon seeing both Englishmen's astonishment, Gezo smirked in sinister enjoyment.

"Do not presume the King of an African country cannot speak English."

It took Forbes a moment to recover, but he did—and he neither liked the subterfuge nor did he take well to the threat. Through clenched teeth he seethed, "King Gezo..."

But Gezo continued in English unfazed, "Ships will continue to pass in my name to the Brazils to carry slave cargo…"

"No," Forbes threatened.

They will bring back goods to us for sale to the world..."

"No! That is not the deal, Majesty!" Forbes warned.

Gezo glared at the Captain, narrowing his eyes. For just a moment Brandon became nervous that they might be killed. But Gezo half-smirked.

"Good negotiations depend on both sides giving up something," he chuckled. "What are you English prepared to give up?"

Forbes looked at Brandon stumped by the question.

Then the king stared at the treaty, "How much the first year?"

Surprised by the turnabout, Forbes hurriedly offered, "Enough for you to acclimatize."

There was dead silence—then gales of laughter from Gezo, followed by his men laughing too.

"*Acclimatize*," Gezo half mocked. "You English. Always ready to make a deal to favor yourselves." He swatted away a few flies and helped himself to a generous portion of lamb sitting in front of them. "Alright, gentlemen. This is how it will go. I will not sign the treaty. Tell your Queen, England is rich enough off our backs. She will leave us alone, let me run my country—and she keeps open the ports to my ships. No negotiation."

Forbes knew trouble lay ahead with this gesture. "King Gezo..."

But Gezo's hand went up to stop Forbes from continuing. He wiped his mouth and raised up to his full six-foot-three-inch height.

"We water graves now. Come."

Moments later, Gezo, the Chiefs, and Emeka escorted the Englishmen outside of the palace compound. They all sat under the umbrellas on the raised platform of the marketplace arena facing the people. Soon, eight naked Amazon warrior women walked out armed with hatchets and scimitars as King Gezo waved his hand to the cheering crowd. Brandon turned to Emeka, "What is happening?"

"We water graves now," Emeka responded nonchalantly.

Forbes then saw several small canoe baskets loaded with people—including one with a girl inside—Aina.

"And who are those people?"

Again, Emeka was matter-of-fact. "They die! You enjoy! We dance. Gods will be pleased. Kill Yorubas."

Forbes and Brandon froze in horror. Gezo whispered to Emeka, who looked at the two Englishmen.

"King say you witness sacrifice," said Emeka.

Brandon's eyes widened as Forbes implored Emeka, "Tell the King...God...tell him, I beg of him, do not do this!"

Forbes pushed Emeka forward. Emeka whispered to Gezo who laughed, waved him off, and danced with several of his warrior wives. The mob went wild with applause.

"Stop this! Stop it!" Forbes yelled.

Brandon clutched his crucifix as Gezo shook his head, his face serious as he spoke to Forbes. "No stomach for our customs, eh? You English killed Africans for centuries to fatten your purses. Today these Africans will die for our gods. You WILL watch. It is a good lesson in negotiation."

He signaled a soldier. All dancing and singing stopped while the Yorubas in the canoe-like baskets were held high in the air by soldiers. Gezo stood majestically and shouted: "I do as my father, Agonglo, and grand-father Kpengla did—going all the way back to King Gangnihessou. Glory to Dahomey!!"

A man in the basket nearest Gezo was placed on the parapet and the King pushed the basket. Amazon warriors roared, while the man in the basket dropped—and a soldier cut the man's head off. Another war-rior picked up the remains and flung it to the mob, which brutally hacked up the body with machetes. Pieces of the mutilated body were taken to a pit. Forbes vomited. Again, and again, with dance and jubilation, sev-eral different baskets were thrust forward, and the beheadings and hack-ings continued…until a fourth basket with Aina inside was readied.

I had been prepared to die. But a higher power had other plans. When I looked up from the basket, my eyes locked with Forbes. His hands were frantically waving in a "stop" movement. There was a kind-ness in his face—a goodness that told me "You shall not die this night." I could hear his bloodcurdling pleas, "No! No! Stop. Please! The girl…I'll pay anything you want. Just don't kill her!" Gezo glared at Forbes, hissing, "She's royal. A Princess. She must die." But Forbes returned the glare, becoming emphatic, "Queen Victoria will not have re-spect for a great king, killing a girl." It took a moment, but Gezo put his hands up and my basket was halted. Always ready to negotiate, Gezo demanded "How much you pay?" Then I watched as Forbes gave Gezo all the coins and cowries he had—and finally offered his flask of rum as well. Gezo opened the flask, drank, then grinned. "More?" "I'll send 50 kegs from my ship," replied Forbes, sensing there could be a reprieve for me. Gezo shrugged, "Okay. 50 kegs. Keep her. I make her a present from the king of the blacks, to the Queen of the whites." Forbes gestured grat-itude to Gezo and the king's soldiers lowered my basket and took me out. I touched Forbes' face and cried for I knew the God of my people had sent him to save me from execution. And though I had no idea what lay ahead for me, I felt safe. Forbes took my hand and walked me away from the ceremony. Away from the palace. The shouting and dancing resumed as another body dropped screaming and kicking in my place...and was beheaded.

"Watering the Graves" execution ritual in Dahomey, West Africa as prisoners in white await beheading in boat baskets on a platform called an *Ah-toh*. (From Volume II of Frederick E, Forbes' 1851 book *Dahomey and the Dahomans)*

Three

The next morning, a pall hung as thick as damp fog in the hut and Forbes, Brandon and Aina had gotten little sleep. They were preparing to leave for Whydah Port, and the events of the previous night had so unnerved them all that Brandon could not stop his hands from shaking.

It was eerily quiet—until Emeka came into the hut as though nothing odd or horrible had taken place yesterday. He threw a skeptical look at Aina then pointed at her with emphasis to Forbes. "She, locky."

Forbes corrected Emeka, "She *is* lucky. Because she is leaving with us, you bastard!"

Emeka ominously smirked. "You locky too."

Not interested in giving Emeka a reaction nor continuing the conversation, Forbes ignored him and gestured to Aina, still in her white execution cloth, to prepare to go. Outside the hut, they all climbed onto a wagon provided by King Gezo for their departure and the transportation of rum back to his palace.

Brandon was relieved. "Thank God. No camels."

"No killings either," Forbes blurted quietly.

Later that early afternoon when they reached the port of Whydah where the HMS Bonetta was docked, Emeka waved goodbye. Forbes barely acknowledged him then joined Aina and Brandon toward the shore. Forbes' men from The Bonetta were already traveling back and forth onto the sand from several Kroo canoes with the agreed-upon 50 kegs of rum and carried them toward Emeka's wagon for loading as the African looked on.

Forbes, Brandon and Aina walked somberly toward the Kroo canoe that would take them to the ship. Brandon was still sullen. Still trying to calm down. "I've been a military man for some time. I've seen my share of battles and conflict," he started quietly. "But nothing like last night. All those people just chopped up like that. It was horrible." Brandon's eyes now filled with tears and he tried hard to control himself. "Where was the honor? The humanity?"

Aina reverentially kept her eyes and head down. Detecting fear in her, Forbes stopped them just before they got into the canoe. Forbes realized she would need more reassurance of their intentions.

"It's going to be alright. You're safe now. Free. You don't have to be afraid. "We won't hurt you," he said gently and smiled at her.

Aina finally looked him in the eye and managed a slight smile. Forbes gestured for her to get into the canoe. As he and Brandon took the oars and rowed toward the Bonetta, Forbes pointed to himself. "Forbes. Me—Forbes." He pointed to Lt. Brandon. "He is Brandon. Bran-don."

As she had done since first hearing Forbes speak English, Aina listened intently for meaning or intent. She realized he may have said his name. She repeated it with a strong Yoruban accent, "Forbes."

"Yes. Captain Forbes. And he is Brandon. Lieutenant Brandon."

"Forbes. Brandon." She repeated.

Both Forbes and Brandon realized Aina caught on quickly, and they kept rowing. Aina looked back and saw that the shore of her former homeland was so far away now. The people on the port docks had become smaller and smaller.

"We're going on a long journey—then you will meet the Queen of England… Eng-land."

"Eng-land," Aina repeated.

"Yes. England."

It finally sunk in for Aina that she had yet to introduce herself, and pointed to herself pronouncing slowly, "A-in-a."

Forbes warmly smiled, "Hello, Aina."

"Hello Aina" echoed Brandon.

To their surprise Aina smiled, "Hello, Captain Forbes. Hello, Lieutenant Brandon."

Finally, they reached the ship where they were helped on board. Forbes helped Aina climb up and all hands were on deck, along with Lt. Gibson and the full ship's complement. As Forbes stepped in front of his crew with Aina, the men stared at her, as did Gibson, who quickly remembered his role, and barked, "Captain on deck!"

The men immediately stood up straight, focused ahead military style and responded in union, "Sir."

Forbes took a power stance, as he surveyed his crew.

"Gentlemen, this is Aina. She is to be treated as our guest."

The sailors looked at Aina with raised eyebrows. Lt. Gibson welled with disgust. None of them had ever been ordered to give respect to a race of people they disparaged. Attempting without success to control his ire Gibson blustered, "Sir, I'm sorry. But I do not wish to work and breathe the same air as a... as her!"

The other sailors' faces revealed shock at Gibson's audacity—even though they were all thinking the same thing. Forbes walked right up to Gibson standing within inches of the Lieutenant's face, "Lt. Gibson, would you prefer two days in the brig for insubordination?"

Gibson swallowed hard and slowly shook his head. Forbes walked the line of crew members and scanned each face delivering a command as intensely as though preparing to do battle with a foreign aggressor,

"Then I expect a generosity of spirit on this ship, and for all of you to treat Aina as a human being. Am I understood?"

"Sir! Yes, sir!" they echoed back in unison.

The deck then fell silent as Forbes found himself grappling with the fact that he had to order and threaten time in the brig to his beloved crew just for them to show basic human decency.

Brandon sensing this, broke the silence and spoke to the men. "You don't know what she went through," he stated somberly. "What we *all* went through, frankly. You'd understand if you had."

But when he turned, he and Forbes realized Aina was gone. She had run off and Forbes and Brandon panicked running immediately to search for her.

"Find the girl!" Forbes ordered his crew.

Everyone went looking. As they searched, Forbes and Brandon alternated calls of "Aina! Aina! Aina!"

Finally, Forbes found Aina sobbing in the corner of the galley deck. Brandon rushed to help Forbes, but Forbes waved his friend away. Carefully, he quietly sat next to Aina as she cried in Fon:

"They hate me. Hate me!!"

Forbes understood what she was saying even though he did not know a word of Fon. It was the centuries old adage that one need not understand a language to know the feeling of what was being communicated. "Shhhh," he assured, "You're an oddity now to them. They just don't understand."

Naturally, Aina did not completely understand his words either. But she found his voice soothing, his manner comforting—and intent meant everything as he took her hand and walked her to his quarters which would be hers as well for the rest of the voyage.

At five that late afternoon, Forbes noted in his Captain's Log and in his personal journal that the HMS Bonetta set sail for London. At first, sounds of the rumbling steam engine frightened the girl, but when she noticed the rest of the crew cheering, Aina was more at ease and managed a slight smile.

She had never been on a ship. Never been out of Okeodan, and all of this was new, exciting and perhaps a bit terrifying. What would happen if the sea Gods came to lay claim on her as she had heard so many slaves were claimed and remanded to the bottom of the ocean? What if she were hurt or dishonored by the male members of the crew without having a place to run to? After all, Captain Forbes and Lt. Brandon, though seemingly honorable men, were still men who might be capable of anything now that the vessel was on the high seas.

Aina started to pray to Mahwah the creator goddess and the other Vodun gods to protect her. Especially since her stomach was now queasy with newfound sea sickness.

True to his word to make sure Aina stayed safe after her introduction to his crew, and knowing she would be nervous and frightened, Forbes set up a separate section in his quarters just for her. He knew no one would dare breach the Captain's threshold. He draped a bed sheet across the room on a clothesline and ordered in a hammock to be hung for Aina's bed. The African received all the privacy she needed and did indeed feel secure in the Captain's quarters.

Each evening she lay awake in her sleeping area while Forbes would recite the Lord's Prayer not only as he had done for himself for years, but on her behalf as well. She listened trying to soak in the words she was hearing, though not completely understanding. But something told her this ritual had to do with his God, and she knew to respect it.

Days passed, and every night Forbes knelt to recite the Lord's Prayer with his eyes closed. What he hadn't noticed was Aina silently mouthing the words.

Through his recitation of the prayer, she found that when she parroted the words, a quiet calm enveloped her. Then one night she unwittingly blurted out loud: *"...and forgive us our debt as we forgive our debtors..."*

Suddenly, Forbes stopped praying, leaped up, and went to Aina's section, where he pulled back the makeshift sheet divider and found her praying like him. She thought he was angry and began trembling.

"No. I won't hurt you," he assured. "You know these words?"

Aina nodded slightly. He then gestured for her to join him in the open area of his quarters. She did. He put his hands together in formal prayer. Aina followed suit and they both recited: "...Our Father, who art in Heaven. Hallowed be thy name..." Then Forbes stopped, looked at her, and waited. Aina continued, "Thy kingdom come..."

They both recited together: "...Thy will be done On Earth as it is in Heaven..."

Forbes smiled—and together they finished the prayer—something they would do each night of the voyage before going to sleep. Forbes became excited that she had so quickly acquired an affinity to the English language, and he spoke to her as though she was already fluent. "...and forgive us our debt as we forgive..."

Then Forbes stopped in mid-prayer and just stared at her. He looked troubled and began to pace. Finally, he came back over to Aina and it took him a few moments to speak as though something were pressing on his soul.

"Aina, I have you reciting our most cherished and beloved Christian prayer, but you are not a Christian. It is wrong. I think we should start with you, at least, having a Christian name."

Aina frowned not because she completely understood what he was saying, but by sensing his body language as he had begun to pace. She knew he was pondering something that involved her. Something she wouldn't understand but currently being stuck on the wide ocean with nowhere to go, prompted her to be prepared.

Suddenly Forbes stopped pacing. "My mother's name is Sarah," he began. "Sarah is a good name. Sarah Forbes. And this is my ship, The Bonetta." He then knelt down next to her.

"You, Sarah Forbes Bonetta," He pointed to her "Aina is Sa-rah."
As she did with the Lord's Prayer, Aina parroted, "Sa-rah."

"Yes! You—Sarah. Sarah Forbes Bonetta." He then gestured for her to go back to her area, as he went back to his bunk to sleep. Aina frowned after him and quietly grunted under her breath:

"Me, Aina."

But I knew, even at that moment, that I had become Sarah Forbes Bonetta for the rest of my life. I did not know it then, but I was to live aboard the good ship HMS Bonetta for a whole year. We had set sail from Whydah sometime in October, 1850, stopping along Africa's West Coast as Captain Forbes completed the remainder of his tour of duty in Africa with his West African squadron trying to convince the native Africans not to sell their own to slave traders. I learned many things aboard the Bonetta, and we would not land in London until 18 October in the year of our lord 1851. I was eleven or twelve years old, or so I supposed…

Sarah Forbes Bonetta at age eleven

Four

ix weeks into their journey the newly named Sarah Forbes Bonetta knew the Lord's Prayer by heart—as well as many passages from the bible. Forbes would read to her from the Christian good book and she loved the bible stories—so filled with challenge, tales of faith, terror, adversity and triumph. She also enjoyed hearing the biblical love stories finding the ones about David and Bathsheba, Jacob and Rachel, and Solomon and Sheba most intriguing.

She thought about Captain Forbes' congenial spirit, and his bravery in rescuing her, then remembered the lines she heard him read from Ruth 1:16: *"Entreat me not to leave thee, or to return from following after thee: for whither thou goest, I will go; and where thou lodgest, I will lodge: thy people shall be my people, and thy God, my God."* Sarah knew that wherever Forbes was taking her would become her new world and she would trust him.

As did the other sailors. For not one of them laid a hand on her or spoke to her in any untoward fashion—including Lt. Gibson. They all had too much respect for Forbes and would never risk censure nor admonishment from him. One evening, Forbes knocked on the door of his quarters to make sure Sarah was dressed and brought her some sailor's clothes. She frowned.

"Sailor's uniforms are all we really have aboard ship as we do not entertain women here," he shrugged. "You should wear these so as not to stand out too much to my crew. Most are not used to seeing a woman, let alone a… one from Africa."

Sarah nodded and started to get undressed right in front of him. After all, most of her tribe were unabashed when it came to nudity since nakedness was a common state of being for them. Rarely did it indicate an inducement to sex—which, as a virgin, she had yet to have.

But Forbes went flush and hurried out in embarrassment leaving the uniform on the floor. Just outside the door he had to get control of himself and rushed off to the deck of the ship—ashamed. He later drank himself into a stupor on deck in discomfiture. This would be the one entry he did not make in his journal which he intended to publish. This would remain private between him and his God.

Meanwhile, over the next months, the sailors and crew went about their duties. Though most were British, many spoke French to each other—including Forbes. Sarah, in her male sailor's clothes, would come on deck listening and learning. Gibson glanced at her every now and then still not knowing what to make of her yet finding himself intrigued by her exceptional mind—especially when she repeated the French phrases she heard him speak to the other French speaking crew members.

Sarah also realized she loved to cook and would help the ship's steward prepare the meals. She quickly learned the various spices he used and helped cut up the chicken or beef portions for the crew. She made up little songs to help her learn both English and French and soon, Ensign Bailey, the ship's cook would sing then back to her to help her learn the languages.

In June, just after leaving the West African Port of Cape Palmas for supplies and fresh water, Forbes, Gibson, Brandon and other sailors were eating in the galley when Sarah took her dirty plate and any others to the cleaning bowl to wash them. Lt. Gibson was still wondering why

Sarah was there. He turned to Forbes and was careful in his approach to his superior.

"Sir. Aren't they all diseased? Most Negroes?"

Forbes was not in the mood that evening but understood why Gibson was asking. His ignorance was stunning, but given Forbes knew so many whites were afflicted with the same massive unawareness he drew in a deep breath to stay calm and explained.

"No. It's a myth white people have created to stay superior—and continue fear of those we know less about."

Sarah overheard, but kept to the shadows to listen.

"What will you do with her?" Brandon asked in a low voice.

Forbes was quiet a while. "I don't know. I just couldn't let that sadistic savage kill her."

Brandon nodded. "Aye. I've never been so scared in my life. I wrote my wife and told her what happened."

"But once she's in London, what's to become of her?" Gibson wondered aloud.

"She'll be free. And alive," Forbes answered quickly turning to Brandon. "Give me your letter, Bran. I'll mail it in Monrovia when we stop there for supplies. Goodnight, fellows." Forbes then got up to leave after refilling his flask with rum.

Sarah looked after him a moment. Then when she finally finished the dishes, she came up onto the deck and found Forbes drinking by himself looking at the stretches of ocean which was all they could see for miles.

The moon was bright enough to illuminate the waves and she marveled at the schools of dolphins leaping and frolicking alongside the ship before them. Forbes managed a smile as the girl joined him, then had another swig of his rum. She looked at the flask. He grinned. "Ever had rum?"

Sarah shook her head.

"And you won't now. You're too young," Forbes grinned as he had another swig.

"Why people drink that?" she asked in her slightly broken English.

Forbes corrected her gently. "Why *do* people drink that?" Then he thought. "It takes getting used to at first," he replied. "But most people drink it to soothe a pain they can't access. To forget. Or to make them feel better, I suppose," he commented absently. "But you must be careful with it—with all spirits actually. They can carry you off to a place of false contentment, and you'll never get anything done. That's why it's better to consume it at the end of the day."

Sarah looked out over the ocean. "So much water. Never see so much water you cannot drink."

"No. All salt water."

"How much longer, Lon-don?"

"Four more months—and then I go home. To Winkfield Place."

"Home," Sarah mused. "You miss home?"

"Very much. Especially my wife, and my children."

"You have Kuanjulli?" Then she noticed Forbes frown not understanding what she meant. She smiled in explanation, "A wife?"

"Yes. For many years."

"Only one?"

"It is all we Christians are allowed," Forbes grinned. Then he thought about his Mary. "And she's a beauty, too. An understanding, perfect angel God sent me. I have four children with her, and a lovely house all of which I cannot wait to see again."

Sarah thought about her own life. About Kua, his death, the death of her family, and the burning of her village.

"No home. No more. No Kuanjulli. No family," she sighed. "I nomad."

"Where did you hear that word? You are not a nomad."

"Gibson say I have no place to belong. No village. No land I live with my people going back through time."

Forbes looked at her and thought. Though he should not have said it to Sarah, Lt. Gibson was right. Forbes had saved her, but his rescue would cause her isolation and seclusion, along with abject prejudice and vagrancy. It would force Sarah to accept everything at every level that was new, different and perhaps even unwelcomed.

Sarah smiled thoughtfully then begged off to go to their quarters. Forbes watched her a moment and wondered if he had done the right thing by her. Perhaps he should have dropped her off at Accra—the last port at which they stopped for supplies. It would have at least left her in Africa where people who looked like her could take her in or care for her. How could he, as a white European man do that? Why did he think it would work? Her going to England. Meeting a Queen. It was the furthest thing from her existence there could be.

That night Forbes entered his quarters having had one too many. He plopped on his sleeping cot. Sarah was asleep on her hammock but heard him enter. She looked over and smiled. Then she began reciting: "Our father, who art in heaven. Hallowed be thy name…"

Forbes sat up remembering this was their routine and joined her.

"…*On Earth as it is in Heaven. Give us this day our daily bread…*" And they continued until they finished their routine. Then Sarah picked up the bible near Forbes' cot and opened it to a page.

"It say, 'You e-eat from the fruit, y-your eyes will be open and you know g-good from evil.'" She smiled. "This book teaches good from bad. I like it."

"Then we shall have to find you more books. They are conduits to learning."

"What means 'conduits?'"

"What *does* conduit mean," he corrected again. Then he had to think first. "It means a method, or an instrument, or channel for something. In this case, a book becomes the road upon which you will learn new things. Open up your mind."

Sarah thought a moment and smiled. "Then, yes. I want to read many, many more books."

Forbes took a moment to be in awe of this young girl. "You are a shining example for your race, Sarah. L'avenir du monde."

"Oui. L'... L'avenir du... monde," she said in perfect French.

Forbes was shocked by how quickly Sarah was becoming bilingual—and the next day he began a letter to Queen Victoria which he would mail at the Port of Monrovia, their next stop. He had to tell the Queen that the mission was unsuccessful, but that he was bringing an extraordinary gift to her from the King of Dahomey.

"...Your Majesty I would like to add a few particulars about the extraordinary present I will bring from King Gezo. One captive of the Okeodan war was an interesting young woman of regal bearing..." it started, then went on for five pages.

Three days later, the HMS Bonetta had docked at the Port of Monrovia. Captain Forbes left the ship with Sarah and others and immediately went to the dock mail station. He gave the Dockmaster letters from his crew for posting, as well as his own to Queen Victoria.

"For the mail steamer to London. Straight away."

The Dockmaster nodded and took the bundle of letters. Then Forbes oversaw the supply of salted meats, seasonings, coffee, potatoes and other longer-lasting vegetables, along with fresh barrels of water as the men loaded them onboard the Bonetta. Then Forbes went down the dock looking to buy some pipe tobacco with Sarah, who habitually followed him everywhere and had become his "shadow" as the men called her. He soon stopped at something and frowned.

In the next berth was the HMS Galtonian—clearly a British ship flying a British Union-Jack flag. But the flag was now being lowered and, in its place, rose the flag of Zanzibar, an East African nation.

Forbes was confused. "Why is a Zanzibar flag being raised on a British ship?"

Sarah watched him as he questioned a crew member of the Galtonian. But the crew member ignored him—as did a couple of others.

Forbes shook his head. Then after purchasing his tobacco, he and Sarah then came back onboard the Bonetta.

That evening, Forbes made a note of what he saw in his journal. Sarah came over and looked at it. "Why you always write in this book?

"These are my journals. I intend to one day publish a book of my travels—especially to Africa, and I don't want to forget anything. It's like a diary. It holds all my thoughts."

"I have thoughts to hold too," said Sarah. Can *I* write a book, too?"

"Of course, you can," Forbes chuckled, then handed her some paper and a pen. "Why not start now. String all those letters from the alphabet I taught you together to form sentences and put your thoughts down."

Sarah smiled and began to write her first entry in a tentative, rudimentary way: "*Hello, my name is Sarah Bonetta. I am on a big ship on my way to a country I heard about from my father. The people are nice on this ship. I hope I will be okay…*"

Sarah looked at her words wishing her penmanship was better but was happy to have this new way to express herself. She loved it.

"Even though I was young at that time, I found that when I put pen to paper I could pour out my heart to myself. No one had to know all my anguish, all my woes, all the wonders. They could just appear on those first early pages and it felt good. I mimicked Forbes at every turn. When he wrote I did too. I described the crew members, what I had learned on a particular day, and how I felt. It was cathartic how this ritual somehow made the uncertainty of my future manageable…

Six months into their voyage, after stops at Accra and Komenda, where the Akan peoples lived, the crew was on deck working. As usual, Sarah watched and learned. She continued her routine of cooking and serving food to the hungry sailors, and repeated English words after Gibson as they ate. Brandon shouted French words, and Sarah repeated those as well. Then Sarah wrote her rudimentary thoughts down.

One evening, Lt. Brandon had his violin out and began playing beautiful music she had never heard. It had a spirit and energy which moved, then emboldened her. With an intrepid curiosity, Sarah came up close to him and watched his fingering on the strings, and the way he held the bow. Brandon could see she wanted to learn how to play the instrument—and so he taught her.

Little by little, Sarah got better and better, first learning the scales, then how to hold the bow to create the intriguing sounds she heard Brandon play. She loved it—and the instrument.

Soon, Brandon played a livelier tune and the crew began dancing and clapping their hands. Suddenly, it was as though the spirit of the ancestors took over Sarah's body and she launched into the African Ya Moto Dance—something she had not done since the murders of Kua and her family. As she danced she counted out the mathematic times-tables to the sounds of the music. "Five times two is ten. Five times three is fifteen. Five times four is twenty..."

Everyone cheered. Even Lt. Gibson was impressed and shouted. "Now do it in French!"

Sarah grinned. "Cinq fois l'un est cinq. Cinq fois deux sont dix. Cinq fois trois..." and so forth. The crew cheered again. Sarah smiled.

So did Forbes—who now realized how brilliant this young African girl was. And over the last two months of the voyage Forbes watched as Sarah's talent for the violin grew, and her mind expanded. He witnessed his men slowly accept the one who was different from them—one they had all had a hand in instructing.

And as Sarah's violin music played on, he thought; "No—leaving her in Africa would have never been the right thing. This was a girl destined for a higher purpose. A greater good…"

…And that greater good indeed lay ahead in London.

Gravesend Port of London (circa 1850)

Queen Victoria in 1845

Part Two

London, England
Fall, 1850

"These are the woes of Slaves;
They glare from the abyss;
They cry, from unknown graves,
"We are the Witnesses!"

Henry Wadsworth Longfellow

Queen Victoria arose at her beloved Windsor Castle with a headache. She did not wish to alarm Prince Albert, but she had been having migraines for over a week and could not understand why—especially since she had been in a constant state of exhilaration for five months.

The inauguration of the Great International Exhibition in the Crystal Palace being erected in Hyde Park for the following May had to be a ravishing success. It was being rendered by designer Sir Joseph Paxton which, in execution, was due to Prince Albert's original designs and the idea of it had at first encountered opposition from high Tories and all sections of society who disliked the Prince. Abroad, monarchs and their ministers condemned it as well and weren't sure they would come. But this was Victoria's pet project, and her wish was for rulers of all countries and/or their representatives to be their guests on the auspicious occasion of its opening, and Victoria would be choosing invitation designs that day.

As she rang for Lady Elizabeth to get some fizz water from Dr. Brown, the royal physician, to alleviate the pounding in her skull, she thought about all the opposition she was enduring regarding the Exhibition. So many foreign sovereigns regarded an assembly of crowned heads in any one place as an inducement to revolutionary conspiracy that could lead to attempts on the Queen and the Prince's lives. A gathering like it could also offer some radical agents in Europe to gather together in London on a specifically innocent pretext, then hatch nefarious designs later.

But Victoria had decided to forge ahead. "Let God decide my fate," she had prayed. Then she flung herself with spirit into making the event spectacular at a much balked about cost of £2 million.

But her dream of happiness was fading. The death of her uncle King Ernest of Hanover saddened her, then Louis Napoleon, President of the French Republic, made himself, by way of a coup d'état, the absolute head of the French Government, with the intention of reestablishing the Napoleonic dynasty.

She viewed Napoleon's accession to almost despotic power, and the means by which he had accomplished it, with loathing. Most especially since he had already made heroes of his country by insisting the West Africans end their practice of selling their own in the slave trade before she could be that shining example for England.

Add to this, a week earlier she had received an odd letter from Captain Forbes to whom she had charged with the mission of remitting a treaty for Dahomey's King Gezo to sign to end his slave selling, telling her the mission was not going well and he had not been successful. Yet, despite the king's refusal, he had tasked Forbes with bringing an African girl to be presented to her as:

"…A gift from the King of the Blacks, to the Queen of the Whites."

"How strange," she'd thought upon reading the letter. Did Gezo not know one did not present a Queen with a human being as a gift? Such an act could be perceived as an unwelcomed affront. Did he not understand that Great Britain had ceased in trading slaves for money for over fifty years and she wanted it to end in Dahomey as well?

And why had Forbes not chosen his words more carefully, so his Queen would not be offended by such an act?

Yet, something in Forbes' letter *did* intrigue her:

"…She is a perfect genius; she now speaks English well, and has a great talent for music. She has won the affections, with but few exceptions, of all who have known her, she is far in advance of any white child of her age, in aptness of learning, and strength of mind and affection…"

Victoria did not know how to process Forbes' failure nor the idea of this so-called gift, but she had Sir Charles Phipps, her Keeper of the Privy Purse, send a note from her to the Forbes home requesting that as soon as Captain Forbes had returned to England and was able, she wanted to see him—and this so-called "gift" at Buckingham.

A week later, on 18 October 1851, the HMS Bonetta docked. All hands began the arduous job of unloading everything on board. It was already snowing—the first snow of the winter.

Sarah was standing on deck with a sweater pulled tightly over her sailor's clothes looking at everything in awe. She had never seen snow nor felt such a chill. She had also never seen anything like London. The bustling port at Gravesend both frightened and engaged the girl. Though the Port smelled of fish, it also smelled of opportunity and potential. She knew that something better lay ahead.

As she watched people hustling about, and fishermen and their crews carrying their bounty to market, she could feel the flakes of snow as they fell on her face. The moisture was cold and strange, and she didn't know what was falling from the sky. Forbes, Brandon, and Gibson came over, grinning.

"Cold, eh, Miss Bonetta?" mused Brandon.

Sarah nodded.

"It's called 'snow,'" he continued.

"Snow?" Sarah repeated.

"We get lots of it here in winter. November through March is very cold here. And it snows. Also, it rains all the time in England."

Sarah stuck out her tongue to catch the snow as if fell. It tasted like cold water but was refreshing.

"You'll get used to it…" Gibson smiled at her. Then he added his own meaning and subdued regret for his former behavior. "…As I have with so many things."

Sarah recognized the apology and nodded to him. Just changing one mind about her, about black people in general, was enough to make her day and she caught the eye of Forbes who was himself moved by Gibson's observation.

Lt. Brandon then handed Sarah his violin and smiled brightly.

"Keep it, Lassie. You're already better on it than I am. It's yours."

Sarah hugged him "I will miss you, Bran."

"Same here."

Sarah and Forbes left the ship and climbed into Captain Forbes' waiting carriage driven by Mr. Humphrey Nelson, an older ruddy-faced man with thinning grey hair who was both his driver and handyman.

The streets of London were crowded with all manner of humanity the day I arrived. I found myself astonished at what people wore and how they behaved. Men tipped their hats to each other and to women. They wore striped pleated long pants with long jackets and waistcoats, and so many very odd hats: tall Stovepipes, Derby's, Boaters, Top hats, Bowlers, even pith helmets.

Women wore dresses with large bustles in back, which hugely enlarged the look of their buttocks; and their waists seemed to be uncomfortably cinched into an unrealistic, small, unbreathable circumference. They carried umbrellas to keep off the snow and many had the artificial look of powdered white faces and painted red lips. It was a thing to behold. I was also fascinated by the architecture.

People lived in houses made of stone, wood or brick and constructed very high. The streets were cobbled with stone or smooth rocks. And everyone seemed to own a carriage like ours.

Forbes had his driver, Mr. Nelson, pull us in front of a dress shoppe on Leicester Square near Coventry Street whose outside window was festooned with fabric, scarves, and stockings. Mr. Nelson helped me out of the carriage and Forbes gestured for us to go inside. I'd never seen anything like it. It was a fairyland of hats, veils, stockings, and gloves—all manner of women's clothing which made me smile in wonder. But it also became my first negative encounter in my new adopted country.

Once inside the dress shoppe, Forbes went to Mrs. Larsen, the sales clerk and proprietor who eyed Sarah furtively. Mrs. Larsen, a thin woman with sandy hair, a plump face, and twinkling eyes greeted Forbes. "May I help you, sir?" she asked in a cheery voice.

"I need an inexpensive dress. Something simple." He then pointed to Sarah. "For her."

Mrs. Larsen was in shock as she looked at Sarah dressed in male sailor's clothes with a sweater over her.

"Oh my," she frowned, "I thought she was a little Colored boy, her hair being so short."

Sarah said nothing and took a few steps back standing just behind Forbes as if for protection. The proprietor took her time and went into a back room. When she returned she had two dresses, one beige and one green, that were actually plain cotton shifts, in her arms. She handed both to Forbes. He held them up to Sarah.

"Well, which do you like, Sarah?"

Sarah hated them both. She had been longing for her comfortable, loose fitting African clothes and a Gele for her head. But wanting Forbes to be happy because he had been good to her, she pointed to the beige one.

Forbes turned to Mrs. Larsen. "How much for this one?"

"Cost you a quid."

Forbes gave her the money. "Can she put it on now?"

After a moment, Mrs. Larsen looked at Sarah who seemed harmless enough. "I suppose she can go back there. But I'll have to help her, and make sure she doesn't steal anything," the proprietress grunted. "You know most of *them* are heathens."

Both Sarah and Forbes were irritated, but Forbes turned to Sarah. "Go with this lady. She will help you get dressed. You'll be a proper lady wearing this."

"Not quite," quipped Mrs. Larsen. "She needs a bath. But she'll be close enough to a Lady to not be taken for a heathen."

She then pointed Sarah to the back room. Sarah handed Forbes her violin and Mrs. Larsen closely followed her into the back room and closed the curtain. "You can take those clothes off." Then she grunted. "Who would put a girl in a man's sailor outfit?"

Sarah shrugged and unbuttoned the shirt and undid the pants of the uniform. She held out her hand for the dress. After Mrs. Larsen gave it to her, it took only two seconds to put the shift over her head. It hung so unattractively on her body that Mrs. Larsen shook her head.

"No. It will never do. You'll need a bodice. Wait here."

Mrs. Larsen went back out into her shop and motioned to Forbes.

"The girl needs to be properly dressed. She needs a bodice. She has breasts which need covering and her waist must be cinched in properly." She then opened a large box on a shelf. Inside were several corsets and bodices. She found a brown one and pulled it out. "This one is fine. It has ribbon for pulling it in and whalebone stays for keeping it put. Cheapest one I have."

"How much?"

"Half a quid."

Forbes nodded and gave the woman the coins. Mrs. Larsen disappeared behind the curtain.

Soon Sarah came out in the dress with her waist defined by the bodice which was laced up in front. Sarah looked feminine and by all conceits like a member of western European culture. Forbes gave her back the violin and smiled. "A perfect lady." His look to Mrs. Larsen dared her to make another disparaging remark about Sarah being African. If she had, there was no telling what he may have said—or done.

Half an hour later, Mr. Nelson pulled the Forbes carriage right in front of Winkfield Place, a three-story Georgian house in the Spitalfields district of London. Before it could even stop, Forbes' wife, Mary, a pretty woman in her late 30's with curly brown tendrils escaping her upswept hair, bolted from the door and jumped into Forbes' arms. He hugged her tightly.

"Frederick! Darling. Welcome home!" Mary exclaimed.

"I couldn't wait to see you," greeted Forbes who kissed his wife instantly and affectionately. They walked inside.

The moment they entered the charming house Jillian McMasters, a hefty, fifty-year-old Scot who was both cook and housekeeper, was grinning along with Rebecca Jordan, another no-frills, fortyish white servant. Rebecca immediately genuflected to Forbes, as she stood with the four Forbes children—Keith, 11, Susan, 8, Elijah, 6, and Ian, age 4. All gave their father a huge hug.

"Papa, Papa!"

Forbes hugged them all tightly, almost moved to tears, "Oh my dears, I've missed you." He stepped back to take in his daughter, "My goodness Susan, are you taller?" Then he looked at his eldest son, "And Keith, you look very fine."

"Thank you, father," the young man responded.

But Mary soon found herself curiously staring back at the carriage and suddenly, Forbes remembered. "I'm sorry, I shall be right back."

He raced out to the carriage realizing he'd left Sarah there. Mr. Nelson was bringing in valises and boxes as Mary, the children, Rebecca and Jillian looked out the window to see why he ran back to the carriage.

Then they witnessed Forbes pull the very brown-skinned Sarah out of the carriage, dressed in her plain beige shift, tightly clutching her violin. Forbes brought Sarah into the house and introduced her to six dazed and confused faces.

"Sarah, this is my wife, Mary, my children, Keith, Susan, Elijah and Ian, and Rebecca and Jillian who work here. Everyone I would like you to meet Sarah Forbes Bonetta."

The name came as a complete shock to Mary as she cautiously extended her hand.

Sarah timidly shook it. "Hello."

"Hello," Mary answered flatly not knowing what to make of it. The children looked on at a loss for how to react to this black girl with their father, in their house.

Sarah, sensing everyone's disquiet, warmly added. "It is so nice to finally meet you. Captain Forbes has told me so much about you."

"And not a word about *you*, dear," quipped Mary looking at Forbes with a side eye.

Forbes quickly interceded. "Rebecca, take Miss Bonetta up to the guest room, please. She'll be staying with us."

Rebecca nodded and showed Sarah up the stairs. Mary watched a moment, then hurried Jillian and the children away. Seconds later, she gave Forbes a "We must talk" look.

Six

A n hour later, in their upstairs master bedroom, the blue skies of marriage were quickly clouded as the loving reunion between Forbes and his wife evaporated. Mary lost all control of herself. With hands on her hips she marched around the room, livid.

"Why you? Why us?"

Forbes grabbed a brandy from the decanter by the bed, but Mary tried to stop him. "Oh no. I'll not let you drink your way out of it this time and forget all manner of thought about it tomorrow. You will tell me why that girl is here."

Forbes shook her off and had his brandy anyway. It helped him gain composure.

"She had nowhere else to go. I was the one who saved her from a brutal, horrible death."

"And that makes you responsible for her here in London? Why did you not drop her off somewhere in Africa—so she could be with her own kind? Why on earth would you bring her here?"

"Mary, please…"

"…And her name? Sarah *Forbes* Bonetta?" Mary turned away.

"Good God, Frederick, was that salvation from a brutal, horrible death, too?"

"She needed a Christian name."

"*Your* Christian name? When she's *not* Christian? Frederick, she's African! Just what do you plan to do with an African in London?"

"She's a human being, Mary! A child needing protection!"

Now Mary was incredulous—and offended. "She is no one's child! Surely you noticed she has breasts!" Then Mary turned away from Forbes unable to look him in the eye. "Perhaps you brought her for another purpose."

Forbes stared at his wife in disbelief. How could she accuse him of such a thing? Never once had anything remotely untoward occurred to him regarding Sarah. Even when he had caught a glimpse of Sarah's body aboard his ship, he had admonished himself mercilessly for he was not that kind of man. He had never been—and certainly not since he'd met and married the love of his life the former Mary McAllister.

"That is shameful—if you mean what I think you mean!"

It was clear from Mary's face she had not meant it. She knew better in her heart. But it was as if evil spirits had possessed her at having to play hostess to a foreign, African non-child. She instantly moved from the prurient to the pragmatic: "And what do you feed an African? Don't those savages eat their own for sport?" she heard herself blurt. "You risk the sanctity and safety of our children by bringing one into our home?!"

Now angered and frustrated Forbes threw his brandy glass against the wall, where it shattered into a million shards.

"For God sakes, stop it! Stop, dammit!!"

Frightened by his uncharacteristic outburst, Mary realized she may have gone too far, and Forbes realized he was out of control. They both had to take a moment to calm down.

They were eerily quiet. Then finally, Forbes spoke first, his head hung in utter frustration and regret. "I had one job to do. Get a treaty signed," he lamented. "And the bastard wouldn't sign it. Instead, I was treated to the sight of a dozen Africans chopped into bits!" He stopped a moment trying to push down the wave of emotion overtaking him. "I had one mission for our Queen, and I failed. That young woman is all I have to show for it. Now she's to be a present for Her Majesty!"

"Her Majes..." Mary was apoplectic but spoke in a low voice forcing calm. "What will the Queen of England do with an African?"

"Who bloody knows. I…I just…I…"

Forbes sat on the bed in complete frustration. Mary sat next to him and he buried his head in her lap. In turn, Mary gently caressed her husband's hair—his beautiful chestnut-colored hair which was still bountiful and unruly—which she loved. Resigned to support him, and knowing his intentions were born of a good heart, she took his face, the face of the love of her life, into her hands.

"Well," she managed a smile. "If Sarah Forbes Bonetta is to meet Her Majesty, she'll need a proper dress, and to be baptized. I'll not have the Queen of England meet a heathen."

I was in the guest room right next door, sitting on the large four-poster bed draped in heavy fabric with tassels. I was in tears. This should have been a happy moment for me. I had escaped from Gezo and after a year, been brought to what should have been an enlightened, uplifting, progressive country with promise and hope for a great future. Instead, I could hear for myself the belittling and berating from the wife of the man who had rescued me from death. And I felt deeply hurt.

I stood and went to the oak bureau and stared at myself in the mirror wondering what was to become of me? Was this my future? I was in a foreign land, with foreign people and customs. The only one I had some attachment to was Forbes, who in my mind, was like a kindly uncle or older brother. A decent man with only the best of intentions toward me. A safe haven. Never once had I ever felt any malignancy from him.

But since coming to England, I had only been met with disdain and mistrust. I had heard the word 'heathen' before, from the shopkeeper on High street, and now Forbes' wife. I didn't fully understand what the word meant, but I surmised from its intonation by both women that it was not complimentary. And sadly, I also knew that Mrs. Forbes was not fond of me which would make my living with the Forbes family uncomfortable. Perhaps even untenable.

Later that day, Mary Forbes knocked on Sarah's door and insisted the girl take a bath.

"It won't do to have body odor, Miss Bonetta. A well brought up young woman must always smell as sweet as a rose." At that she instructed Sarah to take off her clothes and sit in the claw-foot tub while Jillian and Rebecca poured warm water into it. Sarah sat there naked and embarrassed as Mary Forbes insisted Jillian scrub the girl with soap and wash her hair.

"She smells like an open sewage pit. Make sure you clean under her arms and her private parts. Two good scrubbings should do it."

When Mary left, Jillian lifted Sarah's head and comforted her in her Scottish brogue. "Don' pay that much attention to the Missus. Ye been on a long journey. We all need a little soap an' water sometimes. She shouldn't have hurt yer feelings like that." Then Jillian smiled. "By the way, you kin call me Jilly."

Sarah smiled, "Sarah." Though she realized things were so different in this part of the world, she liked Jilly who had the most pleasant personality. There was something warm and comforting about her. She was maternal and loving. While Jilly cleaned her up and washed her hair, Sarah looked around. This room was called a "water closet" or bathroom—which had a toilet, a sink and a tub—all outfitted with what Jillian called indoor "plumbing" to privately accommodate bodily functions with efficiently. Sarah was amazed. In Africa, one just went away into the bushes to do what you must, and Sarah learned that only recently in London there had been only two civilized options: a chamber pot for middle-of-the-night or sickroom use, and the outdoor privy, or outhouse, which meant a trip into the cold to do what you needed.

After her bath Sarah went back into her room to put on her clothes for supper and stayed there for a long while. Finally, around four that afternoon, she tiptoed out lest she be met with animosity from Mary Forbes. She began to smell the aroma of food emanating from the downstairs kitchen and descended the stairs following the scent.

She began to explore the Forbes home to see how it was situated. It had high ceilings and narrow staircases. At the bottom of the stairs to the right was a receiving room, and to the left, a smoking room. Further down was a sitting room, and the two upstairs levels housed five bedrooms. The receiving room had dark painted wood walls and floors, and a brass chandelier with candles that hovered over a large, rectangular table. Ancestral portraits were on walls—including one of a young Forbes that Sarah recognized.

Then Sarah wandered down the hall marveling at all the new technology and modern conveniences of the Forbes house, then she finally found the kitchen—which was in the lower, below-ground level.

By then, Jilly was roasting chickens on a spit. Sweat was pouring from her brow as she wiped it back into her unruly, ginger curls which escaped her white worker's bonnet. To the left of her was an open hearth with water boiling in a big iron kettle into which she tossed peas and carrots. The moment Sarah came in, Jilly smiled. "There ye are. I thought you would hide in yer room through supper," she chortled as she turned the chickens then stirred the mashed potatoes.

"Hi Jilly," Sarah smiled, tipping her head like she saw men do in the street not knowing what the proper protocol was here.

"Ye don' have to bow to me, lassie. I'm just the help. Same as Rebecca. Same as you'll be soon I 'xpect."

Upon hearing that, Sarah reached out her hands to Jilly. "I can help.

Tell me what to do. I can cook English-style. They taught me on the ship."

"I'm fine down here," smiled Jilly, grabbing an open decanter of wine. "But you can take this upstairs to Rebecca for the table. She may need help up there."

Sarah nodded and took the wine up to the fussy, cluttered Victorian dining room with its lace curtains and pressed paper ceiling. There, she found Rebecca setting the table.

"Jilly asked me to bring this up," Sarah said brightly, then offered, "Do you need any help?"

"Yes, thank you," smiled Rebecca. "You can help me set the table. Just put the silverware next to the plates. Like this."

Rebecca showed Sarah where each piece of cutlery should be placed, in the order of its use from the outside in. Two forks went to the left of the plate, and two knives and two spoons to the right. The napkin was atop two plates, one smaller than the other, and all about two inches from the edge of the table. Then Sarah watched as Rebecca placed the wine glasses just above the tip of the meat knife.

Sarah frowned. It was all so different from Africa where everyone sat around a fire or a low table and used their fingers to scoop out corn or vegetables from a gourd or they used a spear or wooden knife instrument to stab meat or fish and ate with it.

Rebecca was a thin, somewhat attractive woman from Manchester, and nice like Jilly. She could see Sarah's curiosity and chuckled.

"You're wondering why so many utensils, eh?"

Sarah nodded.

"It's all rather peculiar, too. But proper English etiquette dictates you start with a salad fork for your salad, it goes on the small plate, then work your way in toward the larger fork and knife for the main course on the bigger plate."

"I see," said Sarah. "And what is a 'course'?'"

Rebecca thought a moment. She had never been asked the question before. "Well, I suppose it's a specific set of food items that are served together during a meal but brought out in separate order. For instance, you can have an appetizer first, salad second, followed by soup, then the main course, and a dessert course last."

"It seems like a lot of food—and a lot of work for whoever has to wash all those dishes."

Jilly, who had come up with a tray of appetizers, heard the exchange and laughed. "She catches on fast, that one."

"Why isn't it all put on a plate at the same time?" Sarah questioned.

"Is that how they did it onboard The Bonetta?" asked Rebecca who had finished arranging the wine glasses.

Again, Sarah nodded. "They didn't have a lot of dishes, so everyone just put what they wanted on their plates and ate. It was simple."

"It's a class issue, my dear," they heard from behind them.

Mary Forbes had entered the dining room and looked over the table nodding her approval. "A well-set table and courses separates the cultured from the barbarian."

Jilly observed Sarah who had looked away. She knew why Mrs. Forbes had said it and hurried back down to the kitchen so not to be in the middle of a discussion on "class."

But Sarah already made up her mind she did not favor Mary Forbes and spoke up. "Captain Forbes is a gentleman, and he ate like that on the ship and like this here. Is he a barbarian?"

Before Mary could comment Forbes entered the room, "Certainly not," he said, motioning his children in. "I've learned in my travels that class, good breeding, and indeed fine manners are found in every culture. And eating habits are diverse amongst different people and their livelihoods. Aboard ship, sailors must be prepared to do battle at the drop of a hat. There may be no time for the 'niceties of four-course meals' when a pirate ship may explode a cannon upon you at any moment." He shot

Mary a look indicating she halt this line of discussion, then looked at the table. "It's a fine-looking table, Rebecca. Thank you."

"Sarah helped, Sir. She picks up fast."

"That's what I told the Queen in my letter to her. Sarah is an unusual girl with a brilliant mind. We're lucky to have her here—however long."

Mary knew all of this was said for her benefit and she held her indignation as Forbes pulled out a chair for Sarah who sat like a guest at the table. Then Forbes held out his hands and everyone took the fingers of the one next to them for the meal to be blessed. Little Ian happily took Sarah's hand and smiled at her. It touched her heart. Then Forbes prayed: "Thank you Heavenly Father for the food we are about to receive, for the nourishment of our bodies. Amen."

"Amen," repeated everyone.

It was not the first time Sarah had joined in a Christian prayer. She had done it onboard the Bonetta and liked the fellowship it seemed to engender—at least for a while. Then she squeezed Ian's hand, smiled at him, and enjoyed the roasted chicken, potatoes, peas and corn like a member of the Forbes family.

And yet, Sarah innately understood she would never be either an accepted guest let alone "family"—for later, she saw both Rebecca and Jilly, the white servants of the house, sitting in the kitchen having their dinner. "Class versus Barbarian," a delicate differentiation she noted, and realized she would take Lt. Gibson's initial, open prejudices based on ignorance, which he overcame, any day to Mrs. Forbes's subtle, learned, but far more hurtful biases.

Seven

Two days later Sarah, Forbes and Mary were at the Rose Chapel with its beautiful, ornate stained-glass windows. The Forbes' had been married there and were still parishioners. The two were standing behind young Sarah, dressed in her plain, beige shift, as Father Francis, an Anglican priest, performed the baptismal rites.

During the procedure Sarah could not help but think how so much was changing so fast. Was she now to completely abandon her own religion and beliefs without her consent? She had been "Aina," who worshipped Mahwah and practiced Vodun, her African root religion, and had to give it up to become "Sarah," a Christian. Where would she go after her death—"Jannah," the place of goodness, or "Heaven?" And did anyone in Europe care?

Suddenly, I felt stripped of my heritage. I was now expected to embrace the spiritual tenets of the image I saw on the stained-glass windows of a white man with long, blond, hair born of the "Virgin Mary." In what context was I to place Mahwah, or any of the other Gods and Goddesses to whom my family, my village, and me had prayed all my life—and centuries before? Were they to no longer to exist for me? And where did they go?

"In the name of the Father, the Son, and the Holy Spirit, amen" intoned Father Francis as he dipped his thumb in the baptismal water and drew the sign of the cross on Sarah's forehead.

With that last "Amen," Sarah turned to Mary, looking directly into her eyes. "No Hee-then now, eh?"

Mary drew back incredulously. But Forbes interceded. "No," he nodded, realizing Sarah heard his argument with Mary, "No heathen."

But when Sarah returned to the Forbes home that afternoon, she continued to pray to Mahwah. She was determined to hold on to some part of herself—or lose the meaning of her existence forever.

The next morning, Forbes was standing in front of his bedroom mirror in his full dress military uniform looking at himself, feeling like a nervous wreck. Today was the day. The day he was dreading. The day he had to report to Queen Victoria and explain his failure with King Gezo in Dahomey, and to present Sarah.

In the guest room, Mary and Rebecca attempted to dress Sarah, as she stood in pantaloons with her hands covering her breasts.

"Today is an important day," Mary noted. "You will meet the Queen of England. The most powerful woman on Earth. You must be respectful."

Sarah nodded as Mary tightly tied the pettiskirt onto Sarah's waist then placed the corset on Sarah and laced it up.

"Must it all be so tight?" asked Sarah, unable to breathe.

"You must be presented to Her Majesty as a 'Lady.' The Queen must always be accorded the highest level of respect and reverence—in both manner and dress," Mary insisted, putting a new blue dress over Sarah's head followed by the bodice and stomacher tied tightly as well.

Sarah hated the constriction and felt like fainting, but Rebecca gave her a glass of water.

"Now. It's imperative you learn to properly curtsey. You will need to do it the moment you are introduced to her Majesty. Like this," instructed Mary who curtseyed in demonstration.

Sarah tried it but was wobbly. Mary scolded impatiently, "No! Right leg behind the left. Then bend. Like this." Mary did it again.

"See?"

Young Sarah mimicked her and was better. Mary smiled and stepped back to look over her handiwork. But once she got to Sarah's hair, she shook her head in disgust. "Oh no. God, no. Rebecca, sort her hair out please. It's…it's…" she sighed in frustration at that which she would never understand nor embrace—African textured hair.

"Do something!"

Rebecca looked at Mary as though she were insane, but still, she obeyed her mistress. Locating a wooden comb in the top bureau drawer, she tried to run it through Sarah's tightly coiled locks. Several teeth in the comb broke. Finally, in frustration, Rebecca stuck a white bonnet over Sarah's kinky hair. Sarah stood there trying to process her feelings.

> *I swallowed my hurt, for it was in that moment I became more aware of that which had been so natural, acceptable and culturally prideful to me, not being an acceptable or desirable thing to white Europeans. My hair, much like my skin color, was a bad thing to them. A disgusting thing. Something to cringe at.*
>
> *Never mind that in Africa our hair was part of our ornament. Our allure. We braided it, or adorned it with ceremonial beads, feathers or mud as decoration. We celebrated the way Allah had designed us and no matter where you looked, we saw us—people who looked like us, people who were a prideful, welcoming, brown people, who accepted everything about our shared heritage, culture, and appearance.*
>
> *But here, we were beasts of the wild. We were thought ugly—and were told so in myriad ways every day of our lives. And it made me ashamed.*

Suddenly, I wanted to be different. To be accepted. To be beautiful and a proper 'Lady.' I wanted to be like them—smart, well-spoken, cultured. I wanted what they had—long flowing, straight tresses that curled and moved. Not something which broke the teeth out of combs and caused grunts of disgust forcing the need for bonnets to be placed on it, to hide it. That was the moment, the first time, I wanted not to be me. To be something other than a dark, unattractive, nappy haired African. I hated myself for that desire. And I wondered if I would ever return to my real self—the proud African—from those terrible thoughts of worthlessness imposed upon me by whites...

Waiting in the sitting room, Forbes, who was still going over his explanation in his head, looked up as Mary and Rebecca presented Sarah with pomp.

"Here she is. Ready to meet the Queen," said Mary, motioning Sarah to show Forbes her curtsey. Sarah did so, and Forbes was impressed.

"That is a very fine curtsey," Forbes complimented. "And you look very fine indeed."

Forbes bowed to Mary and Rebecca, then bowed to Sarah, who beamed. "Thank you."

"So, are you ready, Lady Sarah?" he asked with a smile.

"Yes, Captain."

Forbes then handed her, her violin as Ian ran into the room.

"You look pretty, Miss Sarah," the young lad exclaimed.

Sarah kissed him on the cheek. "Thank you, young Master Ian. Coming from you with your good taste, I'm ap...apre..." she forgot the word—then Forbes helped her. "Appreciative."

"Yes. Appreciative."

Forbes guided Sarah toward the front door, and out to the awaiting carriage. As he turned to wave "goodbye" to Mary, Rebecca and Ian, Sarah drew in a deep breath. Little did she know that the "gift" from the king of the blacks to the Queen of the whites, was on her way to a life altering experience.

At Buckingham Palace, Queen Victoria was feeling good the day she was to meet the "gift" from King Gezo. Her opening and the celebrations of the Great Exhibition had been a tremendous success that May and had only closed the previous week. Reviews of the Crystal Palace were astounding, and Prince Albert's involvement was met with praise. She would never forget how it felt to stand on the Royal balcony to open her cherished Exhibition to a world audience to whom she waved. There were so many hundreds of them.

Now she would settle back into the business of protecting England with the knowledge that something she had envisioned and executed herself, had worked. Her only concern was that the mission she'd sent Captain Forbes on had not succeeded as planned for which she expected an explanation shortly.

Meanwhile, the guards at Buckingham Palace stood at the ready as the Forbes carriage driven by Mr. Nelson entered the gates. Sarah, eyes large and curious, took in the wonder of the grand palace for she had never seen anything like this.

"The Queen lives here? In this big place?" Sarah asked aloud.

"Yes," replied Forbes. "Buckingham Palace is her London residence. But the official abode of the Court is not that far away at the Palace of St. James's. But even with these Palaces, and the queen has several more, her favorite is 23 miles from here. Windsor Castle—the grandest of all."

"Grander than this?"

Seconds after the carriage stopped, liveried footmen opened the doors and helped her out. She stopped to stare at the palace guards with their big black bearskin hats, and despite waving to them, not one broke their regimented, serious countenance.

"Those are Her Majesty's palace guards," explained Forbes. He then pointed to the flag above the palace. "And when you see that flag flying, it indicates the sovereign is in residence."

Forbes and Sarah went inside where there was so much for the young African to be in awe of. Immediately they were met by the Chamberlain, Lord John Breadlebane, who bowed, then escorted them up the famous curving stairs. Sarah stared at the large paintings in gold gilded frames of almost every sovereign to rule Britain adorning the walls. She was clutching her violin and her heart raced for it was if she was about to meet God. When as they got close to the landing, Lord John noted, "Her Majesty will see you first, Captain. I shall keep Miss, er..." Forbes rescued him, "...Bonetta." Lord John continued, "Thank you. I shall keep Miss Bonetta until such time as she is to be presented."

Forbes nodded then looked at Sarah. "You wait here."

Sarah smiled and watched as Forbes went with Lord John through the pale blue double doors into the Presence Room.

Buckingham Palace's Presence Room was long and intimidating. As Forbes entered, he saw on one end of the room, a seated Queen Victoria, and next to her stood Prince Albert. Forbes and Lord John passed a servant by the door, who stood still as Lori, the parrot, rested on the servant's shoulder. Lord John went to the center and bowed.

"Captain Forbes, your Majesty."

As Lord John left Victoria held out her hand. Forbes walked over, bowed, took Victoria's hand and kissed it. Then shook Prince Albert's hand, as he finally gave the requisite royal greeting:

"Your Majesty. Your Royal Highness."

Victoria merely nodded. But Prince Albert was by all accounts more congenial. "Captain Forbes, welcome home. Happy you made it back safely."

Forbes quipped, "As am I, your Royal Highness."

The Queen smiled a bit but proceeded to the business at hand.

"You wrote that the mission was unsuccessful, Captain."

Forbes swallowed hard. It took him a moment, "Yes, ma'am. I...I regret to inform, Your Majesty, that despite our best efforts the mission failed. King Gezo did not sign the treaty."

Queen Victoria, not used to hearing noncompliance, reiterated, "And you told him how important it was for our two countries?"

The memory of what he saw manifested on Forbes' face. "Ma'am, King Gezo is insane. His warriors are cruel beasts, and that includes his Amazon women warriors. They eradicate entire villages, take the people and sell them. Those worthy enough they keep for a god-awful human sacrifice I witnessed where they're beheaded and mutilated in a 'Watering Graves' ritual. Then the King informed me he expects you to allow his ships to continue carrying human cargo around the globe as free labor or suffer his wrath."

Both Queen Victoria and Prince Albert reacted to Gezo's threat, though Prince Albert was more enraged.

"'Suffer his wrath?' Does he mean war? Because we will give him a war which he will never…"

Victoria patted Prince Albert's arm for calm, then turned back to Forbes, "We are disappointed, Captain."

"As am I. On top of all of this, Gezo is trading slaves for guns and ammunition from the French. Without guns, he would have difficulty protecting himself and his people. Any ruler or people who cannot provide adequate self-defense can be captured and sold into slavery themselves. So now, the Africans find themselves emmeshed in a vicious system from which there seemed to be no escape."

"What would be a better solution do you think, Captain?" asked Victoria.

Forbes thought for a moment. "Perhaps one possibility may be for the development of a kind of African coalition, but sadly, these petty African rulers are far too concerned with their own power to contemplate a united activity. Too much European greed feeds African greed, and vice a versa." Forbes then lowered his head. "So I will understand if I am to be relieved of duty."

"Certainly not! King Gezo has proved himself a willful tyrant for some time. The slave trade cannot continue anywhere. What King George, my grandfather, did for the cessation of Trade here, we must do regarding it worldwide. We have much to gain from Dahomey, and I intend to protect that gain."

"Yes, Ma'am."

Victoria pondered a moment, "You shall go back to Dahomey. But this time I shall send Commander Dawson with you. He will lead the negotiations as he is capable of a more...shall we say...forceful application. I am also giving you full authority to act in equal display should Gezo continue his intimidations. Make him sign the treaty, Forbes—or so help me God, he will witness my wrath!!!"

She stopped to collect herself, while Prince Albert and Forbes looked on thrown by such a rare display of ire from the Queen. Victoria then decided to move on to a more positive line of questioning.

"Now. One has a gift from this beastly King?"

Forbes managed a slight smile, "Yes, ma'am." He then nodded to the servant by the door. The servant left, and moments later, Lord John entered with Sarah and her violin.

"Your Majesty: Sarah Forbes Bonetta," Lord John announced.

Sarah curtseyed. The Queen eyed her, noticing every movement, then gestured to Sarah. "Come forward, girl."

Sarah slowly moved forward toward her majesty. She was nervous.

"Take off your bonnet," insisted the Queen.

Sarah removed her bonnet and stood directly in front of Victoria who touched Sarah's hair curiously.

My heart was beating like the Djembe drums of my village. She was much smaller than I imagined—this powerful Queen I'd heard so much about. And she had a vulnerability that was unexpected. Then I looked to my left and saw her parrot. I smiled at it.

Amused, Queen Victoria did the honors of an introduction. "That's Lori. She'll sing when she's so inclined. You have them in your country too, yes?"

Sarah nodded. Then Victoria inspected the girl. She was impressed with Sarah's natural regal bearing and comportment. Also, she found herself impressed with Sarah being unafraid at meeting royalty.

"Captain Forbes tells me you've made a fair acquaintance with our language, and perhaps some French?"

"Oui, ma'am," answered Sarah who couldn't help but show off just a bit and continued in French. "Ravie de faire votre connaissance, Majesty."

The Queen was in shock. Forbes had been right. The girl demonstrated an unusual aptitude for languages that was impressive.

"Extraordinary!"

Forbes beamed with pride, "She would like to play something for you, Ma'am."

He nodded to Sarah who placed her violin under her chin and adjusted the bow in her right hand. She then began to play a rudimentary version of "Rule Britannia."

Delighted, Victoria and Albert applauded wildly. "Well done, child!" Victoria exclaimed. "Enchantée jeune fille. Je suis impressioneé, vraiment. You—are an impressive, talented, smart girl. A wonder, Sally."

Sarah suddenly found herself imbued with her own royal standing. It was bad enough her name had been changed from its African origins of "Aina," to the anglicized "Sarah," she would not have it further bastardized and immediately and firmly corrected: "Sarah."

Prince Albert and Forbes held their breath as Victoria bristled slightly but recovered quickly.

"I shall call you 'Sally.' It will be my special nickname for you. Is that alright?"

Before Sarah could answer, Lori the parrot chose that precise moment to sing 'Rule Britannia" in honor of Sarah's violin performance. This made everyone laugh including Sarah who went to the bird and played with it.

Victoria circled Sarah, and gestured to Forbes, nodding in approval.

"I was going to return Gezo's human 'gift.' But I find I've changed my mind. I shall keep her. She shall make a wonderful experiment for my personal observation."

This declaration took Forbes aback. "Ma'am...?"

Undaunted, Queen Victoria continued, "Have you ever wondered what it would be like if Negroes had the same privileges and advantages as whites in all things? Education, opportunity, social interaction?"

"It is a world I would like to see," responded Forbes sincerely.

Queen Victoria smiled, "As would I. Sally shall be given such an opportunity. A wild, untamed African from the jungle. Developed and educated by English standards. It could be extraordinary. Would you like that, Sally?"

I was bristling with anger as I stood there listening to Her Majesty. As had been accustomed by many in power for eons, they spoke of someone in a perceived lesser station in life, as if they were not present. My own royal standing was screaming to lash out, but my current position as a "gift" — like a horse or a chair, left me no choice but to swallow my indignation at least publicly. My ire, however, coursed through my very being. English Standards, indeed! The same English Standards that killed millions in the Slave Trade, stole Africa's gold, and diamonds, and rendered us as ignorant, sub-human beings, yet we are considered the wild, untamed heathens.

Oblivious to her insults, Victoria continued. "Yes, Sarah will be looked after with due propriety. I shall furnish you with all the necessary funds for her care while I make arrangements for her to be educated and board at the Chambers Society School in Oxfordshire."

Elated that the Queen had embraced Sarah so, Forbes barely contained his excitement.

"That sounds very fine, Ma'am!"

"Until then, have your wife keep a check on her while you're away," said Victoria. She then smiled at Sarah, "You will become the perfect example to demonstrate why England is the greatest, most powerful empire on earth, Sally. I hope you are up to the challenge."

"Thank you, ma'am."

Victoria rang a bell. Lord John entered. Aware this was the signal that their royal audience was over, Forbes kissed the Queen's hand. Queen Victoria then extended her hand to Sarah, who tentatively kissed it. Then she shook Prince Albert's hand, followed by Forbes, who did the same, and the two backed out of the room. Forbes and Sarah exited the palace and headed to the coach.

Once they had distanced themselves from the earshot of Lord John, Forbes excitedly turned to Sarah. "That was not so bad, eh?"

> *I showed no signs of being impressed by having met the 'most powerful woman on Earth' and kept my gaze forward. Indeed, I was still reeling from her self-serving observation that I was some subject of an African safari encounter. Observed prey. 'No. Lady King was pleasant,' said my lips to placate Forbes who had a good heart. But my young mind screamed…*
>
> *…'And full of herself.'"*

Clueless of Sarah's true feelings, Forbes grinned and helped his charge into the carriage. Meanwhile, from the Presence Room window,

Queen Victoria was watching Forbes and Sarah leave as Prince Albert joined her proffering up a glass of port. Concerned about the depth of what Victoria wanted to prove regarding Sarah and, indeed, an entire race, Albert assumed his role of alternate conscience for his *wife*—not his Queen.

"Is this what you want, darling? Truly?"

Victoria turned to her handsome husband—the man whose face she would never cease being drawn in by—or his eyes that had lovingly taken in hers so many times in their now eleven-year marriage.

"I've been told what to want all my life, Albie. By King William, Mother, Prime Ministers. As Queen, I have some plans for England that do not require my seeking permission." She took a sip of the port and moved from the window. "Sally could teach us something about the human condition—and I want to see it through."

Albert regarded his wife—and Queen—and toasted her. She was still the same woman he had fallen in love with. A woman determined to reshape the world. A world that all too often did not welcome such optimism, but repeatedly executed it.

He had to be there for her and stand by her at any and all costs.

or the next six weeks, Sarah lived at Winkfield Place, the Forbes home. She did little odd chores to help them take care of it. Sometimes she would babysit, sometimes she helped carry the dishes to the table, other times she went out and got the newspaper from the vendor on the corner.

Articles of her having an audience with the Queen of England and how impressed Victoria was, were printed in several newspapers including an announcement in the London Times on 23 September 1851 which said she had been presented to the Royal Family as a child who was "a prisoner of high rank kept closely confined for two years" as a slave in Africa.

The girl was becoming a bonafide celebrity in England even though she did not understand what all the fuss was about.

One evening as they all had dinner at the table enjoying Jilly's fine roasted pork and potatoes, Forbes was in a cheerful mood. He complimented Jilly's cooking, then smiled at Sarah who was enjoying brussels sprouts for the first time. "I'm still thinking about how well you did at court. The Queen was so impressed. All the papers say so. She likes you. You are in her favor. And there is nothing like being in the Queen's favor. Not even all of her children are so preferred by her."

"How many does she have?" asked Sarah.

"Seven now, I believe. I am sure you will eventually meet them. A randy bunch I hear—but royal nonetheless."

Sarah drank her tea then looked down and coughed slightly. "Captain Forbes…?"

Forbes looked up from his plate at the girl.

"…Thank you for saving my life and introducing me to Her Majesty," Sarah said in a small voice.

Forbes was prophetic. "We both see your potential…to be greater than your circumstance."

It became quiet at the table that evening as everyone was reminded that Sarah had come through an ordeal and was trying to transition to life in a new country. It was an adjustment for all of them.

But at the same time, Sarah was developing a cough which became worse as the weeks wore on. Sometimes it was bad enough to put her in bed for a day or two.

Forbes had cause to worry. "Could it be our climate? It's very different here in England," he said to Mary one evening.

Indeed, it was. Sarah had been raised in a perennially warm dry climate in Okeodan. She had been eating her native foods seasoned with native African herbs and spices. Now she had gone through a year's trip across the salty-aired sea, experienced seasonal changes, cold, snow and interminable rain which went on for days. Clearly, the girl's health was deteriorating.

But Mary Forbes seemed to be more interested in how and when the Queen would send money for Sarah's care—which was now including doctors. On days when Sarah was unable to come downstairs because she wasn't feeling well, she could hear Mary harping: "When is Her Majesty going to send the cheque?" "When will the money come from the Queen?" "Shouldn't we be hearing about the money for Sarah's care?" All of it meaning, "This African boarder is costing us!"

Captain Forbes had sent a letter to the Queen detailing Sarah's cough and his concerns about her welfare in England. Then four days later, there was a knock at the front door. When Mary answered, there stood an amiable aristocrat in his fifties wearing a top hat. "Good afternoon, ma'am. I am Sir Charles Phipps, her Majesty's Keeper of the Privy Purse. Have I the pleasure of addressing Mrs. Mary Forbes?"

"Yes."

From her upstairs window, Sarah could see the proceedings as Sir Charles handed Mary an envelope. "From Her Majesty the Queen. I am to wait and get your required signature for release of this cheque and to make sure we can send our physician to examine young Sarah."

Mary's eyebrow rose in anticipation and she opened the envelope. When she saw the amount on the cheque, she held her chest. Sir Charles then offered a pen and an inkpot, and she instantly signed his form.

"The money is to be used for Mistress Sarah's clothes and shoes, her necessaries, and whatever else you think best for the next six months." Then Sir Charles handed her another envelope. "And the Queen expects Captain Forbes to be ready to leave for West Africa right after the New Year. These are the Captain's orders. Our doctor will be here tomorrow."

At that, Sir Charles tipped his hat and left.

That night at dinner Mary was uncharacteristically gleeful. "The Queen's envoy brought us the money for Sarah's upkeep. And she wants you ready to leave for Africa in January." But Forbes was looking at Sarah, who was well enough to eat dinner at the table with them but looked peaked and still had her persistent cough.

"How are you feeling, Sarah? Are you any better?"

"I'll be alright, sir." But she still coughed which irritated Mary who turned to Rebecca. "Becky, take Sarah back to her room. Her coughing is no better and will be an annoyance to us as we eat. And since we do not know what she has, we don't wish to catch anything."

Rebecca who was serving, nodded and helped Sarah up to her room.

"We'll send your dinner up momentarily," Mary called to the back of Sarah as the girl went upstairs.

Forbes was peeved as he turned to his wife. "I think that was the most un-Christian thing you've ever done, Mary. Pray, you don't do such things when I'm in Africa. Sarah is in the Queen's care now—and our ward. Treat her with some dignity."

Though she knew she had been impolite, Mary continued eating and instructed the children to do the same. It was only Little Ian who was in low-spirits because he liked Sarah. "I hope she feels better."

"I do too, Ian," offered Forbes.

The next morning, Dr. Brown, the Queen's personal physician, came to call. He was taken up to the third floor, to Sarah's room and examined the girl. From his doctor's bag he retrieved his new binaural stethoscope—a new Irish invention few physicians could own or afford—and moved it around Sarah's chest, he determined that she had an inflammation brought on by stress and the English climate. He nodded to Forbes and Mary. "I'm going to give her some medication, but it is what you suspected. Her constitution is not conducive to our damp air. Her lungs are congested, and I fear after one year here, she will be an invalid." He closed his bag and sighed. "I shall tell the Queen of my results. I'm sure she will have an opinion."

"Indeed," said Forbes who led the doctor out.

"I'll be in touch," said Dr. Brown—and he left.

Sarah just lay there. Now she *was* a nomad like Lt. Gibson had suggested on the ship. A girl who belonged nowhere and to no one. Sure enough, when Sarah did not respond to the medicine that Dr. Brown gave her, Victoria made a decision. Perhaps it would be better if Sarah returned to Africa. Not to Dahomey where she could be recaptured and executed by Gezo, but an area on the West African coast where she could heal, be educated, and happy. Victoria would pay for everything and the Forbes' were informed.

Since Christmas was approaching, Forbes went out and returned with the biggest Douglas Fir evergreen tree he could find and put it up in the corner of the parlor. Then the Forbes family, Jilly and Rebecca decorated and trimmed it.

Sarah, who found it all odd, but fascinating joined in, even with her occasional coughing. After the tree had been trimmed with candles, ornaments, and strung popcorn that created a mouthwatering smell, Sarah and the family stood back and marveled at the stunningly appointed Christmas tree. "Beautiful."

Young Keith grinned. "This one is far prettier than last year's tree."

But Sarah frowned. "What an odd custom—cutting a tree and decorating it for a holiday," young Sarah remarked.

"People tend to think that Prince Albert, whom you met, first introduced the Christmas tree into England in 1840. But it's not true. It was the Queen's grandmother, Queen Charlotte, who put up the first known Christmas tree at Windsor in 1800," began Forbes as he placed the last of the ribbons on the tree. "Legend has it that in 1536, Queen Charlotte's German compatriot, Martin Luther, the religious reformer, was walking through a pine forest near his home in Wittenberg, looked up and saw thousands of stars luminously sparkling amongst the branches of pine trees. This wondrous sight inspired him to set up a candle-lit fir tree in his house that very Christmas to remind his children of the starry heavens from whence their Savior came. Queen Charlotte
followed suit, and we all have ever since."

"So, celebrating Christ's birth is another 'Christian' custom?"

Forbes nodded. "Yes. But Jews celebrate this time of year as well." He tied red ribbon on various branches of the tree. "They celebrate a tradition called 'Hanukkah' which is a re-dedication of the Temple in Jerusalem, and for eight nights they light a menorah—a kind of candlestick," Forbes offered. "Their Temple was built by King Solomon, an ancestor of Jesus."

Sarah shook her head. "There is so much to learn—about your customs, and religion."

"And our societal rules," said Mary.

"All in good time," smiled Forbes who picked up her violin lying atop the piano and handed it to Sarah. "Now, play something for us. Something Christmassy."

Sarah took the violin from him and thought. She had heard a choir of young boys singing Christmas carols outside their window earlier and was intrigued by the music. It was *"Oh Come All Ye Faithful,"* and she positioned her bow across the strings and played the tune from memory. Forbes, Keith and young Susan began to sing the lyrics as she played causing Sarah much enjoyment.

When she was finished, they all applauded, and Sarah watched as Keith, Susan, Arthur and Ian kissed and bid their parent's goodnight and Rebecca took them upstairs to bed. It made Sarah think about her own parents and how she wished they were alive to kiss goodnight. Then she bid the Forbes' goodnight and went to her room feeling lonely even in a home filled with people.

Meanwhile, at Windsor Castle, with her own Christmas tree in the room, Queen Victoria was composing a letter she would give to Sir Charles Phipps concerning Sarah Forbes Bonetta. The letter was then sent from Sir Charles to Reverend Henry Venn, who was head of the Church Missionary Society in Sierra Leone, Africa. It stated that:

"The Queen, having made enquiries... has been anxious that Sarah should be educated in one of Her Majesty's dependencies upon the coast of Africa..."

Thus, arrangements were made for Sarah to attend the Female Institution of the Church Missionary Society school in Sierra Leone. She would be accompanied back to Africa by Reverend Schmid, a white Presbyterian minister and report to the HMS Bathurst in February. It would take time to make all the inquiries, the necessary arrangements, coordinate the ship and its personnel, and obtain proper clothing for Sarah. So Sarah would stay under the care of Dr. Brown, who made weekly visits, until she left England.

In the interim, on a chilly January morning, three days after the New Year, Forbes was finally going on his mission for Her Majesty, Queen Victoria. Valises are piled atop his carriage. His children, Mary, Rebecca, Jilly and Sarah were outside when he appeared. He looked at each of them with longing, hating that he had to leave them a second time in two months.

"I do not know when I shall see you again. I must stay until the mission is completed this time," he said bleakly, then kissed his wife and their children.

"Papa, must you go? It was a year last time." asked Keith, who, at 13, was the oldest but felt like young Ian who was crying at this moment.

"Yes, son. I have a duty to the Queen. She is counting on me."

"But we count on you, too," cried Susan.

It was killing Forbes to leave his family, but as every military man knew—mission first, family second. He looked at Sarah. "Go inside. I don't want you getting a cold. And take care of yourself in Africa. I expect great things from you."

Sarah nodded, and tearfully hugged Forbes for dear life. She ran back inside the house and looked out of the window at his departure. With great melancholy she and the others watched as Forbes got into the carriage. She dreaded the coming of this day. For she would now be without him as her champion both in the house and out. No one would be there to stand up to his wife until she left. Her life could be a living hell with him gone. How would she cope until she left for Africa?

As Mr. Nelson the driver moved the team of brown quarter-horses pulling the Forbes carriage away from the house, and they all waved good-bye, young Sarah was determined to do what Forbes demanded of her:

"Be greater than your circumstance."

She vowed to do just that as Forbes' coach became a speck on the cobblestone road.

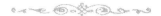

That same evening of her husband's departure, Mary invited her friend Mrs. Willoughby, a widow, to dine with her and the children so she would not think about her distress at Forbes being gone.

Downstairs in the kitchen Jilly was none too happy that Forbes had left. "Saints alive. Now that Mr. Forbes has gone, we'll be worked to death," she grimaced. "The Missus is hell-on-wheels when he's not here. It was something awful just before you arrived."

"'Tis true," echoed a disgruntled Rebecca coming down to fetch the appetizer course for the table. "She treated us like slaves. We hardly got any sleep, nor days off."

Sarah tried to be optimistic despite the building congestion in her chest and the coughing fit that finally subsided. "Maybe she won't be so bad this time."

Rebecca and Jilly only shot her an "Oh please" expression as Sarah helped Rebecca bring up the salad course.

"...Once I was upstairs the truth of Jilly and Rebecca's look became a reality. I placed small salads in front of everyone, and then went to my usual chair at the table to sit down and have supper. Mrs. Willoughby glared at me, then gave Mrs. Forbes a questionable look. Mary Forbes looked at me with an insincere smile. "Oh, Sarah dear, from now on you will eat in the kitchen with Rebecca and Jilly. It's what

is proper in a civilized household." I frowned, "But I've been eating up here with you and the family since I came."

With a glance to Mrs. Willoughby, and employing a firm tone, Mary retorted, "Well, my husband, bless his heart, has a soft spot for the occasional impropriety. But now that he is on the Queen's duties, we must get back to snuff in this house. "But Mrs. Forbes…" I began. Both Mary and Mrs. Willoughby shot me a disdainful look that cut right through me. Mrs. Willoughby lowered her head and softly chastised Mrs. Forbes which I overheard. "My word. Is the Negress talking back to you?" "Of course, she isn't," Mary cautioned, glaring at me. "She knows better."

I gathered my plate and excused myself. With a last look at little Ian, I went down to the kitchen and had my supper. It would be where I would eat from that moment on.

Suddenly, a feeling of foreboding swept over me as I looked up to find Jilly squeezing my hand. "I tell you she's a beast, that one. But don't you worry. Mr. Forbes was right. You're going to be educated. You'll be smarter than her. Smarter than all of us. An' I can say "I knew her. Met her when she was fresh off the boat. Now look at her." I hugged Jilly then finished my meal. Afterward, she showed me the apple pie she had baked just for her, Rebecca, and myself.

But I couldn't help but think that despite having the Queen of England's favor, I had become just another Negro in Britain once Forbes left…"

Nine

Sarah's cough was becoming worse and she was all too ready to leave London. Even though she knew she was not going back to the village or the people she once knew in Dahomey, she did know she was going home to the Continent she was native of…Africa. To things she understood, and to a peace she could grasp.

At the Queen's request Mrs. Forbes made arrangements for Reverend Schmid and his wife to pick Sarah up at Winkfield Place and transport the girl to the docks at Gravesend. All Sarah's belongings were packed in boxes and crates, Jilly made a blueberry pie for the girl. Her favorite.

After many tearful goodbyes between the four Forbes children, Jilly and Rebecca, Sarah, clutching her ubiquitous violin, was off to another new life, and a second voyage across the seas in less than six months. Mary Forbes waved goodbye as the Schmid carriage pulled away with a combination of relief that Sarah was leaving, guilt for feeling that way, and sadness that the Queen's financial support would now be gone.

Once again, Sarah looked in awe at the bustling activity on the crowded docks at Gravesend. As her luggage and crates were being loaded onboard she looked at the large ship which would transport her to Africa. The HMS Bathurst was a 154-ton steam liner which was under the command of Captain Phillip Parker King. The Captain would later come down to meet Sarah as he had been told one of his passengers was a young, African celebrity. He promised to get everyone safely to Sierra Leone, barring pirates, and that is what he did.

After thirty-three difficult, stormy days at sea, The Bathurst finally docked in the harbor at Freetown, the capital of Sierra Leone, where Sarah found the dock far more boring than those in London.

She was instantly coached to the Church Missionary School where everyone was waiting for the African girl who was the Queen of England's ward. She was warmly greeted by Reverend Venn who showed her to her new room at the Female Institution where she would be studying. While her crates and valises were deposited in her new room, Sarah was taken to the community room where a nice party was given in her honor with music and dancing—which Sarah loved. There she met other female students and some of her teachers including Miss Sass and Miss Wilkinson, both white Englishwomen.

She also had her first African food in ages consisting of the traditional dishes she had longed for like Maafe—a groundnut stew, Jollof rice, Fufu, cocoyams, sweet potatoes, and cassava.

Sarah was in heaven. Then after saying goodbye to Reverend Schmid and his wife Cassandra who had accompanied her, she began her life as a student. As the Female Institution was a part of the missionary church society, the first thing Sarah noticed was that many of the missionaries, who were white, didn't think too highly of Africans considering them "primitive" or "savage."

One missionary, Horace Flanders an Australian man in his fifties, who turned up his nose at many of the students, constantly clashed with the African missionaries on tradition and culture. He was insistent that the women of the school dress in the British style—dresses, stockings and bonnets on their heads, while the Africans wanted to be themselves if they wanted. That meant if they wanted to wear printed wrapped skirts and not cover the upper half of their bodies, so be it.

After a tug-of-war lasting over a month, it was decided that Sarah would wear English clothing—which Sarah hated. She was so hoping to go barefoot, topless and free, as had been her life in Okeodan. But as the "Ward of the Queen," no such accommodations were allowed. So, Sarah wore the clothing that had been packed for her and tortured herself into stockings and shoes.

Sarah quickly learned that girls were to be educated to take their place in a Christian monogamous family, to provide moral and practical support for men, and to bring up their children in the new faith. This was especially hard for many of the girls because their various root religions advocated men have several wives.

Girls were to be taught separately from boys by female teachers with a different curriculum which tended to be dominated by sewing. Educational opportunities were only expanded if a woman needed to be a fitting and accomplished marriage companion for an educated man seeking to advance his career in a meritocratic society.

Nevertheless, Sarah took to learning as she had on the ship with Forbes. She absorbed everything, and Miss Sass, who was her favorite, soon became her unofficial guardian. Miss Sass found Sarah to be as brilliant as the Queen had mentioned and pushed the girl toward her "highest and best self." Sarah read voraciously and availed herself to the wonderful library at the school. She also made friends easily and shared some of her clothing with a few of the African girls—especially Abigail Crowther who was older than she and whose father Reverend Samuel Crowther would become the first African Bishop of Nigeria, and she adored Kali Imani with whom she would play and read books to. The three of them soon became inseparable and Kali was the recipient of many of Sarah's English clothes sent by the Queen.

Almost, as if by magic, Sarah's cough subsided, and her spirits lifted.

Now, the only people she missed were Captain Forbes, young Ian Forbes, and, of course, Queen Victoria.

At the school, Sarah learned the history of Freetown and Sierra Leone. She discovered that Sierra Leone was comprised of mostly liberated Africans rescued from slave ships in the Atlantic Ocean during the Middle Passage in a mission by the British after abolishing the slave trade. The Royal Navy—particularly the West African anti-slave squadron, of which Captain Forbes' squadron was one, started patrolling the West African coast and high seas. They seized all slave vessels and transported most of the newly liberated Africans to Freetown. Many of the people who settled in Freetown, were from West Africa—particularly the Kingdom of Dahomey where King Gezo's slavers had almost decimated the Kingdom by selling his black prisoners of war.

Everywhere around Sarah were displaced Africans who had found new opportunities after capture and built good lives for themselves. Part of what the Church Missionary Society did was to help such people rebuild their lives through education, job training and teaching them to embrace Christianity—of which Sarah was already familiar.

Sarah loved Freetown. She loved her mornings there. The air always smelled of food being prepared, especially fish being salted and cured by local fishermen. There was always a cacophony of sounds—dock workers yelling, buyers negotiating, merchants hawking. Life in the marketplace was a continual burst of energy as African women proudly carried baskets of goods on their heads as they gossiped or shopped along rows of open stands featuring vegetables, fruits, fabric, palm oil or hand-made jewelry and beads.

Most evenings Sarah would play her violin for the girls or speak about her visits with the Queen of England and having tea at Windsor or Buckingham palaces. The girls would "Oooh and Ahhh" at all her experiences and beg for more stories as most of them had never been outside of Sierra Leone. Many had been captured in slave raids who managed to escape—as Sarah herself had done.

Then upon noticing the piano in the community room, Sarah began learning how to play it. She loved music and was adept at it, as Forbes had once written to the Queen.

Between the instruments, books, and school she had much to occupy her time, and before she knew it, a year had passed, and then two.

She wrote of her progress to the Queen, who not only wrote back, but was also making large donations to the school and missionary church.

Also, Sarah continued to document her feelings and experiences in her diary/journal which now consisted of several loose pages and Victoria's letters, which she bound with ribbon and prized. She was determined to do those things Captain Forbes had suggested. Especially now that Forbes' own journal he'd been writing for years called, *Dahomey and the Dahomans Being the Journals of Two Missions to the King of Dahomey, and Residence at His Capital, in the Years 1849 and 1850*—a two volume work— had been published in England that fall. Queen Victoria graciously sent Sarah a copy, and in the second volume was a story about her along with her picture. This excited Sarah and further elevated her status as the celebrity student at the school. Life was finally good for her.

News of Sarah's notoriety was far reaching, and eminent visitors to Sierra Leone would request to see the school and Sarah in particular as she had become its star student. One such notable was James Pinchon Labulo Davies, who at 24, was a wealthy missionary and Yoruban businessman on his way to London to sell his merchandise on the docks of Liverpool. James had attended the Church Missionary School in 1848 where he had studied math, English history, geography, and Latin. Then, after completing his secondary education, he became a teacher at the school in Freetown. As a friend of Reverend Crowther, whose daughter Abigail was one of Sarah's best friends, James reached out to Crowther to meet this rare student who was the protégée of Queen Victoria that everyone was talking about. Crowther arranged the introduction the next time James was in Freetown.

When James met Sarah, he was immediately impressed with her poise, her regal carriage and her gift of spoken language both French and English. They took a long walk and James told Sarah about himself.

"My parents had been recaptive Yoruba people. They were liberated by the British West Africa Squadron from a ship about to carry them off to Jamaica as slaves and were brought here."

"The British West Africa Squadron is led by my mentor, Captain Forbes. He's in Dahomey again now."

"Yes, I know who he is. He's doing good work but is up against a formidable tyrant."

"King Gezo. Yes, I know. Forbes rescued me from him. It's how I got to England, and now back here."

"I was raised here. And later, I taught at this very school. Then, as a lieutenant on the HMS Bloodhound during the Bombardment of Lagos, I was wounded and had to retire. Now I am a successful merchant."

Sarah liked James. He was educated, friendly and never once talked down to her. She enjoyed his company and later joined him for dinner with Reverend Crowther, Reverend Venn and their wives. Though James was leaving in two days for Liverpool, he asked if he could write to Sarah some time in Freetown. She accepted not realizing that it would be years before she would see him again.

The next year, news broke which concerned everyone. King Gezo had attacked Abeokuta, another village in Dahomey and was setting his imperialist sights on neighboring countries. It worried many of the female students who had wanted to become missionaries and teachers and teach in their home villages or in other cities. The idea of a crazed ruler like Gezo and his far-reaching armies of soldiers and Amazon warrior women attacking, and decimating cities, towns and villages did not sit well with either Sarah—nor the Queen when she heard about it.

Her Majesty worried that her prized ward could be found, attacked, or kidnapped because her fame was spreading. She was also praying that Sarah's cough had improved. All of this made Victoria reassess the girl's situation. That September, Miss Wilkinson received a letter from Sir Charles Phipps indicating that Her Majesty the Queen was requesting Sarah be immediately sent back to England. Sarah was informed by Miss Wilkinson and fell into her teacher's lap in tears. After two years in Africa, finally adjusting to a happy life she enjoyed, having new friends and acquaintances, and loving her school, Sarah was going back to the place she loathed…London. And she could do nothing about it.

She gave her best friend Kali most of her clothes, and once again valises, suitcases and crates were packed for yet another voyage across the sea. It was her understanding that Queen Victoria was not happy with her "situation" in Freetown. Obviously, the Queen's African intelligence from her Prime Minister and Privy Councilors forced her hand, and back Sarah was to go.

Now for a third time Sarah was standing on a dock, this time in Freetown, waving goodbye to people she had grown to love and would miss. She hugged Kali, Abigail, Miss Sass, Miss Wilkinson, and Reverends Crowther and Venn, and their wives. Then with her violin tucked under her arm, she got into a kroo canoe with Reverend Dicker who would accompany her, and powerful rowers took her to the awaiting steamer ship transporting her back to England.

As she looked back at the shore where her African friends were still waving, she wondered what her fate was now? What was her next adventure? And if she would ever see the wondrous, unique country that was her homeland of Africa again.

Ten

S arah had only been back on British soil for three days when a request for an audience was sent to the Forbes' home for both Mary Forbes and Sarah to see the Queen at Buckingham Palace where the Queen was in residence.

Sarah had soaked in a bath and was wearing one of the beautiful dresses Victoria had sent to Freetown and braided her hair into "corn-rows" the way the African girls in Sierra Leone wore theirs.

She and Mary Forbes dropped into curtsies upon seeing Victoria who smiled warmly.

"Hello, Sally, Mrs. Forbes."

"Hello, your Majesty," both women answered.

Victoria then turned her attention to Sarah. "I regret that I had to bring you back here after you were settling in so nicely as my reports tell me. But other reports, on King Gezo's plans, alarmed me enough to pull you out."

Sarah nodded. What could she say?

Victoria looked at her ward shaking her head in wonder. The person standing before her was not the girl whom she sponsored three years ago, but a woman—a lovely woman, all filled out and almost a head taller than she.

"My goodness you've grown, Sally. Look at you. Not a child at all."

"No, ma'am. I'm thirteen now."

"Of marriageable age, and quite self-assured I see. Did you like your school? We've done everything we can to make it a model institution for the dispossessed and recaptured."

"I did, ma'am. I liked it very much."

"Now if we can stop Gezo's mad nonsense we may not need to dedicate places for marginalized Africans sold into slavery on the high seas." Victoria then noticed the brooch on Sarah's collar. "How nice."

"Open it, ma'am," said Sarah.

Victoria did and was touched at the tiny photo of the Queen inside.

"Oh my. This is quite moving."

"I also had your picture on my wall at school. Every day I could look at it and be reminded of your kindness."

"Thank you. And there is more of that to come. I have made arrangements for you to study at a private school in Oxfordshire. The Chambers Society School for Girls. You are expected there next month, and I can only hope you enjoy it there as much as you enjoyed the Female Institution in Sierra Leone."

Sarah smiled. "I know I will. Your majesty has such very good taste regarding me. I'm sure it will be a singular experience."

Victoria then turned to Mary Forbes. "Until then, Sarah shall stay with you, and I shall send Sir Charles along with monies for her care. I shall also send money for you to buy shoes, stockings and have two uniforms made for her for school. You will also purchase her train tickets with it."

"Yes, ma'am," said Mary.

"I am entrusting you, Mrs. Forbes, to make sure our Sally is well looked after up there when she goes. Write her and go visit from time-to-time, so there is a familiar face. And do send me a report."

"Yes, your Majesty. I will take care of it."

"And, of course, there will be a bit extra for your personal needs."

Mary Forbes nodded. This was indeed good news. The Queen was always generous, so a nice amount of money would be coming.

Victoria then smiled at Sarah. "Despite it all, the illness, Gezo, travel, I'm happy you're back on English soil, my dear. I want people to know my little experiment is well on her way to English greatness."

There it was again. The "experiment." The very thing she never felt like in Freetown, Sarah thought. But then she had to accept that those days were over and new experiences lay ahead.

She and Mary curtsied and left the audience of the Queen.

For four weeks, Sarah did what she was told and took whatever verbal abuses hurled her way from Mary Forbes. All she wanted was to go to Oxfordshire to school. It had to be better than life in the Forbes home without Captain Forbes whom she deeply missed.

Mary Forbes, for her part, gave Sarah's measurements to a local seamstress who made two uniforms for Sarah, and she bought Sarah two pairs of shoes—one for every day and another pair for Sunday and special occasions.

Because Sarah did not wish to be a nuisance nor freeloader, she volunteered to dust, sweep, iron, help Jilly cook, and watch the children, who were now older teenagers. Only young Ian was just under ten. Sarah was especially fond of Ian who had embraced her from the first moment. He would seek Sarah out to play ball, tuck him in bed for his naps, or just to climb onto her lap for a hug. Such a child would surely grow into a loving, honorable man like his father, Sarah thought, and she was so glad to be a part of his life in these formative years.

Sarah also enjoyed Rebecca's company. Rebecca seemed to have a teacher's heart and would show Sarah how to do her various tasks without being condescending—which Sarah appreciated.

But Sarah's absolute favorite was still Jillian. She loved Jilly—who despite a jolly, robust countenance, had a wicked, bawdy sense of humor that kept everyone below stairs laughing. Sarah was often flabbergasted by Jilly's stories which were the most lascivious and provocative tales she had ever heard—especially about Jilly's time in service to a brothel owner in Liverpool. Sometimes even Mr. Nelson hung around in the kitchen when he wasn't driving Mary, just to hear Jilly's randy anecdotes.

"…So, I was assigned to take the sheets off the beds and wash 'em," began Jilly, telling one of her lewd stories one day while she and Sarah were peeling potatoes. "I go into room 8. It was 'spose to be empty an' prepared for the next go 'round. But of course, there was Cassandra—one of the whores who I never understood why was so popular, 'cause she only had one tit. She said a wild dog bit the other one off. Anyway, Cassandra an' a 'john' with a prick the size of a thimble, had just finished up and she threw on a robe to take him back downstairs."

Jilly then tossed the peeled potatoes into the boiling water on the cast iron stove. "Well, I try to get the bottom sheet off the bed an' it's stuck like glue to the mattress," she laughs. "I'm pullin' an' pullin'. When finally I get the damn thing separated, the sheet is as hard as a brick. I coulda cracked it in two from the dried spud…"

"What is 'spud?'" Sarah asked innocently.

Jilly stopped and frowned at her. "Are ye daft, girl? Ye know. Of course, ye know."

Sarah shook her head. She was serious.

Jilly looked at her askance. "The stuff that comes from a man's prick after he's been excited."

Again, Sarah just looked at her. "Prick?" She had no idea of the various slang terms for male genitalia. She'd heard what happens, but never saw or experienced it for herself.

"Saints alive, Lassie," Jilly exclaimed in her Scottish brogue. "Yer too old fer me to be teachin' you about the birds an' the bees? Keep this up an' we'll be taking care of a bastard bairn comin' from ye. Surely ye know where it goes, an' what happens when it's in there?"

Sarah was absolutely embarrassed.

Jilly grinned. "Goodness. Let's start at letter 'A.' Have ye seen a penis before?" Then she added, "The thing dangling betwixt a man's legs that determines he's in fact a man."

Sarah knew Jilly was being sarcastic. "I'm from Africa, Jilly," she snorted. "Not the moon. We don't wear clothes most of the time. In Africa, penises are all you see. In fact, Africa is one big penis."

"That's what I hear," Jilly joked, then lowered her voice. "Must be rivers of spud over there as big as I hear they are."

Everyone broke out laughing. They were so loud Mary Forbes had to yell down to the kitchen for them to use their refined, inside voices.

Jilly sneered. "That one, if ye haven't noticed, is all fer puttin' on airs o' sophistication as though she's 'Lady Mary of Castle Hill.' But she's only a step above me. A housekeeper's daughter she is—who married well." She then added, "An' a saint if ever there was is Mr. Forbes. Don't know how he puts up with her."

Sarah said nothing. She was already on record with her feelings for Mary Forbes and did not wish to further pontificate on it. It was a chore to hear Mary's nightly ravings about any and everything going on in the house including Sarah's presence. So, Sarah kept to the shadows with her head down and tried to be an asset to the house. Every other evening at dinner, Sarah would find herself staring into her food or pulling at loose threads on her dress while Mary went on and on about some concern or other. The only thing to cheer her was when Sir Charles came to Winkfield Place to give Mary the checque the Queen promised. Then Mary felt she could tolerate anything as there was enough for any and all needs. And she was expecting one every other month because Sarah was to have an allowance sent to her at the school. "Walking around money" Mary called it—which she herself now had.

Then a week before Sarah was set to leave, she came down with a dreadful cold. Jilly watched over her day and night like a mother hen, giving Sarah lemon tea and chicken soup. "Come on, Lassie," Jilly would say to the ailing girl. "You've got to get better. Ye cannot be here another second beyond your train leaving." Then they would both recite the Lord's Prayer—just like Sarah had with Forbes on the ship, and finally on the Sunday before her departure Sarah felt better.

When the day came, Sarah re-braided her hair and put on a black hat and silk scarf. She looked like a proper "Lady." Rebecca pulled Sarah aside, smiled, and spoke to her about this next chapter of Sarah's life.

"I almost envy you, Sarah," she began. "You have a chance now to experience something most women are never allowed—the opportunity to be properly educated. Remember, there are those who feel that women should only receive a domestic education. I am not one of those. I know what things one can do with knowledge. You can conquer ignorance, go places, allow dreams to be realized. There are already enough stupid people," she noted. "But you won't be one of those, Sarah. The Queen has chosen you to rise above even the second-class status others put on you because of your color. You get to excel." Rebecca hugged Sarah. "I'm proud of you and wish you all the best. Do what Captain Forbes would say, 'Be greater than your circumstance.' Be excellent."

"Excellent," echoed little Ian—which made everyone laugh.

Outside the house, as Mr. Nelson put Sarah's valise and boxes atop the carriage, Rebecca and Jilly who were fighting back tears—all hugged. Mary walked out with Susan, Keith, Elijah and Ian.

"Mr. Nelson here will take you to the train. Then someone named Mr. Browning will meet you at the station in Oxfordshire. He will escort you to the Chambers Society School," informed Mary who then handed Sarah a few pounds and some shillings. "That money is for anything you may need. Spend it wisely. I shall send more each month in care of the Headmaster."

"Thank you," said Sarah putting the money into her new purse. Then Jilly gave Sarah a napkin folded around a large sandwich cut in quarters. "I made this fer yer lunch. It's ham with lettuce in two nice pieces of that sourdough bread ye like. Don' want ye gettin' hungry, Lassie." Jilly then hugged Sarah. "Now remember what it says in the bible:

"*Those to whom much is given, much is expected.*"

Sarah kissed Jilly's cheek. "I shall miss you most of all" she whispered."

Soon the four Forbes children hugged Sarah for dear life and kissed her cheek as she bent down to Ian's level. "Be a good boy and always mind your mother, alright?"

"I will," he answered sadly.

Then Keith extended his hand and Sarah shook it firmly.

Mr. Nelson helped Sarah inside. Mary nodded her head in an obligatory goodbye, then motioned to Mr. Nelson who snapped the reins and the horses pulled Sarah and her life in the Spitalfields, away forever.

As Sarah looked out of the small square window in back of the coach she saw Mary Forbes immediately go into the house, relieved no doubt that Sarah was going, but the Forbes children, and her two friends Rebecca and Jilly were wiping their eyes and still waving goodbye—and Sarah found herself thinking:

"How many more of these tearful goodbyes can I take?"

Eleven

A lot of people were waiting for the eleven o'clock to Oxford-shire leaving Paddington Station that June morning as Sarah came onto Platform Two. Her heart was racing for she had never been on a train nor traveled unescorted before. She looked around and, in the distance, saw two Negro servants helping their employers with luggage and wondered if she'd be mistreated as a Negro on board.

But soon, she heard the whistle of an approaching train and saw the rising chimney smoke and the billowing steam from the train's locomotive. It all made her heart leap. Once she got onboard the train, her earlier concerns were unfounded for when she showed the conductor her second-class ticket, she was respectfully shown the proper section of the train and taken to a window seat where at precisely eleven o'clock, the train pulled out of the station.

Instantly a huge smile took residence on her face as she could not be more excited to experience this true bit of freedom. She was finally on her way. At a speed of 35 miles per hour the Great Western Railway train, powered by a brand new Penydarren Tram Road steam engine, provided a thrill ride for the former Aina from Okeodan.

She watched as the English countryside whisked by and marveled at how it was all so green and lush. So pastoral. Occasionally she saw farmers tending sheep or cows, and so many horses were meandering or grazing on land that went on forever. As she enjoyed her sandwich savoring every bit of Jilly's baked ham glazed with mustard, she wished she could have shared this experience with Kua, her parents, or even Kali and Abigail in Freetown. It was such a great adventure, and before she knew it two and a half hours had flown by and the conductor announced: "Grandpont Station, Oxfordshire."

When the train stopped, Sarah picked up her valise and with eight other passengers disembarked. As soon as she set foot on the platform in Oxfordshire an air of scholarly sophistication overtook her. She knew from conversations with Rebecca that this was the location of one of the best universities in Europe—the famous University of Oxford. She was so excited to be attending school in this rarified area of education.

Sarah tied her scarf tighter and looked around for Mr. Browning, the man who was supposed to meet her. But no one came forward. As she was the only black on the platform she would not be hard to find. So, she waited. And waited.

She was there a full half an hour when finally, a short, squatty man in his sixties, with eyes too close together approached her.

"Mistress Sarah Forbes?" inquired the man.

"Yes," Sarah responded looking him in the eye, as they were the same height.

"I'm so sorry to be late, but one of my horses had to be put down. I had to change him out," he offered, then extended his hand. "I'm Archibald Browning, assistant to Mr. Barnard Humes, headmaster of the Chambers School for Girls. Welcome to Oxfordshire."

"Thank you," Sarah smiled as she shook his hand. So far so good, she thought. Mr. Browning did not seem bias either as he had extended his hand and didn't grimace upon seeing her.

"Now, we've got another hour and a half of travel to go before we reach South Parks Road where the school is, and there is so much to see along the way," Browning informed her.

At that, Mr. Browning took Sarah's valise and box, and attached it to the back of his coach and deposited Sarah inside. He pulled his team of two horses out onto Abingdon Road and they traveled until they reached the low-lying ground south of the county which was becoming susceptible to winter flooding from the Thames River nearby. The water was now at least four feet onto the land and Sarah saw some people attempting to ice skate. It was a sight.

Eventually, the carriage rattled and rocked down various cobblestone streets on the south end of St. Giles parish. Somewhere between St. John's College and the Taylor Buildings it turned a corner and they came upon a pointed stone monument resembling a church steeple at the intersection of Magdalen and Beaumont Streets. The monument had the sculptures of three men faced in different directions. Browning pointed to it to show Sarah whose eyes were large with curiosity.

"Do you see that statue? It is called 'Martyrs Memorial.' It engenders an impression such as no other in Oxford can."

Sarah looked at it. "It's beautiful. But who are the martyrs on it?"

"Three Protestants tried for heresy in the 16th century and burned at the stake right here in the Square for their religious beliefs and teachings," began Browning with an instructional spirit. "It was during the persecutions in England. The Anglican bishops included the Archbishop of Canterbury."

"One could be executed because you had a different religious belief here in England?"

"Yes," Browning replied. "Terrible episode in our history from which, sadly, we are still reeling. The monument was just finished eight years ago to commemorate the event, so we don't forget our past."

It was then that Sarah told herself not to announce to anyone that she was a Vodun who worshipped Mahwah—instead of a Christian as she had been baptized lest she be executed. After all, she thought, these crazy white people in England might resurrect 'Burning at the stake' with her as their newly inducted victim—and she knew no one would build a statue in the middle of town honoring her martyrdom a hundred years from now.

They rode on, and soon, Browning pulled the coach over and indicated a massive set of buildings and ancient edifices all around them. He turned to Sarah and smiled. "This—is Oxford University, my dear. It's really a collection of architecturally stunning college buildings and I thought you might want to see it up close."

Sarah was overwhelmed. "Oh yes. Please."

Browning helped Sarah out and they walked through one of the university quadrangles and admired the magnificent buildings. The first was the Bodleian Library. "This is one of the largest research libraries in England." As they exited the Quadrangle, one of Oxford's most famous landmarks stood before them. "And this building is the Radcliffe Camera. *Camera* means *room* in Latin. It is one of the earliest circular libraries in England, built in 1749. Do you like to read, Mistress Sarah?"

"Yes. But there were precious few books in Captain Forbes' home. So, I look forward to having the opportunity to read at school."

They walked along the path through the serene Christ Church Meadow when Browning nodded in wonder. "So many brilliant minds, have come out of this institution: Sir Thomas More, Samuel Johnson, John Locke, Percy Bysshe Shelly, Cardinal Thomas Wolsey. Brilliant all."

He stopped and looked at Sarah pointedly. "If you have been chosen by her Majesty to study at the Chambers Society School, you must be something special. Now it's not for me to understand what she finds singular in an African girl of inferior birth with no family, position of power, or wealth, but the Queen has a good eye that I trust."

My teeth clenched causing my jaw and facial muscles to tighten in discomfort. Something inside me was churning and I found I could not let

Browning's comment pass without my innate outspokenness taking me over. 'Mr. Browning,' I scoffed, trying to calm the sharp tone my voice had engaged. 'Before I was kidnapped into slavery and prepared to be executed, I was the princess of my village. I am of royal blood. It may not mean anything to you as it is African royal blood, but I am in no way of inferior birth. I just want that known.'

Browning's eyes reflected the realization he had insulted me. And though he had never had more than two words to say to anyone with brown skin, even he had to recognize I was different. Perhaps it was even the thing the Queen had seen in me. The thing that kept my head up and demanded that attention be paid. I would accept no less. I didn't from Gezo. And I would not from him.

"I apologize for my observation. It was out of…" Browning thought first, then offered, "…an unawareness and inexperience with those unlike me." His eyes moved away from Sarah's in mounting regret. "I shall think of you as unusual and unique from this day forth, and expect great things from you, Mistress Bonetta."

He then pointed the way in the opposite direction. "Now. Let us return to our coach. We must get you to the school in time to register."

Sarah nodded, and they walked back from whence they'd come.

At four that afternoon, they at last reached their destination. The Chambers Society School for Girls was a private school located on South Parks Road in a building converted from a deteriorating Anglican church built in the 1400s. It was bought by a few enlightened clergymen and wealthy, concerned, citizens comprised primarily of women who felt it was time there was an institution of higher learning which allowed women to attend. It opened in 1835, with a full-scale remodel beginning in October 1841. Victoria became one of its ardent supporters when she became Queen, secretly at first, for it appealed to her feminist nature. In these last years, the grounds surrounding the structure had become magnificent. Shrubbery precisely cut; lawns manicured and thick; tall, leafy, oak tree branches billowing in the summer air. Sarah took it all in feeling awed by it.

The front façade of the building retained much of the gothic tradition of the old church from which it owed its foundation. But an ample amount of it incorporated the élan of the great Luxembourg Palace from whom the school's designer/architect, Sir William Mandeville had drawn inspiration. It was glorious and elegant. In the middle of the main building was a superb cupola, the construction of which many had thought too heavy. But upon its completion people were much delighted.

The class of girls who attended the school in 1835, its first year, numbered fifteen. Now eighteen years later, there were fifty-three girls ranging in age from ten to seventeen. Sarah would be the fifty-fourth student, the oldest—and clearly the only one of African descent.

Sarah and Mr. Browning checked in with the admissions clerk, Miss Winterbourne who, after frowning at Sarah, looked at her chart.

"Yes. Sarah Bonetta. A Fifth-Form student. Assigned to Gaia House, Room 10." She then pointed "Through those doors on the left."

Browning nodded and escorted Sarah through the main hall as Miss Winterbourne shook her head in disgust. When they reached the courtyard a few haughty girl students who were known as "The Heras" were chatting. Sarah smiled and waved at them as she passed, but the girls did nothing but stare at her as though they'd witnessed a living demon. It would be something she would have to overcome here, as everywhere she had been in England.

On the western end of the courtyard could be seen the two student Lodges for those who were boarding. They were spacious, splendid and finely finished in the Doric style. The two buildings had been given names of Ancient Greek deities. Thus, the building on the left was called

Gaia House, and to the right was Athena House. Each Lodge had a Housemistress in charge of the residential, social and academic well-being of the female house-members, and each House had thirty rooms for boarding. This system had been carefully copied from the very popular Rugby School for Boys—founded in 1567 in Warwickshire, England, and it worked very well here these last years.

Sarah registered at Gaia House with her new Headmistress Miss Calvin, who gave her a box containing a small silver pin. "That is your Fifth-Form pin. You are to wear it on your uniform at all times on your left shoulder visible to all."

Sarah smiled, took the pin then she and Mr. Browning proceeded to Room 10 on the first floor where Sarah would live while she was at school. She entered the small room with Browning who sat her valise and box down near the door.

"This is as far as I go," said Browning. "Good luck, Mistress Bonetta." He tipped his hat and started to leave.

But Sarah stopped him. "Mr. Browning. Thank you. I appreciate you bringing me here and for our outing today. I enjoyed everything I learned about the university and the city and all. I'm truly grateful."

Browning was touched and smiled warmly. "You're welcome. Now take care of yourself. And do big things." He then left.

Sarah closed the door and looked at her new surroundings. It was a serviceable room perfect for homework and reading. It had wood floors with a rug in front of the small bed. There was a side table with a lamp, a chest of drawers and a plain wood armoire for clothes. There was also a small desk under the window which looked out onto the courtyard framed by white lace curtains with pullbacks.

Sarah opened her valise and set out her two uniforms. One of them she hung in the armoire along with the dress shoes. The other uniform consisting of a blue plaid skirt and white blouse she laid on the bed along with her white stockings and looked at it. When she put it on would it truly make her like all the other girls? Would it distract from her being different? Being black? Being an 'other?' She hoped so. She prayed so.

And she could not wait for tomorrow to get started.

The converted Chambers Society School for Girls, Oxfordshire, England, circa 1870

Twelve

Inside the Windsor nursery, Royal Physician, Dr. Robert Brown had been examining Prince Leopold, now age one and crying his head off. He was a small, sickly boy with sallow skin and a body riddled with dark bruises. A boy who chronically cried and had trouble sleeping. Victoria looked on worried as Dr. Brown shook his head in frustration.

"He is getting no better, Majesty."

Victoria stroked Leopold's puffy cheeks, "Poor dear. I would give anything for him to be out of pain."

Dr. Brown's expression took on the look of trepidation subordinates acquire when they want to offer a good idea, yet risk it not being taken positively. Victoria could see his hesitation.

"Speak your mind, sir."

Brown turned to his Queen and drew in a deferential breath. "Your majesty, would you consider alternative medicines? It is my understanding they are doing great things with Hemophiliacs in Spain. Were I you, ma'am, I would start investigating it."

Victoria looked back down at her son so weak and fragile. The living embodiment of lost hope. "Check into it for me, Dr. Brown. I just want Leo well no matter what." Dr. Brown nodded, bowed, and left the room. Victoria stroked Leopold's dark head. He opened his eyes, stopped crying, and for a few moments the room was quiet.

Victoria thought. How many arguments had she and Albert endured based on where they supposed the disease came from. Which of them was responsible? Who had the malady in the family? Prince Albert had no ongoing hereditary diseases plaguing his line on either side. But Victoria did.

Perhaps Hemophilia was a related blood disease of Porphyria of which her family was riddled. Queen Anne suffered from it in the 1700s.

Then there was Victoria's grandfather King George III whose well known bouts of it resulted in his son, her great-uncle Prince George, to first become Regent and finally King George IV upon his father's death from it. The disease caused what some in the palace called the "Madness of George III," and its symptoms were legendary. The king's urine turned purple, he began talking to trees, running naked in the halls, and speaking for hours on end.

Eventually he was placed in a straitjacket and kept in the bowels of St. James's Palace. He never even knew when his wife Queen Charlotte, Victoria's grandmother, had died.

But of Hemophilia, Victoria knew that neither her mother Viktoria, the Duchess of Kent, nor her deceased father Prince Edward, the Duke of Kent and fourth son of King George III, had any signs of it. She had heard her father had bastard children but coupled with this gossip was no indication of illness amongst the offspring. Besides, it was also her understanding that the bastard children had been fathered with his various mistresses who had other lovers. Duke Edward himself never had any children except for Victoria—and that was very late in his life at age 50. Still, there was no indication of the blood disease.

So where had it come from?

Leopold had been sickly from birth and Victoria blamed herself. She had insisted on the use of a new drug called Chloroform said to ease the discomfort associated with childbirth. Prior, there were no such kind of anesthetics used when a woman had a child, and there were far too many obstetricians who believed that painful contractions during labor were *"the natural physiological forces that God ordained women to endure and suffer through"* based on observations in the Bible. Of course, thought Victoria, the Bible had been written by and large by men—none of whom had ever had a child, and having agonized through seven pregnancies, she had no desire to experience that pain again.

The Queen had inhaled the drug for fifty-three minutes from a handkerchief administered to her by Dr. John Snow and called it "that blessed chloroform" and its effect which was "soothing, quieting and delightful beyond measure," she wrote in her diary.

But when the country discovered the Queen of England could have endangered her child with its use, they criticized her for it.

What they did not know was that the Queen enjoyed an active, robust physical relationship with her husband. In fact, she loved having sex with Albert. But her chief complaint was always the results of it—pregnancy. She referred to it as "the shadow side of marriage." Having suffered through the unbearable pain involved in her previous seven gestations, she welcomed the idea of giving birth without agony and sought out Dr. Snow after reading about his discoveries in his paper published in 1847 entitled: *"On the Inhalation of the Vapor of Ether."*

But now, a year after being dealt the blow of Leopold's condition, she wondered if she should have put off the use of it, until such time as the drug had been more readily in use and its effects on the babies investigated. Victoria put a finger to her lips kissed it and placed her finger on little Leopold's forehead. She nodded to the nurse and left.

Victoria headed for her study determined to finish some correspondence and make some entries in her diary which she hadn't done in some time.

Upon entering the room where she and Albert worked desk-to-desk, she thought about all she wanted to do for England as Queen. How she desired to bring it into the modern age, and ensure the country remained the most formidable in the world. With those dreams, her beloved Albert had been helpful.

But she also had to keep a tight rein on him.

It had become too easy for Albert to assume that simply because he was a man, he knew more than she about running the country. Time and again they argued over who should make decisions and always right after she'd had a baby when he would assume power by meeting with ministers and signing documents intended for her. Too often Albert would forget that he was the consort—not the sovereign—and resort to treating her "like a female" from which she would recoil. He found her fiery temper so upsetting that he chose to settle their numerous marital arguments by letter even though they were in the same house. Then there was his exasperating way of making her feel inadequate, and his intellectual and moral inferior.

Upon that point, Victoria was not the only one who could see these disagreeable traits in Prince Albert. He could be prickly, and there were those who thought it based on his Germanic heritage—which Victoria always dismissed. But he did seem to make himself available to her Privy Councilors and ministers, and many thought Albert's meddling in politics made him unpopular in the country, especially when it was leaked that he felt himself "King" in all but the title.

What Albert failed to grasp was that Victoria's blood also ran with cold hard steel, and her commitment to her Hanoverian birthright as a sovereign was unparalleled. Yes, she did desire to be the perfect wife to the Prince Consort, but her role as Queen and protector of Great Britain took precedence. It was a tiring job for a woman, she thought, but it was *her* job. No one else's. One for which she had dedicated her whole life. She didn't wish to be a good Queen, but a great one—like her idol Queen Elizabeth in the 1500s. So, as she sat before a never-ending stack of correspondence and bills to sign, Victoria sipped a glass of port, and began her duties. Neither a sick child, a misogynist husband, nor what might be a probable war on the Russian horizon, would stop her forward movement toward continuing England's stature as the "Greatest country on Earth."

After an hour of correspondence, Victoria finally began making entries in her diary—the personal notebook she kept in which she recorded her thoughts as well as her private desires on areas she wished to improve in herself—things like her temper, her selfishness, and her loss of self-control.

Then she thought about Sarah Bonetta.

Thoughts of Sarah's well-being, talent, and intellect were uppermost in her mind. When she considered what she could do for the African, who only narrowly escaped death, she felt proud. Helping Sarah was one of her most unselfish acts as Sarah could answer a great many questions about Negroes and their alleged inferiorities. Sarah could represent the future of Britain regarding parity.

And with that in mind, she dipped her pen into the inkpot and began a letter:

26 February 1852
From Victoria, Queen of England
Windsor Castle

To Miss Sarah Forbes Bonetta
Chambers Society School for Girls
Oxfordshire

Dearest Sally,
Greetings from London…
How much we miss seeing you and hope you are well…

Thirteen

arah arose early and quickly put on the white stockings, new shoes, blue plaid skirt and white blouse of her uniform as she reflected on how different her life had become. She was excited. She was going to be a "Fifth-Form" student but did not understand what the term meant and hurried out of her room to ask the House Mistress, Miss Calvin.

She soon learned that historically, a "Form" was the long backless benches on which rows of pupils sat in the classroom to receive lessons. In smaller schools the entire school would be educated in a single room, with different age groups sitting on different benches. But in Sarah's case the Chambers Society School had three classes grouped into Forms for ages eight to eleven; twelve to fifteen and sixteen to eighteen. Sixth Form students were those studying for their "A" level or Advanced level preparation—or college continuation.

"Because of your special status of being entered at the behest of the Queen herself, you were not tested. Instead you were immediately given the status of 'Fifth Form' instead of 'Sixth-Form' as befits your age," Miss Calvin informed her. "The school will evaluate your knowledge base to make a determination of your ultimate Form later."

Sarah nodded then asked about breakfast or if there was a school kitchen. Miss Calvin pointed to a communal room further down. "The kitchen commissary is the third door on the left down that hall past the library. Breakfast is served from six o'clock to eight-forty-five in the morning as classes start at nine o'clock sharp. Lunch is from eleven until twelve-thirty, tea is at four and supper from five to seven."

Sarah thanked Miss Calvin and hurried down the hall. Suddenly a sight caught her attention and stopped her in place.

It was the school library.

She slowly walked inside and froze with delight as she looked around. There on each wall, on oak bookcases from floor to ceiling and in aisles, were hundreds of books. Leather-bound, gold or silver leafed books of every ilk, subject, paper texture and printing style. Sarah could not stop the patter of her heart as she browsed the shelves in front of her separated by tables for reading or study. Her fingers glided over the covers of *Jane Eyre, Sense and Sensibility* and *Wuthering Heights.* Further down she perused books written by Lord Byron, Daniel Defoe, George Eliot, Mary Shelley, Charles Dickens and Mary Wollstonecraft. Any book she had ever thought about reading was right at her fingertips.

"Do you wish to borrow one?" Sarah heard the librarian ask. "All I need is your name, room number, and to see your school pin."

Sarah smiled then decided on "Sense & Sensibility." She went to the librarian's desk, signed her name, and showed her the pin affixed to her sweater.

The librarian nodded, "You have three weeks to use it." She then sent Sarah on her way with her first borrowed book from the school library having no idea how much it excited Sarah to have it.

Now carrying a prized Jane Austen tome Sarah continued down the hall toward the commissary. She was just about to turn the corner into it when she came upon a black maintenance woman in her fifties on her hands and knees scrubbing the floor. Sarah smiled at her. The woman stopped scrubbing and smiled back. "Hello," the woman said cheerfully.

"Hello. I'm Sarah Bonetta. I'm a student here."

"Mabel Darcy. It's nice to see you 'ere… as a student."

Sarah could hear an accent of some sort in Mabel's voice. "Are you from London?"

"No. Kingston, Jamaica. My first master brought me and my mama 'ere when he got married again, 'fore slavery ended. Then I married Mr. Darcy. Been 'ere ever since."

Sarah then thought. "Your last name—Darcy—did you know it's the same as a very famous character in a Jane Austen book?"

The woman shook her head.

Sarah nodded. "*Pride & Prejudice*. The character, Mr. Darcy, represented the 'Prejudice' part of the title. I just borrowed another Austen book "Sense & Sensibility." If I find "Pride & Prejudice" in the school library, I'll get it for you."

Mabel acknowledged amiably but turned away.

"No necessary, Miss Bonetta. I kin no read. But thank you anyway." She went back to scrubbing the floor and shifted her weight to her left knee to move slightly away from Sarah in embarrassment.

Sarah looked at her a moment longer, then moved on. This, she thought, was the fate of most Negroes. No education created a limitation of opportunity preventing most blacks from succeeding and becoming more than domestics or laborers. It was why Sarah so relished this chance she had been given by her Majesty to go to school. But she also remembered what Jilly told her—that *"Those to whom much was given, much was expected,"* and paying an opportunity forward could be as good a way to pay back a favor as not. Perhaps helping Mabel Darcy could be that payback.

When Sarah entered the commissary, there were fifteen other girls including the ones she had seen in the courtyard the day before, already there having breakfast at the two long tables. They stopped and stared at her then grimaced at each other. One of them, Madeline Gray, glared at Sarah.

As Sarah quickly went to the serving table she could hear one or two of the girls smirking: "A Negro?" said a red-haired girl.

"Is she the new maid?" said another girl, "She can't be a student."

"Then why is she wearing a uniform?" answered the red-haired girl.

Sarah ignored this and picked up a plate, napkin, and utensils at the end of the table and went to Miss Sherman, the server. She held out her plate and smiled. The woman took her time ladling scrambled eggs, porridge and a biscuit onto Sarah's plate making no secret of her disgust. "I'd heard there would be a blackie attending this school. But I never thought I'd see the day up close," she grunted.

But Sarah ignored Miss Sherman's insult and held out her hand. "I'm Sarah."

Dismissing Sarah's hand, Miss Sherman snapped, "I don't care who you are. It's a disgrace."

Sarah took a moment. Then chose not to let it affect her. Instead, she took her food over to a table. But the other girls made it obvious they did not wish her to sit with them, so she sat at the far end of the table by herself and quietly ate alone. She would not allow herself to be hurt by the foul display because there was too much she could benefit from the school experience. Just being in the library had excited her, and she imagined all the books she could read. All she had to do was make sure the librarian saw her school pin. Yes. She could get used to being by herself if only for that. Books.

But suddenly she heard: "May I sit here?"

Sarah turned to find an unusually tall girl with dark, curly hair, freckles, and horn-rim glasses smiling at her. She had a plate of food.

"Yes. Yes, please," Sarah offered.

The girl sat and grinned. "I don't know a soul here. Do you?"

"No. No one. It's my first day too."

"I'm Linda Beekman. From Yorkshire."

"Sarah Bonetta. From London."

"*Born* in London?"

"No. In Dahomey—West Africa."

"Goodness. You're a long way from home. Are your parents still there, or are they in London?"

"No. My family is… they're all dead."

It was the first time she had said it out loud, and she stopped eating. Linda touched Sarah's hand. "I'm sorry. I did not mean to bring up any unpleasantness. I was just being friendly. My father told me—insisted really—that I make friends. I tend to put people off."

Sarah was grateful to Linda for wanting to sit with her as she could've gone to any other girl and made her acquaintance. But she chose Sarah. Why? Especially when the other girls looked at Sarah with disgust which Linda saw.

"I'm Jewish," said Linda out of nowhere. "My family has suffered greatly from people who looked at them and only saw a conventional, cliché of Jews and mistreated them." Linda looked over at the other girls, "Like those girls over there did to you." She then took a bite from her biscuit and looked at Sarah. "I do not like when people won't give you a chance to prove yourself first. And, I can tell you, I have had my share of good fights. I have thick skin and good fists."

Sarah laughed. She liked Linda.

"You and I are here at this school because we're good," Linda continued. "Not just because we're different. I have to assume that. Why else would *you* be here?"

"I'm here because the Queen of England sent me here."

Linda almost choked. "Are you joking? Queen Victoria?"

"No, Queen Susie," smirked Sarah.

"Oh. A joke. I see you're being funny."

"I'm sorry. It just blurted out."

"But honestly, did Queen Victoria send you here?"

Sarah nodded. "She's my benefactor."

Linda put down her biscuit and stared at Sarah a moment. "Were it me, I'd rub it in those arrogant girls' faces."

"No," confessed Sarah. "I intend to be excellent. To be better than them."

Linda smiled. "Good girl. Then count me in for support. I love a good fight. And believe me, you're in for at least one a day."

Sarah grinned and shook hands with Linda. To her surprise and shock, she had indeed made her first friend—and an ally.

At nine o'clock, Linda and Sarah separated to go to class. The school had three teachers and a Headmaster—a fifty-six-year-old Welshman named Mr. Barnard Humes, a tough taskmaster. Sarah's class was across the courtyard in Building Two run by Miss Eleanor Rawlins, a skinny red-haired woman of forty-two, who could have made herself far more attractive if her personality were not so rigid, and her face not consistently reflect a scowl. It also did not help that Miss Rawlins employed a Birch walking stick and tended to flog students who were belligerent or unruly. It created her nickname "Old Stick & Bones."

When Sarah entered the classroom, the first thing she noticed was the sea of white faces irritated by her presence. Miss Rawlins pointed to a seat and Sarah instantly felt a glare of fire burning into her flesh. Miss Rawlins made it a point to make Sarah's life unpleasant at every turn.

She was not the only one.

Everyone hated her from Mr. Humes to the school mistresses, to the six highborn Sixth-Forms who had created a clique of rich bullies calling themselves "The Heras" after the most powerful goddess married to Zeus. At first Sarah kept her head down and her mind open to knowledge. She practically lived in the school library, read voraciously, and turned in her homework on time. She always received a perfect score of 100. And yet she was not advanced to Sixth-Form as she ought to have been.

Day after day Miss Rawlins ignored Sarah despite her brilliant mind. Night after night Sarah would forge ahead, study hard, keep her nose in her books—and out of trouble.

Occasionally she and Linda had breakfast together—but always supper. It was Sarah's favorite time with her new friend. Linda would read the letters her family sent, and Sarah was pleasantly surprised when in one letter Linda's father wrote: "Say hello to your new friend, Sarah." It touched Sarah deeply to know that some people were more understanding and thus more thoughtful than others.

Sarah also told Linda all her concerns and frustrations. As both girls felt displaced and segregated by their racial, social and religious differences, they commiserated with each other and became each other's sounding board as well as father confessor.

Linda admitted one evening she wished she had a straighter nose and less curly hair. "If there is such a thing as reincarnation, I'm going to ask God to send me back here as a pretty girl, and not so boy-like. My father says I lack charm and feminine pulchritude. He says I'll never find a husband the way I am."

"I wish I had a father to tell me anything," Sarah confessed, thinking back to the day her beloved father was killed. "I wish I had pretty hair like you have that you hate. Or the convenience of your skin color that yields you the privilege I'll never have."

Linda drank her tea and stared into space. Then she turned to Sarah. "Maybe we should just change the world exactly the way we are—two awkward women who are smart therefore hated by the jealous and the insecure."

"Here, here."

But as much as Sarah wished things were different, she spent the next three months in continuing frustration at being disregarded for her blackness. When Miss Rawlins would write on the chalkboard, turn to the girls, and ask a question, whether mathematical equations, or about proper English grammar, hands would go up including Sarah's. But, as expected, Miss Rawlins would choose anyone else other than Sarah— despite Sarah's perfect record—until one day in April, Sarah had enough.

In math class when Miss Rawlins asked, "What is 72 divided by 2 times 4?" Sarah did not raise her hand. Instead, she blurted:

"One hundred forty-four."

"Wait until you are chosen, Miss Bonetta."

"I'm never chosen."

The other girls gasped in shock. Miss Rawlins slowly turned to Sarah red-faced and fuming.

"What did you say?"

"I said. I am never chosen. You never choose me."

"And that is my prerogative," Rawlins glared. "You do not run this classroom. Nor do you speak when you are not asked to or you will suffer the consequences."

"I already suffer the consequences. I am striving for academic excellence, yet all you do is ostracize and shun me."

Suddenly Sarah felt the pain of Miss Rawlins' stick smack her hard again and again across the back and shoulder. "You will be quiet, young woman! Some time spent in the Cage will silence that tongue!"

Miss Rawlins went to the door and called down the hall. A few moments later, a large man, the school guard, came into the room and Sarah felt herself being dragged out of class by the two of them.

Miss Rawlins and the guard dragged me down a never-ending set of stairs into the basement of the building where it was cold and damp. After opening a particular door, I was pushed into the room and the door was shut and locked behind me. I could not see as there was no candle or oil lamp provided. Just a mattress with a dirty sheet on top, a stool—and a chamber pot. I was in total, dark, solitary confinement.

I sat and cried having no knowledge of how long I would be there or

what other external punishment awaited me inside. As there were not any
windows, the stench of my own urine and excrement was overwhelming
and I fell to my knees in constant prayer. I was so alone in this school. So
unhappy. And for the first time in my life I wished that King Gezo had
killed me that day in Dahomey.

Two days later, when Sarah was released from the Cage, she could
hardly walk, and her eyes had to adjust to the light. She was taken to her
room and told to think about her actions or end up in the Cage again.
She laid across her bed in her small room and teared up. To whom could
she complain? She had no loved ones. She had no family, and Forbes
was far away. Should she write the Queen? No, she thought. She could
never allow the sovereign to know she was peeved at being ignored and
mistreated for speaking out about it. She just couldn't. Not when this
was a school the Queen championed.

So, she decided to stay in her room and not have supper that evening. Perhaps she would read *Oliver Twist* by Charles Dickens, a writer she
heard wrote about the downtrodden of London; or *Moll Flanders* by Daniel Defoe, or *Gulliver's Travels* by Jonathan Swift. She would just take a
bath and go to bed early. Or play her violin since her music soothed her.

But there came a knock at her door. When she answered, it was
Linda. "I heard what happened. Madeline and The Heras were only too
eager for me to know they threw you into the Cage." She took Sarah's
hand. "Is it as hideous as I have heard? Are you alright?"

"I shall never be alright again. A room such as that should not exist
in an enlightened place of learning such as this. Neither corporal punishment nor imprisonment should be acceptable here. Not for a girl."

Sarah sat on the bed. Linda sat next to her.

"Well, do not let them see you cry," insisted Linda. "It is precisely
what they want. To break you. To see you falter. Don't give them that
satisfaction. The whole time you were away, they wanted me to feel badly

because I knew and liked you. I nearly threw hot soup on one of them."
She looked at Sarah pointedly, "I will next time."

Sarah's face managed a smile. "How do you know there will be a
'next time'?"

"Because I know you," smirked Linda. "It's far too hard for you to
keep your intellect a secret, and Miss Rawlins, or one of those demon
girls, will make you lose control and be thrown right back in the Cage."

"True."

"So, tame that inner beast—and let's have supper." Linda got Sarah's sweater. "Stand with your shoulders back and your head up and
show them you are alright and back in the saddle. Be brave and confident." She threw the sweater over Sarah's shoulders.

Something about Linda moved Sarah to action. "Alright. Let's."

The two confidently strode down the hall and into the commissary,
where a hush fell over the room. Everyone looked at them as they got
their plates and utensils and came through the food line with the proud
bearing of aristocracy as Madeline and The Heras, seated at one table,
looked on smugly.

Sarah and Linda went to another table as though nothing had happened to Sarah. These days, another girl, Lucinda Echols, called Luci—
a pretty blond girl from Manchester with large eyes and a big smile,
would occasionally join them to eat. She, too, wanted Sarah and Linda
to know not every girl at the school was as callous as The Heras and the
other biased students who disregarded them. Lucinda hurried over with
her plate and sat across from Sarah.

"Are you alright?"

But before Sarah could answer for herself, Linda jumped in.

"She's fine—and we'll have no more talk about it."

Lucinda nodded and looked at Sarah who smiled slightly. "I'm alright, Luci," said Sarah softly. "It was bad, but not unbearable. Let's just
enjoy our supper."

After a few minutes relishing their roast beef, rice, and green peas, Linda found herself grinning with latent excitement.

"I almost forgot to tell you. I'm Sixth-Form now. They promoted me yesterday." She showed off her new silver school pin affixed to the blouse behind her sweater. "See? My Sixth-Form pin!"

"Congratulations," said Luci. "How did they decide?"

"They gave me a test day before yesterday," answered Linda. "Then yesterday they said I got a hundred percent right. Now I'm Sixth-Form."

But Sarah was quiet and said nothing. She pushed her plate away. Linda noticed her disquiet. "What's wrong? Are you not happy for me?"

"I am. Truly. But why has no one given *me* a test to see if I can be Sixth-Form? I get perfect scores on my homework and class tests, too. Fifth-form is far too easy for me."

"I know it is. Everyone knows it is," said Luci.

"Have you spoken to anyone about it?" asked Linda.

"Did *you,* before they gave you your test?"

"No," said Linda. "Mr. Humes came to me on Monday morning and told me to go to Room 3 to take a test. I did, and yesterday he gave me the news."

"Ask your House Mistress. Maybe she'll know," offered Luci.

"I will," said Sarah. Then they heard: "Were I you, I'd learn to hold my tongue—and keep my nappy head quiet." It was Madeline and two other of The Heras standing there with dirty plates on their way to deposit them. Linda stood up and walked right up to Madeline's face.

"And were I you, I'd hold my own tongue before I embellish the floor with your teeth."

There were some gasps. Madeline was taken aback by the threat. After all, Linda was a girl—even if she was a head taller than Madeline who smirked, "An arrogant nigger protected by an un-ladylike Jew. What is this school coming to."

"Progress," snipped Linda whose face registered a challenge.

Madeline was disgusted. "My father will hear about this. You can be sure." And she started to turn away. But Sarah was furious.

"And the Queen will hear about you," snapped Sarah. "Her Majesty is my personal patron. Can your father trump that?"

Madeline and the other girls just glared at Sarah then backed off. They turned and walked away.

A slight smile graced Linda's lips. "I would bet that will hold them for at least a week." She then turned to Sarah. "Now let us go to the Housemistress and see after your advancement."

Sarah Forbes Bonetta at school

Fourteen

fter supper, Sarah and Linda headed to the office of the House-mistress of Gaia House. They knocked at the door and were admitted. Miss Calvin was just finishing her soup.

"Miss Beekman, Miss Bonetta. How may I help you?"

It took Sarah a moment, but she said what she came to say.

"Miss Calvin, I was told at the first, I would be evaluated to see if I should be a Sixth-Form student, instead of Fifth-Form. But almost four months have passed, and no one has asked to test me."

"Tests are conducted at various times. Perhaps your time has yet to come," said Miss Calvin with a hint of irritation in her voice.

"I was tested on Friday, and I was moved up yesterday," declared Linda. "I have since discovered that three other students were tested on Friday as well. Why wasn't Sarah?"

Miss Calvin looked at Linda sharply. "Why is that your business, Miss Beekman?"

"Sarah is my friend."

"And are you to see after all your friends by insisting we change our methods to suit you?"

"No."

"Then stay your concerns." Miss Calvin then turned to Sarah. "As for you—take this up with the Headmaster. Mr. Humes sets the testing schedules. And…" she gave Linda a reproachful glance then turned back to Sarah, "…I would suggest you not bring your 'friend' here to fight your battles. Good day."

At that, Sarah and Linda left Miss Calvin's office.

As they came down the hall Linda turned to Sarah peeved by the Housemistress's response. "We shall go the Headmaster's office then," she said.

"No," Sarah stated. "*I* shall go. Miss Calvin was right. I shall fight my own battles. Alone. It's time I developed my own thick skin—and formidable fists."

Linda understood and patted Sarah on the back. She nodded, then turned left at the corner as Sarah turned right toward the Headmaster's office.

Mr. Barnard Humes, Headmaster of the Chamber's School, was watering the extraordinary plants in his office. He loved how well they were all doing—particularly his Philodendrons this winter. He'd grown them from cuttings taken from his mother's house in Portsmouth two years ago, and now they were large and bountiful. As he watered his Ferns, Scheffleras, and Pothos, he was humming his favorite melody by Beethoven from 'Violin Sonata #5', while sipping Earl Grey tea. Humes was quite content to remain in this, his private space, all day without bother…

…Except that Sarah knocked on his door.

When she entered his 'sanctum sanctorum,' Humes put on his wire-rimmed glasses, frowned, and sat his teacup down.

"So, the Queen's dark new toy has graced my presence. I understand you just spent two days in the Cage for belligerence."

"Yes, sir."

"And what did you learn there?"

"To be more patient and less outspoken."

"And are you?"

Sarah thought a moment. She wanted to make sure this wasn't a ploy to send her back to that horrible place.

"Yes, Headmaster. I keep a more civil tongue now."

"Then why have you come?"

Sarah drew in a deep breath and looked at him, then at his stunning plants. She touched the elegant Pothos leaves shiny and glistening from proper care.

"Your foliage is quite healthy and beautiful, Mr. Humes. They seem to be well cared for and thriving."

"They are indeed."

"Things that are cared for—looked after and nourished—grow to be magnificent and become the fulfillment of their destiny," she began carefully. "They make us happy and we are proud of them. As you must be of these plants."

Mr. Humes was ahead of her. "And you say that to say what, dear girl?"

Sarah swallowed hard and made sure her voice was on an even keel devoid of emotionalism. "Since I have been here, educationally, I have not been properly looked after. I feel I have not been given the mental nourishment necessary for me to grow and flower to my fullest potential. This, despite the Queen's desire for me to excel. I am not thriving."

Humes just looked at her. Despite his innate dislike of Negroes, this one was of intrigue to him. She was the first well-spoken Negro he had ever come across. Maybe the Queen was correct about her.

"And how has this, shall we say, 'lack of mental nourishment' man-ifested itself?" he asked.

"I realize I am the first, like me, to attend here, and many are finding themselves confronted with their own personal opinions about the forward movement of someone like me whose blood flows beneath duskier skin than theirs."

"You mean you are being mistreated because you are a Negro. Welcome to the world, my dear," Humes mocked.

Sarah was peeved but controlled herself. "In an enlightened society we all benefit from the achievements of educated people who can become inventors, teachers, creators, politicians, painters, scientists and otherwise enrich and elevate the society as a whole. But here, I have been treated…as an inferior. I am ignored, thwarted in my efforts to advance to Sixth-Form as I should, and the perception of 'elitism' or in my case a lack of it, prevails, which does not allow me to develop and grow."

"We cannot change how people disparage minorities."

"But an example can be set which the school will adhere to if prevailed upon. You, sir, could set that example."

"And how would I go about doing that?"

"Test me so that I may progress to Sixth-Form. And make a rule that everyone in this school has an equal opportunity to the education they deserve. Reward each student equally for their academic achievements. And, punish the practice of racialized ridiculing—which sadly, I experience daily."

"Why would I do that? Especially in light of rich patrons and contributors who pay for our existence?"

"Is not the Queen of England one of those sponsors?"

Humes bristled. Sarah had now invoked the name of the Queen. A useful card she had played brilliantly. "She is."

Sarah thought long and hard, then tried a different tact. "I've been reading about your William Wilberforce who fought for twenty years to help the Queen's grandfather, King George III, to end the Slave Trade in England. He stayed at it, and finally, thankfully, his bill passed through Parliament. He has only been dead eighteen years, but in history, he is already considered as a great man. A great emancipator. It was he who said: '*Already we have obtained, for these poor creatures, the recognition of their human nature, which, for a while was most shamefully denied.*'"

Sarah moved closer to Humes' desk and looked at him pointedly. "One hundred years from now, what side of history will you be famous for? Shall you have a statue in the middle of town dedicated to your ideas as an exclusionist? Or as a revolutionary Headmaster responsible for equal opportunity in the British school system."

Humes stood and came from around his desk. He sized up this dark beauty who was suddenly appealing not only to his intellectual critical thinking and sense of self-worth, but to his masculine nature despite his every effort to quell these sensations.

"Your command of the English language is impressive for one so young and so new to our country," he said with newfound respect. "Return tomorrow at three to be tested for advancement to Sixth-Form."

Sarah smiled. "Thank you, sir." She started to leave, but Humes stopped her. "Miss Bonetta. You will need to make sure you do not go to the Cage again. Or I will not be able to help your cause."

Sarah nodded, then left his office.

At three the next afternoon, Sarah was sitting in Examination Room Three taking the test. Mr. Humes was there along with Miss Calvin, Sarah's Housemistress, to make sure she did not cheat. Sarah had been given a list of thirty questions that were prepared for her and several sheets of blank paper for her answers. She was finished at four-ten when she handed both the questions and her answers to Humes who looked at the answers and tried to mask his astonishment. "I'll have the results tomorrow afternoon. You're excused."

Sarah nodded then left.

Humes looked at her answers again. He then handed the papers to Miss Calvin rubbing his temples in amazement.

Miss Calvin had to sit. "You could have given her your answer just now. It is a perfect score, Mr. Humes," she uttered. "100%."

"And she did it in an hour and ten minutes," Humes intoned shaking his head. "I chose the hardest questions in math, English, literature and current science for her. Harder than any other student I've ever given the test to. I wanted to knock her down a peg or two from that sanctimonious perch she's placed herself on." He looked at Miss Calvin. "But we cannot deny the girl what is hers by right—and by achievement. She's brilliant—and she's now Sixth-Form."

"I'd like to tell her so. If I may, sir."

Humes nodded and as Miss Calvin left his office, he looked at his thriving plants. A bit of water and care, he thought. "My God."

That evening at Gaia House while they were at supper, Sarah, Linda and Lucinda looked up to find Miss Calvin standing there.

"Miss Bonetta? I shall take back your Fifth-Form pin please."

Linda frowned, looked at Sarah, then at the Housemistress.

"Why should she?"

"For once in your life mind your own business, Miss Beekman." Miss Calvin then held out her hand to Sarah. "I will have your pin."

Sarah undid the pin from her blouse and gave it to Miss Calvin.

"Thank you. You shall no longer need it." Miss Calvin reached into her pocket and pulled out a small box which she handed to Sarah and smiled, "Because it shall be replaced with this one. Your new Sixth-Form pin. Congratulations, Miss Bonetta."

Sarah, Linda and Luci screamed with excitement.

"Ladies, please," said Miss Calvin as she winked then left.

"Sixth-Form!" exclaimed Sarah.

"You did it!" grinned Linda. "I knew you would."

All three girls jumped up and down happily—to the consternation of Madeline and The Heras who witnessed the entire event.

I was so excited by my achievement that I immediately wrote to Queen Victoria the moment I arrived back in my room. I sat at my writing desk in front of the window. My hand shook as I dipped the pen into the inkpot and began what I hoped would be a series of correspondences with her Majesty with no ability to contain my delight. I wrote:

To her Majesty Victoria, Queen of England
Buckingham Palace, London
Dear Majesty, I write to you today to tell you of my boundless joy at having been promoted to the rank of Sixth-Form here at the Chambers School for Girls to which you have so generously sent me for my education. I cannot thank you enough as I know if I can continue with excellence on this journey it may even be possible for me to consider education at the university level. Though I have made few friends here, my love of books and learning grows boundlessly as does my appreciation for all that you have done.
With enduring gratitude,
Yours, Sarah F. Bonetta'

I placed my letter in the 'outgoing post' basket sitting on top of the Housemistress's hall desk at Gaia House. But I had no idea my letter, nor any of my letters, would never reach Her Majesty. Nor did any of Her Majesty's letters ever reach me. My enemies were too numerous, clever and far too maniacal.

A week later, all teachers and staff were gathered in Headmaster Humes' office to listen as he told them what the new standard of behavior would be accorded all students attending Chambers Society School.

"Every effort shall be made to provide equal attention, opportunity and learning conditions to every girl," cautioned Humes. "The white ones…" then he looked at Miss Rawlins specifically, "…*and* the black ones."

A collective groan emanated from the gathering.

"Our environment must be without reproach," he continued. "The last thing we need is for the Queen of England to withdraw her support and parade this school forever in the general mind as biased."

Miss Rawlins stood there knowing the entire meeting was aimed at her—and she did not like it.

"I will not be made a scapegoat, Mr. Humes. Sarah is not in your classroom. She is willful and obstinate. When you do not cater to her every whim, she runs off to tell the Queen and the world we're all racists. Well, I shall not have a student be so insolent as to talk back to me, nor shall I be indicted for overlooking her in favor of other students. I've taught here for five years."

But Humes stayed calm. "Miss Rawlins, all of us must examine our deepest hearts and find a way to adopt the new thinking. And that will include you."

Miss Rawlins walked out.

Fifteen

Sarah stood looking out of the window at the courtyard. Evidence of Spring was everywhere that May—new buds on trees, shrubs standing tall with new growth, grass emerald green and perky.

News of the Spring dance was buzzing all around the school. It was an annual event for the male students at the nearby McMasters School for Boys to be invited to the Chambers Society School for a dance held in June, right before Summer break. Everyone dressed up in their finest dresses and gowns to dance to music from a string quartet and drink punch. Families of the girls were also invited, and the staff and their spouses would be in attendance as well.

Sarah desperately wanted a new dress for the event but had yet to receive any of the stipends she was told by Mary Forbes she would get each month. So, she had no way of buying a gown for the dance. But she refused to be upset. She looked over at her side table and saw the pretty collection of books she had now acquired with her previous allowance money and smiled. There were now ten books which in the endpaper she wrote "Property of Sarah Forbes Bonetta."

She remembered the day she and Linda took a stroll on a Saturday afternoon and happened onto Chester Street where, next door to Charing Haberdashery, she found Sutton's Book Store. From that moment on she experienced the exact same feeling she had when she discovered the school library. Only this time, if she wanted (and could afford it), she could buy the books and own them. They would be hers to read over and over or mark passages she loved. And she started her collection then and there.

Mr. Sutton was curious about the dark skinned African who kept appearing at his shop every Saturday and inquired about her interest. When she said she was a student at Chambers School, he began to pull down special books he thought she might like to read. When he had used copies, since he traded for them, he would offer them to Sarah at a deep discount and she used the money she first came to Chambers School with. Her joy ran over at her ability to own these treasures. Yes, his first reaction upon discovering she could read and was highly intelligent was to exclaim, "My word. A smart darkie," to which Linda, who was with Sarah that day, countered coolly: "No. A brilliant *woman*, sir."

Mr. Sutton never made that mistake again and tried to redeem himself by helping Sarah to build her personal library. Now Sarah's little collection had grown to ten books and she was pleased with herself. That, and the addition of her promotion, caused a faint smile to emerge as she touched her school pin. Had she carved out a bit of happiness at last? The equality she so desperately coveted?

She thought about Captain Forbes. How happy and proud of her he would be—and she wondered where he was or if his mission was any more successful than when she had first been rescued by him in Dahomey almost five years ago. She had been so hoping for a letter to answer these thoughts, but she had not heard from him, and wondered if he thought about her at all. He, who had once been her champion. Now she had to be her own.

Little did Sarah know that her beloved Captain Forbes had found himself, along with British Commander Dawson, in an interminable standstill. Gezo would not change his mind nor sign their treaty, and all their efforts to insist he did were met with failure.

Finally, Forbes wrote to Queen Victoria and insisted she send more West African Anti-slavery fleets to Dahomey to stand guard along the coastline of Whydah ready to shut it down and board any ship leaving the port carrying human beings and release them. It was a bold move, reminiscent of Foreign Secretary Palmerston's in Brazil, but Gezo only seemed to respond to such moves. And this one was no different. Victoria dispatched her West African Anti-slave trade fleet and a month later twenty ships were in Whydah harbor awaiting orders.

Forbes and Miller, a rugged, stern man of 50, had been in Dahomey for seven months trying to reason with King Gezo. They were either ignored, laughed at or dismissed and sent back to their detention hut under arrest. At least this hut, thought Forbes, was better than the last time he was there. And somehow the food and water were better. He was told by Emeka that King Gezo sent the food over from the palace.

Finally, a full year after they had arrived, the two were summoned out of the blue on a Saturday afternoon and escorted by several Dahomean soldiers with new rifles to Simbodji Palace.

When they arrived at the throne room, the men were asked to sit on rugs in front of Gezo's throne. Forbes could see new African prisoners from another village dressed in white loaded into small boats. He knew what that meant, and desperately wanted to bring Dawson's attention to it, but King Gezo appeared before them with his ministers, chiefs, and several of his warrior wives who carried new rifles.

"Gentlemen, I see you have not left Dahomey, and neither has your fleet positioned in my port. My own ships cannot seem to leave our waters."

"No, your Majesty," stated Dawson, ready to show Gezo who was boss. "Neither we, nor *Queen Victoria's* fleet has left *Queen Victoria's* port."

Gezo shook his head and sat. So did his entourage. The wives stood in back with their rifles and just stared. "And why is that?" asked the King of Dahomey.

"We are in a time of great change. The old ways no longer work. Not for Africa. Not for the world," began Dawson, hoping to influence and thus persuade Gezo with reason. "Great Britain rules the sea with the world's largest and greatest navy. The sun has never set over the extent of hers—the world's largest empire. In this time of great change, brought about through rapid progress, new inventions and modern industry, neither slavery nor the Trade can continue to exist—certainly not in the British Empire nor its territories or holdings. And it certainly cannot exist in countries who have a claim on Britain's friendship…"

As Forbes was specifically told not to lead the negotiations he remained quiet. He watched and listened to Dawson's impassioned pleas have no better effect on Gezo than his own had last summer. But what was also of grave concern to him was the number of African prisoners dressed in white being led to the staging area which he continued to see from his vantage point.

Oblivious to what Forbes was observing and obviously understood, Dawson hardened his stance.

"…So, I am afraid we are insisting this treaty be signed. Until then, our Queen will keep our Naval forces in Whydah Port and will not allow your ships, nor any others carrying stolen or human cargo for sale, to leave. And if you insist on rejecting her request, her Majesty will use other methods."

Gezo did not like the threat. He scanned Dawson's face for a moment, his eyes narrowed into slits save for the ominous yellow in the whites of them burning into Dawson.

"'Other' methods?" He then motioned to one of his Amazon wives to bring the rifle she was holding—one of Gezo's favorites.

Forbes now panicked. Would Gezo shoot them?

But Gezo caressed the rifle as though it were a woman and stared at Dawson. "How will she stop us? As you can see, the French king trades us with guns and bullets for money. We have a lot of them now. Better deal. Gives us power. You British trade only for palm oil." He grinned at Forbes and Dawson intently. "Which you think we prefer?"

Dawson was not amused by Gezo's tone and did not respond. Forbes leaned into Dawson, "The fucking French have dug our graves," he whispered under his breath.

Gezo, sensing their frustration, grinned at Emeka. "Take these Englishmen back to detention. Clearly, they must find much better incentives—or they can rot there. Meantime…we water graves!"

To punctuate his point, Gezo fired the rifle twice in the air. Soldiers and people cheered as Forbes' head fell into his hands, disgusted. The small boats with African prisoners in white were lifted up.

"What is happening?" asked Dawson in confusion as soldiers pulled he and Forbes up by the arms and pulled them through the throne room.

"Remember what I said? About the human sacrifices?" Forbes replied as they were yanked along. But before Dawson could answer he saw for himself as the first victim was pushed over the precipice and hacked into pieces. He nearly fainted and looked at Forbes scared to death. As Forbes was dragged out, he looked back at the human sacrifices wishing he could keep the proceedings out of his psyche.

But he couldn't.

Then he saw an African woman in one of the boats. There before his eyes, the woman became Sarah. His sweet Sarah. Pleading for her life. But this time, this woman could not be saved—and she went over the side. Her screams never left his mind—along with thoughts of the girl he did save—praying she was alright and thriving in London. Little did he know he would be in Dahomey another two years under house arrest.

As the Spring dance at the Chambers School was forthcoming, the school had included dance classes in the curriculum. The furniture had been removed from the second community room and only a piano remained. Dance classes were for an hour and a half a day, and each student had a specific time to be there depending on their Form. Six girls from the Chambers School Glee Club were also brought in to play for the lessons and got 'extra credit' for it. Sarah had been chosen to play the violin with the Club by the Mrs. Harrison, the music teacher, who had been astonished by Sarah's talent. Sarah was the only violinist in the Club.

Sarah's waltz class included most of the Sixth-Forms in the school for a total of sixteen. A dance master, Mr. Weyburn, had been hired to instruct the students. He was tall and thin and carried on dramatically with an exaggerated speech that Sarah found very effeminate. He reminded her of two male villagers she knew in Okeodan that her mother said were "men who liked men instead of women." But Mr. Weyburn was a good dancer and she liked the way he taught the dance movements.

When the glee club members entered the waltz class that day Sarah immediately saw that Miss Rawlins had her infamous birch stick. She also noticed that Miss Rawlins employed a ritual she used to determine who would dance with whom. It was reminiscent of Sarah's experience in Dahomey when King Gezo would determine who would be killed in the "Watering Graves" ceremony amongst his prisoners.

After Miss Rawlins had chosen the dance partners, two rows of young women faced each other.

"Now, we shall go down the row and those of you on the left take the Lady's hand in front of you and ask her to dance!" instructed Mr. Weyburn with a hand flourish.

The female pianist hired for the classes along with the glee club began a spirited waltz and the girls on the left stretched out their hands, and the girls on the right accepted to dance. This process would switch the next time so the girls on the left could be "asked" to dance.

The music continued, and the couples commenced to waltz. Many were clumsy and ill-suited to find the three-four beat as Miss Rawlins counted out aloud, "One, two, three; one, two, three" pounding her birch stick on the beat of one for emphasis.

Sarah played her violin in concert with the glee club members and tried to stay in the background and cause no undue attention to herself.

"Now remember. The waltz was once considered daring because of its strong rhythms, and the holding close of male and female bodies," Mr. Weyburn detailed with his high-pitched voice. "Years ago, a young woman had to get permission from a teacher or parent to dance it. But now, thankfully, we've loosened those traditions and can appreciate in its performance, the display of grace and elegance of which the human figure is capable while waltzing."

These dance lessons went on for a week like this before Miss Rawlins singled out Sarah for some unforeseen reason.

"May we stop please," she motioned to the glee club. "Why is the violin so loud and playing its own rhythm?"

The music stopped, and everyone looked at Sarah. Madeline smirked. "You expect an African blackie not to play jungle music?"

Other girls snickered, but Mr. Weyburn frowned. "I hadn't noticed anything unusual." Then he turned to Sarah, "But Miss Bonetta if you would keep your tempo to three-four like the rest it would be fine."

"But I was, Sir," Sarah protested.

"Are you speaking back to the instructor, Miss Bonetta?" snapped Miss Rawlins.

Sarah said nothing but looked at Mr. Weyburn who came to her rescue. "Let us begin again, please…" And his hands went up indicating they start playing the music to which the dancers would dance.

But as the girls danced, something in the music began to stir images and spirits within Sarah. She was angry to be the one singled out for a mistake she didn't make, and the rhythm in the music soon brought forth sounds of the distant Djembe drums of her West African homeland in her head. Suddenly she saw her fiancé, Kua, clear as a bell, dancing the Ya Moto Dance in front of her. He was beckoning her to join him. His arms outstretched.

Sarah could feel the drumbeats under her feet. She started to move to them while she played. In moments her music was a sound all its own. She was free—playing in pulsating rhythms and chords unconnected to the piano or the Glee Club. Though her eyes were closed, she saw Kua's body undulating in the same syncopated pulsations as their wedding day.

Linda, who was watching, covered her mouth with her hands, and the pianist and Glee Club stopped playing. Mr. Weyburn, Miss Rawlins, and the other girls thought Sarah was possessed as she continued to play the violin to her own explosive sounds of drums echoing in no one's head but hers.

But all of it suddenly crashed to a halt—silenced by the whack of Miss Rawlins' birch stick on the back of Sarah's legs. Sarah yelled in pain. Madeline grinned and joined her friends in the Heras watching.

Livid, Miss Rawlins yelled, "Miss Bonetta! What kind of devil possessed spirit is in you!" Each word articulated with a smack of her stick against Sarah's body.

"Stop hurting me, you witch!" Sarah managed to slap her teacher, who held her cheek then beat Sarah savagely as Sarah screamed.

Mr. Weyburn was stunned. "Miss Rawlins, I'm sure the girl knows not to do it anymore," he said, completely repulsed by the brutality he was witnessing. Some of the other girls snickered. But Linda did not. She was angered over the mistreatment as Miss Rawlins pushed Sarah toward the door. "Into the Cage! These black demons will come out of you—if I have to beat them out!" the teacher screeched.

Linda could not take it and went to Mr. Weyburn. "Do something. She's hurting her!"

But Mr. Weyburn did not know what to do and ran out of the classroom. Linda now ran to Miss Rawlins in fury.

"This so wrong. You cannot take her. You've already beat her, there is no need to put her in the Cage. She will lose her Upper-level status!"

"Perhaps she should have thought of that before she raised her hand to me."

"She's not an animal!" Linda tried to pull Sarah away from the teacher, but Miss Rawlins pointed her birch stick at her.

"Careful, Miss Beekman, or I will make sure you lose your status as well."

This made Linda stop. She looked at Sarah in tears forced to watch as her friend was dragged down the hall and disappeared.

The Chambers Society School for Girls Glee Club (circa 1860)

Sixteen

ictoria was feeling down as she entered the parlor. She had just seen Prince Leopold whose coloring was worse than ever, and she wondered if he would even last the night.

Albert glanced toward her and she shook her head. Tea was being served at Windsor and the parlor was filled with footmen, family and guests which included Victoria's mother the Duchess of Kent, British Prime Minister Aberdeen, Sir Charles Phipps—the Queen's Keeper of the Privy Purse, as well as eldest daughter Princess Victoria called Vicky, second daughter Princess Alice, eldest son Prince Albert Edward, called "Bertie," his friend, Sir Roger Carlyle—and Lori the Parrot.

With concern shadowing his face, Prime Minister Aberdeen cautiously approached Victoria. He took a sip of Earl Grey tea then began.

"Your Majesty, the situation in Russia regarding Turkey is now critical. Tsar Nicholas' Russian army has crossed the Pruth River into Moldavia, and in response Turkey declared war. Three days ago, the Russians destroyed the Turkish fleet at Sinope on the Black Sea coast. They sank seven frigates and other ships. We are going to need to send troops to help our Turkish allies."

Victoria became alarmed. "Minister Aberdeen, I do hope we are not talking about declaring war ourselves!"

The Prime Minister tried a less-measured but firmer approach.

"Ma'am. Part of my duties are to make sure Her Majesty is informed of Parliament's intentions. In fact, the Turkish Ambassador requests a visit."

Victoria sighed then glanced at Albert unsuccessfully attempting to mask her distress. "It's really too bad. I received word from Captain Forbes who says we must keep our West African Anti Slave-Trade squadron in Dahomey. King Gezo continues to be uncooperative."

George Hamilton-Gordon, the 4th Earl of Aberdeen, and a liberal Whig, sighed. He enjoyed having the trust of the Queen which was still important for a Prime Minister, but he had a concern about the type of relationship Britain should have with France. He was especially worried that France's ruler, Louis-Napoléon Bonaparte, nephew of the famous Napoleon, set himself up as an Emperor, and he was vexed by the rising political dominance of the Russian Empire in eastern Europe and the decline of the Turkish Empire—England's allies. He had to be cagey in his answer to Victoria and shook his head.

"With our naval supremacy I would expect a quick victory, your Majesty. But we should be prepared to assist France in an all-out assault on Russian forces in the Crimea. We need to seize the naval base at Sevastopol." He paused a moment realizing he hadn't answered her concern directly. "So, if we *do* go to war, I'm afraid, *all* naval forces will be deployed to the Crimea. The Trade will no longer be a priority."

"Tell that to the thousands of Africans sold into slavery, sir," glared Victoria who marched away vexed and frustrated. She knew Lord Stanley to be a pleasant man and she had a modicum of respect for him. But he could make her teeth rattle with his constant belittling and postulations as though she was a child instead of a thirty-nine-year-old woman with eight children. As she headed toward her offspring standing with Sir Charles Phipps and Sir Roger Carlyle, she could not help but wish her beloved Lord Melbourne was still her Prime Minister. Theirs was a special relationship, one even bordering perhaps on affection many thought on observing them together but fixed and cemented in respect and fidelity. Oh if only Lord M could form her government again, she thought. But that was just a wistful dream. She sauntered past Sir Charles, Alice, Vicky, and Bertie, and stopped in front of Sir Roger who was stuffing himself with hors d'oeuvres, one after another.

Finally, he turned to find her staring at him, and swallowed hard resembling the cat who ate the canary—literarily.

"Sir Roger. Do they not feed you at home?" Victoria teased. "You're here or at Buckingham nearly every day gorging down our food. Shall we name a room after you?"

Young, handsome, charismatic Sir Roger Benjamin Carlyle grinned and poured on his celebrated "Carlyle" charm.

"I cannot help myself, Majesty. There is no honor so great as being in your presence which forbids me to leave. That—your chef's marvelous cuisine…" he then pulled her into his arms, "…and no pleasure so sweet as dancing with your beautiful self."

Though Victoria teasingly spanked his shoulder with her fan, Roger danced the Queen around the room as everyone watched in amusement. After all, they had each witnessed Sir Roger's magnetism before, and Victoria was known for her love of male beauty.

She grinned. Nothing pleased her more than a handsome man paying her a compliment. She had relished it—from Lord M, whom she adored, to Albert, whom she married. So privately, she loved that Roger had the capacity to make her laugh or blush—or worse—wish that he, instead of her blood child Bertie, was her son. She absolutely adored Sir Roger. But now, she feigned admonishment and chided him humorously. "You are quite a shameful flirt, Sir Roger." She then turned to Bertie, "Find Sir Roger a wife, son." She gave Sir Roger a wink. "He absolutely cannot continue to be unloosed on the unsuspecting women in London."

As his sisters giggled, Bertie smirked, "Trust me, mother. The women are not as unsuspecting as you think."

Vicky and Alice nodded in agreement as Sir Roger and Bertie joined them. Victoria took that moment of levity to continue her real reason for coming in that direction—to speak with Sir Charles.

As she pulled her Keeper of the Privy Purse away, her voice became serious and hushed. "Sir Charles, have you heard from my ward? There hasn't been a word since Sally left for Oxfordshire."

On that inquiry, Sir Charles realized that it was not his social graces desired by the Queen, but an update on Sarah Bonetta. He tried to hide his disappointment.

"When I inquired of Mrs. Forbes, she said Sarah was doing well."

But Victoria shook her head. "No. No, I do not like it."

"But, Ma'am…"

"…No," she interrupted, pacing slightly in front of him. "Something is wrong. I can feel it. I've sent letters and there has been no response. It's odd. Make some arrangement to go up there when you can and check on her personally for me. Do it *before* you send the school's or Mrs. Forbes' next cheque, please."

Sir Charles nodded in acknowledgement as Victoria turned to everyone, and with her royal hostess demeanor in full force again, declared: "Shall we go through for dinner?"

Meanwhile, Sarah was now in the Chambers School Cage for a second time. While inside, she'd had another birthday and now at age fifteen was changing. She was hardening and realized the western world was an arduous place to navigate—and the school she attended was a microcosm of that world.

The conditions of her solitary confinement in the Cage were identical to before—dark, unsanitary, odorous, depressing. She was in Hell. All that was missing was Lucifer himself.

But this time her coping mechanism was different. She called upon

Mawu and the goddesses of Vodun to work with Jesus and the God of her new Christian religion. She called upon the ancestors, her parents and siblings killed by Gezo's men, and her own strength to get her through this unyielding time and deliver her.

She thought about the books she'd read about people who over-came obstacles to achieve greatness or personal happiness. She thought of the Bible—of Christ's crucifixion to bring redemption to mankind and his ultimate resurrection. She thought of the Charles Dickens characters who seemed clever enough to transcend their circumstances and survive. *Oliver Twist*, for example, was mistreated and surrounded by crudeness for most of his life. But Oliver was an innocent, and his charms drew the attention of several wealthy benefactors just as Sarah had done with the Queen of England.

She thought of *Jane Eyre* written by Currer Bell, who the school librarian informed her was actually a female author named Charlotte Brontë. Orphaned as a baby, Jane struggled through a nearly loveless childhood, survived a bullying cousin, suffered imprisonment in the same room in which her uncle died, only to become a governess at Thornfield Hall and found love with Mr. Rochester at the estate.

Would Sarah live a life of cruelty and maltreatment before finding happiness somewhere? She did not know. But she had to be the author of her own life and journey and prayed for that very salvation. She thought about what Forbes had demanded of her in London:

"Be greater than your circumstance."

Two days later, she was released and brought before Mr. Humes prior to being allowed to bathe. The Headmaster looked her over while holding a kerchief to his nose.

"Will you make a liar of me, Miss Bonetta? You do not help your intellectual cause by acting like a rabid African beast in class and refusing to obey Miss Rawlins with whom I have stood in your defense."

Sarah could only look away in embarrassment.

Humes' eyes narrowed angrily. "I do not like being made a fool of—and I warn you again. One more trip to the Cage and you will be taught a lesson the likes of which you shall never forget—after which you will be expelled. Now get out! Your grace period is up!"

Sarah ran from Humes' office and sprinted down the hall upset. On her hurried way to her room she failed to see Mabel Darcy mopping the floors and, in an instant, tripped over her. Mabel's bucket of water spilled everywhere, her mop flew into the air, and both women crashed hard to the floor.

"Are you alright, Miss Darcy?" Sarah questioned after seeing the older woman on the floor holding her head moaning in pain.

"I be al'ight, child," the older black women answered slowly sitting up. By this time other girls and Miss Calvin came running to help both women up.

"I'm so sorry, I wasn't watching where I was going," said Sarah in earnest. She turned to the other girls. "Does anyone have a kerchief?"

"I do," and instantly Linda proffered a white cotton one trimmed with lace. She and Sarah held it to Mabel's head.

"I'll fetch someone to wipe up this mess," said Miss Calvin, and she darted down the hall.

"Let's get her to my room to lie down a moment," said Sarah. Linda nodded. But when they got Mabel to her feet, they noticed she had a hard time walking.

"Hip hurts a little," winced Mabel. "I be okay after I sit a spell."

Linda and Sarah got Mabel to Sarah's room as the other girls watched. Once inside, they sat Mabel on Sarah's bed while Sarah took Linda's kerchief and poured water on it from the water pitcher and wash basin. She gave the kerchief to Linda for Mabel's head.

"My husband gon' be so mad," Mabel groaned. "He don' wan' me workin' 'ere."

"Why do you, if he does not want you here?" asked Linda.

"I like bein' 'round the learnin,'" Mabel answered. "I keep t'inkin' some o' it will rub off on me." Mabel looked around Sarah's room. "You got a lot o' books. Like a library in 'ere."

Sarah smiled. "I like books. I'm swept away by the stories or just the information I learn. Most of these are my school books, and some I borrowed from the school library." Then she went over to the beautiful leather-bound books on her side table. "But I own these."

Mabel was in awe as she held her head with the kerchief. "You own yer own books? Wit a library right 'round de corner?" she asked in her thick Jamaican accent."

Sarah came over and sat on the bed with Mabel. "I walk to Sutton's Books on Chester street almost every Saturday and just look around. I like the smell of books, their paper, the printing ink. Each one creates such escape for me," she offered. "Mr. Sutton knows I like books and he always recommends something. If I can't find it in the school library, I go back the next Saturday and he sells it to me at a good price. I buy it with my allowance."

"Yes. But he calls you a 'smart darkie'," Linda chided.

"Small price to pay for a good book."

"Too large a price if you ask me," Linda retorted. "But then, I'm not a Negro. I do not know how much disrespect I could take without a fight."

"Fights engender retribution," Sarah reminded Linda as she took off her smelly uniform and began to wash up with a towel dipped in soap and water. "It's why I end up in that horrible Cage smelling of manure. Better I read." She started washing out her uniform blouse.

"True," Linda agreed turning to Mabel. "She reads like a sieve. You can't stop her," she joked. "She would not eat—if it meant not finishing what she was reading. If you ask me, she's too smart for this place. It's why she gets into trouble all the time."

"You get into trouble fer knowing t'ings, child?" asked Mabel.

"Yes," nodded Sarah. "I just came out of the Cage. Could you not smell me…?"

"…Her second time in there," added Linda.

"…and Mr. Humes threatened me with expulsion if I ever go back. I was upset and ran out of his office, then tripped over you."

"But this time, she went in the Cage just for dancing," said Linda flatly. "Granted it was wild African dancing—like nothing anyone anywhere had seen before, but still, it was just dancing, and they threw her in the Cage for two days. I've written to my father and I asked for two things: to send me and my sister's first ball gowns so Sarah and I will have something wonderful to wear to the Spring Dance; and for him to speak to the Headmaster about this business of 'going into the Cage' as punishment. It's barbaric."

Though Mabel commiserated with Sarah she was cautionary. "You best keep yer good brain more a secret, child. White folks don' know wha' ta do wit smart black folk." She looked at Linda with slight contrition, "I not count you cus you seem to be a tolerant white girl raised wit some kinda Christian goodness." Then she looked back at Sarah. "But you? You need to use yer knowledge for a higher purpose but be quiet about it. Else it be beat outta you. My first born, my Orsoli, he wus smart too. But he be dead now."

"I'm so sorry. How?"

Mabel thought about her son then stopped dabbing her head with the kerchief as though the throbbing ceased long enough for a moment of clarity to articulate her loss. A loss she wouldn't—or couldn't—fully understand or accept.

"My boy wus always interested in learnin'. He wanted to know how things wus put together. How they ran. My old employer, Mista Sanders, had once been a slave owner until slavery ended. He wus never happy that he now had to pay his slave workers or they wus free to find work elsewhere. Many o' dem left him jus' cus he wus a mean man. Terrible cruel. Beat you if you talked back or disobeyed him. My boy, Orsoli, wanted to draw an' build t'ings. But Mista Sanders white daughter, Millie, tol' him he needed to know numbers. Math. He asked her if she would teach him. Millie ain't thought nothin' o' it, an' they went to the barn an' she starts teachin' him numbers."

Mabel's eyes watered as the memory became more and more painful. She began to rock back and forth. Sarah and Linda looked at each other knowing a heartache was coming. "One day, Mista Sanders caught de two o' dem in de barn," Mabel continued sadly. "An' he accuses my boy o' rapin' his daughter. Even though Millie say he ain't touched her, Mista Sanders tied my boy to a tree an' took a whip to him—an' he jus' keep on whippin' an' whippin' an' whippin' 'til de skin come off my boy's back. Mista Sanders other two sons held me back an' made me watch. De whole time my boy wus bein' beat to death he jus' kept recitin' his numbers. One plus one is two, two plus two is four. Like that. Then he died. And they dragged him over to me an' dropped his dead body in my arms."

Mabel tearfully looked at Sarah. "Keep yer smart mind to yerself— 'til you can use it fer good t'ings. Don' let white people beat it outta you."

At that Mabel wiped her eyes and gave Linda back her kerchief. She stood up and slowly headed for the door with a pronounced limp.

Sarah and Linda were in tears too. Neither could speak—and they let the older Jamaican woman leave.

A memory like that deserved quiet processing—and some solitude which they all understood.

Seventeen

For the next few days, I sat in Miss Rawlins classes and said nothing.
I neither raised my hand nor participated in any way. In dance class I
waltzed like the other girls, and in the commissary, I quietly ate my meal,
chatted for a few moments with Linda and Luci, then went to my room to
read and study. The firm words of Mabel Darcy constantly echoed in my
head.

"…Keep yer good brain more a secret, child." "…Use yer knowledge
for a higher purpose but be quiet about it. Else it be beat outta you."
And I had received enough beatings for a lifetime.

On Thursday, two large boxes were delivered to the school for
Linda Beekman who carried them both to Sarah's room after
supper. Sarah had been reading but was excited to help open
the boxes to find two ball gowns. One was canary yellow brocade, the
other pink chiffon. The smaller pink gown was for Sarah courtesy of
Linda's younger sister who had outgrown it.

"Oh Linda. Thank you. It's beautiful," said Sarah, excitedly.

"You're welcome," Linda beamed.

"I will be the belle of the ball," then Sarah looked at the yellow gown
Linda was holding. "And so will you."

Both girls tried on their gowns and spun around holding hands.

"How will you do your hair, Sarah? Can you style it another way?"

"I could braid it."

"No. Don't braid it." Then Linda thought. "I know. Put some Baby's Breath in it. It will look like a halo. You'll look like a beautiful angel. I'll get some for you tomorrow."

Sarah was thrilled. "How did you know your sister's gown would fit me?"

"Three years ago, Anne was smaller than me when we first went to the Circle Ball in Brighton. But she sprouted up like a weed. Now she's taller than me if you can believe it. And already married. We grow tall in my family. My mother is six feet. My father six-four. So I thought, why waste a perfectly good dress. I hope you don't mind pink."

"I love it. Tell your father I'm grateful."

"Speaking of Papa. He's quite upset about the Cage. He said he'd be writing a letter to Mr. Humes about it and plans to give him a piece of his mind at the Spring Dance." Linda took off her gown and folded it back up into the box. "And the one thing you do not want is Papa on his bad side. He can be quite formidable." Linda then poured a glass of water. "Have you heard from the Queen?"

"Not yet. And I've been hoping for a letter—from her or Captain Forbes or someone. But nothing."

"Well, don't worry about it. I shall have my family send you letters. It's all they do. Write about the weather, write about the neighbors. Write about who's getting married to whom. I have sixty letters already."

"What I would give for just one." Then Sarah looked at herself in the mirror wearing the pink gown. "I wonder if anyone will even ask me to dance. I'll be all dressed up, sitting by myself at a table. The lowly, ugly African no one will touch." She took off the pink gown and hung it in the armoire.

"I'll dance with you, Sarah," smiled Linda. "I will not let you be all dressed up at your first school dance—and not, well, dance."

Sarah grinned and hugged her friend. What a saving grace Linda was—and how she adored her.

The following day, Sarah was back in Miss Rawlins English class. Miss Rawlins wrote, *"To Be"* on the chalkboard then turned to the girls.

"Instead of using one word each for the infinitive, past tense, present participle, and past participle, the verb *to be* uses 3 words for the present tense, and 2 words for past tense for a total of 8." She came from around her desk and stood in front of the girls. "So, who can conjugate the verb *To Be?*"

Sarah saw Madeline's hand go up. Although she knew the answer she had not been participating of late. Miss Rawlins picked Madeline who stood.

"Be, Being, Been…" but she began to falter, "…and, uh…"

Irritated by her stumble, Miss Rawlins interrupted without hesitation, "Anyone else…?"

Sarah looked around. No one else's hand was raised, and she found herself surprised to find her own hand go up. The other girls rolled their eyes, yet none dared to be humiliated like Madeline. Thus, through tight lips barely hiding contempt, Miss Rawlins was forced to call upon Sarah. "Miss Bonetta."

Sarah stood up brimming with confidence. Though Linda smiled, she was nervous. Sarah had a way of intimidating and infuriating one with her excellence and she expected trouble.

She did not have to wait long.

"The Infinitive for 'To be' is—*Be*; Present Tense—*Am, Is* and *Are*; Past Tense—*Was* and *Were*; Past Participle—*Been*; and Present Participle—*Being*," Sarah declared, then sat down.

Miss Rawlins said nothing because naturally, Sarah was correct.

Madeline sucked in her teeth sneering, "Nappy-haired, know-it-all!"

Now Linda's eyes closed knowing what would come next. "Oh no," she moaned.

Sarah was furious and as hard as she tried nothing kept her ancestors, Mabel's words, or even Captain Forbes' demand that she overcome her circumstances, from summoning the devil within. Something inside her just snapped. Fed up from months of mistreatment, Madeline and The Hera's bullying, and forcing herself not to display her own intellect, Sarah pushed Madeline so hard, the girl fell over backward.

But Madeline was equally angry and jumped up. She landed a punch in Sarah's stomach. "Don't you ever touch me, you wooly-haired blackie." To her own surprise, Sarah came back at Madeline with righteous vengeance, and with a maniacal glare swung her fist and began pulverizing the girl. A fight ensued replete with kicking, slaps, hurled fists, and swearing.

Miss Rawlins pulled Sarah and Madeline away from each other and hit Sarah over and over with the birch stick. Red-faced and seething Miss Rawlins spat, "This is not the jungle!"

Madeline made "monkey" sounds, which caused a few of the girls to giggle, though neither Linda nor Luci found it amusing.

"Then make her stop calling me 'Nappy haired' and 'blackie'!"

"You *are* a *blackie!*" Miss Rawlins hissed. "A wild, uncultivated animal not fit to be here! And you will not talk back to me again. That will be two days in the Cage! Your last two!!" She grabbed Sarah and dragged her out of the room.

Sarah cried out in pain, "Stop! You're hurting me! I will tell the Queen about this! Stop!"

Sarah summoning the Queen's name only made Miss Rawlins pull harder. "Then I suggest you tell her why you are going to the Cage, and why you are being expelled!"

That Saturday, four days later, the Spring Dance had come to the Chamber's School. The exterior of the building was decorated with bells and streamers, and the interior was filled with fresh cut flowers of every variety. Beautiful azaleas, chrysanthemums, roses and lilies filled dozens of vases set on each table in the main hall. Carriage after carriage brought handsome young men from the McMasters School for Boys, or parents, family, and spouses of teachers to the school.

All the girls were in beautiful ball gowns and dresses as befitted the first major dance of the season. Madeline, resplendent in white, was holding court along with her proud parents and two of her "Hera" friends. Even tall and gangly Linda looked pretty in her yellow gown standing next to her parents.

But she was worried. She had not seen Sarah since she was taken to the Cage last Friday, and she knew Sarah wanted to attend the dance—especially wearing the sister's pink dress her father had sent. Sarah had never been in the Cage beyond two days and she was concerned and told her father so.

"Papa, my friend Sarah, who I wanted you to meet, is not here. It's not like her. She went to the Cage last Friday. It's vile in there."

Sanford Beekman, a six-foot-four-inch man of 57, looked at his wife, Helen and thought a moment. "Where is the Headmaster of this school? I wish to speak with him."

Linda looked around until she finally saw Mr. Humes standing with Madeline Gray, her parents and another teacher. She alerted her father.

"There, Papa. He's next to the girl in white—the one I was telling you about who is an absolute menace to both Sarah and me."

Mr. Beekman walked through the crowd of dancers, faculty, and students and approached Mr. Humes.

"I am Mr. Sanford Beekman. This is my daughter Linda, a student here. Are you the Headmaster of this institution?

"I am. Mr. Barnard Humes, at your service."

Humes held out his hand for a handshake, but none was forthcoming from Mr. Beekman. Embarrassed in front of Madeline and her parents, Mr. Humes withdrew his hand.

"How may I help you, Mr. Beekman?"

"You can help me by explaining why you send female students of this most prestigious and refined school to something as undignified and despicable as the 'Cage', which I hear is a monstrous place."

Mr. Humes swallowed hard, and his face turned pale. He quickly glanced at the wealthy parents of Madeline Jones, then tried to genially explain it all away.

"It is a punishment room of sorts, yes, where a student sits to reflect upon their infractions. It is not pleasant. But then it is not supposed to be. The student comes out later that day, grateful for a second chance to redeem themselves and they write an essay on why they will never cause trouble again. It works wonders for the student."

"Reflect?" Linda frowned and turned to her father. "Papa, ask the Headmaster if there is any light in the Cage, or clean sheets on the filthy mattress they leave on the floor, or even clean out the chamber pots. Ever! Ask him if there are rats! Ask him if there are circumstances under which students stay in the Cage for days on end—as in the case of Sarah Bonetta, the African student who has been in there three times and may still be there!"

Mr. Beekman then looked at Mr. Humes. "You heard my daughter. Where is Miss Bonetta?"

Humes gave Linda a threatening look then half-smiled to Madeline's parents who were very interested in his answer as well.

"Miss Bonetta is no longer a student here. She was expelled. I do not know her whereabouts since she left here."

"Liar!" shouted Linda. "She would never leave here and not say goodbye to me. I am her best friend. We share each other's secrets. Sarah is still in the Cage I tell you!" Linda turned to her father. "Papa, please.

Do something. She could be dead!"

"I want to see Miss Bonetta!" demanded Mr. Beekman.

"I told you Sarah Bonetta is not here."

"Ask him to show you her room. I will wager her things—her favorite books, her violin—are still there," insisted Linda. "And she would never leave her violin!"

Suddenly music and dancing stopped as everyone began to look over at the altercation. Miss Rawlins ran up. "What is going on? This is our annual Spring dance! Everyone is here! Take this up to your office—or mine—but not here!!"

"I shall not take it up at all," fumed Mr. Humes. "Mr. Beekman is not a parent, guardian, nor patron of Miss Bonetta. He is not entitled to any information on the whereabouts of a *former* student."

Humes then gave Mr. Beekman a malicious look. "And, I am afraid that under the circumstances, sir, your daughter, Linda will no longer be welcome at this institution either. We do not countenance hostile elements here, and her belligerence has become unmanageable."

"I can certainly attest to that!" chimed Miss Rawlins.

"Me too!" echoed Madeline, "All of us in Sixth-Form can!"

"Now just a moment, young woman," Mrs. Beekman exploded. "We have heard quite a lot about your cheeky behavior here!"

"Silence!" Humes held up his hand for quiet. "Mrs. Beekman, I suggest you and your husband gather Linda's things and leave. I will have her paperwork sent to your home for her relocation to another school. Good day, sir, madam." This foreclosed the issue.

As Humes walked away, the Beekman's were left stunned.

Madeline chuckled and led her family and friends away as Mr. Beekman looked at his tearful daughter. He put his arm around Linda as she cried. But Mrs. Beekman's hands found her hips in annoyance, and she began to pace. "We should fight this, Sanford. You know Linda will never get into another good school with an expulsion hanging over her transcript and behavior record."

"We cannot, Sylvia. We haven't the power. The Queen of England is Sarah's patron—and it did not stop Sarah's expulsion."

"But Papa, Sarah was *not* expelled," cried Linda. "I know she wasn't. She is still here. In that dungeon downstairs! I know she is!"

"Nevertheless, we are done here. We must get your things."

Miss Rawlins went over to the string quartet and demanded: "Play, all of you! We are not paying you to eavesdrop. Play!"

The music began again, and the students and others slowly started to dance. But for the Beekman family, it was the end.

Later that day Linda could not stop thinking about Sarah. Despite her own expulsion, Linda knew Sarah was still in the Cage and would have to be released at some point.

So, she wrote Sarah a letter. If Sarah was alive she would get it. If she was really gone from the school, it wouldn't matter. She just wanted Sarah to know that their friendship was the most cherished she had experienced thus far in her life and wanted Sarah to keep in touch if possible. She wrote down her address in Yorkshire and slipped the letter under the locked door to Sarah's room.

After that, she and her family gathered all of Linda's belongings from her room and left the Chambers Society School for Girls.

But as the Beekman's travelled away, their carriage traversing the long dusty road back to Yorkshire, Linda had an epiphany. She looked at her father and a faint smile crossed her lips.

"I shall write the Queen of England. I will ask after Sarah's whereabouts and well-being, and I'll tell Her Majesty what transpired here."

"Good girl," smiled Mr. Beekman. "*That*—is how you can help."

Mrs. Beekman nodded and agreed. "Yes. The Queen will not be ignored."

"Nor expelled," determined Linda.

Eighteen

Two of Windsor Castle's court Pages brought the box of personal correspondence and the red leather box of "official" correspondence to Prince Albert. The Prince Consort assisted Victoria in handling the voluminous amount of mail she received each day. He would go through and place in order of importance the one's she should respond to immediately, the ones she could wait on, and he would throw away and disregard what he considered "junk" mail.

Today as he opened the Queen's various letters, he came across one which was marked "Urgent – For Queen Victoria Only." When he turned it over he saw the postmark was from Yorkshire.

Too curious to put it aside, the Prince opened it. Upon reading its contents his face dropped, and he ran out of the office down the hall to the Drawing Room where Victoria was doing needlepoint with her Ladies-in-Waiting and her mother.

The moment Albert entered the room and held up the letter, the Queen knew to excuse herself and leave with him. When they reached the hall, he gave her the letter and took her arm.

"It's from a friend of Sarah's in Oxfordshire. She says she got expelled from the Chambers School for suggesting to her parents and the Headmaster that Sarah was *not* missing or expelled, but in some hideous dungeon in the school basement called the "Cage." She says Sarah is in grave danger. Hurt—or worse, dead."

Victoria gasped and read the letter. She grabbed her chest and held her cheek with her other hand. "I knew something was wrong. I could feel it. Fetch Sir Charles Phipps. He'll get to the bottom of this. Tell him I want him in Oxfordshire straight away."

Albert nodded and hurried off.

At eleven o'clock the next morning, Sir Charles Phipps was in Oxfordshire at the Chambers Society School for Girls. He had taken the last train the previous evening after Victoria and Albert told him about Sarah, and he stayed overnight at the Melody Inn. Now he was seated in front of a stoic Miss Rawlins standing at the side of a grim-looking Mr. Humes. The Headmaster was in the midst of a one-sided verbal rant and character assassination of Sarah.

"...We had to make a hard decision regarding Miss Bonetta who is a wayward, incorrigible young woman…"

But Sir Charles was clearly not fooled by Humes' non-answer, and circled back to the term he found most disturbing: "But what is the *Cage*?"

Miss Rawlins stopped Mr. Humes from answering with a hand on his shoulder and responded in a manner intended to stop this inquisition. "The Cage is for our more belligerent students. And you would not believe how petulant and argumentative Miss Bonetta can be, sir."

Once again, Sir Charles stayed focused on his mission, "I am here to see Sarah Bonetta. Bring her to me. It is the Queen's orders."

Miss Rawlins finally showed concern and looked at Humes who cleared his throat and dared to utter, "That is not how we do things here."

Sir Charles stared him down fuming, "Sir, I am the Queen's Keeper of the Privy Purse. Her Majesty is Miss Bonetta's patron. The Queen has had your school painted, the roof repaired and sends a generous check to this facility each and every month—which she is prepared to withhold immediately if you do not bring Miss Bonetta to me now. Either that or take me to her!" Sir Charles then leaned into Humes pointedly. "And not adhering to my request won't bode well for this institution nor its reputation!"

Miss Rawlins could not look either Humes nor Sir Charles in the eye. Humes sighed and opened the drawer to his desk. From it, he extracted a set of keys. It took him a moment.

"I shall go and fetch her."

"No," Sir Charles now insisted. "I shall accompany you."

Humes sighed.

Moments later, Sir Charles was following Mr. Humes and Miss Rawlins down the endless set of stairs until they reached the door in the cellar. Sir Charles was already sickened by the bleakness of the walls and the subterranean smell, which he noticed had the extra putridness of urine as they got to the door, which was padlocked. This further alarmed Sir Charles and he watched Humes fumble with his keys to find the one to unlock it. When Humes finally did find the key, his hand shook as he opened the door nervously.

They walked in. Sir Charles had to fetch his kerchief to cover his nose as he was immediately struck by not only the dampness, the cold air, and the darkness, but the horrible sewage stench. Miss Rawlins also covered her nose as Humes lit an oil lamp.

Sir Charles gasped. When his eyes adjusted there was Sarah, seated on the floor rocking back and forth, oblivious to their presence as she weakly recited the Lord's Prayer. Her hair was unkempt as she kept scratching her head, the reason Sir Charles assumed could only be from lice. He turned and saw that her chamber pot overflowed with feces and urine—the source of the stench. He then noticed her uniform was torn and when he slowly approached Sarah she jumped as though she would be attacked. But all she would recite was, *"Our father, who art in Heaven. Hallowed be thy name. Thy kingdom come..."*

Sir Charles looked back at Humes and Miss Rawlins aghast.

"How long has she been in here?"

There was no answer from either Rawlins or Humes.

Sir Charles lost all control and rushed toward Humes grabbing the Headmaster by the throat and pushing him against the brick wall with the fury of a thousand beasts. Miss Rawlins became terrified.

"How bloody long has that poor girl been in this filthy, monstrous, dungeon?!"

Mr. Humes couldn't catch his breath from being choked. He could barely speak as he tried pulling the death grip of Sir Charles' hands from his neck. Finally, he barely uttered:

"A month."

"A *month?*" Sir Charles was apoplectic and punched Humes in the stomach. "The Queen will hear of this straight away—and Heaven help you, you depraved bastard!"

By late evening the next day, in Buckingham Palace's Throne Room, a visibly nervous Miss Rawlins, Mary Forbes and Mr. Humes were standing in front of Queen Victoria receiving the tongue-lashing of their lives.

Sir Charles Phipps and Prince Albert were fuming as Victoria turned the full force of her wrath on Captain Forbes' wife Mary.

"Are you mad? Or deaf?" Victoria began, "Were my instructions in any way unclear, Mrs. Forbes? Did I not request that you look in on my ward from time to time? See to her needs and give me a report?

"Yes, ma'am."

"Then do you habitually ignore requests from your Queen?"

Mary could say nothing and just nodded her head as Victoria paced in front of her in unbridled fury. "It has been almost two years and you never visited her once! Never wrote to her and *lied* to us about her well-being. Captain Forbes will be made aware of this immediately. By God he will!"

Mary's face turned beet-red and she began to sob as Victoria continued. "You will no longer receive any money for the well-being of Sarah who was clearly mistreated and alienated. *And* you will repay the Crown for the money you stole by not sending it to her at the school the last several months. You will do this—or face imprisonment."

Victoria then turned her wrath onto Miss Rawlins.

"And you, Miss Rawlins. Who gave you the authority to beat my Ward and place her in a—a basement cell—like an animal?"

Miss Rawlins gulped, before her feeble attempt to justify it all.

"She is a willful, uncontrollable girl, Majesty. Given to fits of rage and self-aggrandizement…"

"…I do not care whether Sarah thinks she's the Virgin Mary herself. You do not punish that which belongs to the Crown!"

"Ma'am," Mr. Humes interrupted, hoping to leverage that excuse, "We thought it wise to teach the girl the English manner of obedience."

Victoria gripped the brocade skirt of her dress to keep from slapping Humes' face. She spun around to him turning her righteous indignation in his direction.

"*English manner?*" she bellowed. "Mr. Humes, I have been told that Sarah has head lice, was living in cold, dark, unsanitary conditions, and was severely beaten. Is that the *English manner?* For if so I would deeply enjoy you having a dose of it yourself this very instance." Victoria came right up to Humes' face and glared at him. "Are you aware to whom Sarah belongs, sir? If not—allow me to articulate. Sarah belongs to the Crown. Her well-being, opportunities and education are all verdicts of this court. No decision regarding her may be born without consulting me. And you, sir, shall no longer have charge of it."

Humes bowed in deference, "Yes, Your Majesty." As he came up expecting to see a somewhat softened Victoria, Humes was instead met with her still prescient fury directed at his colleague.

"Brook no argument, Miss Rawlins, I have informed the school that you are to be relieved of your duties." She turned back to Humes. "And you, sir, will take a six month leave of absence so you can consider your folly! And, I demand to know what happened to the letters Sarah wrote to me and to Captain Forbes, which were never received. Or my letters to her which I hear she also never received."

Humes looked down and said nothing. Victoria hands went to her hips in ire. "Did you hear me, Humes? What happened to the letters?"

"Destroyed, ma'am" he said in a small voice.

"I beg your pardon, sir. Speak up!"

"They were burned, ma'am," said Humes in a louder voice.

Prince Albert frowned. "Burned? On whose orders?" He was as distressed as his wife.

Finally, Miss Rawlins spoke, albeit softly. "Mine, your Highness."

Victoria's fists balled up and she almost stabbed her palms with her fingernails. "Get out! Get out all of you! I never want to see your faces again!" She waved them away and turned her back in disgust.

Devastated both Humes and Miss Rawlins tried a look of appeal to Sir Charles, but he was as stone-faced as Victoria.

Meanwhile, it finally dawned on Mary how her indifference and negligence toward Sarah might negatively impact her husband and she wondered in what way the Queen planned to "make him aware."

Miss Rawlins and Mr. Humes bowed and hurriedly backed away. Sir Charles' eyes followed them as they left, then he turned to Victoria and saw the pain in the Queen's eyes brimming with tears.

"I failed that poor girl," she cried.

Albert held his wife whose arms encircled his body openly. "I had hoped I was giving her an education—a new life filled with wondrous expectation. Instead, I only taught her of man's eternal viciousness."

Sir Charles wished he could do something but was forced to inform his sovereign of Sarah's needs. "Majesty, Sarah must be examined to by a specialist. More could be wrong with her than we know."

Though Victoria was crestfallen, Sir Charles and Prince Albert soon saw her spirit become imbued with a sudden resolve and firmness, which appeared in her as an epiphany.

"I shall have Dr. Brown, our own doctor, treat Sally from now on for we shall keep Sally with us until she is fully recovered. In fact, Sally shall become my Goddaughter with all the rights and privileges the title holds. Hopefully, that will stop all of this color persecution. Now make it known, Sir Charles."

Elated by her declaration to embrace Sarah as an adopted "royal daughter," Sir Charles nodded, bowed, and left the room.

Once he was gone, Albert smiled at Victoria. "'Goddaughter?' That is brilliant, darling. I wish I had thought of it."

Despite what she knew Sarah had endured, Victoria nodded to herself. She genuinely wanted Sarah to have a much-needed chance in life, and she knew she could help facilitate it.

"I know what it feels like to be an ignored, neglected child. Left to one's own devices and not cared for, Albie. It's the reason my relationship with mother is so…" she paused a moment and sighed, "…tenuous." She reached up and touched Albert's face and managed a slight smile. "So I shall not hand this opportunity for Sally over to anyone else. I shall take it on myself—and within the confines of my favorite palace."

"Windsor Castle?" Albert smiled.

"Windsor Castle. And all Sally has to do—is get well."

The next day Sarah, silent, battered and bruised, was in Buckingham Palace's medical room—an unadorned chamber with a medical bed, examination table, shelves of medical books, tables filled with instruments, bottles of medicines, potions and salves. Sarah was on the examination table, her hair wet from a medical solution to treat the lice, and she had a slight but persistent cough. Dr. Robert Brown, the Royal Physician, moved his stethoscope around her chest. "Breathe in deeply and exhale," he instructed.

Sarah drew in a deep breath and let it out as told. But she coughed.

"Again, please," instructed Brown, moving the stethoscope to another area of her chest. Again, Sarah breathed in and out.

"And again," the doctor insisted. Moving the instrument to yet another part of her chest. Sarah repeated the procedure coughing again. Dr. Brown withdrew the stethoscope from his ears and hung it from his neck. He frowned.

Sarah turned away and stared at the books on the shelves. She didn't care what the doctor was thinking or had found regarding her health, she just wanted to die. It was as though the real her had vacated her body and was replaced with someone else—someone bedraggled and subjugated. Someone whose demeanor was sullen and withdrawn with lifeless facial expressions and a broken spirit.

She just didn't care what happened to her.

Dr. Brown went to one of the tables and poured a powder from a bottle and an elixir into a cup and added another liquid from a larger bottle and mixed it all. He brought it back over to Sarah. "Drink this quickly. Trust me. It will not taste good."

Sarah drank the medicine swiftly. Dr. Brown was right. It was so horrid she was induced into a coughing fit. But it finally subsided, and she turned back toward the bookcase and closed her eyes.

Soon, there came a knock. Dr. Brown turned as Victoria entered. The doctor bowed, and Victoria acknowledged him, but went straight to Sarah. She touched the girl's shoulder. Sarah turned and looked into the Queen's eyes. Something in them made her smile slightly.

"Hello Sally. How are we feeling?" Victoria asked.

Sarah didn't answer.

Victoria wondered if she still suffered from shock—or if Sarah was angry with her. But before she could inquire, Dr. Brown motioned to the Queen then led her away from his patient. There was an uncharacteristically troubled tone in his voice. "We used a lice comb to remove the nits then washed the girl's hair with a medical solution containing tea tree oil, mercury and vinegar which should kill the lice and larvae," he stated. "But I am worried about something else, ma'am. She has the same bad inflammation in her lungs that she developed before. It concerns me it could be our climate, but she has also been traumatized. If something is troubling her within her mind, it is far beyond my medical skills, I'm afraid."

As he looked at Victoria waiting for her response, he saw that she was fighting back tears. Victoria quickly composed herself.

"I want you to do whatever is needed to help her, Dr. Brown."

The doctor nodded in affirmation as Victoria went back to Sarah and sat next to her. Victoria rubbed Sarah's face in a soothing maternal way that comforted her. "I shall never allow anything to happen to you again, Sally. Please forgive me for thinking that the Chambers School could do more for you than we could ourselves," she said gently. "So, I have made arrangements for you at Windsor Castle. You shall stay with us there, where you shall heal, be educated, and develop into your highest and best self, without harm."

As before, Sarah didn't respond. She turned her head away and coughed with a pronounced, phlegm-filled rattle.

Victoria frowned and looked at Dr. Brown whose head dropped, and he, too, looked away.

Part Three

Windsor Castle

1853

"Our most significant opportunities will be
found in times of greatest difficulty."

Thomas S. Monson

Queen Victoria's favorite pets—Her beloved "Dash," a King Charles Spaniel is on the footstool, and "Lori," the red parrot is in front.

Nineteen

⟡❋⟡

The first time I saw Windsor Castle I was overwhelmed. I had left Buckingham Palace where I had convalesced for two weeks, then Queen Victoria sent a carriage and driver to transport me to Windsor. She had gone ahead with the family and traveling staff.

My carriage pulled past the magnificent Copper Horse—a statue of King George III on horseback erected on Snow Hill—and ambled onto the two and a half-mile stretch of road called the 'Long Walk' leading to the center of the South Wing entrance to the castle. I held my chest struck by the rows of ancient oak trees which were artfully planted yet had a seeming randomness to them which could obscure one's view of the vastness of the palace grounds. It was on a small hill which added to the allure that you were deep in the English countryside and between the trees, long vistas of emerald-green lawns rolled before me gently sloping down toward a pond surrounded by the dense, tangled growth of shrubs, horse chestnuts and hedges.

The castle, I was told by my coachman, was built in the 11th century by William the Conqueror who chose the site high above the River Thames on the edge of what was then a Saxon hunting ground. Construction began around 1070, and 16 years later Windsor Castle was complete—and glorious.

When we finally reached the George IV Gate at the entrance of the *castle fortress, a footman helped me from the carriage. I was clutching my violin as though for support while another footman retrieved my valise and the box containing my beloved books acquired while I was at the Chambers School. I was so relieved that Sir Charles Phipps thought enough about me to make sure I got them all—especially upon seeing my name inscribed within them. Those books and my violin were all my precious belongings in the world. Then I entered the lower ward of the Castle.*

Inside, there was a flurry of activity taking place as scullery maids, housekeepers, under butlers, Grooms in Waiting, Ladies of the Bedchamber, and various other staff were going about their jobs.

My spirit was still damaged, and my cough seemingly became more aggravated upon the realization this would be my home for however long. I began to wonder what it would be like for me here after the horror that was the Chambers School. It seemed I was starting another new chapter in my life…in a book that seemed to be writing itself despite me.

ir Ian Paul, Windsor Castle's Lord Chamberlain, rushed over upon seeing Sarah enter with the footmen. He was surprised. "Miss Bonetta. My goodness," he exclaimed. "You are already here. We were not expecting you until after three. I am Sir Ian Paul, Lord Chamberlain. Welcome to Windsor."

"Thank you, Sir Ian."

"Follow me. Your room is ready thank God."

As he took Sarah up the stairs, various staff had second looks while Sarah took in the splendid Rococo and Baroque furnishings and wall coverings. Lori swooped by and then flew out of a window. It made Sarah grip her violin tighter.

"Pay no mind to Lori," chortled Sir Ian. "You will get used to her."

They continued on. Sir Ian introduced Sarah to several members of the personal and household staff as they appeared, most of them curious about the new African woman now in the palace.

"This is the Marquis of Allesbury," Sir Ian introduced. "He is Prince Albert's 'Master of the Horse.' This is Lady Harriet, Duchess of Sutherland, senior Lady of the Bedchamber; and Mary Smythe, Duchess of Ancester; Frances, Baroness Barham; and Carolina Augusta, Countess of Mount Edgcumbe, the Queen's Mistresses of Robes…"

I nodded to each member of the Queen's support staff that I met. Later I would have to learn the names and positions of two vice-chamberlains, four pages of the backstairs, six ladies of the bedchamber, a necessary woman of the Queen's private apartment, a clerk of the stables with six assistants for horses, two equerries, two pages of the presence chamber, five coachmen, five postillions, two physicians, and various others too numerous for me to fathom let alone remember. Just the thought was exhausting.

Finally, Sir Ian escorted Sarah to the third-floor apartments. Along the way he showed her eighteen elegant rooms decorated to showcase the Hanover dynasty's obsession with Palladio architecture. She loved the silk walls, painted ceilings, gold gildings and tapestries which dominated throughout Windsor.

But the real delight was evidenced by one room.

"Here we are. The Queen Mary suite. Your personal apartment," said Sir Ian as he opened the door. Seeing that Sarah was delighted, he smiled. "The Queen hoped it would please you."

Sarah was awestruck as she visually took it all in. The apartment was dazzling in matching powder blue brocade drapes and bed covers swathed in ornate rococo ornamentation. To the left was a large oak armoire, and to the right was an oak dressing table replete with a silver trimmed comb and brush set and crystal perfume bottles set atop lace doilies. The footman placed Sarah's box and valise in the room then left.

"Her Majesty will send for you shortly. Until then, should you require anything else I am at your service." Sir Ian pointed to a burgundy velvet rope shining from wear. "Simply pull that rope and it will alert me of your need. I shall be here with haste."

Sarah's hands covered her mouth as she placed her violin on the bed and looked around the great rooms, one leading into another.

She threw back the brocade drapes and let in the light. "My goodness," she exclaimed upon seeing the grounds.

> *It was three times the size of the Forbes' entire home and I could not believe it. I found myself touching the bedding, smelling the soft scent of the cut lilies in vases, and then looking out over the gardens from the beveled glass windows…"*
>
> *Then I heard someone from behind me say, "Beautiful, is it not? Windsor is very old, very grand…and very boring."*
>
> *When I turned, there stood a beautiful raven-haired girl around my age who eased into the room uninvited. She leaned in, and her voice dropped to a whisper. 'All this arrived this morning a hair's breath before you.'*

Sarah looked at the girl not knowing how to act. Who was she? A Lady-in-Waiting? A royal family member? An aristocratic visitor?

The girl smiled and offered the answer while extending her hand.

"Her Royal Highness Princess Alice—recalcitrant third child and second oldest daughter of the Queen. But call me Ally. And I shall call you Sally." Then she laughed, "Ally and Sally. Now there's a pair."

Though she seemed very odd for a royal, Sarah really enjoyed Ally's effervescence. It was so different and refreshing from the girls at school.

"Pleased to meet you, Princess Ally," Sarah curtsied.

"No, no. Not 'Princess' Ally. Just 'Ally for you. We're going to be good friends you and I."

"Alright, Ally."

Sarah liked the princess instantly. She reminded her of Linda, who, at this very moment she missed terribly. Then Sarah indicated not only the room—but, in fact, the palace. "My goodness, it is so large. How many rooms are in this castle?"

"917, I believe, give or take a couple suites."

Sarah nearly fell over. "917?"

"And they all have names you must learn. I'll quiz you myself."

"Really?" Sarah frowned.

"No. I'm just joking. You only need to learn the names of 300."

Sarah laughed. "The staff must be enormous. How many people work here? A hundred?"

"312, actually—excluding our traveling staff who go back and forth with us between residences."

Sarah gasped. "312 all in one place?"

"Yes. But do not be impressed. Windsor is a horror! It boils in summer, freezes in winter, and bores all year."

Alice then looked around, "So let's get you sorted. Where are the rest of your trunks and clothes?"

Sarah shrugged and pointed to the one valise and the one box.

"You *are* joking," Alice exclaimed.

Sarah shrugged and shook her head causing Alice to realize. "I see. You're *not* joking." She went over to the valise, opened it, and pulled out Sarah's two school uniforms, now cleaned from her time in the Cage, then she opened the box. Inside were ten books, two other dresses—the blue one, the pink gown, and two pair of shoes. Alice furrowed her eyebrows. "Ten books, two uniforms, two sad dresses, two pairs of shoes—and a violin? You must be an indigent."

Sarah shrugged again. "Apparently. As I am now living on the good graces of your mother."

Alice's cheeks turned the color of a ripe pomegranate. "Ugh, I am such a dunderhead. I forgot. Yes. You're some kind of African princess, mother said. Saved from beheading by an insane King, then hurled into a nightmare school. Ghastly. Just ghastly. Beheading was better."

She quickly turned to Sir Ian. "Send for Lady Eaton. Please tell her to bring someone over tomorrow to take Sarah's sizes. Tell her we're going to need...a dozen silk and brocade ball gowns, a croquette outfit, a riding outfit, 6 tea dresses, stockings, ribbons, and two dozen pairs of shoes at least, for... 'Princess' Sarah. Tell her she's about my height and size."

Though Sarah knew she was an African royal, because of Alice's skewed sense of humor, she couldn't tell if Alice was being sarcastic or sincere.

Meanwhile, Sir Ian bowed. "Right away, your Highness." Once he left, Alice turned back to Sarah genuinely heartfelt. "Whatever happened to you, know that you are safe here. I'll send my Lady in to dress you in one of my gowns for tea. Dinner is at 5." She started out, then turned back after looking at Sarah's short afro which she thought was untidy and unkempt. "And I'll have Lady Eaton bring in my black formal wig which you can keep. I have at least ten. That should take care of your hair, uh, 'situation.' You will look splendid."

Sarah wasn't sure she should be amused or insulted. Then Alice grinned. "Sarah, I think you should know. We are all hopeless eccentrics here…"

Sarah felt Alice's sincerity—until Alice winked and added:

"...So trust me, you'll fit right in."

At that, Alice flounced out of the room leaving Sarah flummoxed and wondering "What have I gotten myself into now."

It was teatime in the parlor. Victoria was playing with Lori the Parrot now atop its cage as the gathering of family and guests were served tea by the Footmen. As Prince Albert talked to the Duchess of Kent and Turkish Ambassador Jimonpur wearing a gold turban, Vicky chatted with Bertie, while Alice flirted with Sir Roger.

Suddenly Alice's flirtations ended abruptly as her mouth dropped at the sight of something just beyond Sir Roger's shoulders. All eyes seemed to turn to follow Alice's in slow-motion, and each face registered an emotion of wonder, shock, or in Bertie's case, indignance.

Sarah had entered the parlor and all chatter halted. She was stunning in Alice's beige silk gown. Her hair had been tucked under a black formal wig which hung with curls below the shoulder and fresh Baby's Breath was tucked into it. She walked with the elegance and bearing of a royal to where the Queen and Prince Albert stood.

Vicky leaned into her sister Alice in surprise. "Ally. Is that not your dress?"

"Not anymore," said Alice smirked enviously, torn as to whether she'd done the right thing by allowing Sarah to wear it, yet proud that she had.

Meanwhile their grandmother, the Duchess of Kent, leaned toward Victoria not at all amused. "Is that her?" she asked Victoria in hushed tones, "My God. She's so black."

"She's African, mother" quipped Victoria, irritated by her mother's insensitivity. "Shouldn't she be?"

The Duchess nonchalantly snapped open her fan and turned to get tea as Sarah came over to the Queen and curtsied. She had barely come up before Alice pulled her aside, "You fix up quite nicely, my dear."

Now understanding that blunt humor was a defense mechanism Alice used to be liked, Sarah grinned, "Thank you. I think."

Alice gave Sarah another quick inspection, "I just told my sister Vicky you can have the dress. I'll never look that good in it again."

Sarah smiled at her new friend but shifted her body needing comfort. "I appreciate it. But must English clothing have so many corsets and bodices and pantaloons all tied so tightly? I can barely breathe."

"No 'Lady' can. So welcome to western womanhood. It is all designed so we collapse after one sip of water," Alice jested. "It is why it's called 'swooning' I expect. Now. Let me tell you who everyone is."

As Sarah was given a cup of tea by a footman, Alice identified everyone at the gathering under her breath.

"Mother and Poppi you know," she began. "The older man in the turban is the Turkish Ambassador Mr. Jimonpur—he's growing on me. Seems we may go to war to help the Ottomans. Anyway, over there is my older sister Victoria. Call her "Vicky"; the woman next to them is my grandmother—the Duchess of Kent. She can be snippy. Next to her is my intractable older brother Bertie—the Prince of Wales. He 'invented' snippy; and the utterly divine creature next to him is his most agreeable friend Sir Roger Carlyle."

Sarah looked at Sir Roger and smiled. "I concur with your assessment of him. He is *quite* agreeable—even for an Englishman."

"Trust me," Alice mused. "Every noblewoman in England wants him—or has had him."

Sarah looked at Alice in mocked shock. This was, once again, vintage Alice.

Meanwhile, as Alice continued her running commentary on all the guests, across the room Sir Roger could not take his eyes off Sarah.

"Who is that dark, celestial goddess?" he queried Bertie.

"Mother's new pet," scoffed the Prince with a condescending expression. "May as well be that damned parrot."

But Sir Roger ignored Bertie's slight for he was besotted. "She's exquisite."

Ignoring Sir Roger, the Prince of Wales finished the rest of his tea and handed the empty cup back to a nearby footman. "Roger, stick to chambermaids and tarts. There is no need for you to forage into an ethnic cesspit."

Upended by Bertie's gibe, Sir Roger turned his gaze away from Sarah and sneered at his oldest and dearest friend. "*You* stick to chambermaids and tarts. They're more *your* type." He put his own teacup down. "As for 'ethnic cesspits' you're just upset that girl from Bombay gave you a dose of something requiring a six-week cure last year."

"You are such a prude," snickered Bertie unfazed. "No one cares what people do in bed, who they do it with, or what they catch, as long as they don't do it on public streets and frighten the horses."

Bertie snickered as Sir Roger shook his head and moved away, but ceased upon realizing his best friend since childhood, was walking over to Sarah who was still chatting with Alice.

Alice saw Sir Roger on his way and cautioned Sarah. "He's coming this way. Act aloof."

Sir Roger stopped right in front of Sarah and cleared his throat. Before Alice could make the formal introduction, he had bowed and did his own honors. "Sir Roger Carlyle. Captain of Her Majesty's 3rd Dragoons. To whom have the Gods given me the pleasure of meeting?"

It was as though everyone in the room froze in place leaving Roger and me alone. Up close I found Sir Roger more handsome than he was from across the room. In fact, I had never seen a more striking man. His dark curly hair could not be contained by the bow he'd used to tie it back, and it fell in haphazard tendrils around his face. His piercing green eyes were almost haunting, and he had a playful smile as he engaged me. Alice had to indeed be right about him, for I was convinced Roger had broken many a fair maiden's heart worldwide. And yet, despite recognizing that as a fact, I still found myself responding with infatuation as I reached out my hand to him. "Sarah Bonetta," I responded, my heart pumping madly, "My pleasure as well." Sir Roger kissed my hand, and I felt my fingers tremble as well as my knees. I just knew anyone near me could hear them knocking together. Thankfully, a footman was passing by with a tray of fresh tea and I reached for a cup to steady my nerves as I'd never felt the sensations I was experiencing in the presence of a man. Not even with Kua whom I had loved. I found myself in that first moment confounded. I was also quite incapable of breathing. Who was this white man so disturbing my peace of mind? And why was I so giddy in front of him? I looked away a moment attempting to gather myself and drew in a deep breath—almost embarrassed by my behavior. Clearly, I was intrigued, and captivated.

"Miss Bonetta, I understand you are an associate of the Queen?"

"I am, Sir Roger. She is my Godmother and has chosen to be the kindest guardian of my being, and I am so grateful for her favor."

"As am I for having met you through her."

Sarah's heart was still pounding. Was this a British mating ritual? Was he letting her know he liked her? Was it now time to show him she might like him as well? What to do, she thought nervously, finding herself smiling at him—her eyes never leaving his, nor vice-versa.

Seeing this interplay rendered Alice speechless as she watched the chemistry between Sarah and the very man she had been flinging herself in front of for weeks, growing. With a wide but respectful grin, Sir Roger gestured to Sarah, "May I sit next to you at dinner, Miss Bonetta? I should like to be near the most intriguing woman here."

Sarah blushed as the hand holding her teacup shook. Alice watched as Lori flew over and landed on Sir Roger's shoulder. Sir Roger loved animals, and Sarah giggled again, now very much aware she was attracted to a European man. How could that be? After all, they would always be "the oppressors" to her.

Victoria noticed not only her parrot, but also Sir Roger's seeming interest in her new Ward. She came over and knowingly smiled.

"Careful with Sir Roger, Sally. All women love him. Even Lori here." She put out a finger and Lori flew to her. "We have a name for his type, you know. Cad."

But Sir Roger had a line for every occasion. "Oh Majesty, you know I only have eyes for you. But alas, Prince Albert got there first."

Victoria gestured to Sarah. "See? Careful with this one."

As Victoria put the parrot back in her cage, Sir Roger extended his hand to Sarah to escort her to the dinner table.

"I truly love her Majesty. She's like a mother to me. Always has been. Especially when I lost my own dear mother and father at sea."

"Both of your parents? At once?" Sarah frowned.

Sir Roger nodded. "In 1841. I was nine. They left my sister and me at Uncle Benjamin's estate in Liverpool while they traveled to New York on business. They booked a return passage aboard the S.S. President— then the largest steamship in the world. Stormy seas had already weakened and twisted her hull which was poorly constructed with a third deck on top of it making the ship too top heavy. She would roll excessively in bad weather and be underpowered. The ship was the slowest of any transatlantic steamer. My parents were aboard her third eastbound voyage back to Liverpool."

Sir Roger looked down, the story making him emotional. He had not thought about his parents for a long time and accepted a glass of claret from a footman and sipped it.

"The ship was overloaded with cargo and encountered heavy gale winds her second day out," he continued finally. "I remember the day my uncle came to me and Carolyn, my sister, and sat us down. He told us that the ship our parents were on encountered a storm on the seas between Nantucket Shoals and Georges Bank. It went down with all 147 passengers and crew onboard. Including our parents."

Sir Roger and Sarah sat. "I can still smell mother's perfume on the kerchief she left in my jacket pocket."

Sarah felt badly and touched his hand. "I am so sorry, Sir Roger," she said softly. "It is a terrible thing to lose one's parents. I lost both of mine horribly too."

"How?"

"It is a story I will tell you one day. Not tonight."

A footman offered a glass of wine to Sarah as well. She took it and sipped. Roger looked at her—and nodded.

Alice now trudged back over to Vicky and Bertie, and all three watched Sir Roger and Sarah talking.

"Jealous, little sister?" Bertie chortled. "I know Roger. And that African appears to be his next conquest. Where does that leave you?"

"I have to agree," said Vicky. "Something *is* going on with them."

"Shush, both of you," Alice chided, pouting only slightly. "I am not in the least upset. I only wanted to give my maidenhead to someone attractive—before I'm arranged to marry some prig I'll hate!"

Bertie grimaced at his younger sibling as though she were possessed by a demon.

"God, Alice. The things you say."

Later, in the Windsor dining hall, a long table was half-filled with family and invited guests for dinner. Victoria was at one end, Prince Albert at the other. Everyone else was in-between. Roger and Alice were on either side of Sarah as Footmen brought in an array of food courses. Soon, Victoria tapped her wine glass for quiet. "I would like to thank you all for coming this evening. Fate has brought to this home a new member of our family. A princess from a distant land whom I hope you will welcome as my new Goddaughter. Sarah Forbes Bonetta."

Everyone applauded, except Bertie as Sarah stood graciously.

"Thank you, your Majesty, Prince Albert and all of you here. I do not know what Gods I favored to bring me to this wonderful place, but I thank them and pray they bestow great good fortune upon you and this family."

The guests applauded again. As Sarah sat, Roger leaned into her,

"Do you dance, Miss Bonetta?"

Sarah hesitated in her response remembering her punishment at the Chambers School for her impromptu dance and violin "performance."

176

Finally, she smiled wryly, "Unfortunately... yes."

"I love dancing, Sir Roger beamed, elated by her answer. "We shall do so later."

Sarah nodded as everyone continued to chat and enjoy themselves. Sarah looked over at the Queen who winked at her. Sarah smiled. Then she glanced at Sir Roger who could not contain the smile on his face. A smile his friend Bertie across from him noticed and was annoyed by.

In the Ballroom after dinner as a string quartet played a waltz, the guests danced or engaged in lively conversations. Victoria, Albert, Bertie, Vicky, Alice and Ambassador Jimonpur were among the dancers, while Sarah and Sir Roger chatted. Sir Roger essentially gave Sarah an overview of his life.

"...Bertie helped me to run for Mayor of Weymouth. I lost. My youth worked against me. But it developed my thirst for what one can do to make a difference in the world. One can do that if you are in politics."

Sarah was intrigued by Sir Roger's disinterest in ruling the world in favor of doing good. Though she still felt that what he was doing now might speak volumes for where he was actually headed—if anywhere. "How are you fixed now, Captain?"

Sir Roger detected the subtext behind her question and responded accordingly, "I'm the youngest officer in the British Army. I plan to stand for a seat as a Member of Parliament in the Commons, and perhaps someday become Prime Minister."

"Ah, a man of ambition," Sarah smiled. "Well, I have no doubt of your success."

With that vote of confidence, Sir Roger held out his hand to her. "Shall we dance?"

Remembering the waltz lessons at the Chambers school before she was unceremoniously hurled into the Cage, Sarah affirmatively smiled, and took his hand.

He led her out to the dance floor, and they began to dance—a delicious sight for all to see as they were exquisite in their movements. Victoria's mother—the Duchess of Kent, and Bertie, however, were unsettled by the couple.

"What on earth is he doing dancing with a … with her?" winced Victoria's mother. "Does he not know how unseemly it appears?"

"Do not worry, grandmother. I'll handle it in due course," assured Bertie equally vexed by seeing his friend with an African.

However, Sarah and Sir Roger were oblivious. Each only had eyes for the other. "Perhaps tomorrow you will come riding with me?" Sir Roger invited, with eyes hopeful for a nod from her. "You do ride, do you not?"

Sarah feigned insult. "We do have horses in Africa, Sir Roger."

Horrified that he may have offended her, Roger for the first time stumbled over his words. "I-I'm sorry. Yes, yes. Of course. I just… wanted to make your better acquaintance."

Sarah giggled. Realizing she was teasing him, Roger giggled too.

Across the room, the Duchess of Kent gave Bertie a look that clearly indicated he *go and handle this now*. Bertie immediately approached Roger and Sarah and interrupted their much enjoyable togetherness by tapping Roger on his shoulder.

Roger and Sarah stopped dancing, and Bertie extended his hand to Sarah, glancing at Roger sharply. "I'll take over, old boy."

Reluctantly, Sir Roger bowed and stepped back to allow the Prince of Wales to dance with Sarah. It was obvious to Roger—and Bertie—that Sarah did not wish to change partners, because she had not taken Bertie's hand yet. But finally she did.

Bertie was miffed that an inferior 'African' took so long to accept a normal dance custom—and with the Prince of Wales no less. He whisked her into their first waltz, then suddenly became venomous.

"Miss Bonetta, I know you're new here. But let me make myself crystal clear," he bristled making Sarah's bones rattle. "Mother picks up mongrels and foreigners like shoes then abandons them as quickly. While you are here—for the *short* time you will be here—do not insinuate yourself into our inner-circle expecting to advance. Their interest will only last as long as mother's. Briefly!"

At that, Bertie abandoned his hold on Sarah causing her arms to drop sloppily.

"Now. That's quite enough. I won't have it said that the Crown Prince was seen dancing with or extolling the virtues of a Negress."

He walked away leaving Sarah embarrassed.

Alice, who saw it all, quickly went over as did Sir Roger. But Sarah outpaced them both as she hurried away toward the entrance hall.

Sir Roger called out, "Miss Bonetta...!"

Dejected by Bertie's words, Sarah stopped and turned. "I'm sorry, Sir Roger. Tomorrow will be quite impossible." And she ran off leaving both Roger and Alice bewildered. Neither knew what to do.

Victoria, who saw the incident from afar, frowned and walked over to her son. "What did you say to that poor girl, Bertie?"

Bertie turned to his mother as though she was insane to ask him anything which caused Victoria to repeat:

"Are you deaf? What did you say to my goddaughter which caused her to leave?"

"Goddaughter, indeed," Bertie finally snapped. "I told her not to think she had become a member of this family, for there is precious little affection from you for those of us who are actually of the blood."

Victoria was outdone as her son excused himself and went to his room—but not before motioning to Lady Rose, his bed choice for the evening, who, after a moment went up to join him.

arah ran into her room and slammed the door behind her. She immediately pulled the baby's breath out of her wig and threw the flowers on the floor. She then tried to take off her gown but couldn't by herself. She realized she would need help. Exasperated, she sat on the bed becoming overwhelmed by thoughts of her life thus far in England.

> *Image after image rummaged in my head, accompanied by the vile voices I had been subjected to hearing:*
>
> *Lt. Gibson aboard the Bonetta: "Aren't they all diseased?" Mary Forbes declaring: "The Queen will not meet a heathen." Madeline, at school, "Wooly haired know-it-all." The malicious Miss Rawlins, "These black demons will come out!" And now Bertie's: "Mother picks up mongrels, and foreigners like shoes." I couldn't help it. I began to sob despite doing all I could not to. My tears were then interrupted by rattling coughs that forced me to fall across my bed. And before I knew it, I had cried myself to sleep.*

The early morning light was peeking through slits in the closed brocade drapes in Sarah's room. Splayed across the bed asleep Sarah still had on Alice's gown. Her wig was askew, and she stirred a bit when the chirping birds outside the windows became nature's alarm clock.

Soon, she heard a rapid succession of knocks on the door. Clumsily, she lifted herself up from the bed. "Yes…?"

Victoria walked in alone and concerned holding a book in her left hand. Sarah straightened. "Your Majesty?" She struggled to get up, but Victoria gestured her to stay put, and she finally noticed Sarah's clothes. "You slept in your gown?"

Sarah touched the gown, now creased with the lines from the bedding. "I'm so sorry, Majesty. I…I could not get it off."

Victoria noticed the baby's breath on the floor and shook her head. "Of course not! You need a Ladies Maid. I should have thought of it."

Sarah was embarrassed for Victoria to see her so disheveled in Alice's beautiful gown. "No, ma'am. You have already done so much. Too much."

"Nonsense." Victoria began to help Sarah out of her dress. She went to the armoire and took a silk robe from it, and assisted Sarah into it. "Do not allow what Bertie said to upset you. You should pay no attention to him."

Sarah was diplomatic, "Your son will be King of England one day. He cannot be ignored, ma'am."

"I do. He's been a boil on me since he was in the womb. Horrible pregnancy. Horrible child. I'm shocked I haven't poisoned him."

Sarah almost grinned. Victoria knew she was raising Sarah's spirits and continued. "Besides, I intend to live for years. By the time Bertie becomes King you will be a great-grandmother."

Sarah laughed, "Hardly. I understand these things usually require that which I do not have—a husband."

Now Victoria laughed, covering her mouth like a school girl. Then once she composed herself, she smiled warmly at Sarah and handed her the book she was holding. "I have a gift for you."

Sarah looked at the smooth black leather of the book but noticed the inside was blank.

"It's a diary," offered Victoria. "I want you to put down your thoughts every day because what you are experiencing is something you will want to remember. As you get older things become fuzzy—and you'll want to track your life. I have twenty-six of them already. All filled with my thoughts and memories."

Victoria rose from the bed and went to the door and turned. "I'll send someone in to dress you. As regards Bertie, just remember, the only way to defeat a bully—is to bully back—and I hear you do that quite well."

Sarah smiled, and Victoria left the room.

That morning in the Dining Hall everyone was engaged in lively conversation over breakfast. As usual, Victoria's family, as well as the Queen's overnight guests were there including Ambassador Jimonpur, and Sir Roger Carlyle. All were enjoying juice, tea, eggs, bacon, and toast.

Sarah entered with Alice. Sir Roger held out Alice's chair for her and she sat. Then he pulled out the seat next to him for Sarah—to the ire of Bertie and the Duchess of Kent seated across. Platters of eggs and breakfast meats were brought over to the two latecomers and a footman offered sausage to Sarah who frowned. "What is this?"

Bertie smirked. "Surely they taught you what sausage is at that posh girl's school mother spent a fortune on for you."

But Sir Roger interceded turning to Sarah. "It's a kind of ground meat stuffed into a gelatinous wrap. Try it."

Sarah had a bite and liked it. She smiled at him. "We have something similar in Africa. Mashed up meats wrapped in chicken skin."

Soon, the footmen began bringing in small cups and saucers followed by copper coffee pots from which they poured thick, dark coffee.

Victoria rang the little dinner bell for attention, "Everyone, we are going to try this coffee which Ambassador Jimonpur generously gifted us. It's from Turkey. Quite strong I hear. Made with Cardamom. It's called..." Before she could try and pronounce it, Ambassador Jimonpur interjected, "...Kahvalti."

The Royals, Sir Roger, and the other English guests took a sip and were clearly dissatisfied. It was far too strong for them. The Ambassador felt offended and Sarah saw it. As others tried not to gag, footmen proffered sugar to the Queen and moved to other guests who wanted it as well. Bertie pushed his cup away turning to his mother. "Any more of these odd culinary delicacies—as we're casting our English net so far?"

Sarah understood his underhanded insult was not aimed merely at the Ambassador, as did Sir Roger and Victoria—who gave Sarah a look of permission to "handle the bully."

Sarah smiled intently at Bertie, and in a soft, direct voice replied, "Who knows what you'll find in a net. Sometimes a pure delight. Sometimes a tribal cruelty."

Bertie was incredulous. "Do regale us in all things *tribal*."

Sarah's smile dropped, and her eyes narrowed. She peered directly at Bertie which discomfited many of the family and guests.

"Your Highness, *I* was captured in a net after witnessing my parents and siblings beheaded. Dragged three miles to a cruel King who stripped me of my clothing and dignity, wrapped me in cloth, then placed me in a boat to be beheaded and mutilated."

Sir Roger was stunned. Now he knew what happened to her family, and his face, like the others at the table, reflected horror.

Bertie was snippy. "Such lovely breakfast conversation."

Sarah ignored him. "But thanks to a widely cast English 'net' I was rescued and brought to this place. Healed of my wounds, treated as a human being, and thought of as someone worthy of educating to make the best of themselves. So, it is to Queen Victoria that I raise my cup..."

Victoria looked at her warmly, as Sarah raised the small cup of coffee. The others followed, except for Bertie, who took his time raising his as Sarah continued, "...Let us drink Kahvalti to her Majesty, in hopes she always stays curious about all things *not* familiar in her net."

Everyone joined Sarah in the coffee toast, "Here, here."

Bertie nodded to his mother and finally took a sip of the coffee himself—peeved that this African girl did not have more respect for him than to shamefully humiliate him at his own family's breakfast table. Ambassador Jimonpur smiled in gratitude that his coffee gift was far better embraced this time. He felt honored and nodded to Sarah.

Victoria raised her cup to Sarah and also nodded. Sir Roger looked around the table at all those who, with more tolerance, engaged Ambassador Jimonpur in conversation, and added cream and sugar to his coffee—but drank it without complaint. Roger smiled then leaned into Sarah's ear, "Are you sure you cannot come riding with me today?"

Later that morning, Lori was perched on an old oak tree in Windsor Great Park. The parrot looked about, inspecting her territory around the palace. Soon, she saw two riders on horseback dart out from beyond the stables galloping out onto the massive countryside and swooped toward Sir Roger and Sarah, who was riding astride and without a saddle. Lori's flight dropped to shoulder level and appeared to challenge them to a race, which they obliged until Lori soared up and away back to the palace. Roger and Sarah grinned.

As Sarah galloped along, taking command of her horse and allowing the feeling of the animal's power beneath her to take her spirit away, she realized she had not had so much fun or felt so free since arriving in England. Her horse, an all-black Arabian named Onyx, had been a gift from Victoria's Uncle Leopold, King of the Belgians, and was fast and beautiful with a thick, long, wavy mane. Sarah rode him as though she were back in Okeodan—with the African air whipping against her skin, and her eyes closed. She and Sir Roger raced all over the large expanse of the park which was five thousand acres of gently sloping, undulating landscape. As they rode Sarah was struck by the sweeping vistas and coppices accentuated by ancient oak and maple trees. They rode along the small river in the north part of the park called the "Battle Bourne" which ran to the Thames, then raced across to a pond to the south. Sarah had not laughed so much since leaving Africa, and she loved challenging, competing, and drawing closer to Sir Roger who felt like a special gift dropped out of the sky as her friend.

Sir Roger, too, had never met anyone like Sarah Bonetta. There she was, a woman guiding and controlling her horse with the power of her thighs—like a man, and the beast obeying her every move and command. It was unusual and wondrous. He knew he had met a different kind of woman the evening before. An independent spirit. One who was not impressed by the powerful and would challenge him. Keep him on his toes. One he could not control. She was a woman he would have to show his truth to. No other woman ever made his heart leap like this one, and he had wanted and had many women.

Sarah was different. He had to accept he was completely out of his comfort zone. As they rode together Sir Roger tried to deconstruct what it was about her that was drawing him in so intensely. He was used to being with Bertie and accompanying him on sensual jaunts with inappropriate women whom they discarded like old newspapers. Sir Roger was not as prolific as the Prince of Wales, but he did introduce the Prince to a few hat shop girls and a tart or two. They had even frequented a brothel in Manchester once and shared a whore who taught them things neither chose to ever do again in or out of bed.

But unlike Bertie, who accepted he would likely be arranged into a loveless, but appropriate royal marriage, yet intended to exercise the "Divine right of Kings" and keep a mistress, Roger knew that somewhere out there was the "divine right" woman for him. One he would build a life with. One he would not diminish through infidelity and love forever. In that regard, he was like his beloved father—faithful to one woman.

The problem was Roger never found the one woman…

…Until last night. And because of last night, Sir Roger found himself questioning everything. Was he drawn to Sarah because she was confident? Exotic? The Queen's new darling? Was it because Sarah was unlike the noblewomen he usually met—predictable and pretentious, taught not to show emotion, but manipulating nonetheless in a quest for a suitable royal marriage? Indeed, yes, he thought. Did he care that Sarah was African, untitled and without a pittance? No. Would others? Absolutely. But did he care they may talk? No.

But then Sir Roger Carlyle always did what he wanted—and he always got what he wanted. And what he wanted was to impress Sarah. His just being an aristocrat would never be enough for her.

The two finally arrived back at the Windsor Stables, tired, sweaty, and out of breath. They dismounted their horses and gave the stable hand the horse reins. Sarah looked at all the other animals around them in wonder. "It's like a private zoo here!"

Sir Roger nodded. "Indeed. A royal menagerie. The Queen loves animals. They have replaced the hundreds of dolls Bertie told me she once owned." He pointed to a few in the stable. "That is Her Majesty's Sardinian pony, and those are the Windsor goats, her donkeys, Nero her greyhound, Hector her Scottish deerhound, her Pomeranian, five collies, and then there is Lori."

They walked back to Windsor enjoying each other's company.

"You sit a horse well," said Roger admiringly.

Sarah frowned, but Roger continued, "It was a thing to behold, your equestrian command of Onyx with one leg on each side of his back and no saddle. Riding like men do with your thighs controlling the beast. Patrician women usually ride side-saddle."

Despite his commendable tone, Sarah became irritated by yet another comparison of her African life and ways to those of the English, and she lashed out. "African women do not subscribe to your European female customs, or British social graces, Sir Roger. When we need to get from here to there we walk or hop on a horse and go."

Roger was slightly chagrined. "You need not be so defensive. I did not mean harm. It was only an observation. A compliment really."

Sarah became instantly contrite. She realized she had placed the one blameless person she liked into the same company as Bertie, Humes, Miss Rawlins, Madeline, and Mary Forbes—people who thought her an inferior and "an experiment" because she was black.

"I-I'm sorry, Sir Roger. That was thoughtless. You've been entirely considerate. A complete gentleman, and a fun outing partner," she said ruefully, wishing she could take it all back. "It's just that... here in England I seem to be an oddity to be scrutinized, or disregarded or..."

"...Abused," added Sir Roger sympathetically.

Sarah finally nodded slightly, then looked away with a melancholy overtaking her. "It's hard not to think about my life in Africa, and how it was all just snatched away."

Roger remembered what Sarah had told him. "I was so sorry to hear how you lost your family. It must have been hard."

Sarah nodded, "As with you—with yours."

As they walked on Sarah found herself taken back to Okeodan. "I remember how my brothers, my mother and my father, Chief Derefaka, the Omobo Prince, would sit outside our large, grass palace with umbrellas held over our heads by our servants. I was Omobo Aina, 'Princess Aina,' and I enjoyed seeing my father give advice to villagers who loved his kind manner, his good heart, and wisdom."

"So your real name is 'Aina'?"

"It means 'difficult birth' in Yoruba. The name given to a child born with its umbilical cord around their neck." Sarah turned back to Roger, "I was the Ebado Omobo—the Yoruban princess. I wanted to be a respected Oluko, a teacher, like father. But here, I am so often considered a savage being transformed into a 'Lady' by you enlightened British."

Sir Roger was moved by what she said, "You are better than any 'Lady' I have ever met. And you are already a teacher. You're teaching us, more than we're teaching you."

They walked a bit further, then he took her hand. "I promised to meet Bertie at the Norman gate. We're playing Polo with a couple of chaps today, so I'll go to the other gate, and leave you to it."

Sarah nodded and turned to go through the North gate in front of them. But Sir Roger stopped her. "Sarah, I return to Weymouth tomorrow, but I shall be at Buckingham for the Queen's birthday in May," he stated with a sheepish sincerity creeping over him. "I would very much like to see you again."

Sarah smiled moved by his slight awkwardness for someone she knew was much more cunning with women. "You have a kind face, Sir Roger, and I had a nice time today. Yes, I would very much like to see you at Buckingham."

Sir Roger beamed causing his dimples to appear as though two fingers had poked the sides of his cheeks. "Then I'll see you at tea later." He kissed her hand, his mouth lingering as he held it.

Sarah grinned, slowly removing her hand from his. She turned to go, but only got a few steps away when she stopped to look back. Sir Roger looked back as well. His face still reflecting a disarming smile. Sarah returned his smile with an air of pleasure then went inside the castle.

Unbeknownst to either of them, from his third-floor apartment Bertie was standing in the window taking in the view of the River Thames while his dresser, put his Polo jacket on him. Just as he turned from the window he saw Roger and his mother's "experiment" walking together, growing close. His blood boiled, and his cheeks became flush.

"That will be all," he said to his dresser, motioning for him to leave. Then Bertie turned back to the window watching Sir Roger and Sarah together. He was annoyed and not pleased. He was not pleased at all.

Twenty One

...The moment I stepped inside the castle's north gate, Alice was there. She began quickly pulling me along the corridor and finally up the stairs. "Where have you been? I was looking everywhere for you."

"I went riding with Sir Roger," I responded to which Alice grinned. "Riding, eh? Sounds promising." "It was just riding, Ally," I reminded her. "Not a marriage proposal."

"Marriage proposal, indeed." Alice chided. "Certainly not from Roger. He—and marriage—are polar opposites."

I had to shake my head. My friend Alice was nothing if not a character and I asked her why all the fuss?

She said that Lady Eaton was already there to take my sizes and she and Lady Cleveland had brought along several dresses she was already working on to fit to me. "Oh, you should see the fabrics, Sally," Alice exclaimed. "They're wonderful."

When we reached my suite, three women were inside with a dress form, scissors, tape measures, pins and glorious fabric was everywhere. But the moment they saw me enter the room with Alice they became as still as church mice with dropped mouths.

"Is this her?" asked Lady Eaton, the heavier-set of the three, who frowned. "Yes," Alice replied nonchalantly, going to the bed and picking up a piece of silk brocade fabric. "This is Princess Sarah Forbes Bonetta.

Sarah, this is Lady Cecilia Eaton, your dressmaker, Lady Cleveland, her assistant, and Lady McBurney, your new Lady-in-Waiting."

I curtsied. But the three women did not. They didn't know what to do and looked at each other in confusion. I knew it all had to do with intolerance and protocol. These were women used to working for white establishment nobility. By now they would have dropped into deep curtsies for royalty. But I was African and thereby of suspicious birthright, thus inferior. To them I did not require the time-honored respect of a curtsy. But in truth, I was not even expecting such treatment.

Alice, however, would have none of it. "I'm sorry, ladies. Did I stammer?" she snipped just enough to alert the women that they had been disrespectful. "I said this is 'Princess' Sarah Forbes Bonetta from Oke-oban in the Kingdom of Dahomey, West Africa. Surely your upbringing presupposes she be given reverence."

The three women instantly dropped into curtsies.

"Much better," Alice chided. "Hello, Princess Sarah…" adjusted Lady Eaton.

"'Sarah' is fine," I offered, desirous to remove them all from the perilous hook Alice placed them on.

"Mistress Sarah then," insisted Alice, giving me side-eye to indicate protocol and decorum was to be observed in the palace of Windsor. The women nodded, then I went to the bed and looked at all the pre-made gowns, and fabrics.

The cloth was lovely. I had never seen such fabrics. "What is it," I asked, feeling the texture of one of the dresses. Lady Cleveland grinned. "Silk chiffon, Mistress. From China. Isn't it wondrous? Just look at the shimmer."

I picked up the blue dress and danced around with it as Lady Easton continued. "I had started this dress for Princess Victoria. But when the Princess told me she did not like blue I stopped work on it. But it looks perfect against your skin color."

I smiled at Lady Eaton. "I love blue. I love pink. All colors really. I do not have a preference."

Lady Eaton then smiled. "Good. Then let us get started, shall we? I want you to have the smartest wardrobe of any royal this season."

It was like I was in fairyland. Yes, I closed my eyes more than once and opened them again to make sure it was all real. That was the day I felt like a real princess of the court…

eanwhile, Bertie left his suite and went down the back stairs, through St. George Hall and out of the Norman Gate where he was to meet Sir Roger. He was still irked by Roger's behavior when Roger came up.

"It's good weather for the match today," said Roger. "I can't wait to show that rascal Lord Randolph my new underhand swing. It's much better than last time." He then noticed Bertie's mood. "What's wrong with you?"

"I won't have you besotted by that African," Bertie threatened.

Sir Roger looked at him stunned, "*You* won't have…?" His hands went to his hips glaring at his best friend. "Bertie, I am not nine years old. You were not this meddlesome when I was seeing Lady Weston—and she'd slept with every Peer in London."

"…Every Peer in *England*, old boy." Bertie reminded.

Sir Roger shot him a look.

Bertie shot one right back, "Still—she was one of *our* crowd."

"Meaning?"

"Meaning the fastest way for you to never be elected or become Prime Minister—is to stay on this path."

Now Roger was incredulous. "Was it not you who told me no one cares what people do in bed or who they do it with, as long as they don't do it in the streets?"

"God, you're so literal," snapped Bertie. "This is different."

"How is it different—if not for the obvious, bigoted reason?"

The Prince of Wales was outdone. "Were you raised in a monastery, away from the world and all reality? Sarah is some unlettered, untitled Zulu who fell from the clouds into our home because Mother is indulging in another of her overly generous, charitable experiments. She is not a woman for you. I won't have it."

It took Roger a moment. "Again, with what *you* won't have. I am ashamed to know you, right now. And to think that one day a man who thinks like you and behaves in such a way to his supposed friends will be King of this great nation."

Sir Roger started off into the castle leaving his horse. "Thank God one doesn't vote on who becomes 'King' or I'd leave your medieval thinking in the dust."

"Remind me why we're still friends?" snapped Bertie.

"I was just thinking that. Why indeed." Roger scowled, "I shall let you know when I'm back here for your mother's birthday. Until then, forget about polo today. I'm packing my things to leave for Weymouth."

"Roger! Come back here!"

"And she's not some Zulu," Roger called out as he kept going.

"Roger!!"

Bertie was outdone, as his best Polo playing partner marched away in disgust and never looked back.

Upstairs like giddy children, Sarah, Alice and the women in the bedchamber measured, cut, pinned and sized Sarah like a rag doll. She was outfitted in so many lace, silk, chiffon and brocade dresses in every shape, color and configuration that her head was spinning. And the shoes. There must have been dozens of them. Though she enjoyed the fuss being made over her, she experienced a general sense of foreboding: What if all of it was taken away tomorrow? What if it were all a dream?

After all, she had felt excited and thrilled to be attending the private exclusive Chambers Society School, and then was horribly mistreated. Could a similar fate await her in this seemingly wonderful place?

Her new Lady-in-Waiting, Lady McBurney seemed to sense Sarah's foreboding and soothed her fears.

"I know what you're thinking, lass. Can it all be real?"

Sarah nodded.

"I know. Tis a lot to take in all at once. But from what I hear you're a tough one, and a smart one, too. You'll do just fine."

Her Lady smiled and so did Sarah. Lady McBurney was from Edinburgh, Scotland, but her accent was different. Not harsh, guttural intonations like Sarah's friend Jillian from Captain Forbes' household, but a refined modification developed by education and breeding.

As Sarah coughed a bit, Lady McBurney began the process of tying on corsets, then layering the various pieces that created Sarah's new dresses—which Sarah modeled for them—and they would applaud.

Finally, when the afternoon ended, Sarah thanked each woman for their efforts and saw them out of her suite.

Alice smiled. "Well, I think that should do it for today. I'm going to have myself dressed for tea and will see you downstairs." She started for the door, then turned. "You do know how to get down to the parlor? It's quite a large palace."

"Yes. 917 rooms. Each with names I plan to learn."

"Just don't get lost." Alice grinned then left the room.

Sarah turned and smiled at her image in the mirror. She looked and felt like a proper English aristocrat. But would she ever truly be, she thought. It was then she saw her new diary sitting atop the bureau.

She went to it, opened it to the first blank page and began writing down her thoughts. It would be the first of hundreds of entries.

Half an hour later everyone was in the Parlor having tea. Sarah looked around, frowned, then went over to Alice. "Where is Sir Roger?"

Alice looked around. "That is odd. He would not dare miss an opportunity to see you, that is for sure."

Sarah blushed as Alice went to her mother. "Where is Sir Roger?"

Victoria also looked around then motioned Bertie over to her. "Bertie where is Sir Roger? I thought he wasn't leaving until tomorrow. Did you two not play Polo today?"

Bertie breathed in and sighed. "No. We had words, and he walked off leaving us all high and dry. He went back to Weymouth this afternoon."

Victoria smirked. "I'll say this for you. You certainly know how to clear a room."

Bertie moved away leaving Victoria, Alice, and Sarah whose face registered disappointment which Victoria saw.

"I know, dear. Sir Roger has that effect on people. But don't worry. He'll be back. He and Bertie are longtime friends and he can't stay away for long. Besides, he now seems to have a new reason to see us." At that Victoria winked at Sarah and moved off for more tea.

It was an odd sensation, but for Sarah not seeing Sir Roger again after having such a glorious morning riding with him, proved a let-down and she was disappointed. She had two cups of tea and some inconsequential conversation with Vicky and Alice, but after dinner she went upstairs to her room and began playing her violin. The instrument had become a safe haven and comfort for any and all anxieties. It was her friend, her steadfast companion—and the lover who would never leave.

Her violin would prove itself time and again in the next few months as Sarah learned the ways and customs of the aristocracy and tried to fit in as the royal goddaughter to the Queen of England.

Not having to return to the Chambers Society School for Girls enabled Sarah to be privately tutored by Sir Douglas Raynesworth along with Princess Alice and Princess Vicky. As Vicky and Alice watched, Sarah showed off her progress in musicianship by playing a more complicated piece on the violin in the music room. The sisters applauded her skill and complimented her. The two sisters became Sarah's sisters in a way—and she loved them.

Bertie, however, was another matter. At every turn he made her life difficult. Negative commentary at the dinner table became de rigueur. Evil quips and wisecracks were an expectation. But Sarah was given permission from day one to give as good as she got, and she shot back insult with insult knowing there was nothing Bertie could do about it.

Out on the grounds, Alice patiently played tennis with Sarah, who was as terrible a player as Vicky. So doubles with Bertie was always a disaster which he made clear. When sequestered in her room, Sarah would read or play her violin only for the amusement of herself with her eyes closed.

One day, Victoria and Alice were in an altercation about why Alice would not be allowed to receive the attention of Sir Michael McFerrin of Devonshire Downs whom Alice liked, when they walked past Sarah's room on their way downstairs. Victoria stopped at the door and listened for a while. Pleased with what she was hearing, Victoria gestured to Alice for them to move on and leave Sarah to her music.

As Sarah played, images of her homeland, family and the good times in Okeodan ran through her mind. Surprisingly, she thought of Sir Roger—and it staggered her. She stopped playing. Roger was such an unlikely man for her to be captivated by. He was nothing like the one other man she had cared for, Kua. And yet, Roger was so easy to have feelings for. His sense of humor, his soft smile, his way of being were all intrigues which kept her interested—more interested than she could imagine, and she found herself wondering what it would feel like if he ever held her—or better yet, kissed her. Then she admonished herself. No. Roger would never kiss her. He liked her to be sure, but to care for her enough to kiss her? It was madness to even think it. Surely there were laws against interracial relationships in England. And if not, there was rejection and ostracism.

For someone like Sir Roger Carlyle, an aristocrat from an old, respected peerage, there were expectations and conditions. He probably had to marry another aristocrat, someone his family and peers approved of. Someone arranged for him. Someone who would elevate his status in the world. Sarah already knew he wanted to be Prime Minister someday. How would she with her brown skin and wooly hair fit into this lofty goal of his without causing undue harm? No, she thought. This was a racist, colonialized country and no one would stand for, nor advocate, a genuine relationship of affection between a white British peer and an African woman, whether she was a princess or not.

So, she put it, and Sir Roger, out of her mind. At least for now. This was the time to learn all she could to improve her mind and enjoy her growing social circle of friends. Having access to the Queen and her family would be of more significance than a budding romance with a handsome, ladies-man Captain. So, Sarah spent the next few months learning Greek, Latin and French from her instructors, along with mathematics, science and painting with Alice and Vicky.

These brought her many pleasures especially since she and Alice had developed their friendship to that of near sisters.

After a piano lesson in early March, Sarah left the music room and ran into Sir Ian Paul, the Chamberlain, who was coming up the stairs.

"Sir Ian, where is Her Majesty?"

"In the nursery, I believe."

Sarah thanked him and headed to the Nursery. When she entered, she found Victoria looking at her sickly son Prince Leopold in his bed. His body was still weak and badly bruised. Victoria held out her hand for Sarah to come closer and join her.

Sarah looked at Leopold, "He doesn't look good."

Victoria hated hearing that, but knew Sarah was right, and lamented, "Such a sweet, sickly little thing."

Sarah, finally took notice of the bruises, "Why is he so bruised? It looks like someone beat him up."

Dr. Brown walked in to examine Leopold, while Victoria explained. "He has Hemophilia and had a terrible bleeding episode this morning." Sarah then remembered her upbringing and the many natural healing methods used in Okeodan.

"Dr. Brown, if you can find some aloe vera, rub the pulp on Prince Leopold's skin. Then have him drink orange juice with ground cloves. We had a bleeder like this in my village, and our Bohudu healer used it."

Dr. Brown frowned at this interjection of what he considered an African version of a midwives' tale, but Victoria nodded to him to do as Sarah requested. She kissed Leopold and left. Sarah followed her out.

As Victoria and Sarah walked down the hall arm-in-arm, Lori flew over them. Melancholy and utter bereavement engulfed Victoria as she shared with Sarah about Leopold.

"It's so hard on Albert. There is no history of the disease anywhere in his family, nor mine." She then brightened slightly. "But enough sadness. My dear, Albert and I are most pleased with your progress. We think you may be ready to be presented at Buckingham."

Despite all of her time so far in England, Sarah was not familiar with all things English or royal, "Presented...?"

Victoria smiled, "I want to gauge responses to my 'experiment'."

Sarah registered slight annoyance. ...*Ah, yes. The "Experiment."*

Victoria noticed her annoyance. "Do I detect piffling indignation?"

"Ma'am, will you extend the same privilege to others like me? I don't interact with any blacks. There are none are here at Windsor nor at Buckingham. Even Queen Elizabeth had a Moor serving her in 1500s."

Victoria grinned at Sarah's knowing about that fact, "Progress comes slowly, dear. But if anyone can move it along, it is you."

Later on, Victoria was pacing in her private suite as Prince Albert watched her—clearly a routine between them. He finally walked over to her and put his hands on her shoulders, "What has—or is about to happen, my love?"

Victoria was pensive, "Albie, are we truly doing right by Sally?"

Not willing to risk the wrong answer, Albert frowned. "Meaning?"

Victoria turned to him pained, "She said she doesn't have any Negro friends. We don't have any working here nor at Buckingham—and that—is an astute observation. No Negroes are employed at any of our palaces and we have twelve. Let us not turn a blind eye to other black sufferings in favor of the one black person I've countenanced."

Albert nodded. He knew in situations like this that Victoria had a plan and would handle every detail with or without his interest, consent, or help. So, he kissed her forehead, then blew out the candle for bed.

His Royal Highness Prince Albert and Queen Victoria (1843)

our royal coaches were waiting outside Windsor for the family trek to Buckingham Palace. It was now Spring, and the new season meant a move back to their London residence.

Sarah said goodbye to her lovely suite of rooms at Windsor and came down the stairs with her violin and a valise filled with her favorite books. She learned that the royal family did not stay in any of their twelve palaces very long, so it was c'est la vie Windsor, and hello Buckingham. During the year there would be Osbourne House, Frogmore Palace, and Balmoral in Scotland. But for now, it was Buckingham.

Victoria, Albert, and their Lord and Lady of the Bedchamber got into the first coach, followed by Alice, Vicky, Bertie, and Sarah who stepped into the second one, Sir Ian, the head chef, and four Ladies and Lords of the Bedchamber for the Prince and Princesses were in the third. Finally, the traveling staff, three of the royal dogs, and Lori the parrot were in the fourth. The other staff at Windsor were to close up the castle leaving a minimum crew and would come later.

As the four royal coaches traveled across several roads to Buckingham, people from various stations of life looked on in either awe, indifference or disdain. Along the way, Victoria waved as a new steam engine train, one of the exciting results of her growing industrial revolution, roared by with its billowing smoke emanating from the chimney and its whistle blowing in deference to the Queen. The conductor waved. Victoria and Albert waved back.

Twenty-three miles later, after stopping for some refreshments on a stretch of lawn, the coaches arrived in front of the magnificent Buckingham Palace. Footmen awaiting their arrival immediately descended upon the coaches to unload and bring in trunks, luggage and the valises, as well as help the Queen, Prince Albert, Alice, Vicky, Bertie and Sarah out of their respective coaches. Additional staff assisted with the animals.

Sarah stood in the foyer of the palace with its black and white tiled floor and marveled at the wonder of it all. She had not seen it since coming there as a girl of twelve, and realized Buckingham was so much smaller than Windsor. Though it only had 775 rooms, its garden was the largest private garden in London which she loved.

After Lord John Breadlebane, Buckingham's Chamberlain showed Sarah to her personal suite on the third floor, Sarah settled in all her belongings and began to wander around the palace. After all, it was the most famous, iconic palace in all of Europe and the envy of many a foreign monarch. As she came down the curving red and gold carpeted stairs she looked at the paintings of the various kings and Queens who had lived there. Starting with King George III and his wife Queen Charlotte, then King George IV and his hated wife Queen Caroline, then King William IV and his Queen Adelaide, and now Queen Victoria who was the first to make Buckingham the principal royal residence in 1837 upon her accession to the throne. She became the first monarch to formally live there as her London home—instead of St. James's Palace across the mall which had been the seat of power for the English monarchy since Henry VIII commissioned its conversion from a hospital to his royal palace in 1531.

As Sarah wandered about, she happened upon a room of serious interest to her—the royal library—and her body just drew itself inside as if possessed. She could not believe how many books were there from floor to ceiling lining every wall. Her hand clutched her chest as volume after volume of beautifully gold leafed, green leather, red leather, burgundy leather, black and/or brown leather books just seemed to call to her much like the experience she had when she first saw the library at the Chamber's School for Girls.

Moments later Victoria entered surprised to see Sarah, who was likewise startled by the Queen who indicated the library with pride.

"I am so proud of his library. It is the finest collection of books in England. I come in here to read, or get away from it all, or just look at the volumes."

Sarah smiled, "*All* of Buckingham is a marvel, ma'am."

Victoria beamed, "It was just a private estate called 'Buckingham House' when my grandfather King George III bought it for my grandmother, Queen Charlotte. She loved books and was not unlike you."

Sarah was puzzled, but Victoria grinned, "A story I shall tell you soon enough." Then she indicated the palace. "But look at Buckingham now. My uncle George IV is responsible for adding the east and west wings to the palace and most of its grandeur. He was an idiot with women who completely mistreated his wife, and he was a manipulated Whig, but by God, he had such unyielding good taste in everything else—paintings, flooring, architecture. Just unparalleled." She then shook her head and sighed absently. "You know they're planning a ridiculous spectacle for my thirty-fifth birthday as if I don't know anything about it. But I know everything going on in my various homes. I hope you're ready, Sally. God knows I certainly am not." Victoria grunted. "Ugh, thirty-five! I'm ancient—and I feel it."

"Not so, majesty. In Africa, women are most revered when they reach their fifties. It is the time of 'Omo bey Abo'— the great beauty. There is a big celebration and all the men come over to her to tell her how beautiful she is as a mother of the village. It's very special. And in China I read that a woman is just in the season of her life when she celebrates her 'Conriki'—and that is age sixty."

"Sixty. My goodness."

"So you see, you are still a baby."

"A baby who rules a nation quickly aging her to her 'Conriki.'"

They both laughed. Then Victoria put a hand to Sarah's face. "In many ways I envy Negro women. You never seem to show your age— even under stress and tribulation your skin glows and exhibits characteristics of youth that is unmatched."

Sarah smiled. "Well, at least God gave us something to envy."

Victoria patted Sarah's face then walked out of the library. Sarah looked after the Queen for a moment and thought. How could a powerful woman, an influential woman married to a wonderful man, and a mother, remotely care about anything as inconsequential as aging. But then for most people she understood, the grass was greener in someone else's yard. Never their own—no matter how beautiful.

At that, Sarah forced herself to tear away from the library—which she planned to make her favorite place while at the palace and went back to her own suite where soon Lady McBurney, whom lately Sarah was given to calling "Lady Mac" as a nickname, came in to dress Sarah for the Queen's birthday celebration.

Lady McBurney arranged the new formal wig on Sarah's head and applied a hint of lipstick and a bit of dark kohl on Sarah's eyelids. As Sarah looked at herself in the mirror Lady McBurney smiled. "I just wanted to give you an especially glamorous look for tonight because I've heard that Sir Roger Carlyle will be attending."

Sarah perked up. "How do you know about him?" asked Sarah.

Lady McBurney smiled as she finished the makeup careful not to use too much on such a young girl. "You know, the ancient Egyptians regarded beauty as a sign of holiness. Everything the ancient Egyptians used had a spiritual aspect to it, including their use of cosmetics," Sarah's Lady informed her charge. "Tonight will be special because not only is it the Queen's birthday, but it's your 'coming out' into royal society. You are being presented tonight by the Queen, and there to witness it will be a man of whom you are fond—as he is of you, or so I have been told."

Sarah did not know her affection for Sir Roger was that obvious.

"So, for such an auspicious occasion as this," continued Lady McBurney, "I am adding to your already evident dark beauty, the cosmetics of the ancient Egyptians, your continent kinsmen, so that you may draw to yourself all that you desire and have a huge success."

Lady McBurney pulled out Sarah's light green satin gown with black lace trim and the black opera length gloves.

"Look at yourself in the mirror, milady. I want you to be the envy of the ball. Are you ready?"

Sarah looked at the bed where her violin and bow laid, and she nodded with confidence. "Yes, Lady Mac, I am ready."

Torches and fireworks illuminated the evening sky. Fabulous coaches entered the gates carrying all of the British nobility for Victoria's birthday celebration. As various Footmen opened doors to allow the aristocrats inside, one of the footmen stood out, Davis—an exceptionally tall, muscular, dark-skinned black man in a formal white wig.

Inside, guests witnessed pure spectacle as they entered. There were jugglers, massive amounts of food on tables, music and dancing. Footmen proffered drinks and hors d'oeuvres while royals and courtiers waltzed to music from the string quintet on an upper deck. Victoria and Albert met their guests as they are announced and presented.

Sarah wandered about with a glass of wine. When she finished that glass, a new one was proffered up by Barnes, another black footman she had never seen. He nodded. She nodded back, as he moved on. Sarah looked over to Victoria who smiled slightly. Sarah gestured her approval, then wandered over to Alice and Vicky who was with a handsome man in his early thirties.

"Oh Sally, have you met Prince Friedrich Wilhelm of Prussia?" Alice exclaimed. "He came all the way here just to see our Vicky."

Princess Victoria blushed in embarrassment. "No. No, I'm sure Friedrich has other state business to attend. He's not here just for me."

"But I am," said the Prince. "And call me Fritz. You do realize I haven't seen you since the Grand Exposition at the Crystal Palace. You're pretty hard for a man not to think about Vicky. So when I received an invitation to your mother's birthday celebration, I jumped at it." He then held out his hand. "Do you waltz?"

"I do indeed, Fritz," grinned the Princess Royal.

He took her hand and the two danced as if nature had placed them together only for each other. Alice and Sarah grinned watching them. The Prince was adoring of Vicky, and for most of the evening, the two were in the other's company. Alice sighed.

"Now there's a man with whom I could be arranged into marriage. He's mad for her and has been since she was 14." Then Alice grimaced. "I'm finding myself quite jealous of my own sister. I may kill her and marry him myself."

Sarah laughed and moved on to meet other guests finally finding a group who were chatting. She listened to their gossip.

"…I hear the book is quite risqué," said one guest. "It's called 'Fanny Hill.' Purchase it at Phillips Print Shop on George Lane."

The other guest was appalled. "Not the place where abolitionists meet? The one in the Grub area?"

Sarah reacted as the first guest nodded. "Yes. That's the place."

The second guest grimaced, "Ugh. The Grub area is a horror. Too many whores, pubs and dance halls attended by low class, poor Negr--"
The guest stopped upon seeing Sarah then chose to adjust her response,

"'…people.' Oh no, no. I'll send my maid for it."

Sarah moved away—but thought about what she heard. Could it be true that abolitionist meetings were still ongoing in London—and at Phillips Print Shop which was renowned for its political meetings going back as far as the 1760s? She had read that people like the famous Thomas Clarkson and William Wilberforce met there in 1787 when Wilberforce was trying to get his very first bill to end the Slave Trade passed through Parliament which did not happen until 1807. And that Olaudah Equiano, Hannah More, and Grandville Sharp helped Josiah Wedgewood sell his famous china to raise money for the cause. If it were true, Sarah knew she had to go there—if only to absorb the ambiance and history of the place, to know she was standing on the same hallowed ground as people who vigilantly fought for the freedom of her people as she wanted to do.

A smile crept onto her face at the thought of it and moments later there was a tap on her shoulder. It was Lord John Breadlebane, Chamberlain at Buckingham. "It's time, Mistress Sarah."

Sarah gave Lord John a nod then went to get her violin sitting on a bench just behind the Queen's royal presentation chair. When she was ready she saw Victoria come to the center of the room and all became quiet as people sat in the arranged chairs facing her.

"Many of you know that a while ago, the Prince and I were fortunate to bring a young woman into our midst who impressed us so much we chose to give her an advancement in the world. So special is her talent that we chose this occasion of my birthday, to present her to you. Ladies and Gentlemen, Miss Sarah Forbes Bonetta."

There was polite applause as Sarah picked up her violin and bow, then bowed slightly to the audience of Peers. She placed the instrument on her shoulder, positioned the bow then closed her eyes, for she had determined this performance would only be for her. No matter how she was received by anyone in the glorious palace that was Buckingham, the music that would emanate from her cherished violin tonight would be in testament to her own intestinal fortitude and strength. To her own perseverance. To her mother, father, brothers, Kua and all the members of her village in Okeodan no longer alive who now formed a spiritual circle of love around her. And then she began. Everyone listened to Sarah who was incredible as she played Mozart's Violin Concerto #3. She was in her own world. The Queen was bursting with pride and almost cried. Albert beamed as did Princess Alice.

But none more than Sir Roger Carlyle who was seated right in front next to Bertie.

When Sarah finished, she opened her eyes to great applause. Then she saw Sir Roger who was grinning and wildly clapping. He stood. She smiled. For when he did—so did the others. It was a standing ovation from all. Sarah took several bows and acknowledged the Queen and Prince Albert, then left the center stage area to massive, sustained cheering. She was overwhelmed.

As Sarah walked toward Sir Roger, Bertie and Alice, many people congratulated her performance. She was shocked when Bertie nodded with a compliment. "It was not bad, dear Sarah. Not bad at all."

Despite her feelings for Victoria's eldest son, Sarah smiled. "Thank you, Bertie. You honor me with such praise."

"I wouldn't say praise, dear. Just an observation of your presentation from one who knows good from bad. Yours was closer to good." Then he moved on.

Sarah grinned. It was too much for her to expect full accolades from Bertie. But she would accept this as one anyway.

Soon, the Duchess of Kent walked over to Sarah who braced for an insult…which was indeed forthcoming. "Who would have thought an African could play classical music so beautifully?"

Though intended as a sincere compliment, its wording proved yet another slight Sarah had to swallow. "Thank you, Duchess."

Sir Roger, who saw Sarah's vexation, started toward her, but was thwarted in his efforts to get to her before Lady Astor walked up and smiled at Sarah.

"Is your wig made of negro hair? I've never felt Negro hair." And before she obtained Sarah's permission, she patted Sarah's wig then turned to the Duchess in awe, "No, it's not like hay. It's made of Caucasian hair." She then moved away with the Duchess.

Sarah was outdone, then started away. Sir Roger was right behind her as Victoria's birthday cake was rolled out. The Queen took a knife held by a footman and cut into the cake. Thirty-five live doves flew out from it astonishing the guests. It was pure spectacle.

But when Alice looked around, she saw that Sir Roger was hurrying to follow Sarah who, once again, was in quick retreat from the room.

Bertie chortled. "That girl's exits have become far too dramatic."

"Especially when she's insulted," quipped Alice.

Sir Roger caught up to Sarah and gently pulled her into the nearby greenhouse where Sarah wanted to explode. In trying to calm her down Sir Roger took a soothing tone of understanding. "I know, I know," he said gently. "You're a specimen people want to study..."

Sarah was seething, "...Yes. Like Tom Thumb, or the Hottentot Venus. I—I had to leave or scream. Next, I'd be asked if I'm the same color all over." She started to pace. "People amaze me."

Sir Roger kept pace with her, "The Queen's mother was right about one thing though—you played magnificently. I was so moved by your musical expression and feeling. It was wonderful."

Sarah stopped and turned to Sir Roger. She managed a smile, "I'm glad you came. You left without saying a proper goodbye at Windsor."

Sir Roger winced, "I had to leave. I was angry. Bertie... proved to be an indignant irritation. But, I've thought of nothing else but a hope to see you here." Then he blurted: "You would tell me if I was being too forward, would you not?"

Sarah grinned, "You always dance on the edge of it."

The corners of Sir Roger's mouth rose in mocked seriousness, "Because I really do want to know if you're the same color all over."

Sarah looked at him a moment—then burst out laughing. Sir Roger laughed as well. After a moment, their laughter settled. Then, as if compelled by outside forces, they moved closer to each other. Roger looked at Sarah's mouth—and touched it sensuously which overwhelmed her.

"What are you doing, Sir Roger?" She nervously whispered.

Roger leaned in looking at her mouth. "Kissing you," he whispered. "They do kiss in Africa, don't they?" He didn't wait for an answer. His lips found hers—and his arms wrapped around her body holding her close, her arms encircled his neck. It was the kiss they both had desired. Even after they stopped, Sarah's eyes remained closed—for nothing would replace that first glorious kiss between two people—aching for the touch of the other. Finally, Sarah opened her eyes. Roger looked at her adoringly stroking her face with a finger. "I've wanted to do that from the first moment," he whispered.

Sarah smiled, "Me as well," And they kissed again as a hot tide of passion raged through both of them. Just then they heard the explosion of fireworks outside the windows and looked out. With Roger's arms around her, Sarah witnessed the spectacular burst of display which brought to an end the celebration of Queen Victoria's thirty-five years of life on earth. And Sarah's first grown-up kiss.

When his lips touched mine, I became overwhelmed by the sheer magnitude of my own desire. It was all I could do not to surrender to his masterful seduction as my body vibrated with liquid fire. I had to be careful. For the Queen was right. Sir Roger would prove hard to resist...

Twenty Three

On the Buckingham Palace grounds the next day, Sarah and Alice rode their horses behind Bertie and Sir Roger on their own horses. Clearly, there was tension between Bertie and Sir Roger which Bertie had to address.

"Am I to ever be forgiven for my outburst last time? Or will you stew in it like boiled potatoes forever?"

Sir Roger rode along for a moment trying to formulate his words.

"Our friendship has been longer than your bad behavior," he started, then looked over at the Prince of Wales. "But Bertie, do not ever question my life choices again. They are not yours to make. I am my own man."

Bertie smiled slightly then hit Roger playfully with his cap. "Alright, mate. I shall keep my opinions to myself."

Sir Roger smiled and the two continued on. But where Sarah was concerned, Bertie had no intentions of allowing the relationship to flourish. He would just have to work his influence in another way.

Alice kicked her horse and trotted up next to Sarah bursting with curiosity. "So…" she asked mischievously. "Did Roger kiss you last night?"

"None of your business," Sarah smirked.

Alice pouted, "I am your best friend. Tell me."

Sarah feigned shock, "You presume I'm not chaste."

Alice leaned toward Sarah and whispered, "What I presume is—you liked it."

Sarah threw Alice a look of mock astonishment. Then both girls giggled. "It was perfect!" Sarah glowed. "Not that I have much experience. There was only one other kiss. My fiancé. I was ten."

"You were engaged?" Alice exclaimed.

"On our commitment day celebration, Kua kissed me," Sarah said fondly before her smile faded. "Then Gezo killed him and everyone in my family."

Alice took a moment to acknowledge Sarah's comment, then pondered. "Two kisses. I'm almost jealous. I've never been kissed once."

Sarah laughed, "That can't be. You're scandalous."

Alice smirked, "All bluster and strut. I'm never allowed to be around boys without a chaperone or leave the palace." Alice then innocently mused, "Strange Roger should kiss you before me."

Sarah was insulted. "Why? Because I'm African? Because he finds an African attractive?"

"No... I mean... I..."

"...Please. You were thinking it. You feel he's far too superior to me. But I'm royalty, too."

Livid, Sarah dismounted her horse. Alice dismounted hers, as well. Sir Roger and Bertie, still engaged in their verbal jousting, were not paying attention to the brewing rift between Sarah and Alice and continued ahead. Alice boiled with frustration, "Why must you bring color into every facet of your being?"

"Because it affects every facet!" Sarah snipped.

Alice recoiled at Sarah's outburst and Sarah suddenly became remorseful. "I'm sorry. I should not have said that. You and your mother have been good to me."

The silence between them was thick enough to slice through.

"Alright," Alice finally admitted. "Perhaps it was what I was thinking. Not the part about you being attractive—because you are. But, yes, because you're African. I was thinking why would an aristocrat—a Captain and would-be MP—want to subject himself to the scrutiny such a relationship would create? He would be the source of constant barbs and ridicule for which his enviable charm will not spare him. Not to mention his exclusion from fashionable society and aristocratic functions necessary for his advancement. It could wear on him and he would eventually resent you."

"That's honest," said Sarah grim faced. "Hurtful—but honest."

Alice said nothing. Sarah looked at Alice, thought for a moment, then slowly smiled, "But, since we're friends, I may be able to help you get a kiss. But it requires subterfuge."

"Oooh. Sounds sneaky..." beamed Alice. "...and fabulous."

Sarah drew closer to Alice and in a conspiratorial voice offered, "Tomorrow, Roger and Bertie are going hunting with a friend. Meet me at eleven, and dress like your maid—no frills or Royal accoutrements."

Alice beamed broadly and nodded.

The next morning, after fortifying themselves at breakfast and telling no one, Sarah and Alice snuck out of the palace gate dressed like two scullery maids at precisely eleven o'clock the next morning. They exited the King George gate, got into a coach, paid the coachman not to tell, and took off.

Just north of Downing Street, where Prime Minister Aberdeen presided and wielded power, were magnificent carriages carrying the well-heeled and members of the nobility. In the park, couples strolled along taking in the views or promenaded with parasols and high hats enjoying the sweet smell of the various flowers making their spring appearance.

Yet, as Sarah and Alice ventured further east, into St. Giles Parish,

Cripplegate, the contrast was striking. Sarah was reminded why she was desirous for the Queen to be more vigilant regarding the status of minorities. Along the streets of the Grub area was wretched poverty and decrepit buildings. There was no improvement from a century earlier when Queen Charlotte and King George had stumbled onto the street in 1762. Beggars, Negro and white, were boundless, and women of all ages worked as prostitutes, some as young as twelve. Sarah turned to Alice disheartened. "This is how too many of us live, Ally. Sad, isn't it?"

Alice patted Sarah's hand gently and they continued until finally, they reached George Lane—and Phillips Print Shop where the coach pulled up to a building in stunning difference to Buckingham's surrounding areas. Sarah motioned to the coachman.

"Wait here. We shouldn't be long."

She and a scared Alice—whom she was forced to pull out of the coach—went inside Phillips print shop.

As they entered the print shop, they were met with the distinct odor of urine. Looking to their right they saw Negro workmen in the printing area urinating on the disassembled presses and block letters on the floor, then brushing, mopping and cleaning them off. Sarah was befuddled and stared. Alice saw this and gasped.

Then they heard from behind them: "For some reason, urine cleans the presses better than anything else."

It was the owner, Paul Phillips, Jr. who came up to them grinning with an explanation. "Something is in it that dissolves the buildup of oil and ink quite well, so we clean our presses with it once a month."

"My word," Sarah chortled. "How do you know this?"

The man extended his hand. "Because I'm the owner, Paul Phillips, Jr. My father owned this place before me, and his father before him. A lot of political history here. Particularly regarding the cessation of the Slave Trade."

Alice shook her head. "Imagine. Pissing for a living."

"We give them lots of Ale," laughed Mr. Phillips, and all three of them laughed. Then Phillips looked the two women over. "So. Are you here for a book? Or the meeting?"

"The meeting?" asked Alice, "What meeting?"

Curiously, Sarah, who had wandered to a bookcase filled with leather volumes, saw some people going through a back door.

"The Abolition of the Slave Trade," answered Phillips.

Sarah quickly chimed in before Alice could respond. "Yes. We're here for the meeting."

As Phillips led them to the back-door Alice frowned at Sarah.

"I thought I was here for a kiss."

"This is better."

"Not better than a kiss," retorted Alice.

When Alice and Sarah entered the back room, there were at least thirty people of different races seated in chairs facing a lectern. Alice kept her head low. Both women sat in back with the other women and watch the proceedings. Sarah also kept her head low as she found a seat near a plainly dressed white woman with a pleasant face and cockney accent who held out her hand to her.

"Hello. I'm Elizabeth Schoen." She indicated the man next to her. "My husband the good Reverend James Schoen. Welcome."

"Sarah Bonetta. Thank you." Sarah indicated Alice. "My friend Alice."

Sarah and Alice sat next to the Schoen's and Sarah looked around. She began to notice a number of Quaker women from their clothing and bonnets. But the hierarchy was still the same: most women, whether white or black, were seated in back, and men in front, which again disturbed her.

Then, Paul Phillips, owner and President of the Society, stood, pounded his gavel, and called the Society for the Worldwide Cessation of the Slave Trade to order. He asked the group for suggestions on how they could effectively organize a larger body of concerned citizens and raise money and awareness for their cause. An older woman raised her hand and introduced herself as Dorothy Clairemont. She suggested that perhaps Mr. Phillips could donate his services to print fliers for placement in windows and trees. Mrs. Schoen suggested they raise funds through bake sales, book sales, and the selling of cast-off clothing, and use those funds for advertising placement in newspapers.

Both women's suggestions were appreciated by the male majority, but they were asked to approach their husbands about the use of their homes for meetings, to get the word out. They requested the women help with cooking meals and baking products for the various sales. Dorothy and the other women were offended by this.

"I am not married, sir," snipped Dorothy. "Can we women not be of service without the assistance of a man? Must we transpose the second-class condition of slaves to that of women?"

The other women applauded, and Sarah could see the tide was changing with more vocal female commentary. This pleased her. Finally, after a half an hour of informal conversation, Paul Phillips had several petitions which he passed out.

"I need your help to gather at least 3,000 signatures on this petition attacking the worldwide slave trade," he implored. "We need a global initiative, so all countries will join together to end this practice. Now is the time. I've been collecting evidence against the trade from all over the world, and I could stand here and give you horrifying accounts which I've personally received from slaves who've suffered aboard slave ships. But I find it far more compelling when those who have survived the ordeal can expound on it themselves. So, I introduce to you three of the 'Sons of Africa' who have been traveling with me—John Daniels, Miyo Obatunji, and Winston Benjamin. These men, heroes all, have had much experience with the atrocities of the middle passage and slavery first-hand."

Three African men came forward from the back of the room. The first to speak was handsome Winston Benjamin, whose story of his arduous, unexpected journey to London and freedom, struck an unanticipated familiar chord within Sarah. There was something about him. He had acquired a lilting, clipped southern American accent, and his face had the comfort of an old friend. It was as if she knew him from the old country. It was then that she noticed a small piece of wood hanging from a leather cord around his neck.

Winston smiled at everyone and said 'welcome' in Fon.

"Mi kwabo."

"Mi kwabo," everyone repeated, including Sarah shocked to hear Fon—her native tongue.

"There is an old African proverb the ancestors say," he began. "If you speak the words of your life aloud, you gain new perspective on the truth of it—even if no one hears your words." Winston smiled slightly. "This is my truth. My name is Winston Benjamin, but I wus born Mwako Arbuta. I wus fishin' with my father an' brother in West Africa. It wus a beautiful day, an' we had a good catch..."

In her mind, Sarah could see Winston's story unfold in her head. Images of a younger Winston spearing a fish and placing it with the dozens of others in the catch as his father and brother grinned.

"...We planned to have mama cook the fish for the Village. But other African men we did not know came upon us. They threw nets over us an' dragged us away..."

Sarah now remembered the net tossed over her own head as she ran from her predators in Okeodon. How she couldn't get out and was dragged away.

"...We wus chained two by two, right leg and left leg, right hand an' left hand, packed tightly together in the air-less bowels of a slave ship docked at Whydah port." Winston continued. "We lived in our own vomit an' feces and couldn't move or change positions. Once a month we wus allowed on deck to be washed down wit sea water. Most o' us ill, dyin', or dead…"

Winston had to stop as the memory upset him still after fourteen years. "…Like my father who had died still chained to the men on either side of him for four days. I had to watch as they threw his body overboard like garbage that had rotted away an' smelled," he despaired, choking on his own anguish. "It was not unusual to see schools of sharks darting in an' out of the wake of our ship—or any slave ships filled with human cargo traversin' the Atlantic. They'd follow the battered, moldy vessels for miles waiting to attack and eat the disease ravaged or dead black bodies tossed into the ocean—or those who had jumped willingly.

Two months later I was in the Colonies—in a 'Pest House' in Charleston. The manacles cut so deeply into my flesh I developed an infection and dysentery. They eventually put me on the auction block where I wus inspected, an' my teeth examined as I stood there along wit a dozen other naked slaves being sold. I heard the auctioneer chant: 'WhatamIbid', 'WhatamIbid for Prime Negro specimens.' Mr. James Benjamin bid the highest an' I wus sold to him. He tol' me to get into his wagon where we ended up on his plantation where I wus branded and given the name 'Winston Benjamin' so I'd be Christian."

Sarah nodded. For she, too, had been given a Christian name.

"Massa Benjamin kept his slaves in a terrible way—one shed for 200 of us. Every time I ran away Massa Benjamin's dogs would find me, an' he beat me…" Winston took off his shirt to further illustrate his tribulations revealing the permanent scars so visible and deep upon his back that Sarah's tears could not be held back—nor Alice's.

"But one day a new slave came. Her name wus Lucy an' her face wus like sunlight shining on my heart. We came to care for each other, an' the next year we jumped the broom. She became my wife. But Massa

Benjamin, he would take her any time he wanted an' she had two children for him—til she couldn't take it no more.

She shoved a stick inside herself to get rid of the last baby. When I found her, she had bled to death." Winston stopped a moment to wipe his eyes. The memory was too much and he took in a deep breath.

"I ran away to the docks an' tol' the ship owner I wanted to work on his ships. He wus British—an' hired me. Said I could sail wit his crew to London. What I learned while aboard is slave grown an' harvested cotton, tobacco, an' sugar is big business. It maintains the need for slaves. An' even though the English ended the trade years ago, Britain still profits from the labors of the enslaved elsewhere. When I got here I stayed because you're free on English soil. But even though that is true, we must stop the Trade everywhere. Slavery must end everywhere, an' the products sold from the practice should be boycotted, my friends. Over the nearly four centuries of slavery an' the Slave Trade, millions of African men, women, an' children were like me—savagely torn from their homeland, herded onto ships, an' dispersed all over the so-called New World. An' although there is no way to exactly establish how many people perished, it's estimated that between thirty an' sixty million Africans have been subjected to this horrendous triangular trade system an' only a third, if that, of those people survived."

Sarah wiped her eyes for the sheer number was staggering.

"Sadly, I realize that we're taught that white people come to Africa an' capture slaves for sale. But I know now that it is my fellow Africans who are also complicit. They assist the white slavers. They capture my people an' sell them to the whites for money. So, we must stop that practice first. Stop the trade at the African level *an'* at the white slaver level," Winston concluded. "We must remember that there is no such thing as emancipation without freedom. *Real* freedom."

There was applause as Winston came back to his chair and sat. Mr. Phillips returned to the podium as Sarah, Alice and Mrs. Schoen tried to pull themselves together. Winston's speech had been emotional for everyone.

"Thank you, Mr. Benjamin. Now I think you understand why we must pool all of our resources together and do all we can to eradicate this worldwide menace to humanity. Now, I would like for anyone else here to share an experience or story to help us with these goals. Anyone?"

Sarah, still moved by Winston's message, began to think. Her own story had similar themes and she was a woman—no other women had come forward nor been recognized, and soon she found her hand raise. It reminded her of The Charter Society School when upon raising her hand she would be punished or ignored. But instead, Mr. Phillips pointed to her.

"Yes. The lady in the blue dress. Come forward, please.

Sarah stood. All eyes were on her as she slowly, nervously approached the podium. Alice was in shock and her hand went to her mouth as Sarah looked out at the gathering of like-minded abolitionists and began.

"I think Mr. Benjamin is correct about our ancestors and their insights. If you speak the words of your life aloud, you *can* gain better perspective on the truth of it," she drew in a deep breath. "So, this is my truth."

Sarah looked around the room. Everyone was waiting with baited breath for her to continue. It was so quiet Sarah could hear horses whinnying three blocks away. She closed her eyes for a few seconds, then thought about her family in Africa that was no more, and once she started, she could not stop.

"I was born Princess Aina Okonjo in the village of Okeodan, in the Kingdom of Dahomey, West Africa. I am an Egbado Omobo. Yoruba royalty. King Gezo captured me too—but he could not take my bloodline nor my pride from me. Throughout my ordeal, I held onto the knowledge that my forefathers imbued in me a strength to allow me to always rise above any negative circumstances—and so I have done…"

Sarah told her story of happiness in Okeodan. Of capture and escape, her voyage to London, and of her introduction to western society.

But she could not bring herself to talk about the Queen, Windsor Castle or her royal family relationships. She did not understand why and instead stopped short at having seen things no other African former slave had experienced in the great city—and left it at that.

Later, after others had spoken, everyone was talking, having tea, or cookies and getting to know one another. Alice found herself fascinated by Winston's friend Miyo another abolitionist who told a similar story of his capture and middle passage experience to Jamaica while Sarah wandered over to Winston.

"Your story wus very movin'," said Winston with a slight smile.

"Yours motivated me to come forward," Sarah nodded.

"Okeodon is not too far from my village of Komenda where I wus taken." Winston then saw Sarah's tribal markings on her shoulder. "The Princess of Okeodan is very pretty. I'm glad Gezo did not take that either."

Sarah blushed. Then Alice came over with Miyo. Winston introduced him. "This is my friend Miyo Obatunji."

Sarah pointed to Alice. "My friend Alice," Sarah offered.

Alice suddenly did a curious thing and began speaking in an unusual cockney accent which left Sarah puzzled.

"We're chambermaids, she an' me."

"Really?" Miyo wondered. "Where?"

"Buckingham Palace," Alice answered quickly. "But we only work on Monday's an' Friday's."

Winston stood and put on his hat. "Listen, Miyo an' me are goin' to the Crows Pub. They've got good ale an' dancin'. Come wit us. Let's have some fun."

Sarah nodded. So did Alice. They waved to Mr. Phillips who nodded. "Don't forget next month. The meeting is on the ninth."

As Sarah, Winston, Alice, and Miyo came down Grub Street, Sarah smiled at the fact Alice and Miyo were laughing and enjoying themselves as she and Winston talked and got to know each other better.

"Our stories are so similar," Sarah commented.

"Yes. But it sounds like you got some education along the way."

Sarah was taken aback because she'd hoped that she hid any hint of an education to make the chambermaid story credible. Not wanting to reveal how Sarah thought quickly and lied to cover this slip-up.

"My...our...employer taught us."

Winston looked at her whimsically, "I'd be somethin' wit schoolin'. No tellin' where I'd be now."

Sarah stopped him, "You're something now." He locked his arm in hers and they went into the Crows Pub. Alice and Miyo followed.

Inside the Pub there was music and dancing as the four sat at a table. Winston held up four fingers to the waiter, who after a few moments, came over with a tray of four glasses of beer and put them on the table. Winston distributed the ale to everyone. Alice sipped hers, never having had beer and grinned, then drank it licking the foam from her lips gleefully. So far for her this was a glorious experience. Men, a pub, beer and her good friend Sarah. What could be better?

"So tell me more about what you saw aboard the British ship on your journey here to England," Sarah asked.

Winston sipped his beer. "The ships start out in Britain wit goods, then they sail to Africa to trade or buy slaves under a flag that's not British. A flag from, say, Tanzania or Zanzibar."

Sarah gasped. "I saw that with Captain Forbes in Accra. A British flag lowered on a British ship, and a Zanzibar flag raised."

"Yes. Zanzibar is a favorite port and flag ploy," nodded Winston. "Then they sail to the islands or America sell the slaves for money an' go back to England wit' tobacco, sugar an' cotton. So even wit' slavery an' the trade ended—England still gets rich."

Sarah and Alice exchanged looks of anger, as they realized the slave trade was still being exploited by British commercial ships.

Suddenly Miyo burped. Everyone laughed, then for solidarity sake, Winston burped. Sarah and Alice looked at each other and decided: "All for one." The two women burped as well. Laughter erupted, and Winston held up his fingers to the waiter for four more beers.

Later, the rousing music and dancing rose to a crescendo and was too tempting to ignore. Winston held out his hand to Sarah. Miyo held out his to Alice. They all danced along with the other patrons. Alice was hilarious since she had indulged in too much beer and was tipsy. She couldn't dance, and it was a humorous sight for everyone around them.

But Alice didn't care. She was having the time of her life and ignored the looks. And eventually so did Miyo.

Though Sarah was also tipsy, she and Winston were soon overcome by the need to be themselves. True Africans inspired by the sounds of distant djembe drums. It was as though they heard it at the same time and both started doing a version of the Ya Moto Dance.

Soon, Miyo joined in—and so did any other Africans in the Pub. Alice did not know the steps, but she valiantly tried anyway—and they all danced freely.

Sweating and feeling satisfied after the music stopped, Alice pulled Sarah away. But she forgot her cockney accent.

"The time! We have to get back to Buckingham!" she said to Sarah panicked. Sarah looked at the Pub's clock. "God. We have to get back!"

Both Miyo and Winston reacted because Alice had said they only worked on Monday and Friday. "But today is Tuesday," said a perplexed

Miyo. Alice thought fast on her feet, "Special guests for tea today."

Unfortunately, she said it using her normal voice, which was not lost on Miyo. "Where is your accent?" he asked suspiciously.

Sarah chimed in quickly, "Oh, uh, she always rehearses to sound proper for when we're at Buckingham. Well, goodbye," she said quickly, pulling Alice away toward the door.

Winston and Miyo followed right behind them. Winston grabbed Sarah's hand. "When can I see you again?"

"At the next meeting? At Phillips?" Sarah answered quickly.

Winston smiled, "Until then... Aina Okonjo."

To hear her name—her real name—the person she felt she was inside, said aloud, touched Sarah and her eyes welled-up. Winston kissed her hand with deference. Following Winston's lead, his friend Miyo took Alice's hand to kiss it, too. But Alice was determined to accomplish what she came with Sarah to do—and she took Miyo's face in her hands, leaned in and boldly kissed his lips. She giggled and ran off with a shocked Sarah—leaving both men astonished yet grinning.

"I should court more chambermaids," chuckled Miyo.

Sarah and Alice ran back to their carriage snickering like two naughty schoolgirls. They were tipsy as they jumped in.

"Miyo's lips were like big, soft pillows," Alice said breathlessly.

Sarah grinned. "Ally, I hope you learned more than how to kiss."

Alice stopped giggling a moment. "I did actually. I've never felt such sadness and the inability to do anything. What Miyo and Winston—and you have gone through, is so wrong."

Sarah returned Alice's look with more intensity, "Then I hope you'll do better, Ally. You're too insulated, and the world outside the Palace is vast and cruel."

An expression of understanding rushed over Alice's face and for the rest of their trip back to Buckingham, they rode in silence.

Twenty Four

Sarah and Alice came through the King George gate and snuck back into the Palace. They tipped up the backstairs to their respective suites to get out of their chambermaid clothing and into the attire befitting tea. It took Alice twenty minutes to powder and attempt to arrange her hair and she was emphatic that Lady Jane, her Lady-in-Waiting not say a word about her coming in improperly dressed and bedraggled.

Sarah took less long as she did not need powder nor a hairdresser, but found herself telling innumerable lies to Lady McBurney, her own Lady-in-Waiting, as to her whereabouts. Both girls had gotten their stories together so would be in sync if they were asked.

Tea had already begun when Sarah and Alice rushed into the parlor and pretended all was well and proper. Everyone was already there. Victoria was irked as was her mother and Prince Albert.

"Where have you two been? It's half past four," the Queen asked.

Alice and Sarah looked at each other. Sarah glanced away to allow Alice to answer her mother with their prepared excuse.

"So sorry to be late," Alice started. "Sally and I went riding and her horse went lame. We had to walk back."

Bertie smirked. "Why not take your horse? Two can ride a horse."

"M-my horse... ran away," Alice lied.

"Where is the lame horse and the runaway horse now?" asked Bertie.

"I…I don't know," snipped Alice becoming annoyed. "Wherever lame horses and runaway horses go when they're lame or run away." Then she burped.

Sarah sighed as Alice dug a deeper hole for them both. Bertie began to chuckle and looked at his mother. Victoria frowned as she moved closer to Alice and smelled her breath.

"My dear, have you been drinking?"

Alice said nothing but burped again—which gave her intoxication away. She swallowed hard then looked at Sarah. Victoria's hands went to her hips as she looked at Sarah as well.

"Would you like to tell me where the two of you were, Sally? And let me advise the truth—since our chambermaid has confessed to lending Alice a dress."

Sarah now looked at Alice. The ruse was definitely over.

"I gave her a shilling not to tell," Alice lamented.

"I gave her two," retorted the Queen. "Now, where were you?"

Sarah held up her hands to Alice not to lie anymore. "We went to Phillips Print Shop on George Lane—an unfashionable area of London. I advised Ally not to dress regally."

"George Lane? Why did you go there?"

Alice could not hold her tongue being indeed tipsy. "Because I wanted to be kissed," she said boldly.

Victoria tried to contain her temper, but Prince Albert lost his.

"And were you kissed? Along with drinking alcohol like a common tramp?"

"Yes. He was a nice man—and I kissed him," Alice retorted flippantly to her father. "I wanted to know what it was like. And I found out."

Prince Albert was livid. "You kissed a strange man we do not know, in a poor area of London where God knows what could have happened to you? Go to your room."

"But Poppi…"

"I said go to your room! And no supper for you."

Alice huffed off. Sarah started off behind her until she heard:

"Not you, Sally," cautioned Victoria.

Sarah turned. Victoria's mother was furious.

"Why the print shop, Sarah? My granddaughter could care less about books. How could you let her be kissed or consume strong drink? You should know better," scorned the Duchess of Kent.

Before Sarah could answer Bertie chided to his grandmother. "*Know better*? Sarah?" he turned to Victoria. "You see, mother. This is what happens when you give Negroes too much leeway."

Finally, Sarah held up her hands. "Please. Everyone. Stop. It was a ruse. I wanted Alice to accompany me. I had heard abolitionist meetings went on at Phillips and I wanted to go. I thought she'd learn something, I didn't want to go alone, and afterward, we both had ale."

Victoria groaned in annoyance. "This gets worse by the minute."

"I suggest we all finish our tea and concern ourselves with this matter later," snapped Prince Albert. He turned to Sarah. There will be no supper for you either."

Sarah nodded and went up to her room. She was there perhaps ten minutes when there was a knock.

"Yes…?"

"Sarah? It's Ally. May I come in?"

"Yes," groaned Sarah, as Alice entered.

"Well, you're not battered or bruised, so I assume you emerged unscathed."

"Not unscathed. They're disappointed in me," Sarah shook her head in frustration. "Ally, why would you tell them you were kissed? We might have escaped with a mere dressing down. Not a banishment with no supper."

"I don't know. Rebellious I guess."

"And I noticed you stopped short of saying it was a Negro you kissed."

"Rebellious, not insane!"

At that, both girls had to chuckle. Then it settled. Sarah sat on the bed, Alice on the settee. Alice looked off slightly. "But I'd do it again, you know. If I had the chance. Just being out—with you—and dancing. Having a good time with Winston and Miyo. Being kissed. I'd do it all again—despite being punished."

She wandered to the window and looked down at the grounds at nothing in particular. "Sometimes, I just want to have some fun before I have to settle down to the business of being a royal wife. It seems as though everything is always planned for me—who I see, or not. Where I go, what I study, how I must behave. Just once I wanted to do what I wanted without restraints." She looked over at Sarah and smiled. "You gave me that chance."

"Well, I got us into this. But I must admit I've never met a girl more rebellious than you—and the Chambers School was filled with them."

Alice went over to sit on the bed with Sarah. "I guess I'm like my grandfather Edward. He was rebellious too. He drank too much, smoked hashish, and had a mistress for 28 years. At least there were no bastard children there."

The two said nothing for a moment as Sarah thought. "Ally. I need to apologize to your mother and father. They expect more of me than I gave them today. So I'm going to find them."

"You, my dear, are a glutton for punishment," chortled Alice. And the two girls left the room.

Barnes, the new black Footman, had just brought a glass of apple juice to Victoria who was in the nursery with Albert. They were looking at their young, sickly son Leopold. Victoria drank the juice. "I wish I could hold him," she lamented.

"I do too," responded Albert. "But I fear he'll break in two he's so weak."

"Why is my stomach always churning? I can keep nothing down except juice. Must be nerves."

"Indeed. Nerves called Alice," grunted Albert.

"We must get her married soon, Albie. If not, she'll be the ruination of our family's reputation."

Albert smirked. "Dearest, your grandfather George had only one legitimate grandchild out of twenty. Not to mention the bigamists, sodomites, and rapists. So let us not lay the *ruination of our family* on Alice."

"Nevertheless, let's invite Prince Friedrich here. Alice needs a husband."

"On that, I agree. I will arrange it."

There was soon a knock. "Yes," called out Victoria.

Sarah came in somewhat nervous and sheepish. "Majesty. May I have a word?"

Victoria nodded.

Sarah took her time and chose her words carefully. "I want to apologize for sneaking out with Alice. I know I've disappointed you both by doing so."

Albert's arms folded indicated she was correct. Yet Sarah forged ahead. "But while I was there, aside from the beer and Alice's kiss, I was very moved by the speakers. They were all stolen from Africa in the slave trade and sold in America—their stories horrifying. It made me want to do something. Is there any word from Captain Forbes on his mission?"

"No—and he's been there for months. He and Captain Miller may be dead."

"Oh no!"

"In his last letter, Forbes said King Gezo and his men were being supplied rifles and ammunition by the French to cease selling slaves to France."

"But the rest of the world still buys slaves," said Sarah. "Something must be done."

"Yes, but what? How? It's been our conundrum for years now," responded Victoria bleakly.

Sarah became steely and thought. "Then I would suggest you send two dozen ships to blockade Whydah Port and not allow Gezo's slave ships out. If he protests, burn his ships, his palace, and his prized marketplace. Then pour red paint in the main water well. It will look like blood and the superstitious Dahomeans will turn on him for bringing the wrath of their Gods to the town. Amazon warriors will neutralize him."

Albert looked at Victoria. Could this calculating girl in front of them be the same one they met four years ago?

Sarah continued. "Prince Albert, perhaps you could talk to the French? Or maybe speak at one of the abolitionist's meetings?"

Victoria looked at Albert and nodded.

"Sarah, I am actually President of an anti-slave trade society," Albert admitted. "The chapter I head doesn't meet often. It's comprised of mostly Peers, but I spoke out in 1840 to them and little changed."

"Then perhaps you could have an event arranged so that they could hear the atrocities for themselves," Sarah suggested. "Maybe move other countries to act. Sir, the tentacles of slavery keep even free Blacks from the promise of their potential."

"I know this issue is important..." started Prince Albert...

But Sarah was adamant. "...Yes, because I was a lucky one!" she blurted out. "But what about those who are not as lucky as me. Western civilization must be opened for all to enter or be demolished by those excluded."

"Sarah, change comes hard for most people."

It was all Sarah could do not to scream. "Yes, to most people who do not look like me. Most people who wear nice clothes and live in lofty homes, in exalted positions with weekly balls…"

"That's enough," Victoria admonished.

"…Most people who have never felt discrimination, or inequality…" Then she pulled down the top of her dress to show her back.

"…Or the lash!"

Victoria was in shock. "Oh my dear girl!" she cried out upon seeing the permanent welts and raised wounds on Sarah's flesh.

Sarah's eyes filled, and she held herself with her arms folded across her chest. Then she fell to her knees almost in prayer which disconcerted both Albert and Victoria.

"I am calling on my ancestors, and speaking my truth aloud…"

Sarah closed her eyes then she paused. "…When they threw me in the Cage the first two times, I prayed to just stay and bear the two-day hell." Tears fell from Sarah's eyes. "But the third time was worse. The third time, Mr. Humes, the headmaster himself, locked me in…"

Victoria grabbed Albert's hand anticipating a horror story. She did not have to wait long.

…It had to be said. I had held it in for too long. Well over a year. I had convinced myself, prayed to myself that if I ignored it, didn't think or talk about it, the day that destroyed me would go away. The day that silenced my hope for a happy life in England. The day he hurt me. The day he damaged my sense of self forever.

I thought back to that awful moment when I was led down the stairwell to that dark basement Cage by Headmaster Humes who was carrying an oil lamp. Miss Rawlins, who had been with us, stayed behind at the top of the stairwell while he unlocked and opened the door. He pushed me inside the Cage, then came in behind me and locked the door. He put the oil lamp on the floor which threw odd shadows and flickers of light on his face making it more demonic than he was already. "A wild African in a God-fearing school like this. The Queen must be mad," he sneered. I was frightened as he backed me up against the wall. "You need to be taught the proper English manner of obedience," he threatened. Then I heard it. Plain and clear. "Take off that uniform."

I shook my head. "No." But Humes was manic. "It's a disgrace for you to wear it. Take it off I say!" He grabbed at my blouse. But I hit him. "No! Leave me alone," I screamed. But Humes tore then yanked off my blouse as the buttons flew. I tried to run but couldn't get far. Humes caught me and forced me to the floor. "Damn blackie. Think you can hit a white headmaster? Do what I say!"

He slapped me. Then slapped me again. Soon he overpowered me, slamming my head on the brick floor. I screamed in pain for I could feel blood oozing from near my left ear. Then Humes took off his belt and hiked up my uniform skirt. "No. No, please!" I pleaded. But his trousers were down. I felt the stabbing pain of him violating me—and my inno-cence—which I had so guarded like a jewel. Then I felt the agony of every strike of his belt as he beat me over and over and over, deriving sexual pleasure from every lash as he forced himself on me while I screamed…

What Sarah didn't know was that Miss Rawlins was standing on the top landing of the stairwell. She wiped away tears—for she knew what was happening. She could hear Sarah's screams, pleas for help, and crying out, and she wanted to do something. But didn't. She did nothing. In-stead, Miss Rawlins, herself a woman, accepted the demonic actions of a sexually deviant Headmaster—and walked away.

Back in the nursery, Victoria was in tears having heard the story.

Sarah finally opened her eyes and sighed in the misery of her memory.

"I no longer have my virtue to give the man I marry. Humes took it—along with any honor I may have had. And he did it—because he could. Being white, he could violate me any way he wanted because it would be his word against mine. Because to him, blacks are considered less than nothing."

She turned and looked at Prince Albert. "That is why you must speak out, sir. It's why you must be a voice—for the voiceless."

Victoria took Albert's hand. He nodded. Sarah stood up, brushed herself off, then turned and left.

Victoria had to sit to calm her nerves. Then her tears flowed in a way that frightened Albert who could do nothing but hold her.

Sarah had a lot on her mind as she ran down the hall on her way back to her own room. Sir Roger was coming up the stairs with a napkin package when he saw her.

"You are exactly who I was looking for," he smiled. "I heard what happened with you and Ally." He gave her a napkin package. "This is for you. It's biscuits, roast beef and pie from dinner since you had none."

"Thank you." Said Sarah starting off again, but Roger stopped her.

"Will you watch me play tomorrow? I'm a good Polo player."

"Alright."

She tried to move on a third time, but Roger pulled a blue silk scarf from his pocket and gave it to her.

"Then wave my scarf to cheer me on. You give a scarf to the girl you like—so you'll see it—and be inspired when she waves it."

"Sir Roger. Now is not a good time…" warned Sarah who desperately wanted to get away to be by herself.

But Roger put a finger to her lips to stop her. "Sarah, nothing you do will upset me—unless you tell me I do not have a chance. And I very much want a chance. Wave my scarf?"

She could deny him nothing and nodded. He smiled, then gave her a sweet, respectful kiss and left.

Sarah looked at his scarf, but her mind was on her spoken truth. The truth she had just revealed to the Queen and prince. The truth about what happened at the Chamber's Society School for Girls. A truth she was sure would now change how the royals thought of her.

She came inside her suite and never lit a candle or the fireplace. She just sat in the dark. She couldn't think about Sir Roger now. All she could do was pray that perhaps her revelation would exorcise any demons left inside her associated with the molestation.

She sat in the dark all night. Wide awake.

Meanwhile, Victoria paced in her robe as Albert watched. "I'm sending an invitation to the French Emperor. I want him to visit here with his wife. And I want you to invite Duke Friedrich. Albert, we have to invite as many people of influence as we can have here so we can help eradicate this menace." She finished her glass of port and looked at Albert pointedly. "And I want Humes arrested for rape."

"So do I." Albert blew out the candle and held his wife.

Clearly Victoria was still upset for her tears began again. "What that poor girl went through. What I allowed to happen by sending her there."

"No. Victoria," appeased Albert. "Your heart was in the right place. You cannot blame yourself."

But Victoria tears still flowed. For she knew she would blame herself the rest of her life.

Twenty Five

A mallet hit the Polo ball and in a smash, the polo match was off on the east grounds of Buckingham Palace. Sir Roger, Bertie and other players were fiercely competitive against an opposing team comprised of many members of Parliament and other nobles. Roger and Bertie had obviously made up from their dispute of last April and gave each other pats on the back when they did well. In fact, Bertie was surprised because Roger had been right. His backswing had improved exponentially and the horse he rode seemed keen on maneuvering splendidly with Roger's every move.

Alice, Sarah, Vicky and others were watching intensely from the stands built for the match. Victoria and Albert watched from lawn chairs with umbrellas, arranged in a raised royal spectators area, cheering the players on. Specially invited military officers and various guests including Sir Charles Phipps, Prime Minister Aberdeen, Ambassador Jimonpur and several Ladies-in-Waiting chatted while the game played. Everyone seemed to be having a good time.

Sarah had Roger's blue scarf and was waving it whenever Sir Roger rode by and Alice kidded her mercilessly.

"Oh, my. Waving his scarf are we?" she chided. "Things are certainly progressing fast."

"Can you not see I'm ignoring you?" quipped Sarah continuing to wave the scarf. Sir Roger saw it and waved back, tossing an air kiss.

"Goodness. He certainly doesn't care who sees him."

"I should hope not," Sarah admonished. "Since it would mean something is wrong with him blowing a kiss at me." Sarah then narrowed her eyes at Alice. "Is there something wrong with me?"

Alice knew better than to forage down this terrain as it would mean another long exhaustive argument on racism which she would simply not have today for she was too happy. The object of her own affections, Sir Michael McFerrin of Devonshire Downs was playing today, and she wished she had his scarf to wave—even though he was on the opposing team to Bertie and Roger—and quite married.

An hour into the game there was some commotion as two men on horseback rode up to the royal stand. One of them, a messenger, gave Lord John Breadlebane a note for the Queen—which he handed her. Both messengers then rode off.

Alice frowned. "What is that all about. No one would dare disturb mother during this yearly competition."

Sarah looked over at the Queen whose shoulders dropped, and countenance fell. Victoria clutched her heart as she slowly stood waving her hands for quiet. The game stopped, and people moved closer to her. Everyone was worried because Victoria's face was sullen, and it appeared the life had just drained from her body.

"Ladies and gentlemen, I must ask that all military men here in service to Her Majesty report to your posts," she intoned.

Now there were rumblings throughout the crowd as she continued. "England, and our allies France and Sardinia, have declared war on Russia. Troops will be deployed to Crimea in a fortnight."

Everyone gasped. Prime Minister Aberdeen motioned for his secretary and ran from the stand to his carriage to get back to 10 Downing

Street to conduct the business of Parliament now that England was at war.

Alice looked at Sarah who looked at Sir Roger pained in the knowledge that he would have to go off and serve, and there was a chance he might not return alive.

Roger jumped off his horse and ran over to her thinking the same thing. What if he never saw Sarah again? What if he died in Crimea? What if England lost the war and they all ended up under the control of the Russian Czar?

Sir Roger grabbed Sarah and held her tightly in front of everyone. Now was not the time to stand on ceremony.

"I'm so afraid, Sarah. This cannot be happening."

"Roger. Oh Roger," Sarah cried.

Once everyone returned to Buckingham there was no question a pall had overtaken the palace. No one said a word as they all went to their respective suites to change for tea then dinner.

Sarah entered her suite solemnly and sat on the bed. She just stared out. Then she looked at Sir Roger's blue scarf in her hand. What an awful week it had been. First the aftermath of sneaking out to the abolitionist's meeting and being punished with no supper, then her revelation of being raped by Mr. Humes at the Chamber's School, and now war with Russia and her beloved leaving for God only knew how long. Was she ever to find lasting happiness?

Lady McBurney came in to dress her and quietly laid out two dresses of which Sarah chose the light blue. Like an automaton she allowed her Lady to put the clothes on and neither said a word to the other.

That evening at the dinner table as Victoria, Albert, Bertie, Alice, Vicky, Sir Roger and Sarah ate, all anyone could hear was the cutlery against the china as almost no conversation was had. Even Bertie left the table early because he simply wasn't hungry. Roger picked at his food, and Victoria and Albert saw that Sarah mirrored this by not eating at all. She even turned down the opportunity to have Victoria's favorite claret which she loved because a general malaise had enveloped her.

No one wanted to dance that night either. Victoria and Albert retired early as did Ambassador Jimonpur who quietly had his Kahvalti and begged off to go to bed early. He wanted to leave the palace in the morning as it was important he be with his Turkish kinsmen since they had called for war in the first place.

In fact, Sarah begged off, nodded to Roger, and slowly headed for the greenhouse since it, besides the library, had become one of her favorite rooms. She sat in the window seat amongst a myriad of potted plants and budding seedlings and stared out. Moments later she was joined by Roger who sat next to her. Neither said anything.

"My first war. My first command. And yet I don't want to go," said Roger grimly.

"I don't want you to go either. That is the problem. But you must." Sarah stood up to go, but Roger grabbed her hand. "No, Sarah. Please."

"I need to be alone, Roger. So much is happening all at once."

"Come riding with me again tomorrow. Let's face this together. Please, Sarah, I need you."

She squeezed his wanting fingers and smiled slightly. She nodded then left for her room.

Roger stood there trembling. If only he didn't love her. He could take anything. Go anywhere. Be brave in the face of war. But how could he leave her now when his feelings ran so deep.

The next day, Sarah and Sir Roger were on horseback riding along together on the grounds of Buckingham's "Pleasure Gardens," which encompassed an area of over forty acres including a lake. It was a chilly, cloudy, overcast day on the verge of a downpour, and they could feel and smell the dampness in the air. Yet neither seemed to care since the weather matched their mood.

"I must report to Fort Amherst next week after which my regiment and I will be deployed to Crimea," Roger began quietly. "I don't know when or *if* I'll see you again."

"Please don't say that. You're resourceful. You won't get killed."

Suddenly, at that precise moment, as though God ordained it, the skies opened up and there was a downpour of rain soaking them instantly.

"Oh God!" Sarah screamed.

"Follow me. I know where to go. It's closer than trying to make it back to the palace." He rode ahead of her as Sarah followed. Soon, they were in front of a picturesque octagonal cottage at the top of a small man-made summit which had a steepled roof. Roger helped Sarah off her horse, tied the horses off, and they ran to the front entrance. Roger searched the stone planter pot, found the key, and unlocked the door. They went inside.

The cottage was ornate. In the center was an octagon shaped room, with eight lunettes painted in fresco by eight well-known artists of the time. To the right was another room decorated in the Pompeian style, and a third embellished with romantic designs, suggested by the novels and poems of Sir Walter Scott whom Victoria loved. Straight ahead of them was also a kitchen with a large fireplace.

"I'll make a fire and some tea. We may be here a while with this storm," said Roger as he went into the kitchen, gathered some wood from the wood pot, and placed them into the fireplace. He then put a few logs into the cast-iron stove, and pumped water into a kettle.

Sarah looked around. "Where are we?" she asked as raindrops created deafening noise crashing against the roof.

"This is the Garden Pavilion," Roger began. "Prince Albert had it designed as a private 'summer cottage.' But neither he nor the Queen use it anymore. Mostly Bertie and I come here."

"And bring women?" Sarah turned, looking at Roger pointedly.

Roger was almost embarrassed. It took him a minute. "We used to. A long time ago. I haven't..." he stopped and looked at her seriously. "...I haven't in a long time, and certainly not since meeting you."

"Well, that's something."

When the fire took hold, Roger began to think. He knew with everything happening, now was the time for truth with Sarah. There was only two weeks before he'd be at war and she had grown important to him. No secrets could be between them.

Sarah knew much was on his mind and that he was trying to admit or share a truth and she had to let him find the words by himself.

Finally, as thunder roared outside the cottage, he confessed.

"Sarah, because of Bertie, I have a reputation with women. But it's not true of me," he began. "I do not have a woman in every port, nor a girl under every bed. That's Bertie's mien. He's really the cad. But since I'm his best friend they say 'birds of a feather'—you know the rest."

"Still, you like being the man whom every woman wants—or has had, so I've been told..."

"Sarah, no..."

"It's alright, really. No one wants someone no one else wants," Sarah admitted. "But understand. I'm not in London to be a plaything nor a 'what if' experiment for the Queen in racial and educational equality," she paused a moment and looked away slightly. "Nor a sexual conquest for a white man who has never been with a black woman before."

"Is that what you think my motives are? To bed you so I can laugh with my friends that I've added an African to my list of carnal exploits?"

It took Sarah a moment. "Isn't it?"

His eyes examined her face. "God. Why are you so beautiful?"

Sarah said nothing and looked away. No man had ever said that to her and she was moved. But she had to be careful. Even the Queen warned her Roger could draw a woman in.

But Sir Roger moved closer unable to stop his thoughts. Why did her skin glow and her large brown eyes beckon even without her awareness? And those lips, large and full, framing gleaming white teeth when she smiled. He felt guilty for always wanting those beautiful lips on his mouth—on his body. Why couldn't she understand that his world had changed the moment he met her? That he had thrown caution and his past to the four winds to possess her.

Finally, he answered her. "I do have a confession. I have wanted you from the first moment. It was visceral and urgent—and primal. Something came over me and I just had to talk to you. To be near you. It was unlike anything I have ever experienced with a woman. And the more I kept telling myself how upset it would make Bertie or how insensitive and unsympathetic my friends would be, the more I found myself still drawn to you. Please do not hold that against me."

"I won't. It's rather complimentary, actually. Still…"

"…Still, I like that you at least don't find it offensive as you have so many other comments of mine in the past." Roger smiled. "It's a start."

Now Sarah had to smile. It was true that she found fault in some things Roger had said in the past, but it was because she always felt on guard and mistrusting.

"Well, it's because Bertie can be so awful and, as you said, 'birds of a feather…'"

Sir Roger took a moment to think. "It's important you understand that part of me likes having my erudite crowd to be around—to belong to. Being a part of the Prince of Wales' inner-circle has a certain privilege attached to it, I suppose," then Roger's tone changed. "But I am not him. In so many ways I'm not Bertie, Sarah. Not just that I will never be king, but in basic human kindness. Bertie can be bad-tempered and doesn't mind belittling or hurting one's feelings. It's why I left Windsor a day early when you first came. I'd had enough of his contrary opinions and demands."

"Then why do you stay friends? Why stay so close if you don't really respect him?"

"How do you refuse the next sovereign of England? There is no telling what he may do once he's in power, and he has an ugly, spiteful side." Roger made them two perfect cups of Earl Grey tea. "Make your decision about me purely for me. Please don't judge me by Bertie," he said looking into her eyes softly.

"How can I when you're a Peer who's handy in a kitchen."

Roger grinned. It was then he noticed her dress. "My God, your clothes are soaking wet."

"So are yours," said Sarah softly.

They met each other's gaze—and suddenly there was no more to be said. Roger set his cup and then hers on the table without breaking eye contact. Slowly, deliberately, he pulled her to him. She didn't resist. In fact, before she realized it her fingers had touched his face, as he ever so slowly eased her into his powerful arms. His mouth found hers and their kiss was so tight she could hardly breathe. Soon they could not help but give in to the raging passion which had them both possessed. Roger's body pushed hers onto the table while he rapidly, desperately took off layer upon layer of restrictive pettiskirts and corsets. Sarah found herself neither objecting nor rescinding. Rather, she accepted the inevitable, perhaps even welcomed it—relishing it as the most exciting, sensuous experience she had ever had with a man undressing her.

This was indeed different. Better. It was not the cruel, beastly corruptions of a demented headmaster taking her by force and hurting her, but her willingly giving herself to a man she genuinely wanted. Every moment of this was thrilling.

They made love there in the kitchen—and in one, sublime, stormy afternoon, months of forbidden, pent-up frustration was finally released.

Later, Sarah's dress, pettiskirt, and Roger's clothes were drying in front of the roaring fire Roger had made earlier, but the two of them were lying in each other's arms on the rug in front of the fireplace. Everything had blurred into one sensual extraordinary explosion—and Roger was now introspective.

"For so long I've thought of nothing but this moment," he whispered, almost absently. "And now that it's here, I fear that it is all it will ever be—one fleeting, luminescent moment."

Sarah turned to Sir Roger kissing him softly. Her body tingling with sweet sensations.

"Then let's have our moments as they come—one at a time." She nestled in the crook of his neck. "You see, I never thought I'd want a man to ever touch me," she continued. "Or to be so vulnerable and completely exposed emotionally. But here we are."

Roger kissed her neck and then the tribal marks on her shoulder.

"I am in love with you, Sarah. Truly in love with you."

"You don't have to say that."

"But I do. I may die on a battlefield. I don't want to talk about our differences. Only the truth between us."

"I…am afraid to love you," Sarah whispered. "Everything I love is always taken from me—my home, my family, my tribe, my name."

"I cannot bring any of that back. But I can help to change the circumstances that brought you here. I'll fight to end the Slave Trade worldwide. I'll help you fight if you want. I will never leave you."

But Sarah knew better. She knew Roger was 'in the moment' of his passionate affection for her and his heroic but romanticized view of *"I'll help you fight"* had yet to become a reality. She knew that as soon as that fight became arduous, he would be gone. He would retreat to the world he understood—to the erudite crowd into which he admitted he enjoyed belonging and socializing with the Prince of Wales' inner-circle and its attached privilege.

She smiled prophetically. "You *will* leave. But I'll understand when it happens. For us, it must be one day at a time, Roger." She removed the red necklace ribbon from around her throat and gave it to him. "Carry this with you when you go. Just come back from Crimea safe."

"It's what will get me through it. Coming back to you."

They kissed again, then fell back onto the floor.

…By three o'clock the rain had stopped. Sir Roger and I dressed and left the Garden Pavilion that became our trysting place for the next two weeks until Roger had to go. We met three times a week and enjoyed every moment of our closeness and deepening love.

By the last time we were together, the day before Roger would leave with his regiment for Crimea, I found myself overcome with emotion and took Roger's head into my hands. As I gazed into his green eyes longingly I heard myself finally say the words Roger had wanted to hear from the beginning.

"I love you. I'm scared to death. But I love you."

That was the day Roger vowed to God to forever be his servant if he would allow him to return to me. "I'm going to marry you, Sarah," he told me. "Marry you as soon as I return." God, how I lived on those words…

On their ride back to the palace from the Garden Pavilion that day, Victoria's mother was in the window and saw the lovers together. The Duchess was disdainful when she saw Roger kiss Sarah before they walked through the side gate, and she moved away from the window.

"It cannot go on, Victoria. Roger and Sarah. You must stop it."

"Mother, the lad is going to war. He'll be gone for some time."

"Sir Roger Carlyle cannot continue to expose himself to mockery and derision for his feelings for that girl. It's time you sent her away."

"Mother…!"

"…There are those of us who feel this 'experiment' of yours has grown tiresome," groused the Duchess. "Now it's yielded a good result.

Sarah is brilliant, your point proven. Move her on."

Victoria was affronted. "I will—when *all* Negroes can move on to non-discriminated lives."

"And you call yourself a Queen…"

"I *am* Queen…"

"…Then act like one. How many battles do you intend to fight before you realize the way things are—are how they will stay. You will be waiting for racial equality forever. That girl should be with her own kind. How much more gossip and whispers behind your back can we take before someone, like your son, Bertie, decides to call into question your sanity and have you removed from your position."

The Duchess of Kent left the room as Victoria stood there wondering if, even as Queen, she would ever have the true power to make the changes she thought the future England deserved.

She sat down finding herself enveloped in frustration. Her mother, once again, had successfully reverted her to her 13-year-old self—ridiculed, insecure and deeply disparaged.

Lori seemed to understand Victoria's mood and flew over to her. He lit on her shoulder—and for just a moment, the bird seemed to brighten the Queen's spirits.

he Scots Fusilier Guards were parading in the early dawn of a
bleak March day, en route from the Wellington Barracks to
Portsmouth to embark for the Black Sea. Lined up in formation outside of Buckingham Palace were the Queen's regiments—
Redcoats, Cavalry, Journeymen soldiers, and Infantry members on
horseback and on foot. Also seated on a horse in full dress uniform was
Sir Roger Carlyle in a glum mood.

Queen Victoria walked out onto the viewing balcony with Albert,
the Duchess of Kent, her children—and way in the back on the side,
Sarah, as Victoria went to the edge of the balcony. The crowd, which
included members of the public and the soldiers' families, roared their
approval. She waved for silence as she prepared to bid her troops goodbye and deliver a speech she dreaded having to give but needed to inspire
her beloved soldiers.

She remembered her role model Queen Elizabeth and the inspira-
tional military address she gave at Tilbury to her troops going into battle
in Calais in 1588. Those troops were victorious for Elizabeth and England—and Victoria needed to be just as inspiring now. So she drew
strength from Queen Elizabeth, and began:

"The British Empire along with the French and Sardinia have linked together in our cause against Russian encroachment and will defend to the death our way of life. Like good comrades we must aid each other to the utmost of our strengths. My fearsome, gallant soldiers, though we have before us many months of struggle and suffering, when the time comes that you realize there is no longer anything to be done, remember that the battle is not to the strong alone; it is to the vigilant and the brave. And this army, *my* army, is the bravest on Earth!"

Victoria paused a moment to embrace the crowd that loved her but had to accept England's decision to send its young men to war—and she harkened on her role model's 1588 plea:

"Our inimitable Queen Elizabeth once said: *'I know I have the body of a weak, and feeble woman. But I have the heart and stomach of a king, and of a king of England too!'* Well, so do I!"

The crowd roared upon hearing that and it gave Victoria the impetus to continue with bravado.

"So, there is no retreat but in submission. Our chains are forged! Our resolve is confident. We will wage war by land and sea with all our might against a tyranny never surpassed the grievous accounts of human error. Our goal is victory! Victory over tyrants! Victory despite terror! Victory however hard won! For without victory, there is no survival! So onward troops! Onward to English VICTORY!"

Victoria raised her right arm amid great cheers rising from the crowd and from the soldiers until they all began to chant:

"VICTORY! VICTORY! VICTORY!!"

As the chants continued, Sarah edged forward to wave Roger's blue scarf. Roger saw the waving scarf, and then her, and he pulled Sarah's red ribbon from his uniform's breast pocket and waved it back to her. They locked eyes. Sarah's eyes began to well up, as Sir Roger gave her one last nod.

Then he and all the soldiers marched forward—it was now on to battle—to months, perhaps even years of absence and uncertainty.

As Sarah sadly watched Roger ride away, Alice looked over at her friend and knew what she was feeling. She couldn't help but go to Sarah, feeling badly for her, and gave Sarah a hug. Sarah fell into her arms.

"I love him, Ally."

"I know you do." And the two friends just hugged each other.

That evening Sarah was in her suite. She had closed herself in there since the troops left and refused to come down for either tea or supper. All she wanted to do was play her violin—and the tune was as haunting and melancholy as her feelings.

All she could do was think about Roger and their intimate time together. She thought about how his hands felt when he touched her. His fingers caressing every part of her. His mouth kissing her lips, her neck, her breasts. She had marveled at his tall sinewy body with its broad shoulders, the dark hairs which accented his well-formed chest—and his ass. His beautiful, round, muscular ass that she found herself absently squeezing with relish. They had loved each other in as many ways as two people who could not get enough of each other did. And when they were thoroughly sated held each other tightly—neither wanting to let go of the other. It had all been magnificent. But now, Roger was gone.

Sarah wondered if she would ever experience such pleasure again. Just the sheer and complete ecstasy of giving one's self to another person without fear, without recrimination, without guilt. Was it all in her past? But her reverie was soon interrupted by a quick knock immediately followed by Victoria's entrance. Sarah stopped playing and was about to curtsey, but Victoria gestured for her not to as she came closer.

"Sally, you didn't come down to take tea or have dinner."

"No, ma'am. I wasn't hungry."

Victoria was careful. "I know Sir Roger has gone off to war," she started gently, knowing how Sarah must have been feeling. "And I know that you are fond of him."

Sarah looked at Victoria intensely.

"Fond? I'm more than fond of him, ma'am. You know that. I am in love with him."

"That doesn't surprise me." Victoria shook her head. "So, I suppose I am probably the last person you want to see—as Parliament's decision and my agreeing with it, is the cause of Sir Roger having to go—and a possible reason for his not returning alive."

They said nothing to each other for a moment. "Such a somber, awful time. So many young men in harm's way for the good of our country," said Victoria who taking Sarah's hand as both sat on the settee. She looked off in fond memory a moment.

"I remember when I first met Albert. I was so struck by his charm and his undeniable good looks. It was all I could think about. Especially when he kissed me that first time. And when he left, there was actually an ache for him. I wanted to see him again so much. And I wondered, hoped and prayed for him to feel the same." She turned back to Sarah. "I know love when I see it. But I also know fear. You are afraid Roger won't come back. I am afraid he will…" Victoria looked away not wanting to face Sarah. "…, and your relationship could become…tenuous."

It was quiet for a moment as Sarah sighed. "I see. He's white and a Peer. I'm not right for him in your mind. You weren't expecting me to fall in love with one of your own."

"Sally…"

"…And what happens to Captain Forbes and his West African Squadron of ships? Do they abandon us as well?"

Victoria looked at her ward at a complete loss. "Oh dear girl. I now realize I have moved away two of the men who mean the most to you and placed them in harm's way in one fell swoop. I am so sorry."

Sarah nodded and looked away. Victoria formed her words carefully. "I'm afraid Captain Forbes and the West Africa Squadron have been redeployed to Crimea. We are going to have to forget about the

Trade for now as all our ships are needed in Russia."

Sarah found herself feeling alone and rudderless—the way she felt when Forbes left England and she was sent off to the Charter Society School alone with no friends.

"Then I want to go back to Phillips Print Shop."

"What on earth for?"

"Helping to end the slave trade is my goal. A personal goal."

"Sally, I do not like you going there."

"You seem not to like me going anywhere." Sarah found herself growing irate realizing she had changed and needed defined parameters to her court life. "…Am I a prisoner here?"

"Certainly not."

"Then I do not understand why I cannot come and go as I please. Like free people."

"Because I am responsible for you."

Sarah stood when she heard that. It was all she could do not to scream. "My parents are dead. I have no siblings. Captain Forbes is now in Crimea with Sir Roger," she retorted. "I am responsible for me. I am of age."

Victoria was shocked by the intensity of Sarah's response. "Your insolence astonishes me. Are you unhappy being a part of this family? Because I have bent over backwards to make you welcome."

"Welcome?" Sarah countered, reminded yet again of her otherness—an otherness which kept her beholden to the Royal family's largess—and her role as "Experiment to the Queen." It took all her reserve to swallow her indignation and employ another tact.

"Ma'am, I am simply asking—to have an occasional afternoon to myself. To be with people like me—who look like me. Where I can commiserate and exchange ideas and laugh and talk about my homeland and culture which I miss—something you have no relationship to, or even an understanding of," she gently pressed.

"I see." It took Victoria a moment, but she stood, then nodded her consent. "Very well. Go to Phillips. But let me know whenever you do." The Queen then left the room as Sarah returned to her violin.

As she went down the hall Victoria could hear Sarah's melancholy violin playing again. She knew the girl was hurting, but her own fury at what Sarah had said and, more importantly, *how* she said it was uppermost on her mind. Frustrated by her tête-à-tête with Sarah, Victoria briskly approached Lord Everly coming from the opposite direction.

"Where is Bertie?" she inquired.

Lord Everly, cleared his throat. "Uh, I believe he…is in his suite, ma'am."

Victoria nodded a 'thank-you' then turned to continue down the hall. As she rounded the corner toward Bertie's suite she heard the familiar moans of lovemaking emanating from his chambers and realized why Lord Everly hesitated to answer her.

Victoria's hands went to her hips in disgust, then without knocking she barged right into Bertie's room and saw exactly what she presumed was happening.

Bertie was there in bed with Miss Gordon, one of the chambermaids, who let out a horrified gasp at the sight of the Queen.

"Mother! Why do you think they call it a door!" snapped Bertie as he rushed to find his overrobe. "Learn to knock!"

The chambermaid covered herself with the sheets as Victoria's arms folded in fury. "Miss Gordon?" charged the Queen.

The chambermaid looked up in embarrassment, with cheeks turning bright red. She was shaking. "Yes, Your Majesty?"

"It would appear you are about your 'work' quite late today."

"Yes, Majesty, everything was so…dusty" Miss Gordon stammered, then quickly gathered her clothing and jumped from the bed hoping to run out covered in the sheet.

"One moment, dear."

The chambermaid froze in place as Victoria icily walked past her to retrieve a feather duster and apron still lying in a heap at the foot of the bed. After giving Bertie a caustic look Victoria brought the items to the chambermaid with sardonic cynicism. "Here, my dear. Evening dusting is so difficult without your… 'tools' of the trade."

Miss Gordon grabbed the feather duster and scurried off having gone blanch from humiliation. Victoria shook her head and scornfully looked at her 20-year-old son. "You're pathetic, Bertie. Miss Gordon is the third chambermaid in as many nights," her voice as accusatory as Bertie had ever heard. "Your appetite for fleshly desire appears as insatiable as all your Hanover uncles and grandfathers. Why could you not have adopted your father's sensibilities in this area?" She threw his over-robe at him. "Is there no end to the Hanover men and their penchant for common women?"

Before Bertie could respond she held up a hand, glaring. "No need for an answer. It was rhetorical. Get dressed. I have a question."

Bertie sighed. There was no stopping his mother from getting her wish no matter how indelicate, impolitic or inopportune the moment.

"What, Mother?" Bertie stated with as much indifference as he knew to muster.

Victoria knew this was his evergreen tactic but forged ahead with her question. "You once told me you met an African in Liverpool who impressed you," she said, as she tried to keep her irritation at his philandering with the subordinate help from escalating.

Bertie was surprised. "I'm shocked you paid any attention to my mentioning him as it was merely small talk at dinner a year ago."

"Who is he?" Victoria insisted.

"James something or other. A wealthy African merchant as I recollect," the Prince of Wales recalled. But really, mother. You interrupt my good time for a question about some commoner I barely know, let alone an African one. Why couldn't it have waited?" he said in aggravation.

"I want you to find him now."

Bertie was disbelieving, and his entire physical countenance drooped. "For God's sake. Not another experiment. We're sick to death of your experiments."

"Of that I am fully aware," retorted Victoria, her eyes burrowed into a stare that unnerved him. "Now do as I ask. Find this man James, get a report on him, then invite him here. I need to have a proper match and diversion for Sarah as Sir Roger will only bring her pain and derision upon himself."

"Well now. Finally, a sensible plan. An African…with an African. Nature's proper order. Bravo."

Victoria ignored her son's snipe. "Do it tomorrow if you can," she said through clenched teeth, then turned to leave. But she turned back quickly adding, "That is unless you have plans for more fleshly entertainment tomorrow as well." She snapped the skirt of her gown back, and stormed out, leaving Bertie sighing from relief.

As he looked at the closed door a moment, the Prince of Wales shook his head wondering why his relationship with his mother was always so regrettable. Victoria was cold and indifferent toward him. In fact, Bertie had never experienced or seen any affection for him from her in his entire life. Still, he loved her and had at least witnessed her deep and abiding love for his father Prince Albert, and perhaps even two of his sisters—the eldest, Vicky and his younger sister, Alice. But why didn't she love him? Why did she not understand him? Why did she not understand men in general, especially the men of her own bloodline? There had never been any one woman in the history of the Plantagenet, Tudor, or Hanover dynasties capable of satisfying their male thirst for carnal knowledge—except his father Prince Albert—a true saint in Bertie's mind. But his father's gene had escaped him.

Frankly, the Prince of Wales felt justified in acting on his inherent sexual genetics as the product of his infamous 15th generation ancestor

Henry VIII, who not only bedded women generously but also married and beheaded them with impunity and frequency. Then, there was his 5th great-grandfather, King George I, the first of the Hanover dynasty, who imprisoned his own wife for thirty-two years for having an alleged affair with a Swede whose mutilated body was rumored to be kept beneath the floorboards of their residence. Meanwhile, George I carried on with not one but three mistresses. Next, his son, King George II, openly bedded Madame de Walmoden while his wife, Queen Caroline, was still alive. Upon the Queen's death he conferred the honor of "Lady" to his lover, who then became the "Countess of Yarmouth" and a ubiquitous presence at St. James's Palace. Then there was Frederick Louis, Prince of Wales, who, having predeceased his father George II, never became king. Nonetheless, it did not preclude him from flagrantly parading his mistress, providing her an apartment in Soho Square and an allowance of £1600 a year for all to comment upon.

Then to add fuel to the Hanover sexual excess, there was Bertie's über extravagant great uncle King George IV, who had earned the contempt of the British people and diminished the prestige of the monarchy by marrying Maria Fitzherbert—a commoner six years his elder, twice widowed, and a Roman Catholic in spite of the 1701 Act of Settlement law, which barred a Royal married to a Catholic from succeeding to the throne. Then there was the Royal Marriages Act of 1772, which prohibited his marriage without his father, King George III's, consent.

When his debts became untenable, George IV was forced to marry his cousin Caroline of Brunswick. Not having his previous marriage annulled made him a bigamist forcing the prior marriage to be set aside. The King upon ascending the throne after his father's death, so hated Caroline that he forbade her to even attend his coronation. Eventually, he left her, had the marriage illegally annulled, and embarked on a string of mistresses and lovers with whom he had several illegitimate children. His only legitimate child, Princess Charlotte, died before George IV did.

Thus, when the King died, the throne went to his brother, Victoria's uncle, William—a man who lived with his mistress and had 10 illegitimate children before becoming king.

It was all a debauched mess. Wives, mistresses, concubines, lovers and courtesans, all part of the luxury of being a royal, and Bertie, with his good looks and guaranteed ascension to the throne, was no different than any other. Little else was on his mind sometimes except women—beautiful women, charming women. Women who made his heart leap.

Which was why he would never understand his dear friend Sir Roger Carlyle's infatuation with an African. What did he see in her? She was as black as any Negro he had ever seen with almost a shimmer of blue coming off her skin. True, she had a fine, thick, kissable mouth and hips that went on forever, but most black women had those traits which he could see drove the average white man into fits.

But not him.

As far as Bertie was concerned, Roger had lost his mind and was mad. Sarah Forbes Bonetta was as unsuitable a match for him as a donkey, worse actually, because a donkey could at least take you from one place to another, whereas Sarah would take Roger nowhere. In fact, she would drag him down and ruin his life and prospects considerably. So, if his mother was hatching a plot to bring Sarah and the African man he'd met years ago together, Bertie would do everything in his power to make it happen and soon. He wanted Sarah and her undue influence, out of the palace and the Queen's life for good and all.

He wanted "the Experiment" over.

.

 week later, Sarah was in the library looking through some books. When she would find what she was looking for, she placed the books in a small valise she'd brought with her.

Moments later, Barnes came into the library with juice that he gave her and started to leave, but Sarah stepped forward. "Thank you. Barnes, but please wait," she asked.

Barnes turned back around. "Yes, m'lady," he said quizzically since he'd brought what she requested. Sarah came closer to him in a friendly *we're social equals* kind of way that Barnes wasn't used to with anyone above his station—regardless of color.

Sarah wasn't sure how to start. She had wanted to have a private conversation with him ever since he was hired but didn't know how—or if it was appropriate. Now it almost didn't matter, and she felt silly for being concerned about it.

"Are you happy here?" Sarah finally inquired.

It took Barnes a few moments as the servant looked at her with a degree of astonishment wondering why that particular question. Was it in actual interest of him—or in wonder for her own well-being. It was, after-all, quite a personal query for a member of the hierarchy to ask—even one who was not an actual aristocrat but an "anointed" royal." And he had to remember that such a question—those four words: *Are you happy here?* could also be a trap.

Yet somehow, he began to feel there was more to it—especially coming from Sarah, who by now, from palace scuttlebutt, he understood had been influential in both his and Davis, the other black footman's hiring. So, under these unique circumstances, he decided to answer and add his own inquiry. "I am—for the most part." He then moved in closer to her pointedly, "But there are those of us here who wonder...if *you* are happy, m'lady?"

Now Sarah was thrown by his question, and her look gave her away. No. She wasn't fully happy and now she knew he and others were aware of it. "Is it that obvious, Barnes? Because it's hard to know who to be. Or where to belong."

Before Barnes could comment further, Dr. Brown came into the library with a few books he intended to return. Protocol dictated Barnes instantly bow—and leave.

"Oh, Miss Bonetta. Forgive me."

"Dr. Brown. You're here early."

"I'm here to check on Prince Leopold," he responded. "How are you?"

"I'm so much better. I don't cough as much anymore. Thank you."

"Must be those native cures of yours. You should have them patented."

The two laughed. Sarah always liked Dr. Brown. He had such a gentle manner and kind face, and he always liked to genuinely engage Sarah in conversation. He also had nicer teeth than anyone else she knew in London.

Then she noticed the books he was placing back on the shelves. He smiled noticing her looking at the titles.

"I was just returning these books. The library here at Buckingham is as good as any in London. Quite impressive."

"Indeed. The Queen was correct in that," she smiled. "I was looking for children's books. And I see you were interested in…" She read the title of the book he was holding. "…Hereditary Diseases"?

"I'm treating Prince Leopold with no success. Hemophilia is a frightful, insidious disorder." Then feeling he may have shared too much about his medical shortcomings, he wanted to leave before he revealed any more. "Well, I must go. Have a good day, my dear," he said, managing a sincere smile.

Sarah smiled back as he left. Once he was gone, she went to the book and flipped through it. Armed with curiosity, she took the book with her as she left the library headed for her destination.

Sarah's coachman pulled up to Phillips Print Shop where she got out and instructed him to return in three hours then went inside with her book valise. Upon entering, Sarah once again sat in the back next to Mrs. Schoen. She looked around and seconds later saw whom she was looking for—Winston Benjamin—who smiled at her. She smiled back.

While abolitionists chatted, Winston joined Sarah in back.

"I was praying you'd come," he said beaming.

Sarah kept him engaged with a smile as she took in a deep breath ready for her confession. "I needed permission to come from the Queen," she revealed.

Winston became confused. "The Queen? What is the hierarchy for chambermaids at Windsor? Wouldn't you just ask your Chamberlain? Why would the Queen be bothered with such triviality?" He then noticed Sarah wasn't smiling. In fact, she was somber.

"I wasn't honest when we first met," she said in hushed tones. "I don't work at Buckingham. I live there. I'm the Queen's goddaughter."

Winston was now taken aback, and it took a moment to process what he'd heard—the expression on his face registering incredulity and amazement. "An' the white lady you were with?" he asked not sure he wanted to know the answer.

Sarah leaned forward to his ear, "Princess Alice. Her daughter," she whispered.

Winston's eyes closed in dread. "Oh God! God, no! An' Miyo kissed her," he said in quiet despair.

That was the moment Sarah realized the position she had placed Winston in now knowing hers and Alice's true identity and the social ramifications for him. So, she had to alleviate his angst.

"Remember, she kissed him—but honestly, she loved it. She had never been kissed, and it's all she talked about." she grinned.

Winston failed to see the humor of it all. "Please don't make light of it," he said genuinely concerned. "She's a princess, and he's an absolute commoner. A pauper." Though Sarah saw how serious Winston was, she just couldn't help laughing,

"And a *black* pauper at that. But she truly enjoyed that first black commoner kiss."

Now Winston had to laugh. "White ladies will never admit to it, but they do love a good black kiss." They both laughed again. Finally it subsided and Sarah opened the bag, and pulled out books, and put them in Winston's lap. "These are for you."

"But I can't read."

"I know. I'm going to teach you."

Winston frowned at that proposition, especially knowing her true position to the Royal Family.

"Mr. Phillips said he will let us work back here," Sarah said as if reading his mind. "Let me help you."

He smiled as she opened the first book and showed him the first page. "Do you see this word? This word is Apple. See this shape? It's the letter A," she started. "A, Apple." Say it."

"A, Apple," Winston repeated.

The lesson went on for the next two hours reminding Sarah of her time on the HMS Bonetta with Forbes as he taught her English and how to read it, then Brandon and Gibson teaching her French and math. She felt so good as she watched him learn and feel better about himself as he began to understand the alphabet as the building blocks of the language he was forced to learn as a captive but could master to educate himself and improve his world. She loved being a part of that growth. She loved teaching.

Equally, Winston looked at her with the utmost gratitude and kept asking himself what wondrous thing had he done to deserve her? Who was this divine creature the gods dropped from the heavens into his life—and he clutched the ancient piece of wood dangling from his neck—his good luck talisman.

They had a lesson every Tuesday and Thursday. Several weeks went by since Sarah began to teach Winston to read. Those weeks soon turned to months, and now they were at Phillips working through a pile of books spread out on a back table, as she continued to teach Winston rudimentary reading and spelling despite the fact that on occasion Sarah wasn't always feeling well. Sometimes her stomach would be upset, and she learned to bring along some "Nature's Miracle"—an elixir that women used for cramps which seemed to help.

But it was Winston she found herself in awe of. Winston was a natural learner. He was naturally curious and caught on quickly—much like herself—and she almost couldn't keep up with how fast he picked up words, numbers and exercised critical thinking.

For Sarah, it was almost as though teaching Winston kept her own interest in learning sparked. One day while waiting on Winston for his lesson she had looked through the books at Phillips and found one that fascinated her. It was called *"Blood Disorders"* and as she flipped through it found herself thoroughly engrossed and bought it. She wanted to learn as much as Dr. Brown so perhaps she could help her Majesty and young

Prince Leopold.

Soon Winston arrived, and they began the mathematical times tables which he did aloud, and then later Sarah graduated him to reading children's books aloud which she had borrowed from the palace library.

On this particular day, while Winston was reading an Aesop fable called "*The Tortoise and The Hare*," Sarah found herself beaming with pride. When he finished the tale and looked up he saw Sarah grinning and grinned back.

"It's kind of a silly story really. The hare falling asleep and the tortoise beating him at the race."

"But you read it so well, Winnie—and more importantly, understood it. That's the real prize."

Sarah had recently been given to calling him "Winnie" which he loved. It was her private nickname for him and he felt her decision to use it was bringing her even closer to him. Especially since he only called her "Aina."

But Winston did something strange. He took her hands, squeezed them and pointedly looked in her eyes. It almost made her flush with excitement. "No. The real prize would be if I could kiss you," he confessed.

Sarah didn't know what to do and slowly withdrew her hands to pull herself together. She knew he was serious and did not wish to hurt his feelings. She liked him too much to lead him on—especially when her feelings for him did not mirror his for her. She touched his face and smiled slightly.

"You're doing so well. Why don't we continue with our lessons without any distractions or unrequited agendas? I want you to be as intellectually possessed externally as you already are internally."

There was no question this was not what Winston wanted to hear, but he nodded because he wanted to be smart too. Smart for her. He'd rather see her and have her close to him by teaching him, than to frighten her away with his silly romantic notions—gestures he knew he had to control. It was too early in their relationship to think about loving her—which he did—let alone her returning that love. Sarah was that rare jewel who could be a true partner if he played his cards correctly and developed patience. Better he become the smart, clever man she could come to one day care for. He had to develop into someone she could respect. Be her intellectual equal. Then he would have his prize. All he had to do was wait—and learn.

"Then, perhaps, we could move on to a more stimulating story," Winston offered. "Did this Aesop write anything with more substance other than stories like "*The Mouse and the Oyster*" or "*The Fox and the Grapes*"?

Sarah chuckled. "They truly are silly tales on the surface. But they do have a deeper meaning. They're actually little morality fables—tales like extended proverbs." She began to pack away the books. "Did you know Aesop—was African?"

Now Winston's interest was piqued. "An African wrote these?"

"He was from Ethiopia actually. But he lived in Greece. He wrote hundreds of fables. They called him a 'Fabulist' and he had an influence on the reading pleasures of many noblemen. In fact, I read a 1687 biography about him that described him as "his complexion was black.""

Winston nodded. "And I suppose he wrote these morality tales so he could speak a truth to the powerful or Royal—without being arrested. Why else would a black man use animals to speak about political matters."

"Yes. Yes, Winston. Very good. Aesop was clever that way."

"If only I could be a talking turtle," grinned Winston. "I'd spew my opinions on these white aristocrats for their wretched behavior toward us in a thousand fables."

Sarah grinned. "You see? A man with a purpose who can write down his words and opinions. That's you."

"Tell me more about black Aesop."

"Well, he also wrote limericks."

When she saw Winston frown, she explained. "A limerick is a five-line poem. Meant to be humorous."

"Do you know any?"

Sarah thought a moment, then: "*…There was a young man of St. Kitts. Who was very much troubled with fits. The eclipse of the Moon. Threw him into a swoon. And he tumbled and broke into bits.*"

Winston then grinned. "Oh, I know one of those. Maybe Aesop wrote it too. He then recited: *"There once was a girl from Trevises. Who feet were of two different sizes…"*

But suddenly Sarah joined in. She knew this limerick too.

"*…The left one was small. And of no use at all. But the right won her several prizes…*"

The two broke into laughter. Then it subsided as Winston fought his impulse to touch her again. "You—are a brilliant, unique woman. I hope you know that Aina," he said.

"And you are an extraordinary man," Sarah enthused. "One I expect we shall have in front of Parliament before long reading some exceptional speech on abolition. Or writing tales like Aesop or selling his books as an author like Equiano."

"An author like Equiano?" he smiled, basking in her compliment. "Olaudah Equiano is my hero. He sold 100 copies of his book in one day and it helped Wilberforce to get his bill passed to end the slave trade here in England."

"You could be an abolitionist like that too."

Then and there Winston decided he would work as hard as he could, for he would never tire of such admiration from the object of his affection. Indeed, he hoped to one day never have to read a book to elicit such esteem from his beloved again. And after the lesson, Winston held Sarah's hand and helped her into her carriage.

Once she was seated, he held her hand a moment longer than propriety dictated—and kissed it. She smiled back. He gently released her hand as if it was a prized gem, and she immediately waved goodbye as he closed the carriage door. The carriage drove off and Winston remained watching it leave until it disappeared into the setting afternoon sun.

There was no question, Winston Benjamin was completely and unapologetically besotted with Sarah.

When Sarah returned from teaching Winston that day and came down for tea, she noticed everyone grinning at her like Cheshire cats as they entered the parlor. Alice in particular was gleeful to the point of bursting. "Oh, Sarah! She's wonderful! I love her! She reminds me of…well, me."

"Who…?"

They entered the parlor and Sarah could see Prince Albert sipping tea with Princes Bertie, Arthur, and Alfred; and Victoria was smiling as she held conversation with her mother and daughters Princesses Vicky, Louise, and Helena. But one extremely tall girl who was having tea with the women looked familiar to Sarah but was not a member of the family. As Sarah came closer the girl turned and grinned at her. "Sarah…!"

Sarah was dumbfounded as a sweet veil of realization and excitement rushed over her. "Linda?"

The two girls hurried to each other and hugged for dear life.

"Linda Beekman! How are you? It's been so long."

"Too long!" cried Linda. "Oh Sarah, when the Queen sent a personal invitation I couldn't resist. My family made all the arrangements instantly—and here I am. A whole week here at Buckingham Palace!"

They hugged again. Sarah turned to Victoria. "But how would you know who she was? How did you get an address?"

Before Victoria could answer, Linda offered. "I wrote her, Sarah. After all that terrible business at the Chambers School, the Cage, my expulsion, I wrote to the Queen and told her I thought you were still there, maybe even hurt. They'd told my parents you had been expelled. But you would never have left your violin, or your books—and they were still in your room."

Sarah looked at Victoria who nodded. "Miss Beekman's letter is the reason we sent Sir Charles to Oxfordshire to fetch you. God only knows how much longer they would have kept you in that horrid room. She made sure we had her address. I thought you might enjoy a familiar face now—with what's happened."

"Ah. Now it all makes sense," Bertie smirked. "Sir Roger goes to war and Sarah's old and dear friend we have heard nothing about magically shows up here." He turned to Victoria, "Mother, there is no end to your machinations."

"Except in this case, I'm glad Linda was invited," Sarah admitted. "She was a savior to me at Chambers School. She didn't know me or care, but the first day she reached out like I was an old friend, and I will never forget her kindness."

Linda smiled. Then Sarah thought about something.

"Linda, remember Madeline Gray at school?"

"How can I ever forget? She was the most ill-tempered, truculent student there. I hated her. We both did."

Sarah then pointed to Bertie. "Think of the Prince of Wales as Madeline incarnate."

"Ah. Then may I be permitted to be myself?"

"Please," insisted the Queen, smiling."

Linda turned to Bertie and grinned. "Your Highness, I've dealt with bigger bullies than you can imagine. Care to go toe to toe?"

Bertie, outdone by her candor despite his eminence, finished his tea and perused Linda like a purchase. "A bit more blush and removing your glasses would certainly feminize you." He then walked away to the other side of the room to his brothers.

Alice turned to Linda and grinned. "It going to be a long week for you, dear."

They all laughed.

Though Sarah began to feel poorly for much of that week for which she took a tonic, she and Linda got caught up. Since Alice was Sarah's newer best friend, the three girls found comfort and laughter in each other's company often gathering in Sarah's room in the afternoons, or on long walks or horseback riding around the grounds. Linda told stories of Sarah at school, Alice shared her experiences as a "put-upon" royal, and Sarah confessed everything from her rape by Mr. Humes and subsequent convalescence, to her love for Sir Roger.

Then one evening after supper, as the girls were describing their love lives—or lack thereof, Linda became quiet and looked off.

"What's wrong, Linda?" asked Sarah. "You seemed to drift away all of a sudden."

It took Linda a moment, but she teared up suddenly.

"I don't think I like men," she admitted to no one in particular. "Not in the way you do. I have, it turns out, a peculiar attraction…" she paused a moment to wipe her eyes.

"…To women?" asked Alice.

Linda nodded slightly looking away.

"I knew it," said Alice. "It's your mannerisms and feistiness. Not to mention your odd clothing."

"That could be said of you, Ally," Sarah pointed out.

"Please. I am too big a flirt with men—for someone who doesn't know a thing about them."

But Linda continued seriously. "Father has sent me to several doctors and no one knows what to do with me. I like masculine clothing, I loathe interactions with men except as friends, and I'm drawn to things men like to do—building things, hunting, fishing. So I push my feelings down as far as I can, so as not to upset my family. But they already think of me as a spinster they'll have to support the rest of my life—which would be an embarrassing burden on them."

"Oh, Linda. I'm so sorry."

Linda finally looked at Sarah. "You were the first woman I knew I had a, well, knew I liked more than I should have. Maybe that's why I was so protective of you at school. It wasn't until I got back home to Brighton after my expulsion, that I realized my feelings were deeper and, I'm told, abnormal."

"Linda…" Sarah almost cried.

"You don't know what it's like to have your family want to cure you from whom you love. So, my father has found an answer. He's found a man, the son of a trusted friend he expects me to marry. I have been told this man has a similar predilection in addition to an underdeveloped…well…" she stopped then gathered herself. "Father says if we marry, between our two families, our finances and well-being will be more than adequately provided for. But we cannot express our true, private natures to anyone. I am supposed to think about it."

"What will you do if you marry? Wear each other's clothes?" chortled Alice to which Sarah gave her the evil eye. "Not funny Ally."

"Forgive me, but it is—when there is a simple solution to this," Alice disputed. "Marry him. Make your families buy you a home deep in the country then express yourselves how you please. This is just another form of arranged marriage and royal women are perennially forced into them. Trust me, others are like you. I've seen them."

"Where?" frowned Sarah."

"Frankly, with you. At Phillips Print Shop, and at the pub we went to afterwards," confessed Alice. "You were so caught up in Winston, you never saw that there were men dancing with men at the pub while we were dancing with Miyo and Winston. And at Phillips Print shop, my goodness the entire crowd there was positively bohemian. I mistook the woman I was sitting next to for a man—except she was wearing earrings."

"That is no indication," offered Linda.

"See?" Alice turned to Linda. "Marry for money, then you and your husband decide your own course. No one will know what you do behind closed doors. Choose happiness," Then she grinned. "Just don't kill anyone. There are laws against that."

"There are laws against being a sodomite too," cautioned Sarah.

"But first you must get caught," smirked Alice who turned to Linda. "Do not get caught."

By the time my old friend Linda Beekman left Buckingham Palace, she knew what she was going to do, and I reestablished what became a lifelong friendship with many letters exchanged to each other. Linda was married that next May and asked their families to do just what Ally suggested—purchase a home deep in the Yorkshire countryside which they did. But unbeknownst to their upstanding, well-heeled, Jewish families, Linda and her husband established The Sappho Inn there. It was a private, underground "Molly" house for people who had yet to decide who they loved male or female—or perhaps had. They became wealthy—and were never caught as their wealth paid off many a constable in the police department—who frequented their establishment. . . .

Meanwhile, Bertie did what Victoria had asked. Inside the Royal Lodge one day, he was patting the buttocks of one of his regular ladies of the night, who was always ready for a romp during the day—for the right money or trinket.

As his one hand was preoccupied with her nude derriere, the other he used to play chess with his friend, Sir Rhys Langley. As he moved one of the pieces around the board, he finally asked the question for which Sir Rhys had been brought to the cottage.

"Rhys, remember the African man you introduced me to in Liverpool last year?" Bertie inquired innocuously, so not to reveal the real reason was abiding his mother's request—and more importantly his own determination to keep Sarah away from Sir Roger, forever.

"Yes. James Labulo Davies."

"Can you find him for me quickly?"

"I don't see why not. He still trades on the docks in Liverpool."

Bertie smiled slyly. "I need a favor, old boy. One for which I shall be forever grateful."

Sir Rhys grinned. "Anything for the future King of England."

Young Prince of Wales Albert Edward (Bertie)
Future King Edward VII of England

Twenty Eight

wo weeks later, Lady McBurney was laying out Sarah's dresses for tea when Sarah appeared after a lesson with Winston ready to be dressed.

"Did you hear?" Sarah's Lady asked excitedly, "The Queen is having a private performance from one of the world's greatest sopranos."

"Who?"

"Jenny Lind," answered Lady McBurney as she put the pink pannier over Sarah's head. "They say she left her successful American tour to perform for Her Majesty at the Queen's command tonight."

But as Lady Mac tried to fit the satin pannier on Sarah it was too tight and left gaps where the tie-strings interlaced around her stomach and hips. "My dear, I would suggest less beef and potatoes at dinner," joked Sarah's Lady, "Right now we shall have to let out at least five of these gowns. Let's try the yellow one."

"Tie them looser, Lady Mac. You always make it so I can't breathe."

Once Sarah was dressed, Lady McBurney draped five gowns over her arm. "I will take these to Lady Eaton. But I must say you look lovely in the one you're wearing." Lady McBurney left and Sarah went to her bookshelf and pulled down her new book. She had been dying to get to it for several days yet had been pulled in all directions never allowing her enough daylight.

Now, she had some time before tea and she decided to sit in the window seat and read. She was glad she did. For between this book and the earlier one she'd read from Buckingham's library, Sarah was learning all she could about hemophilia. She discovered it was a rare disease in which the blood does not clot normally and was usually inherited and commonly occurred in males.

She also learned that full-blown hemophilia was passed from a father to a son and that women were primarily carriers of the disease. A carrier's son had a fifty percent chance of having the disease. A girl could inherit the dominant gene and pass it to her boy child where it could become full-blown hemophilia, whereas her daughter would be another carrier, or it bypassed her.

It was all fascinating to Sarah as she now understood why the concern over who in Victoria and Albert's family was a potential carrier or who had the fully developed disease. Sarah made notes and charts like a medical student but kept her ideas and theories to herself as the subject of Prince Leopold illness was a sensitive one to the family. She dare not upset anyone with her layman's thoughts.

But her private discoveries were found out when Alice knocked at the door while Sarah was reading and hadn't time to hide her books when Alice barged in.

"What are you reading?" Alice asked innocently.

"Nothing in particular," said Sarah looking like a dog who hid the bone. "Just a book."

"What book?" Alice proceeded to snatch the book from Sarah and read the title. "*Blood Diseases*? Why on earth would you be reading such a topic?"

"Ally, I just want to learn all I can about Prince Leopold."

"Why? You think you can help my brother? Honestly, I don't think he'll live out the year. If you just kiss his cheek he bleeds." She handed the book back to Sarah. "Did you get the book from downstairs?"

Sarah shook her head.

"Then where? Tell me."

Sarah said nothing. Suddenly Alice guessed. "From Phillips Print Shop. Of course. That's where you've been going these last months. I wondered where you got off to without me. But why?"

Sarah said nothing and put the book next to her cherished others.

"I've been teaching Winston to read there."

"Does Mother know?"

"We had a talk. I told her I needed to interact with people who looked like me who were interested in causes for people who look like me. She eventually acquiesced. So she knows I go for abolitionist meetings. But she doesn't know I've been teaching Winston."

Alice grinned. "Then I'm going with you."

"No, Ally. You'll only get into trouble again. I have permission. You don't. It could jeopardize everything."

"What 'everything'? I'd like to see Miyo again."

"Ally, please. No."

"So it's alright for you to see Winston, or Sir Roger, or any other man you want to cavort with, but not me?"

Sarah was taken aback. "Cavort with?" It took her a moment to calm down. "Ally, this is not about me seeing men. I'm teaching a Negro man to read and write to better his life and opportunities. To educate him. You don't know what it's like for us."

Suddenly Alice gave Sarah a strange look. "And were you teaching Sir Roger to read and write to better *his* life and opportunities?"

"W-what?" Now Sarah was nervous.

There was a long pause as Alice moved closer to Sarah lowering her voice. "Do you think I don't know about you—and Roger?"

Sarah's heart was racing as Alice continued. "That before he left for Crimea you were sneaking off to meet him. To have intercourse?"

"That's not true!"

"Liar. I saw the two of you leave together one day. I was furtive, but I followed on horseback and watched you go to the Garden Pavilion. Then three days later you went again and every three days after until he left. Only a moron wouldn't know why you went or what you were doing…"

Alice's revelation shocked Sarah as she continued."

"…Especially now, with you and the vomiting, and upset stomach, and ill-fitting clothes."

"How do you know all that?"

"Twice at dinner last week you excused yourself because you weren't feeling well. You haven't bled in at least two months and haven't ordered any hot towels for your cramps. You and I and Vicky are almost synced together with our monthlies. Then just now Lady McBurney had a load of your dresses she told me must be let out."

Alice crossed her arms and looked at Sarah pointedly. "Sally, are you with child?"

Sarah swallowed a scream as her hands went to her mouth. She could not believe what she was hearing. Her friend knew about it all. Everything she had feared. "Oui. Je suis enceinte."

Alice shook her head. "How do you think Mother will feel when she finds out?" Then she continued with almost a Machiavellian glint in her eye. "The Queen of England's prized 'experiment,' the bilingual African taught to be a Lady, living in the palace with the royal family, educated at the best school, playing the violin for Peers and nobles—'enceinte' with a bastard child like a common slut…"

"Ally please, stop! Please!" Sarah cried.

"She'll feel betrayed, and worse, like an idiot for thinking she could change the nature of a Negro like everyone has been telling her. Oh, and the aristocracy, Sally. The aristocracy will have a field day. Between them and Bertie? You will make mother the laughing stock of England. Why she'll ship you back to Africa for the beheading you deserve in her mind.

And your precious Roger will never be able to show his face anywhere near Parliament—not to mention he'll be booted out of the Queen's Dragoons. Think he'll want you after that?"

"That's cruel, Ally," cried Sarah, her tears flowing openly. "You can't mean it. Please. Your mother can never find out."

"How can she not? You'll be showing any second."

Sarah laid across her bed in a gale of uncontrollable sobbing. Alice went over and sat next to her, then took Sarah's hand.

"Then take me with you to Phillips—and make sure Miyo is there." She gave Sarah her kerchief. "Here. Wipe your nose." She then walked to the door and turned back. "We're friends, Sally. Friends help friends and never betray them. I would never betray you. I have too much fun with you. Or at least I did—when you had time."

She smiled and left. The moment she was gone a pain rose in Sarah's stomach and she ran for her chamber pot. Everything within her—including her faith in humanity—vomited into it.

That evening in Buckingham's ballroom as Victoria, Prince Albert, the royal family, and fifty invited guests enjoyed the spectacular voice of Jenny Lind, Sarah was seated way in back with much on her mind. She chose where she was seated so in case she had to leave because she became ill she could do it less inconspicuously. But mostly, it was so she could think without the prying eyes of the nobles, who, she thought in her paranoid state, were descending on her like vultures for her dishonor.

She could see Alice looking at her. Her look said it all. Alice held Sarah's future in her hands—and Sarah never felt so alone in her life—except perhaps the Cage at Chambers School. And *that* had ended badly.

How could she have allowed it to happen? To become pregnant. To not be more cautious. She was a smart, well-read woman. She knew that what she and Roger did inevitably leads to babies whether wanted or not.

It was simple biology. There were things she could have done, she thought—a douche of mudwort root, or vinegar, sponges soaked in tansy oil, or treated sheep guts for condoms. She should have been more careful.

But no. She and Roger let their passions get the better of them. Now he was gone, and she was left with the result of that passion. What would she do with a child? How would she live? Of course, the Queen will throw her out. And if Forbes knew he would be so disappointed. Her once idyllic life had now turned into an embarrassing disaster. A scandal. And all because she had fallen in love...

...with a white man.

Then she had the worst thought of all. Could she rid herself of the baby? Was there a place she could go, somewhere in London that was safe? Somewhere she wouldn't die in the attempt to correct this situation. There had to be an answer, a fix.

The next morning after breakfast, while everyone was still enthralled with the soprano Jenny Lind, there for another day, Sarah pulled Alice aside.

"Put on the plain blue dress I first came here in. We're going."

Alice became very excited. "Where? To Phillips?

"To the Grub area."

Suddenly Alice was nervous. "We're not going to a meeting? Will I see Miyo? Are you teaching Winston?"

"No. You will be my friend and not betray me, Ally. I shouldn't be alone. So get dressed and come with me."

Alice nodded slightly. But she was worried.

An hour later, the coach had brought the girls down Sweedon's Passage and stopped in front of #32 in the Grub area. All around them was the Dickensian troposphere of hustlers, harlots, and beggars. Sarah then checked the address again and she and Alice knocked on the door.

Moments later, Mrs. Elizabeth Schoen appeared and smiled.

"Ah, Sarah. How nice to see you."

"You too, Mrs. Schoen."

Were you in the neighborhood? Or did the good Reverend an' I forget a meeting?"

Sarah swallowed hard and shook her head. "No, you didn't miss a meeting. I…I'm here for a reason. A personal reason."

"Oh," said Mrs. Schoen glancing at Alice. "Come in."

Alice and Sarah entered the modest house.

As Elizabeth Schoen made tea for the girls, and after some initial small talk, Sarah finally crept her way up to the reason for her visit.

"I need your help, Mrs. Schoen. I am in trouble and need the services of a…" she stopped and looked at Alice who now understood why she was asked along.

"I've made a mistake—and now I'm…" Sarah couldn't go on and looked down in embarrassment.

"She's with child," said Alice in a small voice.

Mrs. Schoen sat her cup down and frowned. "An' you thought I could help you by providing the name of someone who would…correct such a…situation?"

Sarah nodded slightly.

Mrs. Schoen looked at both Alice and Sarah and shook her head. "You girls get into these situations all the time," she said with her exasperated cockney accent. "I can't tell you how many times I tell women to use precaution. You certainly can't expect the man to." She got up and left the room. Sarah tried not to cry but kept wiping her eyes. Alice held her hand.

When Elizabeth returned she gave Sarah a bag and a piece of paper with an address on it. "There are sheep-gut condoms in there. At least four. Keep them moist. After that, you'll have to find an' pay for 'em yourself. As for the other, well, the girls on the street out there tell me there's a woman, Miss Jenkins, in Lemley Market Alley down the road and over to the north. She'll fix you up good as new. Tell her I sent you, else she'll think you work for the bobbies. She's not cheap. But she's good. You'll be able to have children again for your husband—when you get one."

Sarah wiped her eyes.

"If it all goes well, I should see you at the next meeting on the twelfth?

"Yes," answered Sarah in a small voice.

"And me too," echoed Alice.

They all went to the door. Mrs. Schoen then looked at Sarah pointedly. "Why'd you come 'ere. To me, Aina? What made you think I could help you?"

Sarah looked around and shrugged.

"You probably thought since I live in this area, an' go to abolitionist meetings, an' have Negro friends, I'm part of a lower life culture."

Sarah said nothing.

"Well, I'm not. This house has been in the good Reverend's family for 86 years—enough time for us to see how some change isn't always for the good. I jus' want decency an' justice for all of England's citizens—the poor, the downtrodden, Negroes, an' the lost. Remember that when you're down here slumming—from Buckingham Palace."

Sarah was embarrassed, but nodded and hugged Elizabeth. Yes, she had indeed been an elitist. Her life in the palace had only strengthened her one overriding view of the world even though she came from another. She was no different from the poor people outside Elizabeth Schoen's door and she did assume Mrs. Schoen knew someone who could help her get rid of an unwanted baby because her home was in the middle of a demoralizing ghetto.

Then, as she and Alice got into their beautiful, upscale coach that belonged to the Queen of England, she thought perhaps she wanted to keep this baby. After all it was conceived in love. But as she looked around, while the coach took them four blocks away to Lemley Alley, she realized this area is where she might end up—she and her baby—after being evicted by Victoria and rejected by Sir Roger.

So her reality grew omnipresent, forcing her and Alice, trembling and scared to death, up the alley to the green door she was told belonged to Miss Jenkins.

After knocking several times, a large, older Jamaican woman came to the door and answered. "Yes…?"

"Are you Miss Jenkins?"

"Who wants ta know?"

"Me. I'm Sarah Bon…"

"Don' wanna know no last names."

"Well, I…I've come to…" Sarah showed her the paper with the address on it. "Mrs. Elizabeth Schoen told me I should come here."

The woman looked Sarah over. Then looked at Alice who was so scared she blurted out: "I'm not in trouble. I just came for support." She pointed to Sarah, "She's the one in trouble."

"Uh huh. How far along are yuh?"

Sarah shrugged. "I've missed three of my monthlies."

"You married?" asked Miss Jenkins.

Sarah shook her head.

Then the woman opened the door wider. "Come on. If Miss Elizabeth sent yuh, I'll do what I kin."

Sarah and Alice nervously entered the dark, depressing looking home and followed the woman to an area behind a well-worn green velvet curtain separating the front room from the examination room. They saw a rickety table, various medicines on a bookshelf, and another woman moaning on a bed obviously recuperating from a "procedure." Everything was bleak and disheartening. Old furniture, threadbare, moth-eaten rugs, and the stale odor of tinctures and elixirs hung in the air. It was all horrible to Sarah and Alice who were now holding hands.

"It'll cost yuh ten quid. Yuh got ten quid?"

It was a lot of money, but Sarah nodded having brought all the money Victoria had been giving her as an allowance. She opened her purse, counted out the amount and gave it to the woman.

Miss Jenkins stuffed the money down her bosom then found a sheet and spread it on the table. "Take off yer skirt an' pantaloons an' get on de table. Let's see wha' we got."

Sarah looked at Alice who teared up and was more at a loss for Sarah than Sarah. She helped her friend out of her clothes and Sarah got on the table. Miss Jenkins pushed, prodded and probed Sarah's stomach then demanded, "Open yer legs."

Though Sarah was embarrassed, she obliged. Soon, she felt Miss Jenkins' cold fingers probe inside her vagina. "Feels like yuh may be closer ta 12 weeks along," said the woman.

Then Sarah was horrified when she saw the woman wipe off a long metal instrument and bring it over. "What is that?" she asked trembling.

"It's called a Speculum," answered Miss Jenkins. "I'm going ta put it inside yuh ta open yuh up, so I kin take a closer look, then use a copper wire ta snip de fetus from de placenta. Yuh'll expel de fetus in a couple hours."

Sarah began to shake as she felt Miss Jenkins start pushing the Speculum inside of her. Soon, the degrading, humiliating procedure not only caused Sarah physical pain but mental anguish and suddenly she sat up shaking her head.

"No. Stop! Take it out!" She got off the bed and put on her pantaloons and clothes quickly. "I don't want to do this. No." She grabbed Alice's hand. "Let's go."

"Fine. But yuh ain't gettin' yer money back."

"Keep the money!"

Sarah and Alice ran as fast as they could out of the house, down the alley and into their carriage.

"Take us back to Buckingham. Quickly!" Alice instructed the coachman. Sarah cried in Alice's arms all the way.

"What will you do, now?" asked Alice. "I don't know," Sarah sobbed. "But I couldn't let her continue to hurt and degrade me like that. I'll have to explain it to your mother—but I'll have to find a way to have this baby."

Her Royal Highness Princess Alice
(circa, 1870)

Twenty Nine

A lice and Sarah's coach came through the St. George's gate and stopped. Alice immediately went up the back stairs unseen while Sarah entered through the side entrance and came down the hall headed toward the front stairs.

Suddenly she heard:

"A moment please, Miss Bonetta…"

Sarah froze, then slowly turned to find Lord John Breadlebane with a grave expression on his face and employing a tone that indicated seriousness.

"…Her Majesty and the Prince Consort wish to see you in the Queen's office. They said as soon as you returned you were to go straight away."

Now I panicked. They know, I thought. They know about my pregnancy and my plans to end it. Either Alice alerted them earlier, or Lady McBurney told them about my clothes being too tight or the vomiting, or they just guessed correctly. I was worried. How would I tell them? How would I be treated? What would happen to me now? As Lord John announced me and I came into Victoria's cluttered office, I could see Victoria and Albert were solemn. I could feel that things were not right from the moment they turned to me. "Sit down, Sally," said Victoria somberly.

I sat as Victoria came from around the desk she shared with Albert to help divide her voluminous amount of correspondence and Parliamentary business. "What is it, ma'am? Lord John said you wished to see me."

"Yes. I have dreadful news, Sally. Captain Forbes..." Victoria hesitated. "...Captain Forbes...is dead."

Sarah slowing sank into one of the chairs as Victoria looked at her. Though there was a level of relief it wasn't about her pregnancy, what it *was* about devastated her, and her eyes welled with tears.

"No. No. What happened?"

Victoria attempted to answer but couldn't since she was keenly aware—especially in Sarah's presence—that hers and Parliament's decision to deploy ships to Crimea was a direct result of his death.

Sensing Victoria's vulnerability in that moment, Prince Albert immediately came to her aid. "He had been wounded by Gezo—and his leg became gangrenous. But once he and his ships were deployed to Crimea, he was unable to recover. He's been buried at sea." Albert never believed in sugarcoating hard truths—even such truths as death.

"He's dead, and I am alive," whimpered Sarah crestfallen, realizing the irony that this man who saved her from beheading at the command of the manic King Gezo, would himself die as a result of a last attempt to stop Gezo's slave trading. She also realized she was in front of the woman who was at least partly responsible for Forbes not only being sent to Gezo again but not having time to properly heal because England sent him to Crimea. Sarah's tears rolled down her face—a face that had become hardened.

Almost as if she was reading Sarah's mind, Victoria came over and touched her shoulder.

"I know you're angry we can't do more because our ships are in Crimea," she said sincerely conciliatory. But Victoria couldn't go on because she herself was on the verge of tears.

"But Forbes' death has finalized my decision," offered Prince Albert sensing that his beloved was internally struggling. "I am going to lend my voice to the voiceless."

Sarah looked at him curiously through her tears.

Albert looked at Victoria who nodded as he continued to Sarah. "As you suggested, Victoria and I are planning an event. We will invite French Emperor Louis-Napoleon, Peers, MP's and others here to Buckingham where I will speak out against the Trade."

Sarah looked at Victoria who nodded that it was indeed the truth. Then she lowered her head and teared up again. This time, Victoria knelt next to Sarah, lifted her goddaughter's head and peered into her eyes.

"But you are going to speak first Sally, then you will introduce Albert," Victoria declared with a hushed smile.

Sarah was disbelieving. "Me...? In front of everyone?" she asked through her grief.

Victoria and Albert exchanged looks of muted relief, that her reaction wasn't as they feared it might be, which was to refuse to speak and rail against them.

"I'm sure it's like playing your violin," Albert smiled. "Except that instead of musical notes we hear, it will be your powerful words we heed." He turned to Victoria, then looked back at Sarah. "So, invite the abolitionists—those speakers of whom you are so fond," he stated genuinely. "Ask them to speak. I plan to honor Forbes there."

Sarah's tears flowed again, but this time with joy that neither Captain Forbes nor his death would not go unnoticed for all that he'd done for the British Anti-Slave Trade...and for her. She would worry about her personal problem later.

Three days later, Sarah and Winston were sitting in St. James's Park on a blanket for their lesson. Winston had brought wine and for some reason was better dressed than usual. Sarah wanted to ask him to speak at Buckingham the way he had done when they first met, and he impressed her, but she was still mourning the death of the "foster" father who rescued her.

"Captain Forbes was the one who saved me—who protected me. He brought me here to this new life, and I've missed him," she said, looking at Winston intensely. "Please come to Buckingham, Winnie. Give one of your talks."

Winston nodded. "I'll come. But I don't know about speaking out. That crowd is very different from the ones at Phillips."

"But more influential. Your speech could inspire so many others to act worldwide."

Winston just looked at her. She was always teaching. Instructing others on how to be better, more powerful, to live their best lives. And yet he only wanted to live his with her. He reached into his pocket and pulled out a small wooden figure.

"I carved a Mawa for you. I made it from the piece of Baobab tree I kept around my neck from Africa."

Sarah gasped. "I've seen this piece of wood around your neck. You're never without it. Winnie, it's beautiful."

It was only a matter of time now, he thought, as he placed the Mawa he carved around her neck. "It has brought me luck. So I carved it to bring luck to you—for the rest of your life," Then he looked away. "And to think of me on occasion."

"Thank you. I'm touched."

Suddenly, Winston found himself in a strange place and he couldn't look at her. "I miss the smell of Africa after a rain. Don't you? I also miss the taste of my mother's salted pork with corn and cassava." He smiled slightly at the memory.

Sarah smiled at his memory too. It used to be that the memories of others about their families only evoked a deep sense of pain for Sarah and were too often depressing to her. She had found a way to suppress the memories of her own African life with her family prior to being captured by Gezo's warriors, and her life in Freetown which she loved, and only thought of her English life as though she were born again. But when Winston spoke of his African life, it was almost like hearing the story of a fairytale place, in a distant land she had once visited but was unable to see again.

"Tell me, more about your mother."

"She was a potter," he started, thinking back to the woman who had given him birth. "An artist, really. An' she made wonderful bowls for cookin'. Almost everyone in the village had her plates and bowls," he adoringly recalled. "And could she dance!" he laughed. So did Sarah. "She had dancin' hips. They'd swing from side to side and I remember all of the men in my village sneaking looks but making sure my father didn't catch them. She was a looker. A real beauty." Finally, he turned to Sarah. "Like you. Oh, how she would've loved you," he smiled. Then he became serious. "But then anyone meetin' you loves you."

Sarah was not oblivious to Winston's subtext and went into teacher mode. "MeetinG. Please put "G's" on the end of your words," she reminded him. You must speak the King's English correctly."

Acutely aware she was avoiding his intent, he took another tact causing him to break the promise he'd made to himself months and months ago not to push the issue of his feelings for her. Even as the words came out of his mouth, he was hating himself for saying them.

"My 'King's English' words. But have you forgotten our real words?" he asked. "Our real language?" He then spoke to her in Fon:

"*I want to protect you...like Forbes did. Don't avoid me. Marry me. You know I love you. You have to know that by now.*"

Though it was always a comfort to hear her native language spoken to her on those rare occasions it had happened since leaving Africa, it did not allay the uncomfortable response she had to give Winston as she answered him in Fon. *"Yes. But I can't. It's not possible. It cannot be you, Winnie."*

"Why not?"

"I just can't."

Winston was crushed. *"Is there someone else?"* he asked in English.

Sarah looked away. It took her a moment for she knew the truth—that she was in love with Sir Roger and had not only missed him every day he had been gone to war but was now secretly carrying his child.

"I don't know. Maybe." Then she confessed. *"Yes. There is someone else."*

Winston became silent feeling a deep sense of betrayal that Sarah, in all this time, had never shared with him the existence of "someone else."

"Who? Where is he?"

Sarah hesitated not wanting to say but knowing she wouldn't lie to Winston either.

"He's at war in Crimea. He's a Captain."

Winston drew back almost in disgust. "Only white men are officers in the military."

Sarah tried to hide her surprise that Winston correctly guessed that her "someone else" was white. "Yes. That's true. But there are many blacks serving and fighting. There is even a black woman nurse, Mary Seacole, helping to heal the wounded both black and white."

"But *your* man…is white."

Sarah finally nodded slightly.

There was a long pause as Winston had a sip of the wine he had brought. He could not look her in the eye.

"I suppose the Queen chose him for you—since we black men are not good enough for her goddaughter?"

This question triggered Sarah's ire. "Black men *are* good enough—and the Queen doesn't choose for me."

Winston glared at her with deep disappointment.

"You always defend her. Don't you realize the Queen has influenced your every move since you left Africa?"

Sarah was taken aback. She'd never perceived Victoria as influencing her every move, as much as offering Sarah various paths and ideas to choose from to enhance her life in England—an enhanced life now ruined by the death of Forbes and a pregnancy by Roger.

"No, the Queen has not influenced my every move," she snapped.

Winston adamantly shook his head in disagreement. "The life you lead, how you dress, who you are, how you think, the man you want—they're all choices based on her influence."

"I have influenced her just as much."

On that declaration, which from his perspective was another of Sarah's misguided assertions, Winston chose his words carefully to make sure they resonated with her. "Let me use the language of the colonizers that I know you understand—the 'King's' English," he groused. "The language of slaveholders, slave traders, hypocrites—and that white Captain you think you love."

Sarah did not appreciate his sarcasm and folded her arms around herself as he stood up glaring at her with nostrils flared. It sent chills through her.

"Slaves don't influence their masters," he seethed. "And you are enslaved, Sarah. Indeed, your shackles may be gold. But they are still shackles…" Then he spat out the words she would never forget: "…House Negro!"

At that, he walked off in anger and frustration leaving Sarah stewing in her many decisions she now wondered if were truly her own—or the Queen's influence on her. It made her angry.

Everything. All of it infuriated me. Suddenly I ran after Winston with a coil of fever, nightmares, and agony raging inside me and my stomach churning. "Damn you, Winston, "I yelled. "You do not know anything about my life. You don't get to pass judgement on me! Come back!" I ran faster. But I couldn't find him anymore. Somehow, I'd lost him in the crowd near the pagoda on the bridge spanning St. James's Canal. "Winnie!" I called out running first on the lawn of the park, then climbing the stairs on the east bank of the bridge heading toward the west.

Then I saw him. He was marching away still in his angry menagerie of disappointment. "Winston!" I yelled again. He turned and saw me. But then he kept going.

I ran across the bridge to the descending brick stairs toward him. "Stop!" I demanded. Again, he turned around. But the heel of my shoe caught the hem of my dress and I instantly lost my footing and fell down the stairs. Winston's face—and the world—suddenly contorted and spun around me, becoming one enormous blurry jumble. With one false move, I collapsed head first falling like a rag doll, hurling, tumbling and striking every step until all there was left was total darkness, dead silence, and the twisted wreckage of my own body.

The bridge, pagoda, and stairs spanning St. James's Canal where Sarah fell.

Thirty

 ueen Victoria was pacing with tears in her eyes as Dr. Brown examined Sarah in the medical room—the same one in which Sarah had been treated after her ordeal at the Chambers School. Bloody towels were collecting in a nearby basket and Dr. Brown was placing bandages on Sarah's left wrist and head. Sarah herself was unconscious.

"Will she be alright?" asked a distraught Victoria. "Will her wounds heal?"

"They will, ma'am. Her wrist and ankle will take a little time. But the bruising and swelling on her head, arms and legs should go down in a fortnight or so." Dr. Brown then wiped the blood off of his hands and turned to Victoria. "As for the other, well, she was lucky. The Lord took care of it."

Alice was there too, sitting on a chair crying as she rocked back and forth in dismay.

"But how did it happen? Why was she in the park in the first place?" Victoria questioned.

"You should ask the young man who brought her here."

Victoria frowned, "Who?"

"He's been in the hall this whole time." Brown continued.

"And I daresay may be responsible," Victoria retorted angrily as she went to the door and called out to Lord John. "Fetch that young Negro man and take him to the Parlor now. I will be there directly."

Lord John bowed and left.

Though upset, Alice tried to calm Victoria down. "Mother, I don't think you should be rash with Winston. After all…"

"'*Winston*'? Victoria exclaimed in shock before Alice could finish, "Do you know this young man?"

Now Alice was caught. "N-not directly, she lied. "But I've heard Sally speak of him. I just assumed that's who brought her here."

"So he *is* responsible for this!" Now Victoria was angrier than ever. "And all the time she had me believing she was going to abolitionist meetings to help end the Slave Trade. Instead, she's been cavorting with Black men in parks for anyone in London to see."

"Not true, mother. Winston is Sarah's friend *from* the abolitionist meetings."

"Yes. A *friend* who obviously impregnated her!" Victoria became steely and turned to Dr. Brown. "Breathe a word of this to anyone and I will have you sacked with a bad reference. I will not have this matter known."

"Yes, your Majesty," nodded the doctor.

Victoria then left the room as Alice looked at Dr. Brown wringing her hands. "Oh God. This is all wrong. It's so not true."

"I'm afraid it is, your Highness. Sarah lost the child when she fell. But there *was* a child."

"But…" Alice stopped and looked away tearfully. She didn't know whether to tell the truth or protect Sir Roger and say nothing.

She decided to say nothing.

Meanwhile Victoria marched into the Parlor where an unsuspecting Winston Benjamin immediately bowed respectfully. "Your Majesty…"

"…You scoundrel," Victoria spat.

Winston didn't understand and frowned. "W-What…?"

"How dare you show your face here at Buckingham after what you've done."

Winston's head dropped. "I'm sorry Majesty. I should not have left her alone. I walked away, then she came after me and fell. I've been so distraught."

"As you should be. Running away from a woman who tells you she's having your child and you leave her alone in the middle of St. James's Park to hurt herself…"

Now Winston shook his head disbelieving. "Having my child? What are you talking about?"

"You'll be happy to know she lost it. But I should have you arrested—for rape, or…"

"…Majesty, what child? I've never touched her. We were in the park because she was upset about Captain Forbes' death. She wanted me to come here and speak at some event you're having. Then I stupidly asked her to marry me and we had an argument…"

"Marry you? Marry *you*?" Victoria was incredulous. "A brilliant, educated woman brought up in the great palaces of England? Marry *you*?"

Though insulted, Winston was still reeling from the news of Sarah's pregnancy. "She's been teaching me how to read and write. I know she's too far above me, Majesty. But I've never touched her. She turned me down. She said…" Suddenly he realized and had to sit down. His head falling into his hands. "…She told me she was in love with some white officer serving in Crimea. Oh God…"

"It's true," they heard from behind them.

When Victoria turned Alice was there. She came over and immediately went to Winston. She hugged him which shocked Victoria. Winston looked at her.

"You knew? About the baby?" Winston asked in a low, hurt voice.

Alice nodded. "I guessed correctly. It was a secret between us as friends. She didn't know what to do She was scared."

Alice then went to her mother who was overwrought. "It was Roger's child, Mother."

Victoria looked away. "And you felt you couldn't tell me."

"It wasn't my secret to tell. It was Sally's. And she wasn't ready yet. She thought you would hate her—or worse, throw her out to fend for herself."

Victoria nodded, then after a quiet regretful look to Winston left the room as a long impenetrable silence engulfed the parlor.

Finally, Winston looked at Alice. "May I see Aina?"

"She's still unconscious," Alice answered somberly.

"But she'll be alright, won't she? I mean, she won't die."

Alice took Winston's hand. "The doctor says she should pull through. We'll pray, Winston."

"Yes. We'll pray very hard."

And the two hugged.

"Expectant!?" bellowed Prince Albert in shock when Victoria told him. later. "It can't be!"

Victoria was sitting in her bedroom suite staring off. But Albert paced furiously. "Sarah is too serious a girl. She would never do anything so foolish like allowing herself to become pregnant."

"The heart is a capricious organ, Albie," said Victoria teary-eyed. "I mistook the young man who brought Sally here after her accident for the man who impregnated her. But the child is Sir Roger's."

"Sir Roger Carlyle?" Albert exclaimed.

"And Alice knew all about it—yet chose not to tell us out of deference for Sally's feelings."

Albert shook his head. "I will give Alice a good talking to. And I'll send her to Germany if I have to." Then he paused in disappointment.

"But Sir Roger? If that man survives the war I assure you he will never be allowed at any of our palaces again."

"Oh yes he will, Albie," said Victoria ruefully. "I'll not have him punished for what nature urges us all to do. I'm just grateful, sad to say, that Sally's fall ended the unwarranted consequence of the situation. It could have all been so much worse."

Victoria held out her hands for Albert who came over and took them. "That is why we must get both Alice and Sarah married off to appropriate men as soon as possible. What's happened to Sally gives us a second chance to make proper arrangements."

The Prince Consort nodded. "Prince Louis sent a note telling us he will be here for the Ball. That takes care of Alice."

"And Bertie tells me he's been in contact with an African man I think will be perfect for Sally. Let's make it work. No matter what."

Albert kissed her forehead. "Then consider the matter closed."

Victoria nodded in agreement. "We won't speak of it."

Two days later Sarah finally awoke from her unconscious state. She looked around groggily and realized she was in Buckingham's medical room. Finally, when the fuzzy images she saw cleared, it was Alice, asleep in a corner chair having exhausted herself watching over her, that came into focus. Though feeling woozy Sarah tried to sit up but found she could not sustain herself and fell back upon the pillows from pain. Alice awoke and quickly came to Sarah's aid, placing a wet cloth to her forehead.

"What happened?" Sarah whispered.

"You took quite a spill and have some injuries. Your ankle is sprained and so is your wrist."

Sarah could now see the bandages and felt her head which was aching.

"I'll fetch Dr. Brown." Alice ran from the room while Sarah examined her body—her bandaged wrist and ankle, her head—then she felt her stomach which was terribly sore.

"I'm afraid you've sustained some internal injuries, Sarah," said Dr. Brown as he came into the room with the Queen and Alice. "You'll need full bed rest for a fortnight."

Dr. Brown then looked over at Victoria who gave both he and Alice a quick look indicating they should go. The good doctor left along with Alice. Victoria moved a chair to Sarah's bed and held Sarah's good hand.

"Are you in much pain?"

Sarah nodded, then sighed. "How did I get here?"

"A young man, Winston I think his name is, carried you here from across St. James's Park. He stayed here the last two days not wanting to leave."

Sarah looked away. "I..I remember running after him and I tripped down some stairs."

"I know." Then Victoria let go of Sarah's hand. "I also know about the baby."

Sarah was rendered speechless, and it took her a moment as she searched the Queen's face for any sign of forgiveness. "Majesty…"

"…You lost the baby, Sarah. Sir Roger's baby."

Her words stunned Sarah. The baby. Roger's baby—was gone. She'd lost it. And worse, the Queen knew all about it. Sarah sank further into the pillow in despair, knowing this was God's punishment.

"As soon as I'm better, I'll leave, Majesty. I do not wish to bring shame or any scandal upon you or this family when you've all been so kind. This is all my fault."

"Yours and Roger's. A man I know you love."

Sarah nodded. Victoria took Sarah's hand again. "I cannot say I condone illegitimacy. But I will tell you a story, she began. "My favorite aunt was Princess Sophia, fifth daughter of my grandfather King George III. She died only seven years ago, and I miss her terribly. I always wished she was my mother, instead of my own. Aunt Sophia was a lonely child as all of the girls born to King George were. And it didn't help that the King's recurring bouts of madness stopped all would-be suitors from coming forward with offers of matrimony.

When she was 15 years old, my aunt was raped by her eldest brother, my uncle Ernest Augustus, Duke of Cumberland. She became pregnant, and it ruined her life. They sent her away to have the baby of that awful incestuous relationship. She was sent to Kensington Palace where I was being raised. Aunt Sophia was wonderful. But mother hated her because my aunt's wealth allowed mother's friend, Sir John Conroy, whom I hated, to live a rich lifestyle. She gave or loaned him enough money to acquire a house in Kensington for £4000, and other estates for £18,000. She was always looking for genuine affection, never found it—and never married. She never knew love. Ever." Victoria paused a moment.

"You see, my dear, a scandal dashes all hope for a successful life. The whispers and gossip change and affect you. And it goes on for your whole life. That won't happen to you. You were already taken by force by that terrible Headmaster at school whose name I shall never speak aloud. But you also know what it is like to give yourself over to love."

Victoria stood. "You didn't know it at the time. But had you come to me and told me of your 'situation,' I would have told you this story, and provided you with a safe place at one of our estates for your lying-in. I would never have forsaken you—because of what my aunt experienced—and because, believe it or not, I love you. You are everything I hold to myself as dear, Sally. In the future, be careful where you place the love you share with someone else. Do you understand?"

Sarah nodded. Her eyes filled with tears. Then Victoria did something she had not done since Sarah arrived. She hugged Sarah.

"Now. Get better. You have a speech to give next month. We shall never discuss this matter again."

And they never did.

Thirty One

One month later, a six-carriage ceremonial cortège pulled into the main gate of Buckingham. A full complement of footmen and stewards awaited the retinue as it came to a stop. When the door of the main carriage opened, outstepped French Emperor Louis-Napoleon Bonaparte III.

The handsome commanding sovereign of France turned and offered his hand to his new wife, Empress Eugenie—a stunning thin woman with dark curly hair and the most ornate diamonds and other exquisite gems around her neck. This was the cue for his retinue to exit from their respective carriages.

Napoleon, Eugenie and the entourage entered the palace where Queen Victoria, Prince Albert and her family stood in official formation to receive them as Lord John announced: "French Emperor Louis-Napoleon Bonaparte III and Empress Eugenie."

Napoleon bowed, and Eugenie curtsied to Victoria who was almost jealous of the impressive jewels Empress Eugenie wore. It took her aback momentarily. But she recovered with no one suspecting.

"You honor us with this visit, Emperor," said Victoria.

"We, too, are honored, Majesty," Napoleon warmly responded with his distinctive French accent. "My wife and I have been counting the hours to this moment."

Victoria then turned to Lord John, "Make sure the Emperor and Empress have everything they need in their suites." She then turned to Napoleon. "We have given you the Luxembourg suite of rooms. We thought you'd like the idea of that."

Napoleon grinned. "I'm sure it will all be satisfactory, Majesty."

The emperor and his wife followed behind Sir Ian and went up the stairs toward their suite as Victoria looked after them. When they were out of earshot she turned to Albert.

"Did you see Empress Eugenie's jewels? They were spectacular." She then motioned to Lady Sutherland, her Lady-in-Waiting.

"We absolutely must rethink the gown and jewels I'll be wearing tonight. I shall not have that beautiful woman upstage me in my own palace."

Lady Sutherland grinned. "I think we should go with the teal silk and the Queen Elizabeth crown jewels. Also, we should do a feather in your hair for added accent."

Victoria smiled. "Let's get to it shall we? Send Sir Nigel in to start with my hair."

"Majesty, I think your formal white wig is better for this evening," Lady Sutherland insisted. "We need volume, drama...and most especially height for this occasion."

Victoria chuckled, for Lady Sutherland was correct. Based on her diminutive size, tonight was a time to exude power, wealth and unmistakable presence.

Meanwhile, upstairs in her suite, while activity was on-going throughout the palace with all the members of the aristocracy expected tonight, Sarah looked at herself in the mirror. The swelling on her head had subsided and any residual bruising had been covered up with make-up by Lady McBurney. The bandages were off of her wrist and ankle, but both were still sore, and she knew she would be dancing tonight. So, she had been careful not to put much pressure on either these last days.

Then there was a knock followed by Barnes who entered with a letter on a tray he gave her and left. Sarah smiled when she looked at it. It was from Sir Roger—and she read it.

"Dear Sarah. I am with my regiment near Sebastopol where our Allied forces have fought the first major battle of the Crimean campaign. It has been hard for there has been a widespread cholera outbreak in our encampments. I cannot write often and do not know if my letters even reach you, but my thoughts are filled with you. I think about our last days together at Garden Pavilion. I miss your eyes, your lips, the way our bodies entwine, and I keep asking God to allow me to come home, so we may have the life together I so desire. Pray for me, Sarah. I love you…Roger."

Sarah smiled again and hid the letter in her leather diary tied with ribbon and tucked it away in a drawer. She prayed the same prayer as Roger—that he would safely make it back to be with her. She missed him and was finding the void of his absence unlivable, and as she perused herself in the mirror again she wished Roger could see her. Lady McBurney had dressed her exquisitely in a peach colored satin chiffon gown with Queen Anne's lace trimming the neckline and the sleeves. To add interest, Sarah placed Winston's mawa around her neck so she would have just a hint of Africa visible.

Then, as she caressed it, she thought about Winston. How terrible it had all been—and how she would probably never see him again since the accident. How foolish for her to think he might come tonight after learning of her debauchery.

Alice had told her the whole story. About Winston being accused by the Queen of being the one to impregnate her, and how hurt he was to learn of it. She knew he would never look at her the same way again, just as his learning about Roger in the first place caused him pain, their argument, and ultimately her accident. Poor Winston didn't deserve it, she thought. And she wished him well and put any thoughts of seeing him again out of her mind.

But she was still filled with dread. Victoria's revelation about her aunt had moved Sarah and she was somewhat glad she had not jeopardized her life by going through with the procedure in Lemley Market Alley. The trouble was, something Bertie said to her one evening after dinner two weeks ago was still worrying her.

While she was still on a cane and about to step outside the palace to take in the night air with a glass of claret, Bertie asked if he could help her. It was not like him, but she'd nodded affirmatively. He took her good arm and she leaned into him for support as they came out and stood on the small south balcony overlooking the rose garden.

After a few moments, as they were sipping wine, he spoke to her but did not look at her directly.

"I am truly sorry for your injuries, Sarah. I wouldn't wish an accident causing medical attention on anyone—not even my mortal enemy." he began, "But in the future, come to me should you find yourself in the kind of trouble causing you to need help in Lemley Alley."

Now Sarah froze, staring at him nervously. Bertie kept his attention forward sipping his wine. "You see, these situations come up frequently in my world—and I keep a woman on salary who takes care of such matters without the prying eyes of gossipmongers." He finally looked at Sarah. "That way you will not require my sister, Her Royal Highness Princess Alice of England to escort you into unseemly areas of London where she could be recognized, and engender untoward actions like blackmail for example, which could befall my mother, the Queen."

Sarah trembled. "Bertie, I'm mortified," she said in a small voice.

"I know I am an unlikable man to you and I am fine with that. But I love my mother. No matter how cruel she is to me, I do not want anything preventable to bring low her reign. Nor would I want my dear friend Roger to suffer any indignation because he could not keep his prick from the second-class likes of you, however smart and talented you are." He finished his wine in a gulp. "So, come to me—with your inevitable low-life problems, and I'll see what I can do."

He started off leaving Sarah there upset and worried. But he turned back. "And don't worry about Miss Jenkins. She—and her loose tongue—were taken care of." He left.

Two days ago, Sarah learned that the body found floating face down in the Thames, thought to be a suicide, was that of the Jamaican abortionist Abigail Jenkins. There was no investigation. Miss Jenkins was just another black nobody in London—who was now dead.

So goes the power of royalty—in which Sarah lived. She turned away from her reflection and took a deep breath. It was time to rehearse her speech. Time for her to pretend 'All's right with the world in the Palace of Buckingham.' The Slave Trade had to end, and Sarah needed to be the unblemished, unsullied face…of the "Queen's experiment."

That evening, candlelight in the Grand Ballroom flickered on all the fabulous gems. It was a spectacular view of hundreds of aristocrats and noblemen representing most of Europe's royal houses. Indeed, a line of nobles and landed gentry had formed to greet Victoria and Albert as Lord John announced them.

Alice, Princess Victoria and Prince Arthur stood to Victoria's left, and the Duchess of Kent, Bertie and Princess Louise were to the right of Albert. This was European monarchy at its best.

"…The Duke of Manchester," bellowed Lord John.

The Duke bowed before Victoria and Albert and the royal assembly line continued.

"Prince Friedrich Wilhelm of Prussia," announced Lord John.

The Prince bowed before the Queen and winked at Vicky.

"I see you've returned, Prince Friedrich," the Queen remarked.

Alice leaned into her sister. "So…he's back to see you."

"Yes," smiled Vicky with a subtle returned wink to Fritz. "He wrote he was coming."

"…The Duke and Duchess of Suffolk," announced Lord John, and the procession of nobles continued until:

"…Prince Ludwig Friedrich Karl IV of Hesse Darmstadt."

The awkward, slightly overweight, twenty-eight-year-old Prince Louis bowed and kissed Victoria's hand. The Queen glanced at Alice just to her left.

"I am so glad you could come, Your Highness," smiled Victoria. "Princess Alice, my daughter here, cannot wait to meet you."

Alice tried to suppress a subtle "I can't?" look. She knew her mother and now she knew the Queen was up to something that involved her and this Prince—and she was peeved.

Sarah, dressed exquisitely in her peach gown, was among other guests watching the wonder of it all. Barnes handed her a glass of juice, bowed and then winked. She grinned and moved through the crowd—nodding to those she knew, introducing herself to others she didn't. Then she froze.

From across the room she saw him. Their eyes locked and he instantly walked over managing a smile. Sarah smiled too. Winston was smashing in a black brocade jacket, a waistcoat with notched lapels, a gold pocket watch strung across the waistcoat, and velvet trousers.

"Winnie, you look very handsome this evening," said Sarah.

"Thank you. Because I'm scared to death and uncomfortable."

"Why?"

"This suit belongs to Mr. Phillips."

"It can't be! Mr. Phillips is a size larger than you!" exclaimed Sarah looking it over. "This looks like a perfect fit."

"Yes, because I've been sewn into it."

They both laughed.

"Well, I'm glad you went through the trouble for this occasion. Thank you," Sarah smiled. "I didn't think you would come given our last time we were together."

Winston squeezed her hand. "I promised you I'd come. And I won't break a promise," he said looking at her feeling all the love in his heart he had for her. "You look beautiful. How do you feel?"

"I've been better—in so many ways."

He nodded. She took his hands. "Winnie, I know you know—about me…and the baby."

Winston nodded and looked away. "Sir Roger's baby."

She turned his face back toward her. "Thank you for bringing me back home so I could be treated."

But Winston shook his head. It all began to churn up in him again even though he was aware of where he was and had promised himself to behave if only for one evening—because he loved her.

"Yes. Back *home*. Home to the godmother who immediately accused me of getting you pregnant probably because I'm Negro. The Queen who said you were too far above me for me to marry. Yes. I brought you back home."

But Sarah would not engage his outburst. "We are not going to fight tonight," she whispered firmly. "Not tonight. I'm better. You're here, and I appreciate that."

He looked at her. Why did she have to be so devastatingly beautiful, he thought gazing at her gown—the neckline of which showed off her bosoms and his mawa which was handsomely present.

"You're wearing the mawa."

"Yes. I love it."

Winston thought about what he wanted to say. "Aina. I apologize. The things I said that day…"

But Sarah stopped him. "…It's forgotten. Let us move forward."

"But I know it hurt you, and I've been kicking myself these last weeks. Not seeing you has been so hard."

"It was something I needed to hear. You were honest."

"And then, my pride… it…"

She took his hand. "Shhhh. You're here. Just as I asked. That counts for everything.

"I did it all for you. Coming here, the clothes—all for you. For your forgiveness. Please forgive me."

But before she could answer, a strikingly dressed African man in a military uniform came forth and was announced by Lord John. The Grand Ballroom fell to a hush as this was not usual at Buckingham—or anywhere nobles gathered. Winston and Sarah wondered who this mysterious black man was—who looked vaguely familiar to Sarah.

"Lt. James Labulo Davies, of Sierra Leone," announced Sir John.

His name didn't register for Sarah or Winston, but Bertie leaned into Victoria and whispered, "The African from Liverpool."

Victoria brightened as she realized this was the man she wanted for Sarah. "Ah, Lt. Davies," she beamed with her hand outstretched. "Welcome to Buckingham Palace."

With erudite airs of sophistication, James Davies bowed and kissed the Queen's hand. "Greetings, your Majesty, your royal Highness. My heartfelt appreciation for allowing me to attend this auspicious gathering," he said respectfully with a slight African accent. "Later I hope you will allow me to present a gift from Africa to these festivities."

Victoria liked him already. She smiled at Bertie then at Sarah, who returned the smile, but was clueless as to the connection the Queen was determined to make.

Later, as the guests were enjoying themselves, Victoria knew it was time to get to the purpose of the gathering. She stepped before the crowd and everyone became quiet. "Many of you have met my young goddaughter and heard her play here at Buckingham," she said. "But tonight, she has a message to share along with the Prince Consort. Please join me in welcoming Sarah Forbes Bonetta."

Sarah's heart began to beat so loudly it almost drowned out everything else as she stepped in front of the gathering. She cleared her throat and looked out at the sea of influential faces.

"Lords, Ladies and all invited guests here," she began. "We are experiencing a worldwide crisis requiring our humanity and our grace. Our researchers tell us that the yearly loss of life caused by the Slave Trade has now increased to twenty-five percent. Hundreds of thousands of Blacks are annually reduced to slavery with over a quarter of a million dying in the middle passage. The loss to Africa, a rich proud continent bursting with oil, gold, diamonds, and so many natural resources, is incalculable..."

As she spoke, she could see various guests nodding in approval. Winston beamed with pride, as did Victoria. Even James Davies looked at her intrigued as she continued. "...and Africa is capable of so much more than her dark offspring beaten into submission as human mules. So, I would ask that those of you from countries still engaged in the practice, stop," she implored. The guests from those countries looked uncomfortable, but Sarah didn't care. Her mission was more important than a few bruised feelings.

"And those of you with caring hearts stop purchasing the goods gleaned from the broken backs of my people. An open market can be created worldwide for the benefit of us all—if we just put our heads together toward the higher good," she emphasized in closing.

The Grand Ballroom erupted into sustained applause. Sarah smiled, "And now, to truly expound upon this, I would like to present His Royal Highness Prince Albert."

She stepped back to the applause for Albert that thundered throughout the Grand Ballroom as he came forward.

"Thank you, Miss Bonetta," he said warmly smiling at her. "In 1840,

I was induced to preside as president of *The Society for the Extinction of the Slave Trade*, from a conviction of its paramount importance to the great interests of humanity. And to justice. I deeply regret that the benevolent and persevering exertions of England to abolish that atrocious traffic in human beings, at once the desolation of Africa and the blackest stain upon civilized Europe, have not as yet led to any satisfactory conclusion. I sincerely trust that this great country will not relax its efforts until it has finally, and forever, put an end to a state of things so repugnant to the spirit of Christianity, and the best feelings of our nature. Friends, the deliverance of Africa lies in three parts. One: Africans must be taught that capturing and selling their own makes them as culpable as slave traders buying their victims. Two: They must embrace Christianity—the best cure for Godlessness…"

Albert stated this with such admonishment that Winston grunted as Sarah joined him. "Yes. Impose your religion on countries with their own," he said snidely under his breath.

"…And three," continued Prince Albert, "was suggested by a man we respected whom we posthumously honor this evening—our own Captain Frederick E. Forbes."

Applause echoed throughout the crowd for Captain Forbes as Sarah remembered Forbes praying, teaching and protecting her.

"Captain Forbes suggested that Africa learn to harness her own resources for profit. So, under my presidency of 'The Society…' we will strive to make the Africans aware of the benefits of free trade by profiting from their resources versus selling their own people…"

There were nods of agreements all over the room.

"…And, we will instruct the natives in agriculture and science, and show them how to cultivate their land so that they may imitate other great European nations."

Now Winston shook his head disgusted. His breathing began to change, and Sarah could see he was once again churning up toward an explosion. She became concerned for if this first step wasn't received well, it would have all been futile.

Meantime, white European guests were enthralled by Prince Albert as he continued: "So, let us therefore trust that Providence will prosper our efforts in so holy a cause, and that under the auspices of our Queen and Her Government, we may at no distant period be rewarded by the accomplishment of the great and humane object for the promotion of which we have this day met. Therefore, I ask that those of you present who have influence and power, choose the right side of history and refuse to purchase or condone the selling of flesh for money. Our race must show the Africans the better way. We must show them order, civilization, and indeed, the proper way of life!"

Rousing applause and cheers went up as Albert left the center of the room. However, there was no applause from James, who frowned, and none from Winston who shook his head fuming to Sarah.

"Must the European white man be the moral center of the world?" he snapped and then slid into plantation-speak. "Lawdy, what is we darkies 'spose to do wit'out him?"

Sarah was irritated by Winston's attitude. "Winston, stop. The Prince never spoke out before," she said, genuinely baffled by his response. "I think it's courageous and found his speech laudable."

"'Laughable', you mean," Winston snipped, once again shaking his head in disagreement.

But before Sarah could counter him, she felt a tap on her back. She turned to find Victoria standing there.

"Albert wrote his speech by himself," she said evenly trying not to show any emotion other than pride for her husband.

"He was quite good, Majesty," Sarah managed, hoping Victoria had not heard Winston's negative comments. So she quickly diffused Winston's ire with a formal introduction hoping he'd conduct himself cordially. "Majesty, may I formally present Winston Benjamin, a friend."

Winston bowed to Victoria, "Her Majesty and I… have met." He looked at the Queen pointedly. "It's a wonderful event, Majesty."

"It is, isn't it," said Victoria coolly, her eyes narrowing as she looked him over like a dangerous spider.

Grateful Winston did not challenge the Queen about Prince Albert's speech, or her accusatory attitude from before, Sarah found herself momentarily distracted by James Davies who went to the center of the room at the behest of Bertie and waved his hands for quiet.

"Kind sirs and gentle ladies," James began, looking intently at the audience. "For those who do not know, my name is Lt. James Pinson Labulo Davies of Sierra Leone, Africa—a progressive, self-sustaining and eclectic country in West Africa. As a son of Yoruba slaves freed by the British, I chose not to invert into a slave merchant but instead help the Anti-slavery Squadron of the Royal Navy…"

Suddenly it hit Sarah. She and James had met before. In Sierra Leone while she was at school there. They'd had a many-splendored walk together and he had promised to write her. But she was no longer there. Now her hand covered her mouth in shock.

"…While I agree with most everything the Prince Consort has said in his address to you," James continued, drawing in a deep breath and looking to Prince Albert with almost an apologetic expression for having to state what was needed to be said to this audience. "And I echo the sentiments that we must teach Africa what we can. But let us try to preserve her specialness. Let us be mindful that Africa is not, nor will ever be England or Europe. She is her own unique gift to the world…"

A smile formed on Winston's face. For a change, he was elated. He grinned at Sarah without a care that Victoria was just behind her. Someone finally said what these privileged aristocrats needed to hear, he thought—that Africa had a clear and genuine place in the world. One untethered to western conventions.

"Now, there's a Negro worth his salt," Winston commented.

To Sarah's surprise, Victoria put both of her hands on Sarah's shoulders leaning into her goddaughter. "Is Lt. Davies not marvelous?" she said excitedly then whispered. "I want you to dance with him later." Then with a chilly nod to Winston, Victoria whisked away to join Albert leaving Sarah flummoxed. She frowned to Winston. "What is going on?"

But Winston's focus was still on James who impressed him. "Imagine," he whispered leaning into Sarah with a kind of pride. "A fellow Yoruba who has come to this country and made a mark for himself. One that brings him enough respect to be invited to this palace and speak to this crowd by standing his ground for our people. I want to be like that."

"You *are* like that," Sarah encouraged. "And with your ability to read and write there is no telling where you will go. You already speak well in front of people. It's how I first came to be your friend."

Winston winced at the word "friend." It, coming from Sarah, his beloved, broke his heart. She may as well have said he was her favorite puppy or next-door neighbor. "Friend" meant the closeness he had so desired and needed her to feel for him would never be more than sustained "like." It would never move from admiration to love—which is what he felt for her—but what she felt for Sir Roger, and his countenance sank.

James Labulo Davies finished his announcement: "...And to underscore that sentiment, I have brought some dancers from Africa, to perform a ceremonial presentation created especially for this occasion..." he said proudly, then indicated Victoria and Prince Albert. "...And for their Majesties."

Just then, colorful dancers in feathers, beads and tribal makeup, ran into the Grand Ballroom. Guests moved to allow them space. Several drummers began to beat their drums and the dancers performed an exquisitely choreographed, athletic routine that left everyone awestruck. Sarah and Winston were grinning through the entire performance subtly swaying to the music and pulsating movements of the muscular men and unabashed women. When the performance was complete, the crowd burst into applause, including Emperor Napoleon who grinned and applauded the loudest. Victoria was speechless but thrilled as she looked at James with incandescent approval and nodded. James acknowledged her with a slight bow, but Bertie saw this and became disdainful. He had hoped James' little speech about Africa's uniqueness would have backfired so Victoria would send him away for challenging his father, and make him take Sarah with him. Instead, by his mother's overwhelming look of endorsement to James Davies for his 'gift' of performers, Victoria, Bertie felt, had now found another "black pet project."

Another "experiment."

The Princess Royal, Victoria (Vicky) Adelaide

Thirty Two

The evening's festivities wore on into the night as guests waltzed or chatted. Vicky and Fritz once again only had eyes for each other, while Bertie found some slight interest in Princess Alexandra Caroline of Denmark. Alice was happily chatting with Sir Michael McFerrin of Devonshire Downs, the very married Polo champion she liked, who flirted with every woman there as Queen Victoria brought Prince Louis over to her.

Prince Louis bowed and offered his hand to Alice to dance. Alice politely demurred—to the Queen's dismay. But before the Prince could walk away feeling dejected, Victoria pulled Alice from Sir Michael and pushed her to Prince Louis forcing them to dance rather awkward and tentatively together. Sarah saw it all as she and Winston wandered over to Prince Albert with Emperor Napoleon III and Empress Eugenie.

Once Victoria saw Alice and Prince Louis dancing, she set aside her royal matchmaking and approached Bertie and James.

"The performance was splendid," she gushed to James.

"Thank you, Majesty," said James as he genuflected to her.

Bertie grinned, "I told Mother of your good business reports as a merchant, Mr. Davies."

James modestly smiled, "I have been fortunate."

Victoria finally leaned closer to James to lay the groundwork for him to partake, unwittingly or not, in her plans for Sarah. "I understand that you are recently widowed, Mr. Davies.

"I am, ma'am. My dear wife died two years ago of consumption."

"Did Bertie mention there was a fellow Yoruba I wanted you to meet?" said the Queen coyly.

"He said you had an African goddaughter. I'll admit I was stunned, until I saw her just now and realized we have already met. In Sierra Leone.

Now Victoria was surprised. "Then you know she is as unique as you described Africa to this gathering."

James and Bertie followed Victoria's eyes as she looked at Sarah speaking with Prince Albert, Napoleon III, Eugenie and Winston.

Meanwhile, Sarah was praising Prince Albert. "You were 'manifique,' your Highness," she complimented as Winston stood there.

"Thank you, my dear. As were you." Prince Albert turned to Napoleon and Eugenie and gestured to Sarah, "The Queen's goddaughter, Sarah Bonetta."

Sarah curtsied, then said to Napoleon in perfect French,

"Votre Majesté, au nom des Noirs partout, je vous remercie d'avance pour votre soutien à notre cause. Un grand empereur comme vous, qui vole son propre destin de l'ombre de son oncle, est le plus louable."

As Prince Albert looked on proudly, Napoleon, Eugenie and Winston were in shock that Sarah was bilingual.

"Vous parlez notre langue maternelle très magnifiquement," said Eugenie, to which Sarah smiled, "Merci, Majesté, C'est presque une deuxième langue pour moi."

Winston was curious. "What did you to say to him?" he whispered quizzically to Sarah.

"I said that on behalf of blacks everywhere, I wanted to thank him for his support of our cause. That a great Emperor as he is, carving his own destiny from the shadows of a famous uncle, is commendable."

"Oh." Winston then turned to Napoleon. "I echo what she said."

Everyone laughed. Napoleon nodded to Prince Albert regarding Sarah. "The Queen's goddaughter is most impressive."

Prince Albert smiled. "She is indeed.

Across the room, Victoria transitioned their pleasantries to the real reason James had been invited to the palace.

"Mr. Davies, I will not keep you in suspense..." she began. "...It is of great importance to the Crown that a proper nuptial match is found for my goddaughter. One applying all the care for her well-being."

Now James became intrigued sensing where this was going.

"I had you researched," said Victoria. "And you are that man."

James was surprised. He wasn't offended that she researched him—his own success, and the caliber of his British, African and Afro-British social circles suggested he would make a fine match for any woman. But he was stunned that Bertie, standing there with a Cheshire cat grin at the opportunity to be rid of Sarah, hadn't been more truthful as to why he had invited James to Buckingham. After all—he was not to be procured like some paid Lothario on Dean Street. Still, it was the Queen who was encouraging this match with her goddaughter. How could he refuse? Especially when he was already besotted by her when she was younger.

Victoria almost read his mind. "Mr. Davies, I hope I am not encroaching on an already committed relationship." Then she offered with added emphasis: "Because it is also in the Crown's interest to ensure, and thus guarantee, your financial success—should you be interested in such a match."

James looked at her, as he got what she was saying—and smiled.

"While I've seen her loveliness—and, dare I say, feistiness—on display, may I formally meet this jewel of the motherland?"

310

Victoria returned his smile. "Come with me." She took his arm and walked him over to Sarah, Winston, Prince Albert and the Bonaparte's, who were engaged in conversation. Bertie followed behind.

Victoria caught Prince Albert's eyes and gestured toward the Bonaparte's and he subtly maneuvered in front of them carrying on their conversation in French. Before Sarah and Winston could detect what had happened, Victoria swept right up next to Winston.

"Mr. Benjamin, have you seen our gardens?"

Winston, completely caught off guard by her out-of-the-blue question shook his head. "No, Majesty. I haven't."

With a very specific look to Bertie which he completely understood, Victoria instructed, "Bertie, show Mr. Benjamin our gardens, please."

The Prince of Wales obliged and took Winston away—who felt like an intruding child. As he glanced back he saw Victoria nudge James toward Sarah, and finally understood the Queen's reason for his 'to the garden' dismissal.

Victoria smiled at James finally initiating her hope for the start of something special. "James Davies, Sarah Forbes Bonetta."

"Mr. Davies," Sarah said as she curtsied.

Seeing Sarah up close caused James' heart to race. He was awestruck by her beauty which had ripened. "Miss Bonetta," he said kissing her hand and looking deeply into her eyes, "You are more beautiful than when first we met."

"So you *do* remember?" Sarah blushed.

Victoria contained her elation, as she saw that Sarah finally noticed James was still holding her hand.

"As apparently do you. Would you like to dance?" he asked.

Sarah glanced at Victoria, who gestured her approval.

"I'd be delighted," said Sarah to James.

James escorted her to the dance floor where he took her left hand and immediately led her into a grand turn to the music. Though her wrist throbbed as James held it, and her ankle was killing her, the two waltzed as though they had been dance partners for years. Sarah actually enjoyed it, even though she suspected more was going on with him—and the Queen.

Eventually they danced past Alice and Prince Louis as they continued their own waltz. Sarah and Alice exchanged looks.

Seeing that Sarah was now in James' arms, Victoria approached Prince Albert and the Bonaparte's enjoying their conversation.

"I hope my husband has not bored you," Victoria teased.

"Not at all," Napoleon smiled. "In fact, if His Highness does not mind, I would like to ask Her Majesty for a waltz."

"I do not mind," grinned Albert. "But I defer to my Queen."

"The Queen desires to dance," Victoria smiled.

Napoleon held out his hand to Victoria which she took. They glided to the ballroom floor. After a few moments of waltzing, Victoria turned from her social agenda regarding Sarah and James to her political one.

"Majesty, you've been sending French weapons to West Africa in exchange for their not importing slaves to your country."

"Yes, and it has worked effectively."

"But the Africans use those weapons to intimidate and attack other African villages and sell their prisoners to other countries."

"My obligation is to France. Not other countries."

"Perhaps. But France and England are the greatest powers on Earth. So goes our countries, so goes the world. As an example, the war in Crimea which we were happy to assist you in. Maybe you can help us by amending your African policy to stay on the good side of..."

"...of England?" the Emperor quipped.

At that Victoria stopped dancing. "...Of history, Majesty," she stated firmly. "You see, we both have Africa to thank for our heritage. Me—and Queen Charlotte, my *mulatto* grandmother. You—and your *Creole* aunt, Empress Josephine."

Napoleon's concerned expression became one of bemusement. "You are a clever sovereign," he then looked at Sarah dancing with James. "With an equally clever goddaughter," he continued. "I shall extend an invitation for you to visit France—where we hope we may gain your support for some of our causes."

"Of course. It is what great countries, who are fierce allies, do for each other," Victoria smiled. "Je serais ravi."

Napoleon grinned. "I never tire of hearing my native tongue, when I'm away from home."

Albert danced Eugenie over to them, stopped and bowed to Eugenie with appreciation. "Thank you, Empress," he said.

"It was my honor," curtsied Eugenie.

Napoleon III kissed Victoria's hand as they exchanged an understanding look. He danced away with his wife.

Once they were far enough away, Albert turned to Victoria. "Well...?"

Victoria looked coy. "Let's just say, that the Emperor is a true patriot with the best for his country at heart."

"The two of you have that in common," Albert grinned.

"Among other things," mused Victoria, thinking of her reminder to Napoleon regarding their shared African ancestry.

On the other side of the ballroom, when the music stopped, Prince Louis gestured for he and Alice to go to one of the food tables laden with hors d'oeuvres which he tried.

"May we go riding tomorrow?" he asked as he accepted a glass of wine from a footman. "Or perhaps I could read some poetry to you. I'll be here two weeks before returning to Germany."

Though the prince was an amiable fellow, Alice was unexcited by any prospect of being with him—even though she knew her mother was manipulating the situation as she had done for Princess Vicky. Alice's royal duties required she consider the prince. But this droll man would never excite her, she thought. Not when compared to the fun she often had with Sarah—like their outing at a pub in the Grub area with Miyo and Winston. "Have I a choice?" she quipped, trying not to roll her eyes.

Prince Louis wasn't sure how to react and kept eating as Alice emitted a loud sigh.

Meanwhile, James and Sarah continued to converse as they waltzed. James looked down and commented on Sarah's necklace admiringly. "What an exquisitely carved Mawa. My mother had one many years ago. It is said to bring luck."

"Yes. This was carved for me by my friend, Winston. He's here."

"The man you were with when the Queen brought me to you?"

"Yes."

James thought a moment. He did not want to seem anxious but had to ask. "Is this Winston someone important to you? Because I would certainly like for the two of us to see more of each other?" Then he was pointed. "I know your godmother would avidly welcome it."

Suddenly, it was clear to Sarah what Victoria's agenda was and why she had gotten rid of Winston. James was the man she had chosen for her. The man Victoria deemed appropriate for the 'Goddaughter of the Queen of England.' A man who would take Sarah as far away from Sir Roger Carlyle as possible and Sarah was to have no say in it.

...Almost instantly his comment unraveled everything inside me. Dancing and making delightful small talk with me had not been of his own volition. It was all an arrangement and I knew now what to expect. After several more pleasant meetings James would ask me to marry him. Victoria would of course approve and provide a fine living for us, and the whole unpleasant situation with my unwanted pregnancy would genuinely be forgotten. The Queen would have her way—as she always did.

Sarah stopped dancing and dropped her hands. She became snippy.

"If not, Mr. Davies, my godmother would avidly welcome seeing more of you herself." Seething inside, she curtsied politely and left James standing on the dance floor as she navigated her way through the throngs of guests to find Alice.

James frowned as he looked after her and then searched for the Queen. She had to know things weren't going well—thus far.

When Winston's manipulated 'garden tour' with Bertie finally ended, he came back into the Ballroom. He moved as far away from Bertie as possible and looked for Sarah. When he found her, she was dancing with James. Then he looked over and saw Queen Victoria smiling at them as they danced. He, too, understood what was happening as he found himself once again immersed in his low social standing.

But then he saw Sarah curtsey and walk away from James. She appeared irked as she headed toward Alice across the room and Winston navigated through the crowd toward them.

Alice immediately knew something wasn't right when Sarah reached her. "What's wrong?"

"Your mother is playing us like my violin," Sarah fumed.

"Better," Alice lamented, indicating Prince Louis stuffing hors d'oeuvres down. "We're not obligated to marry your violin."

It was then Sarah looked over and saw Winston. She smiled.

Winston didn't. Instead, his smug expression spoke volumes. "Still think your shackles aren't gold?"

He then bowed to Alice and simply walked away. Sarah followed.

James Davies found Victoria speaking with some guests. She then excused herself and the two moved away slightly. "How did it go?" asked the Queen.

"She's extraordinary. And let me say unequivocally that I would be honored to wed, Miss Bonetta," began James…

Victoria saw the pained look on his face and frowned. "But…"

James looked over and saw Sarah running after Winston, who was leaving the ballroom. Victoria followed his look.

"But you would need to assist in this plan," he lamented, as they both saw Sarah disappear behind Winston. "She's rather—reluctant."

Victoria held in her feelings—but was indeed irritated.

Winston briskly strode out of the Palace and signaled a Footman for his coach just as Sarah caught up with him.

"Winston… Why is it always like this with us?" she pleaded.

He turned to her looking into her eyes. "This is how you got hurt last time, chasing after me—and the thought of it still haunts me… but I have my pride, Aina. I may not speak French or be as educated as you. But I know when I'm defeated," he said ruefully.

"You're not defeated. We're friends!"

"I don't want to be your friend," he snapped. "I want to be the man you just met who has the Queen's approval. And if not him, then that white officer two thousand miles away fighting her war—who made you pregnant."

"Stop it!"

"You say you're 'home?' If this is truly your 'home,' ask your god-mother that if England is so magnanimous about endinG the Slave Trade worldwide—why is there a consulate in Zanzibar to protect British slave trade routes to India and Persia? Most of Zanzibar's population are slaves."

"What?" Sarah was outdone.

"You say you have the Queen's ear? Then advise her against that. That is—if you have any *real* influence." He whistled again for his coach.

Sarah shook her head in frustration. "Why are you so hurtful?"

"Because I do not know who you are—and neither do you!" he bleated. "These clothes, that wig, the jewelry. Who are you? Are you an

African? Are you British? A teacher? An aristocrat? Sarah? Or Aina—who I fell in love with." He grabbed her shoulders. "Then ask yourself where you—the *real* you—can do the most good, and have the most influence? Here, with these royals? Or with your own!"

Sarah lowered her head, now feeling like the defeated one.

Winston softened then took his hand and raised her head back up. "I love you. If only you would let me." Then with all the love inside of him he suddenly, impulsively kissed her. But before she could react, he left when his coach arrived.

Sarah stood there in front of the palace—completely undone and confused by everything that happened since the evening began.

A State Ball at Buckingham Palace, 1850's.

Thirty Three

T he morning after the ball the dining hall at Buckingham Palace was a burst of energy. A myriad of guests from the previous evening had all gone home in their golden carriages and shiny coaches, and the cleaning staff had started very early that morning tidying up and transforming the main ballroom back to its original state.

But in the dining hall, several footmen including both Davis and Barnes, the two Black ones, served eggs, bacon, sausage, toast and coffee, to the overnight guests. Emperor Napoleon III, his wife Empress Eugenie, Prince Louis, and James Davies could not stop talking about the positive comments they heard from fellow aristocrats, MP's and guests regarding the ball. It had been a tremendous success. Sarah and Prince Albert's heartfelt pleas to end the Slave Trade worldwide, and James' incredible "African presentation" had topped the evening. Victoria was thrilled because creating awareness for this cause had been the primary purpose of the ball.

As Eugenie delighted Albert in French, Napoleon leaned into Victoria. "Thank you again for your hospitality, Majesty, and for your subtle reminder that I be more mindful of my country's influence in helping to end this wretched business in Dahomey. You have made us feel so welcome. The evening was incredible, and this morning—in this charming, intimate room with just your family and friends—is so special," he smiled.

"You are welcome, Majesty," smiled Victoria. "It is an opportunity for us to share time together without officials around talking policy."

Napoleon nodded, then indicated the sausage. "And the food, manifique. This, this… what is this?"

"'Boerewors,' Majesty. It's a type of sausage which originated in Africa made from pork, beef, lamb, onions and spices we blend and stuff into chicken skin right here in the palace—in our kitchen."

Prince Albert indicated Sarah, "Our dear Sarah taught our cook the recipe and we've been enjoying it ever since."

"It is delicious. I've had seven pieces."

Victoria laughed. "Be careful. Too much more and we'll be letting out your waistcoats before you go."

Indeed, Victoria loved these smaller meals taken in the upper dining hall, because they were less formal than her usual state-level dinners. She didn't have to seat a hundred people and she was able to engage in conversations that wouldn't necessarily launch a war or a political crisis. Just family and friends—no matter the hierarchy—enjoying each other's company. And by the look of it this morning, her secondary agenda— bringing together her daughter Alice and Prince Louis; and Sarah and James seemed to be going as well…

…At least on the surface.

Little did she know nothing could be further from the truth.

The banter between Alice and Prince Louis, and Sarah and James though cordial was merely for show. Louis and James had no idea that both their respective paramours were contemptuous of and bored to death by them. In fact, Alice was only marking time until she could rid herself of Louis and go upstairs to write to her married paramour Sir Michael McFerrin of Devonshire Downs, whose correspondence with her the last three months began bordering on the pornographic. When

Alice would read his letters to Sarah, thrilling to his every word, Sarah would cringe from shock. "How can you permit him to write such things?" Sarah exclaimed. "It is so explicit."

"It is the closest I'll ever get to experiencing the real thing before I'm married," Alice chortled. "Remember, you've had the actual experience. You know what it's like with a man. I can only imagine—or read these letters." Then both girls would laugh, and Alice would read Sir Michael's letters again making Sarah dream about her own letters from Roger—like the one she had received just yesterday before the ball.

Now, as she was seated next to James Davies on her right, purposely ignoring him because she knew he was just another cog in Victoria's self-serving plans to control her, she was thinking about Sir Roger and wishing he was next to her instead. She missed him and was aching for his touch. She turned to Vicky seated to her left and began to chat with her. Vicky had earlier announced her engagement to Prince Friedrich III of Prussia, an arranged relationship that had been ongoing since Vicky was eleven and Friedrich nineteen. The two actually liked each other and had engaged in a beautiful exchange of correspondence over the years that appealed to Vicky—even though they had only seen each other twice— the second time at Windsor while Sarah was in residence.

Prince Frederick had fallen in love with Vicky at first sight as a child and now he wanted his feelings known to the world. The engagement would be for at least eighteen months giving Vicky enough time to prepare for her duties as the future Empress of Prussia, and naturally the Queen was pleased because it was all in keeping with her plan to arrange suitable marriages for all her daughters and her goddaughter. In fact, her desire for Vicky's nuptials had always been to forge a deeper and closer bond with Prussia, and with the announcement of this engagement, her goals were closer.

All these arranged marriages were merely designed to increase the British Empire's stronghold on the world, Sarah thought. But how did *she* fit into this strategy? How would *her* marriage to James improve England's power and world influence? Would it strengthen Britain's ability to end slave trafficking? No. So why should she do it—especially when there was nothing in it for her? Thus, she ignored James for most of breakfast of which James was obviously aware, and the Queen noticed. Something had to be done.

"So. What plans do you young people have for this lovely morning?" Victoria inquired as she pointedly looked at Sarah, James, Alice and Prince Louis.

"I wouldn't mind a walk," said James before anyone else could respond because he wanted to seize the moment to influence a scenario allowing him on better footing with Sarah. "I hear the grounds here are breathtaking."

"A walk would be wonderful," agreed Prince Louis.

"Then it's settled," smiled Victoria. "Alice, you and Sarah take Prince Louis and James on a tour of the rose gardens after breakfast."

Both Sarah and Alice were unenthused which Victoria noticed.

As the breakfast chatting continued, Bertie and the Duchess of Kent were about to enter the dining hall. However, they stopped at the entrance upon surveying the room. Struck by Sarah and James at the table, and Barnes and Davis serving them and others, Bertie grunted to his grandmother.

"God. It's like bloody 'Little Africa' in here," he snipped. "As if last night wasn't enough with all that unbridled undulating and gyrating."

"Don't worry, Bertie," smirked the Duchess. "If things go as planned, Sarah and James will be gone never to return after they marry."

"And if they do not marry? It looks tenuous from where I stand."

"Oh Sarah will marry James," the Duchess insisted. "Or she will lose Victoria's support. It's been decided."

Now Bertie smiled. "At last, some good news," he smirked as they finally entered the dining hall and sat. But just as Bertie sat down, Lori the parrot swooped in from the open window and landed on Bertie's shoulder infuriating the Prince of Wales.

"Mother! Lock this bloody infuriating beast in its cage! It's ridiculous!" he exclaimed.

"Lori!" the Queen called out, "Go home!"

The parrot immediately flew to its cage, but not before leaving a mound of white bird droppings on the shoulder of Bertie's clean navy-blue waistcoat jacket. Bertie went ballistic. "Bloody hell!"

He ran off as everyone tried their best not to hoot—but lost the battle. The entire table burst into gales of laughter including Napoleon and Eugenie who couldn't help themselves. The raucous laughter lasted for at least five minutes as Bertie stormed up the stairs to change—and take breakfast in his suite.

Sarah laughed the loudest.

Now walking along the stone path leading out to the rose gardens, Sarah and James were behind Alice and Prince Louis, who were walking in silence.

"Have you ever visited Germany, your Highness?" asked Louis struggling to make conversation with Alice who had yet to even look at him. "It's obvious their majesties wish for us to be... close," he said hoping Alice had the same wish.

"Close? Or married?" said Alice matter-of-factly, without an ounce of romantic whimsy. "After all, 'close' will not endear our two countries toward the alliance my family—and I suspect yours—truly desire."

"My word, you speak your mind most vociferously, Princess Alice," he said taken aback.

But Alice remained nonplussed. "I just know how mother thinks. Our nuptials are good for England and Germany, and to hell with us."

Now Louis stopped and stared at her. Alice just smiled and kept going. "Sir, if you are planning to marry me, you need to get used to my outspokenness or find yourself in a perpetual state of shock."

"So I see," he responded in just that state. Then he employed a different tact. One he thought would appeal to her more prurient side.

"You may be the type of woman who needs to be disciplined from time to time by her husband. A good spanking perhaps?"

Now Alice stopped and looked at Louis. He didn't seem the type who could even murmur such a thing. Sir Michael, yes. Sir Michael's sexy letters had described his desire to spank her. To dominate her. How it would give him pleasure just to think about what he would do to her after a good thrashing. But Prince Louis? He seemed too weak. Far too obedient and subservient. And yet, she thought, what if this was his nature? Or what if it was she who brought out this nature. What if under his slightly pudgy physique was a tiger who could satisfy her sense of exploration?

"If we did marry, where and how would I live?" Alice inquired, never directly answering his earlier comment.

Prince Louis finally realized that she was now perhaps open, albeit reluctantly, to accept what was likely the inevitable, but only on her own terms rather than his or his family's. So rather than respond with the sheer elation he was feeling inside, he chose to counter her with quasi aloofness.

"In Hesse-Darmstadt. You would become its Grand Duchess. You would have three palaces at your disposal along with staff, jewels and any other accoutrements you desire," he said flatly. "I would make sure you had a life that at least tried to mirror what you have here. Not as many castles, of course, but power. And, of course, love..." it took him a moment, "... from me."

Alice finally looked at him. She realized he was at least making an effort to interact with her on her terms. Perhaps the relationship was doable after all. She started to soften a bit—and Prince Louis could feel the ice melting. He smiled at her. Alice smiled back—and the two began a more lighthearted walk together.

Meanwhile, James was struggling tooth and nail with Sarah. All his attempts to approach her about solidifying their relationship had been for naught. "Make me understand why wanting your hand in marriage offends you, Miss Bonetta?" James said almost insulted.

"It doesn't offend, Mr. Davies," said Sarah trying not to sound dismissive yet clearly irritated. "It puzzles. Marriage usually requires some knowledge and a modicum of affection for each other."

"Affection can be acquired—much like knowledge," he countered.

"I speak of the heart. Not the mind," she retorted, annoyed that he didn't accept her initial refusal.

"I speak of both," he persisted.

Sarah stopped, turned to him, and looked at him directly so he would not mistake her intent nor the fury in her eyes.

"Well, both tell me—no," she said forcefully. "I'm sorry."

She started off, but James grabbed her hand. She swung around affronted that he would touch her in such a forceful way. James immediately dropped his grasp. He was almost confused by his behavior.

"Miss Bonetta. What have I done to provoke such hostility and acrimony from you? I proposed marriage. Not murder."

Sarah almost laughed. "It's the same thing to me, sir. You and my godmother plotting to manipulate me into matrimony, and I have no say in it? I may as well be dead."

"She only wants the best for you."

"And that 'best' is you? How do *I* know that? *I* should decide what's best for me. Not you… and not her."

"Have you become so integrated into royal society that you look down on regular people? Commoners? Have you become the uppity puppet of the aristocratic upper-class establishment?" His voice then turned to acid. "Or is it that you don't want a black man—that we are not good enough for you—I heard you rejected that Winston fellow last night as well."

Sarah could not contain her fury. "How dare you even invoke Winston's name. You know nothing about it—or him—and will never insult me again" She scooped up her dress skirt, "Goodbye, sir. Do not try to see me." Sarah then marched back to the castle.

James stood there embarrassed. He looked over at Prince Louis and Alice ahead of him if not enjoying each other's company at least quipping through it pleasurably. But Sarah had rejected his overtures for the second time in as many days, and James' ego was now bruised and damaged. He was a rich man. He did not have to beg for the affections of a woman. Yet, his heart was breaking because he was sincerely falling for Sarah. Now he had to face the fact that his feelings would never be enough.

Sarah tore down the Buckingham Palace hallway, still reeling from her walk with James when, as she turned the corner toward her room, she saw Miss Gordon, the chambermaid, with Miss Nelson, another chambermaid, cleaning the hall near her room. Neither had noticed Sarah because they were engaged in a lively, hushed conversation which Sarah overheard:

"...The Duchess of Kent has shouted at me for the last time. Calling me loose and licentious when everyone in the palace knows she's the libertine," sniffed Miss Gordon.

"She should be grateful the Queen doesn't know any one of a dozen men other than Duke Edward could be her father," said Miss Nelson just as dismissive.

It was at that point Sarah made her presence known and cleared her throat. "Ladies...?"

Both chambermaids jumped and turned to find Sarah there.

"Step into my room, please," Sarah demanded, "I want to know more about this."

Obliged by protocol, both women nervously went into Sarah's suite and Sarah closed the door behind them.

After tea that afternoon, once everyone realized that James Labulo Davies had packed his things and left the palace in humiliation and rejection by Sarah, the Queen summoned her goddaughter.

By the time Sarah arrived at the Drawing room, Victoria was enraged. "I am greatly disappointed by your decision against marriage to James Davies."

"I'm sorry, but I won't marry a man I don't love."

"Really? With all your education and training, when it comes to a marital union, you choose the heart over good sense?"

"That—is all that matters."

Victoria was outdone. "England could not have expanded to the powerful Empire it has become if its royal overseers married purely for love?"

Sarah held her ground. "You love Prince Albert."

"I was lucky to find love in my arrangement. But it *was* an arrangement."

"Ma'am, England is not my responsibility. Why am I being arranged into anything?"

"You are a ward of the Crown. We have made an investment in you. Your place, your future—is with James."

Now Sarah was angry. "Why? Because he's African? Because he's rich? Or because he's not Sir Roger Carlyle!"

"Sally...!"

"Am I now expected to barter my body and peace of mind for England? The same England still furtively in the Trade in Zanzibar?"

Victoria was in shock and froze into place.

"Oh do not pretend you don't know what I'm talking about," Sarah continued. "You have a Consulate there. Your ships still carry human cargo at its behest."

The veins in Victoria's forehead rose to visibility and her voice attacked. "I know of no such slave ships out of Zanzibar. And you will not stand there orating dialogue to me like we are in a theater. I have spent too much on you to accept ingratitude."

"I did not ask to be your ward."

"Oh, but you certainly accepted its rewards. All the attention, the proximity to royalty, the preferential treatment, privilege…"

"…I was already privileged! I am a princess!"

"And I am Queen!" Victoria snapped, her face as red as a beet. "Brook no argument, 'Princess' Sarah, you will learn respect for that fact, or you will leave here and live somewhere reflecting your life without my Royal protection!"

Sarah was astonished, it took her a moment, and she started out, but turned back angrily.

"Fine. Then before I go, consider this, as you insist I marry a man who in no way suits my heart. I've studied your son Prince Leopold's condition. He has hemophilia—a hereditary disease. But neither Prince Albert nor his family's background evidence the disease you said. So, *you* must be a carrier. But your mother's family also has no history of the disease. Which leaves only your father, Duke Edward."

"What of it?"

"Not only did he have no history of hemophilia, but no children with his first wife, no children after 28 years with a mistress, and no other children with your mother who had two children with her first husband before you. . One might think your 'father' incapable of siring a child…"

"I am not amused!"

"…and your mother had to ensure she gave birth—to a child in line to the British throne. Your mother is the subject of a whispered about affair. Who was it at the time of your conception? Sir John Conroy?"

"Careful, girl…" Victoria fumed.

"…Majesty. Are you truly the legitimate ruler of England? 'Orating dialogue' to me about 'Ward of the Crown' and the virtues of arranged marriages…!"

Victoria was seething and slapped Sarah—who held her face.

"How dare you! Leave here at once! And hold your tongue about these lies!" Victoria marched to the door and yelled. "Lord John! Come in here now!"

Sarah ran out passing Alice in the hall who overheard the entire argument. As Sarah ran up the stairs Alice followed. "Stop. Sarah, stop!!"

But Sarah ran into her suite and pulled her one valise from the armoire. She began packing the few clothes and books she came with very upset and fighting back tears.

Seconds later Alice ran into the room without knocking. "You can't go. You can't Sally."

"Leave me alone, Ally. Just go."

"No! You don't have to leave. Just tell mother you're sorry. You made her angry. That's all. Don't condemn yourself to a grievous life when you don't have to."

"I don't belong here, Ally. I am an outsider, an 'other.' No matter how you dress me I'll just be a spruced up, arrogant African 'experiment' who doesn't know how to stay in her place."

"But what will I do without you? You can't go, Sally. I won't let you!" Alice cried.

"Leave it to you to only think about yourself."

Then Alice grabbed Sarah and swung her around. "Do you think it's any better for Vicky? Or for me? I'm being arranged into an unwanted marriage too. I don't love Prince Louis. I don't even know him. I don't know his likes or dislikes. What if he is debauched and pisses on women?

Or spanks women as he's suggested? What if he's a sodomite who doesn't even like women?"

"But you'll still be rich, powerful, royal…"

"…and unhappy. Just like you, Sally!"

This stopped Sarah as she sat on the bed at a loss. How did it get to this? The idyllic life she thought she had was now gone.

"We're women, Sally," Alice continued. We do not have the gift of choice. Men dictate everything. And sadly, even powerful women like mother continue the tragedy."

The two friends held each other and cried. Finally, Sarah wiped her eyes and took her one valise. She looked around the room she loved sadly—and walked out leaving Alice in tears.

Victoria was in the window watching as Sarah got into a carriage. Seconds later Lord John Breadlebane entered. "I've sent a note to the Prime Minister, ma'am. But the Duchess of Kent is here now."

Victoria's mother entered and curtsied. "You sent for me?"

Victoria wiped her eyes, turned and glared at her mother point blank. "Just who is my father?"

"W-what?" stuttered the Duchess nervously.

"My *real* father. Who is he? Tell me the truth."

The Duchess was shaking. "Victoria, do not become overly excited. You know you're having a baby."

It was true. Dr. Brown had informed Victoria of her pregnancy just two days earlier and Victoria had only told her mother and Prince Albert. But at this moment, the Queen was only interested in answers to her burning question at hand. "Mother, I am aware of my condition. What I want to know is who is my blood father?"

The Duchess of Kent slowly sat down and looked away. Victoria slowly sat too, and she was worried.

Sweedon's Passage on Grub Street (circa 1858)

Part Four

An Independent Woman

1856 - 1862

"…Every king springs from a race of slaves,
and every slave had Kings among their ancestors…"

Queen Victoria

VISIT OF AN AFRICAN PRINCESS TO THE PRINCESS ROYAL'S WEDDING.— The Rev. J. F. Schön, chaplain of Melville Hospital, Chatham, has received a command from her Majesty for Sarah Bonetta Forbes, the young African princess who has been placed by her Majesty under the care Mrs. Schön, at Chatham, for the purpose of being educated, to be present to witness the marriage ceremony of the Princess Royal, on Monday next. Mrs. Schön has received the Queen's commands to attend at Buckingham Palace with the young princess on Friday next, to receive the final instructions relative to their attendance at the Royal wedding. Her Majesty has manifested her thoughtful care towards the princess by forwarding her, within the last few days, a supply of dresses and other requisites suitable to be worn on the occasion. The princess, who is the daughter of a late African king, was brought to this country a few years since by Captain Forbes, of her Majesty's ship Bonetta, and ever since her stay in England the Queen has manifested the most lively interest towards her. The princess is about 18 years of age, and is stated to be highly accomplished.

Excerpt from the London Standard newspaper, 20 January 1858, page 3, announcing African Princess Sarah Forbes Bonetta's royal request to attend Princess Vicky's wedding.

Thirty Four

Sweedon's Passage was located just off Grub Street in a vast lawless slum called a rookerie. The area was famous for its concentration of impoverished, untalented writers, aspiring-but-poor poets, and low-end publishers and booksellers. It was where Phillips Print Shop was located—and the Crows Pub where Sarah and Alice once enjoyed an afternoon with Winston and Miyo.

The street itself celebrated some of London's most outrageous members of society and was set amidst flophouses, brothels, and coffeehouses existing on the margins of London's bohemian scene.

Interspersed along its length were slender entrances to courts and alleys—which is where Sarah was going—to the Schoen's home at #32 Sweedon's Passage.

As she came down the street with her valise she once again felt like a rudderless ship—traveling on no course with no destination. But this time she was scared. She was on her own without the Queen's royal protection and wondered what was to become of her.

Elizabeth Schoen, and her husband Reverend James Schoen, were good Christian people who helped the poor and fed the hungry. The good Reverend had a small church on Plymouth Road and was the Chaplain of Melville Hospital. He did charity work and Elizabeth helped him.

She also took in boarders every once and awhile for extra money. Elizabeth had been especially good to Sarah in her time of need when she was pregnant and was now offering a safe haven for Sarah to stay while she pondered her future.

When Sarah appeared at her door, Mrs. Schoen hugged and welcomed her sincerely. "You're home, dearie. Stay as long as you need."

"I'm glad you invited me. Thank you."

Elizabeth showed Sarah up to the room she would be living in for the time being. Sarah sat her one valise down and looked around.

It was a tiny, modest room in a modest house with only a bed, bureau and chair. But Sarah was grateful to be there. This was her independent new life where she could make her own choices.

That evening, Sarah helped Elizabeth with dinner. She snapped peas, husked corn, and pulled the skin off of chicken so Elizabeth could roast it. The delicious smell of food filled the air and Sarah realized she had not had this experience since staying with the Forbes across town. The difference was the Schoen kitchen was on the same floor as the dining and reception rooms, and the Forbes kitchen was downstairs in the basement. While Sarah helped with dinner, Reverend Schoen was reading the newspaper. He frowned, "Oh my. The Tories are demanding an accurate account of all soldiers and sailors sent to Crimea and the casualties we've sustained."

"Casualties?" Sarah asked nervously.

Knowing what Sarah was thinking, Elizabeth was calming.

"Don't worry, dearie. Roger will be fine Sarah. Trust in God."

But I wasn't so sure, and as we had dinner that night I thought about Roger—where he was, how he was doing, if he thought about me at all. In fact, thoughts of Roger would carry me over the next several months as I settled into my new life. I was just past seventeen and was feeling as the Queen once did about turning thirty-five—like I was being used up and my happiness drying out.

Then came the day I will never forget. Reverend Schoen ran through the kitchen door elated and asked for the good Brandy. 'Oh, happy day, happy day,' he grinned excitedly as he showed his wife and me the headline of The Times which declared:

WAR IN CRIMEA ENDS! PEACE TREATY SIGNED IN PARIS!

Mrs. Schoen brought out the decanter of good brandy and poured snifters for her husband, herself and me while I wondered if I would ever see my Roger again—or if he had survived the war…

More months passed and by that Christmas, a blanket of snow covered the streets of London. Most people were digging out from a horrible December snowstorm which engulfed the city. Sarah helped trim the Christmas tree and looked for work. She would soon discover she did not possess the skills to be either a lady's maid, a cook or a housekeeper—all jobs in which unmarried women were expected to excel. Perhaps she could be a governess, she thought, and began to check the newspaper for those positions.

In the meantime, she paid her own way at the Schoen's by cooking breakfast and lunch and keeping the Schoen house clean so Elizabeth could do her charity work at the church.

The following February of 1857, with an apron on and her real hair covered by a bonnet, Sarah set the table the way she had been taught by Rebecca and Jilly so long ago at the Forbes house. Who would have thought that skill would one day come in handy—even though the Schoen's laughed at her for using all their cutlery like she was setting places for four courses. "Are we expectin' the Duke of Clarence, dearie?" laughed Elizabeth one day. "I've never seen so much silverware for a simple beef, beans and potato meal in my life. This ain't Windsor dearie."

Sarah smiled, as she brought out the salads. "Well," This is the first course, the meat, and potatoes, the second, and dessert, the last. All need their own plates and cutlery."

Reverend Schoen chuckled. "And who will be washing and drying all these plates, forks and spoons for all these courses?"

They all laughed again—because, of course, Sarah had to. And she soon learned to present just the staples—one knife, one fork and one spoon for one plate of food. A simple presentation.

That April when the weather was better, Sarah and the Schoen's went to a meeting at Phillips Print Shop. Winston and Miyo were there, and Sarah and Winston were awkward with each other and said nothing. It broke Sarah's heart because she liked Winston and missed his friendship. But it would be his militant, argumentative nature that always proved his undoing. So, she would nod to him from afar. The death—or even the illness—of their friendship was hard to bear.

But when she returned home to the Schoen's home later that day, there was a letter from Princess Alice waiting in the post.

"Sally, I don't know if you are aware, but mother had a baby girl last Thursday. She named her Beatrice Mary Victoria Feodore. She is the prettiest baby I have ever seen. I so wish you were here to see her. I know you would love her as much as me. I miss you, Sally. We all do, especially Poppi who tells me so all the time. And so does mother, who won't admit it, but she does. Love sincerely, Ally."

The letter touched Sarah and she read it and re-read it over and over. But it changed nothing. She had to live her own life, her way. She wrote Alice to say congratulations on the birth of her new sister, and that although she, too, missed everyone, she was happy where she was. But even after posting the letter, she wondered if that were true. Was she actually happy? Was this the life she wanted to live?

She received her answer two weeks later while walking home with a basket of bread and vegetables for the Schoen's dinner. Ahead of her was a black beggar soliciting money from a passerby. "Help a poor bloke get some food? Help a poor bloke get some food?"

The passerby ignored him. Then he saw Sarah hurrying along.

"Spare a shillin' for a man in need?"

At first Sarah was going to hurry away too. Instead, she stopped and thought. He was in worse shape than she and thus chose to be like the Schoen's and be a good, charitable Christian woman. She went back to the man who searched her face with need. "I don't have a shilling," she began. "But maybe some bread?" She tried to hand him one of two loaves she was carrying, but the man shook his head and refused it.

"I need money, girl. Not bread. Don' know why I asked you anyway. You're jus' another poor blackie on these streets like me."

Sarah stood there staring at the man who went on to beg other people passing by. It upset her so much she ran full throttle to the Schoen house in tears, not understanding why it bothered her. But it did.

"You're jus' another poor blackie on these streets like me."

When she came into the house, she dropped the basket onto the kitchen table, ran up to her room, and lay across her bed in tears. That beggar was right. She *was* just another impoverished Negro on the streets of London without work, without money, and without any opportunities. Suddenly she jumped up, pulled out her diary and began to write how she felt—how disappointed she was with her life, and was she really experiencing happiness.

Then there was a knock. "Sarah. Come on down, dearie. You 'ave company," she heard Elizabeth call from beyond the door.

"I don't want to see anyone, Mrs. Schoen."

"Oh, Trust me, dearie. You do."

Sarah wiped her eyes, straightened herself up and left her room.

When she came into the reception area where Elizabeth led her, she gasped at the man standing there who turned around and smiled.

"Hello, Sarah."

"Roger...!"

Sir Roger Carlyle scooped her up and as he whirled her around they kissed. They kissed for an eternity. Then she pulled back to take a good look at her beloved. Roger had aged in the way war ages you. Slight wrinkling around the eyes and a somewhat gaunt frame. But the best of him—his gorgeous dark hair, his piercing green eyes, his cute dimples, were all the same—and a feast for Sarah.

"How did you find me?" she asked.

"The moment the war ended, I went to Windsor Castle. But Bertie told me you had fallen out of favor for not marrying a man the Queen wanted you to."

Sarah nodded slightly.

"I asked him to tell me where their detectives had located you."

"Detectives?"

"Sarah. You're the Queen's goddaughter. Whether in or out of favor they must know where you and all family members are at all times."

Now Sarah was almost angry. All this time, the Queen had her spies on her like barnacles on a whale. But she said nothing—even though Alice knew where she was.

Soon they were interrupted by Mrs. Schoen wearing her hat and coat and carrying a basket of old clothes. "Sarah, dear, I'm going to join the good Reverend at the church and hand out some of these old clothes. Then I thought maybe I'd help him while he counsels a few congregants."

"Alright," Sarah frowned, wondering why Elizabeth was making a fuss about it. Then Elizabeth gave Sarah a knowing look regarding Sir Roger. "I'll be gone at least—two hours, maybe more. You'll have the house all to yourself. And the good brandy is behind the umbrella stand.

Help yourself," her voice lowered knowingly. "And—I left a bag of 'items' on your bed upstairs—so there won't be another 'undesirable epilogue.'"

Elizabeth gave Sir Roger a wink and left. Roger grinned. "That wasn't at all obvious," he mused—and then Sarah understood. Elizabeth was giving them some 'alone time.'

"But what did she mean by 'undesirable epilogue'?"

Sarah sighed. She knew that if Roger survived the war and returned to her she would have to tell him about her pregnancy. Yet, now that he was standing in front of her, there was a part of her that wanted to forget the whole sad episode and leave it in the past.

"What are you not telling me?" Roger inquired. "I can see in your eyes you're holding something back."

Sarah finally looked up at him, at the eyes that captured her heart the first time she gazed into them and didn't let go in all this time. She took his hand and walked him to the settee. There they sat.

"After you left for Crimea, I discovered that I was having your child."

Roger reacted with a joy she had never seen before. "My child? Oh Sarah. Where is it? What did you have—a boy or a girl?"

"Neither," she answered in a small voice. It died. I...I lost it when I tripped and fell." She couldn't bring herself to tell him the whole truth—that she tried to abort it, became afraid, and ultimately fell down a flight of stairs chasing after another man and that's how she lost it.

Roger held her face in his hands. "I would've loved to be a father. I've seen mixed-race children. They're always beautiful. Ours would've been too—beige skin, curly hair, your large brown eyes..."

"And your personality," she concluded. "Yes. Had I been a married lady I would have been thrilled to have a beautiful child like that. But I wasn't, and the Queen found out and tried to force me to marry a man I didn't love—and now my life has changed."

It took a moment for Roger to realize all the circumstances surrounding Sarah being in this place.

"You have to go back to the Queen until I can make arrangements."

"Make arrangements? No. I won't go back to her."

"Yes. You have to. Beg if you must. Don't let pride keep you here like this."

"This—is how most blacks live."

"You... are not 'most blacks.'"

Sarah pulled off her bonnet—to reveal her actual kinky hair sans wig and she indicated her apron and plain clothing. "But I am, Roger. This is the real me. Living in the real world. And it's best we both understand that—and not pretend. This is not Alice in Wonderland."

Roger just smiled. "Yes, it is," then he pulled something from his pocket Sarah recognized—her red ribbon. Only it had an amethyst ring strung on it. "The Mad Hatter is in love with Alice." He knelt before her. Sarah's breathing began to come in short spurts and her hands shook as he put the ring on her finger. "I love you, Sarah Bonetta. I survived three years in Crimea to marry you like I promised..."

"Roger I won't hold you to that..."

"...I plan to stand for election as MP to the House of Commons," he overrides her. "I told you I only want truth between us. I want to make a difference. I want to be by your side in the fight." He smiled, "I want to have beige children with large brown eyes, curly hair..."

"...and your personality..." she finished.

They kissed. For the next two hours Sarah and Roger made love in her bedroom. True to her word Mrs. Schoen had left a bag of sheep gut condoms in a bag on the bed. But with the revelation of Roger's intent to marry her and her acceptance, somehow the awkward, cumbersome method of birth control was never used. The two lost themselves in each other as though the preceding three years of absence had never occurred. Roger came to the Schoen home every other day and they would have lunch or make love when the Schoen's weren't there. They would walk down the street together comfortable and affectionate with each other completely oblivious to staring passersby.

Then one day Roger posed a question as they lay in each other's arms in Sarah's bed. "It's getting harder and harder to leave you," he whispered as he caressed her. "The other day, I asked Bertie if I could have the keys to the Garden Pavilion for a few months. He asked me why, and I told him…" But he stopped.

Sarah sat up curiously, "Told him what?"

"I told him I wanted to have a woman there, a lover, for 6 months."

Sarah paused a moment to consider the word 'lover.'

"Did you tell him it was me?"

Roger looked off not wanting to hurt her feelings. "No. He would only give me grief about it and I tire of his condemnation. I knew if I told him it was some other woman, he'd agree to it…and he did. I told him I was seeing Lady Penelope Valmont from Liverpool and wanted her to hide out there until her divorce was settled."

"And he agreed to *that?*"

"You know Bertie. He's only interested in social debauchery."

"Yes. As long as it's *white* social debauchery."

Roger said nothing for he had to agree.

"So, you have the keys to our old trysting place," Sarah mused.

Roger nodded. "It's all ours until October. So…" he grinned impishly, "…Come live in sin with me until we marry, and I find us a home here in London."

Sarah lay back on the pillow smiling. She looked at her ring.

"Sin, indeed."

Thirty Five

The "request" was furtively forwarded to Garden Pavilion from the Schoen's in a letter from Alice that delighted Sarah. Alice joyfully announced that her eldest sister Vicky, the Princess Royal, was marrying Prince Friedrich Wilhelm Nikolaus Karl von Hohenzollern, known as "Fritz," only son of Emperor Wilhelm I of Prussia, on 25 January 1858 at Chapel Royal in St. James's Palace.

"She wants you to come and asked me to 'test the waters,'" wrote Alice. "So even though you and mother are feuding, Vicky wants you there—even if you sit in a balcony. At least one of us girls in the family should be happily married, and Vicky and Fritz are mad for each other."

Sarah had started writing to Alice under an assumed name a few months earlier because she wanted to keep up with her best friend, tell her where she was, and maintain at least some connection to the royal family. The two vowed to keep their correspondence, and Sarah's location a secret as had always been their way. Upon discussing it with Sir Roger, Sarah decided to attend the Princess Royal's wedding, but not together to avoid a scandal.

Within a fortnight I received a formal wedding invitation and "command" through Reverend Schoen to attend Vicky's nuptials. Knowing that such invitations were exclusive and reserved for people of distinction such as European royalty, or special friends of the royal family, newspapers revealed my receiving one. It was first announced on 20 January 1858 by the London Standard newspaper, which printed that "…An African Princess Sarah Forbes Bonetta, was to witness the marriage of the Princess Royal." That was shocking enough to me. Then the Illustrated London News published a fuller account on 23 January 1858 on page 79 saying: '…A command has been received from her Majesty for Sarah Forbes Bonetta, the African Princess, to be present to witness the marriage ceremony of the Princess Royal. Her Majesty has manifested her thoughtful care towards the Princess by forwarding her within the last few days a supply of dresses and other requisites suitable to be worn on the occasion…'

Sure enough, at the next meeting of the Society for the Worldwide Cessation of the Slave Trade at Phillips Print Shop, Mrs. Schoen had two large boxes with her. "They were just delivered to you from the Palace." Later when Sarah opened the boxes inside were two dresses, some shoes, a hat with veil, two pairs of gloves, new stockings, and a note that simply said: *"From Her Majesty, at the Princess Royal's request."*

This of course meant that Vicky wanted Sarah at her wedding, but the Queen was still angry. On Monday 25 January 1858, eight hundred guests were crowded into Chapel Royal—the same church where the Queen married Prince Albert, her uncle King George IV married Queen Caroline, and her grandfather King George III married Queen Charlotte. British citizens were excited and filled the streets surrounding St. James's trying to glimpse the royals as they arrived and all the various guests who came from around the world. It was a chance for Britain to celebrate and heal after the war in Russia which ended victoriously.

Sir Roger entered the church first and sat behind Bertie and other family members, greeting them warmly. Then much later Sarah, outfitted in one of the dresses sent by the Queen, slipped into the sanctuary and sat in an upper balcony in back so as not to upset the Queen, but to be seen by Princess Vicky when she and Prince Friedrich came down the aisle. But people knew who she was because she was the only black in the church, and clearly "the African Princess" of whom the London newspapers spoke. Her head had to be held high.

The ceremony began as eight royal bridesmaids, all friends of Vicky's, came down the narrow aisle, and finally the bride herself appeared.

Vicky was escorted by her father the Prince Consort Albert. Everyone sighed in awe. When the Royals turned, it was then the Queen looked up and saw Sarah and their eyes locked for a moment. Then Victoria cast her eyes back to the Princess Royal—and smiled. Vicky was a vision in a white moiré antique satin gown designed by Janet Fife, with flounces of Honiton lace. She wore a headdress wreath of orange flowers and myrtle, and a long white veil and train draped her head and followed. She looked happy.

The service was not terribly long and as she sat in the beautiful narrow chapel with its side-situated oak pews, upper balconies, and tall stained-glass windows, Sarah thought about Alice's words: *"At least one of us girls in the family should be happily married."*

Sarah wondered if it could be true and looked down at her engagement ring—and then at Sir Roger himself seated behind Bertie, his friend. She knew that if Bertie was aware, he never would have allowed her to stay in the Garden Pavilion as she was doing, and she was thankful the Royal family was in residence at Windsor Castle which was 23 miles from Buckingham where the Cottage was.

She thought about her life now with Roger who was loving, attentive, and caring. Together they made a good team fighting for the rights of Negroes and the cessation of the Slave Trade. In fact, Roger had begun to accompany her to abolitionist meetings at Phillips Print Shop. He would listen to the stories, the plans and concerns, then discuss them with her later to devise solutions and strategies. Wisely he chose ending the Trade and Anti-slavery as his platform to showcase his potential as a Member of Parliament for Weymouth—his home city. It was his plan to get at least 2,000 signatures on a petition he would present as he raised awareness for the cause in London, Brighton, Liverpool and Bristol.

But in Sarah's mind, Roger was still too naïve concerning issues of race to assume leadership of a movement to dismantle an insidious institution like the Slave Trade, which had been in place forever. In that regard he was like Alice—an innocent whom she adored—who, despite all her bravado, took people at face value and gave you the benefit of the doubt before passing judgement. Blessedly, everyone was equal in the eyes of these two and both lived their lives in a utopian reverie that one day everyone would embrace their philosophy and join them there.

But Sarah thought about how much the real world was a far different place. An uglier place. A place of the "colonizer" and the "colonized." She felt if she could parley her status as "The African Princess" who got press attention because she was the black goddaughter and ward of the Queen, and an honorary member of the British royal family— while she still had it—into power for Roger's election as MP, then she could contribute to the cause in a furtive but meaningful, significant way. Sir Roger would need white allies with influence. Powerful white friends. And she was surrounded by them here at Vicky's wedding. All she had to do…was be subtle and sly.

So when Sarah saw Vicky and Fritz kiss after being pronounced "man and wife," she waited until the Queen and Royal family left the church then allowed herself to be greeted by various guests and indicated Sir Roger as a hope for the future. Those that did not know Roger quickly sought his acquaintance.

Then Sarah left the church. Outside she made sure she thanked Princess Vicky for the invitation and hugged Alice. The Queen ignored her. Then Sarah stood with the crowd and watched as Vicky and Friedrich waved to the masses from the wedding coach. She saw Alice,

Bertie, Prince Albert—and finally the Queen, who looked happy, following behind. Roger and Bertie spoke for a while and Bertie glimpsed Sarah in the crowd doing her best to be incognito. Then, he patted Roger on the shoulder and joined his family in the wedding coach as it left.

Sir Roger greeted other nobles and guests and chatted about his campaign with Lord Samuel Murray, an influential fifty-year-old MP from Weymouth who owned several banks, among other businesses, and had known Sir Roger's dead parents.

They had been chatting for a while when Sarah finally turned and walked for a long time by herself in the cold. She felt lonely. It was hard to accept the reality that she, although loved by many in the royal family, was now just another Negro in London with a tentative relationship to palaces, crowns, castles and royalty. And as she pulled her coat in tighter against the January chill, she walked to Allen's Cafe on Chestnut street, the designated eatery at which she and Roger had agreed to meet after the wedding since today was not one to upstage the wedding of the Princess Royal by flaunting their controversial relationship.

Inside Allen's Café, Sarah ordered a slice of blueberry pie, and hot apple cider, and while she waited for both, she could hear the conversation at the next table where two friends discoursed on the state of affairs in America and how it may impact Britain.

Sarah was already aware that relations between the northern and southern states in America were tenuous. Things had come to a head with the publication of "Uncle Tom's Cabin" three years earlier. But now, news that the internal struggle between the north and south had turned to an outright Civil War was the topic of conversation at every pub, restaurant and meeting place in London—which included the café in which she was now waiting for Roger.

"They say eleven southern states have left the Union and are now fighting to establish independence by forming their own country. They're calling it the "Confederate States of America," said one man.

"I hear they already have their own President and Constitution to protect the institution of slavery," said the other man.

Sarah surreptitiously moved her chair closer for a better listen.

"Yes, but the North has refused to recognize the new 'country' and has been slowly abolishing slavery."

"They can afford to," chuckled the second man, "There's a steady flow of immigrants, especially from Ireland and Germany with the potato famine, to give the North a steady pool of cheap labor. That certainly diminishes the need to cling to slavery."

"If you ask me, Americans have taken too long on this issue. They could have done what we did years ago. Abolish the bloody institution because it's wrong. Not wait for war to decimate their country."

"I agree. But watch the North try to pull us into their fracas."

A waitress brought Sarah's pie and cider, and she began thinking. When U.S. President Abraham Lincoln vowed to keep the Union whole, war became inevitable, and many wondered how long it would be before England would be pulled into the dispute. England and America had maintained a "Special Relationship" since John Adams so impressed Queen Victoria's grandfather King George III by insisting Great Britain and America be friends and allies after England lost the colonies.

Sarah knew the primary reason for the war had much to do with ending slavery in the south—the net reason the Slave Trade was still so active around the world. And ending the Trade worldwide was the cause both Sarah and Roger were committed to. So when Sir Roger finally arrived, they talked about their goals and how to get there. Roger told Sarah about the people he'd spoken to at the wedding who wanted to be helpful. People like Lord Samuel Murray, the MP and banker who had power and influence.

"He's going to come to one of the meetings at Phillips," Roger told her. "He's heard about them but didn't have an impetus to go to the area. But I told him I'd be speaking there next week, and he'll come."

Both Sarah and Roger were on the side of freedom for America's slaves and an end to slavery and the Trade everywhere. But they also knew that big, influential money always sided with the rich. And people who owned slaves were usually wealthy. Someone like Lord Murray, if he liked Roger and was impressed with him, could be very helpful indeed.

Sure enough, the next week, Sarah, the Schoens, Winston, Miyo and all the regulars were at Phillips Print Shop at an abolitionists meeting. It was crowded that day as people had heard a Peer and would-be MP was going to be a guest speaker.

Sir Roger was confident as he rose from his chair, after a thrilling introduction by Mr. Phillips, and strode to the podium. Lord Samuel Murray with his grey mutton-chop whiskers, puffing a distinctively carved, full-bent Meerschaum pipe, was seated prominently in front. Sarah was in back with Elizabeth Schoen and other women.

Soon one could hear a pin drop as Sir Roger spoke passionately.

"I was brought up in a household of Peers at Fenmore Place in Weymouth who never once thought about how our food was prepared, or our homes cleaned, or bedpans emptied. We had Negro help for such things—and in my grandfather's day they had slaves," Sir Roger began. "All around me growing up was an invisible workforce of people who did all the menial chores of running our home and our lives, creating our comfort, and at Christmas we gave them gifts, patted them on the back, then returned them to the invisible background of our existence. Then my parents died tragically at sea.

In my overwhelming grief, our Negro housekeeper in Liverpool held me and let me cry. To properly mourn. She said it would be okay.

She made me my favorite pudding and told me that time would heal me in my broken spirit. Her name was Helen. I soon spent all my free time with her—and she suddenly became a real person. A loving person—a human being with feelings and a heart and experiences she began to share. I would come down to the kitchen where she and the others worked, and I learned from Helen that her father had been captured in Africa and sold to my family two generations earlier. That he was stripped of his name and freedom and mistreated on his journey here. I learned that almost all of our Negro servants had similar stories. Being stolen from their native land and sold. Being overworked, discarded and thought of as three-fifths a human being as Thomas Jefferson wrote.

Ladies and gentlemen, there is a Trade—one founded in heinousness and derision and carried on still right here in Britain and across the world. When I consider the magnitude of it, I cannot help but want to shine a light on its injustices for it has been examined and gone over and verbalized for eons. Now is the time for action! To do something about it! To stop forever what should be the unlawful buying and selling of human beings and trading them for goods and merchandise and free labor! The Northern states in America are right to want to end slavery in their whole country—their Union—not part of the country. *All* of it. And we here in England should want for there to be no slave trading anywhere! Not in this country, Europe, nor anywhere else in the world!" He banged his fist on the podium, "Not as long as England is a world power! Not as long as England is the greatest power on earth!"

The audience burst into applause, stomping, cheering. Sarah was amazed by Roger's dynamics and intense fervor. Winston was moved too. Roger's audience was galvanized by his words as he continued: "This is a subject I have chosen to undertake as an advocate. This great cause needs a champion who will bring before the House of Commons signed petitions in preparation for a bill in favor of the worldwide cessation of the Trade. And not just the Trade—*all* of its tentacles which keep it in place—which among those tentacles, has come to my attention, British slave ships masquerading as cargo vessels both out of Liverpool and Zanzibar. They do this by flying another country's flag after leaving port, and as a ship now belonging to a country which allows slavery these British merchants and slavers continue the slave trade. I have also learned that we have a British Consulate in Zanzibar which is mandated to protect Britain's slave trade routes to India and Persia. Why? Because over eighty percent of Zanzibar's population are slaves."

Winston suddenly turned and looked at Sarah—who looked away. He now knew Sir Roger got this information from her via him. He wondered if this was her way of getting the Queen's ear? Or helping her white lover to achieve a goal? Or both.

"These practices must be banned," Roger continued. "If I am elected to the House of Commons these will be my first bills presented. I am determined to march forward and justify upon the clearest principles, every resolution at my disposal, the avowed end and the total abolition of the slave trade. And I will not rest until I have helped effectuate its abolition!"

There was massive applause. The people stood, some ran up and hugged Roger. One woman embraced him and kissed him on the lips. Roger's ovation was overwhelming and when he finished receiving his congratulations and praise he found Lord Samuel Murray smiling and nodding to him.

"Come around to my London office next Wednesday at one. It's on Harley Street," smiled Lord Murray. "There are some people you should meet if you are to be successful in your bid. I shall make sure you are well received as you have my favor." A pat on Roger's back concluded Lord Murray's comments and he left. Roger hugged Sarah forgetting where he was in his excitement and audience applause.

Miyo turned to Winston and frowned. "He's very friendly to Aina."

Winston said nothing. He knew exactly who Sir Roger was now, especially when he saw a ring on Sarah's ring finger. He looked away determined not to explode but forced to accept he'd lost her forever.

Later, Sarah, Roger, the Schoen's and others came out of the print shop and were milling on the street. Paul Phillips shook Roger's hand and smiled. "You were wonderful, Sir Roger. Thank you for your insights and courage. I will have those fliers ready for you Tuesday."

Roger nodded. "I appreciate it, Paul." He then took Sarah's hand as Winston came out of the building with Miyo who saw the hand-holding but said nothing.

Winston swallowed his pride and held out his hand to Roger. "It was a very rousing, very good speech, Sir Roger. A lot of information you shared…" He gave Sarah a quick glance, "…was obviously from a trusted source that people needed to hear."

"Thank you, Mr.…?"

Sarah suddenly felt obligated to introduce. "…Benjamin. Mr. Winston Benjamin. And this is Mr. Miyo Olatunji. Both were trafficked in the Slave Trade. Winston and I are old… friends."

There it was again. The word. "Friends." The word that would stick forever in Winston's craw like phlegm. "Yes. In fact, Aina, er, Sarah taught me how to read."

There was a long awkward pause as no one knew what to say about the obvious. Finally, Sarah spoke up. "Winston. Sir Roger and I are…"

"…Engaged. I can see as much." He took Sarah's hand with the ring and looked at it. He then nodded to them both. "Congratulations." Then he turned to go, walking fast so not to display his feelings. Miyo gave Sarah a quick kiss on the cheek, then he turned to catch up with his friend whose pain was obvious.

Roger was confused, and the Schoen's felt badly. But as Sarah stood on the street that day watching Winston Benjamin walk away from her news, a terrible sense of loss enveloped her again.

Thirty Six

When Sarah and Roger finally returned to the Garden Pavilion at Buckingham, they made love. Sarah was so proud of him, so confident Roger had a genuine chance to be elected. All her earlier fears were assuaged. Everyone had loved his speech, his energy, his enthusiasm, and most of all, his commitment to the cause. So many wanted to rally behind the new, handsome political leader, and she could now see him as Prime Minister one day.

"You really took command at the meeting. You were like a young Wilberforce, doing what Wilberforce did 60 years ago in the same place. A man on a mission to change things. To go beyond partisan politics and make the world better for all of us. It was something to behold."

"I was only interested in what you thought," Roger said softly. "Talking about Helen and my Negro friends and workers at Fenmore Place made me realize where my soft spot for you first developed." Roger turned toward her and began caressing her. "Helen was the first person to show me love in an external way as we British are always taught not to show outward signs of affection. She'd squeeze my cheeks and joke with me. Tickle me. Hug me. Oh, her hugs were the best. I can still feel them. She was a real mother to me, and I loved her. Deeply."

"Where is she now?"

"Dead," he answered somberly which made Sarah mournful.

"A growth appeared on her neck," Roger continued. "She kept insisting on her own homegrown African herbs and concoctions, but after two months, it was no better, and by the time our doctor arrived to examine her it was a cancer from which she never recovered. I had her buried in the family cemetery. My uncle hated it, but I wanted the sun to shine on Helen all the time. When I'm in Weymouth I still go out and talk to her. She told me that one day I would meet a woman who would take my breath away and make me believe in God again after my parents' deaths made me agnostic. And when I look at you, I see Helen, and I do believe in God again."

Sarah kissed him. Now it all made sense, she thought. Roger had been in love with his black housekeeper in his adolescent way, and now as an adult, that love had manifested in her. Yet, somehow Sarah didn't care where or how it happened, she was just happy he loved her—especially in this time of uncertainty between her and the Queen. So, she just nestled in the embrace of Roger's powerful arms and prayed that each day to follow would continue to bring them happiness. And they fell asleep in their love nest that was Garden Pavilion.

The next morning, they dressed for the day and Sarah prepared breakfast. The plan was to go to Berkeley Square and pass out the fliers advocating an end to the Slave Trade that Mr. Phillips had kindly printed for them gratis, then go to Gunter's Tea Shop at #7 for refreshments. Roger had raved about the ices and sorbets served there in summer which you could eat in the shop or in one's carriage under the plane trees shading the Square. But as it was winter, they would have tea and lunch inside. Sarah was excited for the experience and was right behind Roger as they opened the door of the cottage to leave.

What a shock they received when they attempted to go.

"Well, well, well. If it isn't the aspiring MP and his dark chanteuse who both take me for a royal fool." The voice belonged to the Prince of Wales standing on the other side of the door, livid. To say that Sarah and

Roger were dumbfounded would be an understatement and neither could say anything.

Bertie pushed his way into the Cottage and glared at his friend.

"Somehow I knew you weren't truthful about Lady Penelope being here. But it wasn't until my sister's wedding and I saw Sarah there singing your political praises to friends of mine that I realized you two were still seeing each other."

"Bertie…let me explain…"

"No. Let me. I want both of you out of here post haste. Our friendship is over as long as she is in your life. And I hope you understand that it also means my favor has been withdrawn as well. No one takes advantage of me."

Then shooting an evil eye at Sarah, Bertie walked out, got on his horse, and galloped away.

"To hell with you, Bertie! You will never bring me to heel! I am my own man!" Roger yelled after Bertie. But both he and Sarah knew that losing Bertie's favor would be a bitter pill for Roger to swallow.

Days later, Sarah found herself back living with the Schoen's. Like every respectable Victorian Peer, and a few not so respectable, Sir Roger was a member of a private Gentleman's Club. His was Brooks's at #60 St. James Street in London—a famous bastion for liberal Whig leaders which at one time boasted MP's Charles James Fox, the Duke of Portland, and the Duke of Devonshire as members. While Roger stayed there, his intent was to galvanize its members toward his cause and to try to forget his former friend's withdrawal of his powerful favor.

But there was no stopping the massive influence the Prince of Wales had on the British aristocracy. One well-placed word in the ear of key Peers and MP's derailed months of forward movement and progress by Sir Roger toward his ambition. Over the next six months, Bertie met with or sent notes to twenty-eight influential MP's and noblemen for the purpose of banishing his former friend to the hinterlands of politics—if only to show Sir Roger the ultimate power of the heir-apparent. He even sought out James Labulo Davies, who had gone back to Liverpool after the disastrous encounter he had the last time he saw Sarah. Bertie took James to an eatery on Hobart Street near the Liverpool docks.

"You must try again with Sarah. It's imperative she marry properly, and Mother is beside herself with disappointment it didn't work out."

"I hear, your mother is beside herself with fury," retorted James as he sipped his tea. "I hear Sarah angered her by refusing to marry me."

"It's true," said Bertie who became quiet a moment.

James looked down at the roast beef lunch Bertie was treating him to. "My reports also say she's involved with Sir Roger Carlyle *and* Winston the abolitionist. I don't understand as neither are proper for her."

"And the Queen will never approve either," Bertie grunted.

"But those two impediments keep her from an attachment to me."

"James, trust me. You answer all the concerns I have regarding Sarah. But we must be judicious in our plan to entice her toward you."

"And just what is your plan—when the heart wants what it wants?"

Bertie took a bite of his steak then a sip of bourbon. "Leave my plans to me. I just want to know that if she changes her mind, would you want her again?"

James looked away. After a moment he had to admit, "I've never stopped wanting her."

The following month, Bertie was at Garden Pavilion and asked his friend Sir Rhys Langley to join him there. After a vigorous chess game which Sir Rhys won, Bertie reached into his jacket pocket and retrieved an envelope thick with cash.

"Make sure it's what we agreed on," said Bertie.

Sir Rhys counted the money and smiled. "Yes. It's all there."

"I want no details. Just get it done and contact me after."

Sir Rhys nodded and shook Bertie's hand. They commenced another chess game.

Mr. Phillips was a good friend of the cause. He would print three hundred fliers at a time for Sir Roger, and not charge a pence. By that October he had printed and helped Roger, Sarah and others pass out over two thousand.

On a crisp afternoon on Piccadilly Street heading toward Regent's Circus, amidst the noise of horse hooves against cobblestone, and chilly air thick with smoke from a thousand chimneys, Sarah and Roger were passing out the last of the fliers and requesting signatures from people for Roger's proposed bill to *"Stop the Illegal Use of Foreign Flags on British Ships."*

They chose Piccadilly Street, which was informally called "Rothschild Row," because so many wealthy people lived there including the many members of the Rothschild family who had mansions dotting the western end of the street. Sarah and Roger felt that perhaps they might be able to generate some decent traction for their cause if they approached people strolling along the avenue and got signatures or gave them a flier.

But on this particular day, a man got out of his carriage and approached them. Upon closer inspection, it was Lord Samuel Murray, recognizable by his distinctive mutton-chop whiskers and Meerschaum pipe. He tipped his hat to Sir Roger. "Sir Roger, may I have a word?" He then glanced at Sarah. "Alone."

Sarah curtsied to Lord Murray and turned to Roger. "I'll find the Reverend and Mrs. Schoen and help them with the fliers." She moved away from the two and walked up the street toward the famous Regent's Circus intersection.

Sir Roger and Lord Murray began to walk together. Lord Murray's heart was clearly heavy. "Sir Roger, you know that I have been an avid supporter of yours since I first heard you speak. I shall never forget being moved by your words and your passion. I have even introduced you to others of influence who have become supporters of your cause."

Roger became anxious because he detected an imminent "but."

"However, let me be candid," continued Murray fulfilling Sir Roger's anxiety. "Your wish was to curry favor with me to secure your election as MP. But I am afraid I can no longer offer it."

"Why not, Lord Murray?"

"Frankly, your personal life is not conducive to my favor."

It only took Roger two seconds to realize what was happening.

"He's gotten to you, hasn't he? The Prince of Wales said something to dissuade you."

"The Prince of Wales, and all of us, are concerned that you are flaunting your relationship with 'that woman' far too openly. It is as though you have no respect for what your constituents or Members of Parliament might think."

"To hell with what they think. It's time we change how people think. That's why Queen Victoria made 'that woman' her goddaughter in the first place."

Lord Murray stopped walking and put his hand on Roger's shoulder lowering his voice. "Sir, some of our colleagues may forgive you in the face of their own 'dark' dalliances. But most assuredly, the majority will pile high their scorn upon your election. They will not take kindly to this sort of thing in Parliament's great halls of power and it is most imperative your conduct be above reproach." His hands dropped from Sir Roger's shoulders. "Sir, get rid of the Negress—if you intend to wield an ounce of that power."

"I shall not," rebuffed Roger, "I am my own man."

Lord Murray took a puff from his pipe. "Then bid your election goodbye," he warned matter-of-factly. "Good day to you."

At that, Lord Samuel Murray strode away and got into his carriage. His coachman pulled the team of horses and his Lordship away leaving Roger standing there nonplussed, then angry, then woefully concerned.

Meanwhile Sir Rhys Langley was seated on a bench in St. James's Park smoking a cigar. Seated next to him was Winston Benjamin who was not appreciating Sir Rhys' words—or tone.

"...Sarah is the Queen's ward and goddaughter, Mr. Benjamin, and you have been interfering with the Crown's plans for her. What is your price to stop communicating with her?"

Winston was annoyed. How much more of Sarah's rejections, the Queen's interfering deputies, and his claimed inferiority was he supposed to accept? "I have already stopped communicating with the Queen's goddaughter," he intoned. "But threats like this may just motivate me to look her up again."

"Do that—and you will be sorry." Sir Rhys then took a puff of his cigar and blew the smoke at Winston. "So, as I've asked, how much will it take for you to ignore her existence altogether?"

Winston stood and tied his wool scarf tighter against the cold. "I'm sorry. But you have me mistaken for a slave, sir. I am not for sale." He walked away.

Sir Rhys crushed out his cigar and also stood. When he put his gloved hands into his pockets, a pistol was evident which he quickly hid.

Thirty Seven

Two nights later, Sarah and Sir Roger were at Theatre Royal, in Covent Garden. The theater had been destroyed by fire in 1856, and anyone with any power or influence was present tonight for the celebration of the theater's reopening. It as a performance of German composer Giacomo Meyerbeer's *"Les Huguenots"* and a celebrity Gala was planned afterward.

Sarah and Roger were seated in upper box seats opposite an MP and his wife. Everyone was enjoying Corrado Miraglia, the marvelous Italian tenor performing the role of "Raoul de Nangis" in the Act One aria. Occasionally, people glanced up or use their opera glasses to spy on Sarah and Roger who had refused to shy away from sitting together.

At the curtain rang down Roger and Sarah stood to applaud. The MP opposite them had a newspaper he furtively placed on the empty seat next to Sir Roger. He quickly left with his wife. Moments later, Roger looked over, saw the newspaper, and picked it up. He frowned.

There on the front page of the Weymouth Gazette was an exaggerated drawing of Sir Roger and a black woman favoring an ape. The headline blasted: *"Candidate Carlyle and African Paramour?"*

When he read it, his shoulders slumped, then he pulled Sarah from the theater. They never attended the Gala afterward.

"What's wrong?" asked Sarah bothered by Roger's behavior.

"We must get you back to the Schoen's."

When finally they returned to Sweedon's Passage to the Schoen's house, Roger handed Sarah the newspaper. She opened it, saw the illustration, and in distress read the article aloud:

I couldn't breathe as I read it: "...Sir Roger Carlyle has for years been in a loathsome relationship with an African whom he intends to marry, the thought of which strains credulity. I ask you, how do we present such an alliance to our wives? What do we tell our children? Is this fornicator of Africans truly the man we want to represent Weymouth when the ruination of both Sir Roger—and indeed our county—now lies in the hands of a slut as common as the dirt? Why, sir, have you not married a worthy woman your own complexion?"

Sarah had to sit. Roger too. "My God, she muttered. And they couldn't look at each other.

"I want to change things, Sarah. I want to make a difference," said Roger softly, a lump forming in his throat. "But I…I cannot if I am not in an MP's seat of power. All of our hard work will have been for naught. I don't know what to do."

Sarah could see Roger was tortured. So torn between his love for her and his love for the freedom of her people—and one of those was the greater good. She looked down at the engagement ring he'd given her six months earlier. With a painful heart enveloping her soul, surpassing all understanding, she removed the ring and after a moment, gave it back to the love of her life.

"I once told you, that you would leave—and that I would understand." She stood up and looked away. "I do…"

"Sarah, no..."

"Go. But you must keep making a difference." As tears filled her eyes, she kissed his forehead. "Goodbye, Roger."

"I will never love anyone else," Roger whispered, not looking at her.

But Sarah walked away leaving Roger sad and regretful. It was a full two days before she could eat or sleep. All she did was play her violin, day and night, trying to submerge her feelings. The Schoens tried to help or comfort her, but Sarah was unresponsive.

"Everything I love I lose," she lamented to Elizabeth Schoen when finally she accepted a glass of wine and the two women sat on her bed.

"Well, I don't profess to have a cure for a broken heart, dearie," admitted Mrs. Schoen. "But I think you did the right thing. You sacrificed your relationship with Sir Roger for a better cause. Now he can run for office with no impediments. Get bills introduced. Make changes for the betterment of your people. Supposin' he becomes Prime Minister. Imagine what he could do for Negroes then?" Elizabeth stood. "You'll find love, one day, dearie. A love that won't create problems for you, him—or society." She went to the door then turned back to Sarah. "Well, I'm off. There's a meeting at Phillips today, and the good Reverend and I will be there. Maybe you should come."

Sarah nodded. Mrs. Schoen left.

I began to pace. Why was I always the problem? This is what I was fighting against. My blackness, my "otherness" always being the concern. Surely there was a life and a lover I could have where my being black wouldn't pose a negative, nor "impediment." But where was that life? And who was that lover? I wandered over to my bureau and opened the drawer. I saw Roger's blue silk scarf and fought back tears. But next to it, I saw the Mawa Winston Benjamin had carved for me. I held it in my hand and thought about Winston's words at Buckingham: "Ask yourself where you can do the most good, have the most influence. With these royals? Or with your own...?" And suddenly I knew who I was—and what I had to do...

Sarah put the Mawa around her neck, caressed it a moment, then left the house. It was snowing that December day when Sarah arrived at her beloved Phillips Print Shop on George Lane. The meeting of the "Society for the Worldwide Cessation of the Slave Trade" was in session. As she entered, Winston Benjamin was at the podium speaking. But this time, instead of relaying his experiences as a victim of the Trade, he was making a speech regarding self-empowerment. He was insisting that those present who were white be proactive about equality and inclusion, and to be instructors if possible.

"Negroes must be educated to be vital, productive members of society. We must have pride in who we are, what we've done and what we have contributed historically. We must learn to be self-sufficient. To know things. To read and help each other become knowledgeable…"

He then saw Sarah, his beloved, and smiled. "I was blessed to have such a teacher. A beautiful African woman who taught me everything she knew—math, language, reading, writing—and history. She made me love books as much as she did. And I am a better man for it. If it takes the rest of my life, I will always love and be indebted to her for that gift."

Sarah smiled, and nodded to him. For it was then she knew Winston had held her heart all along—that together they could conquer anything, proudly, openly, honestly—and without her blackness impeding.

After the meeting some people were gathered outside of the print shop including the Schoen's, Mr. Phillips, and Miyo. Finally, Sarah and Winston emerged. Winston smiled at her.

"I didn't think I would ever see you again, since your engagement."

Sarah showed him her left hand on which there was no ring. "I've been so wrong, Winnie. So blind. I'm sorry. Please forgive me."

Winston face broke into a grin as wide as the Atlantic. "I can forgive you anything. You know that." His arms then encircled her body, and for once she didn't pull away as he kissed her gently, sweetly, right there in front of everyone on George Lane. Reverend and Mrs. Schoen smiled, as did Miyo. Sarah felt warm and contented at last…

...until she opened her eyes and saw in her sight line...a pistol! It was aimed directly at Winston's back. In seconds, before she or anyone could do anything, the white finger squeezed the trigger...and Winston Benjamin fell dead in Sarah's arms. His body slumping as she screamed:

"Winnie!! No!! NO!!"

The man who shot Winston ran off as people gathered around Winston's body in shock and disbelief. All Sarah could do was sob in utter devastation as she rocked his body back and forth, back and forth, back and forth.

On 19 December 1861 Sarah Bonetta tearfully knelt over Winston Benjamin's grave at Rose Chapel—the same church where she had been baptized. She placed several cut evergreen branches in front of the makeshift wooden headstone against which snow was building. It read:

M'WAKO ARBUTA
KNOWN AS WINSTON BENJAMIN
BELOVED FRIEND AND
A SON OF AFRICA
1838 – 1861

Sarah's heart was filled with pain and rage at his killing—and at her loss, especially all the time they could have had together. Then, as she was wiping her eyes, she heard from behind her: "Sally...?"

Sarah turned to find Princess Alice there in tears with Miyo. Sarah was surprised. "Ally. What are you doing here?"

"I told her you were here, Aina," said Miyo.

Alice went over and fell into Sarah's arms. "I am so sorry for your loss. For the loss of both of them, now."

"*Both*—of whom?"

"Winston...," cried Alice, "...and Poppi. Oh Sally, Poppi died."

Sarah stood up as the snow battered her face. She was disbelieving. "No! No, it can't be! Not the Prince Consort, too."

"Mother is beside herself with grief. It was typhoid fever. He was already unwell, then he was in the rain chastising Bertie and caught a chill. He never recovered. He died Tuesday," she sobbed. "Mother says she will blame Bertie the rest of her life."

Alice fell back into Sarah's arms in a gale of tears. "I had to find you. I just had to." She looked up at Sarah, her heartbroken, and overwhelmed by grief. "Come home, Sally. Please, please come home."

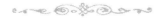

Two days before Christmas 1861, the streets of London were empty. Shops were closed. Few carriages on the roads. All of Britain was in mourning as the great bell of St. Paul's Cathedral dolefully tolled.

His Royal Highness Prince Albert of Saxe-Coburg and Gotha, the consort to the Queen of England, who died at age 42 on 14 December 1861, was honored with a full-court funeral. Victoria ordered all palace flags flown at half-staff. Outside St. George's Chapel at Windsor Castle, an Honor Guard in a black cape, stood at the main entrance.

Inside the church, the closed coffin of the Prince laid in repose in front. The chapel was crowded. Close friends and members of the royal family were present. Queen Victoria, dressed in black, was in the front pew along with daughters, Princess Vicky and her husband Prince Friedrich Wilhelm, Princesses Alice, Helena, and Louise; and her sons Princes Bertie, Alfred, and Arthur. Four-year-old Princess Beatrice, and sickly Prince Leopold were left at Windsor Castle under the care of their governess thought too young or sickly to attend their father's funeral. Lords and Ladies-in-Waiting, special friends, court aids, MP's, Prime Minister Henry John Temple, 3rd Viscount Palmerston—who had succeeded Victoria's beloved PM Aberdeen, and Sir Charles Phipps and his wife sat behind the family. Then there was Sarah, with her head bowed and grieving, who sat a few pews behind them and across the aisle from Sir Roger Carlyle as the Priest spoke:

"...As we look back on the life of the Prince Consort, may we know of his high intellectual gifts of mind; unbounded friendship, true virtue, and deep love for our great nation..."

When the service was concluded, the body of the Prince would continue lying in state, so the public could pay their respects, but Victoria and the royal family came out of the church and headed toward the black funeral carriages. It was then that Victoria noticed Sarah and motioned for Alice to summon her.

Sarah went over and curtsied. "I adored the Prince, Majesty. My sincere condolences on your loss."

"And mine to you...with Winston."

"At least you were able to say goodbye...at the end." Sarah looked away slightly. "We don't all get to do that with the people we love."

"And Albie certainly loved you," said Victoria solemnly. "As we all do. We miss you, Sally..." She became overcome with grief and struggled not to show it as they were now in public, "...*I* miss you."

She put a shaky hand to Sarah's teary-eyed face. "When do you return to the Schoen's?"

Sarah glanced away and saw Sir Roger looking at her. It was a sorrowful look filled with regret. Sarah slowly turned back to Victoria.

"I had hoped not to, ma'am."

Thus, she and the Queen of England shared a knowing moment in which Victoria understood and nodded. She moved on. As did Sarah.

Thirty Eight

That February 1862, in the snow and bitter cold of an English win-ter, I returned to Windsor Castle—to the position of goddaughter under the royal protection and guardianship of Queen Victoria. And for the rest of my life I felt guilty because Winston Benjamin was the one I had sacri-ficed for what I thought was my own better good...

arah's carriage arrived to the gate at Windsor Castle and foot-men were there ready. Barnes opened the carriage door and re-trieved Sarah's luggage.

"Welcome back, m'lady." He helped her out and into the Castle.

"Thank you, Barnes."

When she entered the Queen Mary suite, her old rooms, she looked around. It was still as wondrous and impressive as when she first came to live there nine years earlier, and still arranged as she had it when she left two years ago. But it no longer drew her in. It was just a nicer place for her to sleep as she planned her future.

As Sarah was unpacking Bertie and Alice knocked and came in.

Alice ran over and hugged her.

"I've missed you so much. I'm glad you're back."

"I've missed you, too. But I will not be here long."

"You know I'm engaged and will marry Prince Louis this July. It's all arranged—whether I like it or not."

"I know. But try to make the best of it, Ally. Make it work."

Sarah turned to the Prince of Wales, "Bertie, will you find and ask Mr. Davies to come here to Windsor? I would like to speak to him—that is, if he wishes to see me."

Bertie nodded and left, knowing his devious plan to get rid of both Sarah and Winston, had worked.

The next week, Sarah was seated across from James Labulo Davies having tea in Windsor's red parlor. "I've asked you here because I was very rude the last time we spoke," Sarah began. "I apologize for that."

"Much was on your mind," James correctly assessed. "As now."

"It's very hard for a black woman, any woman really, of no means, to find love, be happily married, *and* make a difference in this world."

"True. Such a smart, rare, extraordinary woman with a God-given purpose would need to find a man who is her equal. A man who would love, understand, and help her unconditionally," said James pointedly. "A man who would put her needs above his own—and champion her." His face turned up easing into a slight, knowing grin. "But such a man is rare and could easily be overlooked."

Sarah's eyes rose to meet his and she understood. She evaluated what he said—and, more importantly, didn't say, and she wondered if she had not been hasty in her dismissal of his original interest. Or, had she been affected by her experiences living with the Schoens, leaving Sir Roger, and Winston's death. Then she knew it was all of those.

James, sensing she was contemplating his words, sat his cup of tea down, his voice becoming soft and thoughtful. "There are some women whose instinct is to choose the shiny bauble. It's prettier, everyone is attracted to it and likes to look at it. But right next to it is a sturdy, tough, durable piece of crystal, not yet shined to its diamond appearance. But in fact, a diamond. It will not break when dropped and warms in your hand as it holds your strength. Which do you choose?"

Sarah then perused James noting his large frame, smooth chocolate skin and confidence. He was fifteen years older than she, so perhaps this also accounted for his self-assured aura as he smiled at her. Confidence and wealth were much to recommend a man.

Later that day, Sarah and Victoria were on horseback riding through Windsor Park enjoying the clear, almost warm afternoon after three days of snow—which was now melting. Victoria was still dressed in widow's black as would be a practice she kept up for the next 40 years until her own death. This day, though she was still mourning Albert and not her usual upbeat self, she and Sarah were relishing each other's company.

It had been almost four years since Sarah had seen the beauty of the Windsor grounds with its rambling trees and wonderful expanse of foliage. Even though there wasn't a leaf on the trees, it was still as enthralling as when she and Sir Roger would ride for hours taking in the surroundings—and each other.

As they rode along Victoria was introspective.

"I thank God you're back, Sally. The last two years have been a horror, and my travails make me feel worse. We're embroiled in a standoff with America's northern states trying to draw us into their Civil War," Then the light faded from her eyes, "…and of course the tragedies, first mother, and then eight months later my beloved Albie." She sighed. "I'm alone. Bad times make you regret bad choices."

"I know," said Sarah ruefully. "Like mine—to remain in England."

Victoria frowned at Sarah. "I don't understand."

"I want to go back to Africa," Sarah began. "I want to be of service to my own. I've learned so much here that I can share with my people."

"But how can you be happy back there after living here in the cradle of culture and opportunity? Look at who you are now."

Sarah realized that the Queen would never understand what it was like to be black. "But I've paid too high a price for who I am not." She paused a moment to form her words carefully as she did not wish to insult the Queen, nor England, but it had to be said.

"Majesty, the English—the French too—have taken great pride in being world powers. But you got that way through plundering and destroying many great nations—raping them of their resources—places like Africa, India, and South Asia. And you've done it without giving a thought to the indigenous people of those lands and how they'd cope."

"There has always been war, Sally."

"I know. My life is the result of it. But did it ever occur to you how hard it was for me?—one of those indigenous people from an English plundered land—an African princess barely escaping execution; my family butchered; uprooted from my homeland and way of life. I was baptized, and my name changed so I could accommodate a religion that was not mine. Then I'm given as a gift to you like a horse or a vase. I'm raped, turned into an 'experiment' to be educated, dressed and wigged as an English 'Lady' to show how much my being an "other" is unsuitable. Then when I find true love with a British Peer, I cannot marry him because my black heritage will 'ruin' his career. And were that not enough, Captain Forbes dies; Winston is killed; it's demanded of me to marry a man chosen for me, and I have no say in the matter. Then, when I refuse I'm thrown out and uprooted again."

"But Sally. Surely some of those things can be forgotten…"

"Forgotten? Ma'am, I have no money of my own, no title, and no identity here—save for my 'royal' association with you. Much of the time I don't know who I am as a woman of color in this country."

Victoria was speechless as they rode along a bit further.

"So, apparently I've made your life a conundrum of disparity."

Sarah paused a moment. "Not completely, ma'am."

Sarah and Victoria stopped at the far east end of the Park and looked out over the River Thames with its winding aspect carving through London. Sarah got off her horse and stood at the precipice of the hill. Victoria did too.

"I know we've had our differences, you and I, but you've been good to me. And I appreciate everything you've done to help me," Sarah admitted. "I've been given opportunities unparalleled to anyone I know who looks like me and I'm grateful." Sarah then looked at the Queen smiling slightly. "I've accepted James Davies' marriage proposal."

Victoria was suddenly overjoyed. "Oh, Sally. That's wonderful. Just wonderful. We must plan the wedding straight away. Oh, this is such good news."

"We are going back to live in Africa where I can make a difference just being me. I can be a teacher."

It took Victoria a moment. But she understood. "My dear, I know you think me intransigent, but I had good reason for my experiment with you. You see, my family has more than one secret."

Now it was Sarah who frowned.

"My grandmother, Queen Charlotte, to whom Buckingham was given, was forced to hide who she really was—a mixed-African," Victoria began the news of which shocked Sarah. "Though her skin was very light, she hid it under white make-up. But she, too, was still an "other" struggling with her identity. Victoria paused a moment to look at the river. "And though King George loved her, the concern was if their children would be brown. I envisioned a world where such concerns wouldn't matter. I was hoping it would start with you."

Sarah was incredulous. "So you, Alice, Bertie, Leopold—all have African blood?"

Victoria nodded. "And the world I want to create would allow for those who are undeniably black equal access." She looked back at her beautiful goddaughter and took her hand. "But sometimes to create that world mistakes are made—like the one I made by insisting you stay here with us—or, force is required, like that you suggested we exact on King Gezo."

Sarah frowned as Victoria continued. "But success was the result of those efforts. Both with you and with Dahomey."

As the Queen told the story, Sarah saw it unfurl in her mind's eye:

King Gezo looked at the scorched earth of his village and palace which was burned to the ground by French and British soldiers.

"We burned all of King Gezo's slave ships in Whydah port and his palace. As you proposed we poured gallons of red paint into his main water well and trust me, he graciously signed our treaty."

An English officer handed Gezo the Treaty to sign—which he did. The officers marched away leaving Gezo to ponder his fate. Soon, homeless Amazon warriors carrying machetes and scimitars approached Gezo—including Emeka. Gezo was ready to accept his fate as their blades rose—and came down on the now *former* King of Dahomey. His blood splashing on their faces as he was chopped to bits.

"Gezo's own warriors sacrificed him in a "Watering Graves" ritual just as you predicted—for bringing the wrath of their Gods on them. The slave trade in Dahomey is over."

Victoria smiled triumphantly. "As is that nefarious business at our Zanzibar Consulate—of which I knew nothing."

Sarah shook her head in awe. "You did all of this in my absence?"

"And much more. Headmaster Humes was arrested for rape. It turns out—you were not the only girl at the Chambers School to come forward with the same story." Victoria patted Sarah's hand and smiled. Sarah smiled too. Maybe this *was* her new beginning.

On 1 July 1862, Sarah was seated in the dining room of Osborne House, which had been converted into a temporary chapel where Princess Alice and Prince Louis had a private wedding ceremony.

Alice looked miserable. The Queen was ushered in by her four sons, who took her to an armchair near the altar. Alice was given away by her uncle, Albert's brother Ernest II, Duke of Saxe-Coburg and Gotha, and was flanked by four bridesmaids: her younger sisters, Princesses Helena, Louise and Beatrice, as well as Prince Louis' sister Princess Anna. Alice's oldest sister Vicky was heavily pregnant and living with her husband Friedrich in Germany and could not be at the wedding.

Even though Alice was wearing a white dress for the ceremony, the Queen had insisted she wear black, in mourning for her father Prince Albert, before and after the nuptials, which angered Alice and further underscored why Alice felt she had no rights at all—even with a new husband. Queen Victoria, seated in an armchair, also in black, struggled to hold back her tears and cried throughout the ceremony.

The weather at Osborne House was dreary. Bad winds blew in from the English Channel, and everyone in attendance felt the service was "more like a funeral than a wedding." In fact, the ceremony was described by writer Gerard Noel, who was there, as "the saddest royal wedding in modern times."

Even Sarah, who knew what Alice was feeling, thought it was indeed a very grim day. When they saw each other before Alice and Louis left in their carriage, they hugged. Alice begged Sarah to "Pray for me."

By contrast, everything about Sarah's wedding the following month was the envy of the aristocracy—and the 'must attend' event of the season. The newspaper headline of the Brighton Dispatch dated 14 August 1862 had revealed to the world: *"Queen Victoria Godmother To Colored Sarah Forbes Bonetta Attends Her Godchild's Wedding."*

The wedding party arrived from West Hill Lodge, Brighton in ten carriages with pairs of grays. It was made up of white ladies with African gentlemen, and African ladies with white gentlemen. There were sixteen bridesmaids and sixteen groomsmen who entered the church. Dignitaries, statesmen and VIPs of the British Empire entered in their carriages then went into the church including the Schoens, Gibson, and Brandon from the HMS Bonetta.

The Royal family arrived last in a carriage. Policemen kept order, barricading the path into the church as Victoria, still in black, waved to the roaring crowd. Bertie, and Prince Friedrich followed

Inside St. Nicholas church it was packed. Blacks, whites, Royals, and commoners sat next to each other watching Sarah at the altar with James. Victoria proudly looked on. Occasionally Sarah coughed to which Victoria frowned. Sadly, Sarah's cough was back.

The wedding vows were exchanged. "...Wilst thou love, honour, and keep him, in sickness and in health; and forsaking all others, keep thee only unto him, so long as ye both shall live?" asked the minister.

Both James and Sarah answered, "I...I will," and the minister pronounced them "man and wife." The two kissed each other almost the way platonic friends do when reuniting after several years' absence.

But Sarah was determined to make the marriage work—and leave Britain. James' goal was to make Sarah as happy as he could until she learned to love him. It became his mission.

At the reception later, family, friends and well-wishers congratulated Sarah. Gifts were piled high on the gift table and champagne flowed. Soon, Brandon and Gibson approached Sarah smiling. "Brandon, Gibson. Thank you for coming," Sarah grinned.

They all hugged. "Congratulations. It's wonderful," said Brandon. "I wish Forbes could've been here."

"Me too. But he's here in spirit," Sarah beamed.

They each kissed her, and the first British friends she made from so long ago moved on. Next, Sarah's mouth dropped when she saw Jilly and Rebecca from the Forbes house approach. They, too hugged.

"Saints alive, Lassie. You found a man to marry," joked Jilly. "Now ask him if he's got a brother." Then Sarah and Rebecca hugged. "You know Mrs. Forbes moved to Scotland after the Captain died. She sold the house."

"I heard," said Sarah. And the three women hugged again. Next Sarah saw Linda Beekman and her husband who came up from Yorkshire. "Be happy," said Linda as she hugged Sarah.

Finally, Sarah looked up to find Bertie standing there with Sir Roger Carlyle next to him holding a small box in one hand and the fingers of a blonde woman in the other. "Congratulations, Sarah, James," Bertie offered, noticing Roger was unable to meet Sarah's gaze. Knowingly, he then indicated Sir Roger to James in faux innocence. "James, may I introduce my dear friend Sir Roger Carlyle, the youngest MP ever elected from Weymouth—and his lovely new wife Lady Lydia Carlyle."

Sarah hid her shock at the news Roger was married while everyone greeted the other. She perused Lady Lydia and thought, of course. She was white, blonde and beautiful. A titled aristocrat no doubt from Roger's circle. The perfect, acceptable woman for his political goals.

"So, Sir Roger, you are a Member of Parliament," noted James.

"Yes. In the Commons," replied Roger, still unable to look at Sarah.

"What is it like having access to all that power and influence?"

"Not always powerful," answered Sir Roger. "But satisfying. In fact, I present my first bill next week— *The Illegal Use of Flags on Cargo Ships.*"

His eyes finally met Sarah's with a look of remorse. But Sarah's face countered with appreciation. This had been *their* cause. *Their* bill. And Roger intended to fight the good fight even without her. Though he still loved her—so much so his heart was bursting—he bowed then handed her the small box he was carrying. "A wedding gift," he offered.

Sarah opened the box, inside was a silver inkpot. She had to grin.

"For when you write in your diaries," Roger managed, then quickly moved away with his wife lest he scream from frustration.

James leaned into Sarah when Roger and his wife were out of range. "I know that was hard. I know about you and him from Bertie."

"Of course you do," Sarah lamented trying to steady herself. But when she glanced over, Sir Roger was looking back at her.

"I swear, you will never regret marrying me," James assured.

"I already have no regrets," she replied, squeezing his hand which made his heart leap. Then he kissed her as Victoria approached.

"Congratulations Mr. and Mrs. Davies."

"Thank you, Majesty," they both said.

"Alice wanted to be here, but her husband would not permit her to leave Hesse."

"I know," said Sarah. "She wrote me. But I still miss her."

"When do you leave?"

"The day after tomorrow," answered Sarah. "We're going to Sierra Leone. I'd like to open a girl's school and teach so women can have an informed mind."

"Well, your life has always been ordained for a higher purpose," Victoria smiled. "Take your dream and your husband to Africa and teach. Make your own experiment. And I'll help in any way I can." Victoria then touched Sarah's face. "I shall miss you, my dear."

"And I, you."

They hugged for a long tearful while, then afterward Victoria slowly walked away from James and her goddaughter as the couple watched her. They knew from the Queen's countenance how sorrowful she was— even in the midst of her great joy at their nuptials.

As Victoria walked past him, Sarah caught Roger's eyes and smiled knowing that even as she stood next to the man she had just married, she would always have love in her heart for Roger. Then she turned away—and her smile now indicated her life had indeed moved on...

...On to that higher purpose of which her godmother Queen Victoria spoke.

The wedding of Sarah Forbes Bonetta
to James Labulo Davies, 14 August 1862

Epilogue

Funchal Bay, Madeira
Portugal

1880

"…If I cannot do great things,
I can do small things in a great way…"

Dr. Martin Luther King, Jr.

1 August 1880

The Kroo canoe carrying James and I was rowed onto the sandy shores of Sierra Leone by four sailors from the HMS Clybourne. When we newlyweds came ashore, we smiled at what we saw.

Our new life. It was 9 October 1862.

I squeezed James' hand and looked out over the African savanna and the hillside dotted with small homes and lean-tos. I was happy. I instantly pulled off my wig, kicked off my shoes, and undid the stomacher, bodice, and corset of my tortuous English clothing and hurled them all into the air. I then ran barefoot into the bush wearing only my shift and Winston's mawa. James grinned at the expression of my freedom.

That night, James and I made love—and created you.

Three months later in Freetown, I was wearing a kanga, a gele, my tribal markings, and the mawa while teaching the times-table and playing a violin to a classroom of girls. I had opened a girls school in Freetown with Queen Victoria's help. She and I wrote each other many letters over the years and her friendship remained one of my most valued. As my girls sing-sang the times-tables—"5 times 1 is 5, 5 times 2 is 10..." I remembered Captain Forbes, Lt. Brandon, Sergeant Gibson—and Winston, to whom I had taught math the same way. The girls did the five times table to music from drummers outside. Sounds of learning and excitement emanated from them. Then I held a few girls by the hands and we all ran outside the school where the drummers were. Suddenly we all danced the Ya Moto. Everyone was having fun, dancing wildly. And the dancing was allowed—and okay.

Sir Roger Carlyle's bill was never voted on because it was never presented to Parliament. The Queen wrote to tell me that, sadly, I had lost my first love.

Three days after my wedding, Roger was killed in a hunting accident. They say his last words were 'Forgive me.' When I heard the news, I mourned him. I mourned for many years but never told James. A woman's heart is a deep well of secrets—and regrets. But to this day, I have his blue silk scarf and the silver inkpot he gave me which I am using now—even though I learned to love your father and have had the most incredible life with him. James is a good man, an understanding man—and a good father to you, your brother and sister. The love he gives us all will stay with me the rest of my life—however long.

By 1865, the Civil War in America ended slavery there. It prompted Brazil, Portugal, the Netherlands, and Cuba to end slavery in their countries. I wished my dear Winston could have lived to see it.

My dear friend Princess Alice, Grand Duchess of Hesse, is dead too. She died two years ago, in 1878, from Diphtheria, and, I suspect, from an unhappy, sad heart. In 1863, the same year Bertie married Princess Alexandra of Denmark, Alice and I both had daughters. She, too, named hers 'Victoria' after her mother. Oh, how I wish you two girls could've met her for I think of Ally all the time—of her outspoken feistiness and her rebellious nature that was finally married out of her.

Soon, it will be my time.

Dearest daughter Victoria, I have been unwell for many years. They say I have Tuberculosis It is why you, your brother Arthur and your sister Stella are here in Madeira—for the better climate so I can convalesce. I am 38-years old and have been told I will not survive the summer. But I am hopeful. All I wish is to finish this diary, so my written words can serve as my truth since illness no longer permits me to speak them...

n 1867, Sarah and James had visited Queen Victoria and brought along their first child Victoria Matilda Davies. Sarah wanted little Victoria to meet the woman for whom she was named that she had loved, fought with, and respected.

The Queen was thrilled because she felt the match between Sarah and James was successful and she fell in love with four-year-old Victoria. "I shall make little Vicky my goddaughter as well. And I will provide an annuity for her for the rest of her life," smiled the Queen to Sarah.

Sarah did not know it then, but this would be her final trip to London and the last time she saw her beloved Queen. James and Sarah would go on to have two more children—a son, Arthur, and another daughter, Stella. When it was time, Victoria Matilda was sent to London to be educated at the behest of the Queen. So important was Sarah and her family to the Queen that she gave standing orders to the Royal Navy that should there be an uprising in Lagos Sarah, James, and the children were to be evacuated.

But Sarah's cough got worse and James felt it best to move her to a hospital in Funchal, the Capital of Madeira on the Portuguese shore. He would do anything he could to keep her alive and make her happy.

James' business had gone very badly, and the financial troubles they were having, coupled with its court case hanging over their heads, so concerned Sarah that it had aggravated her condition, and she did not want to tell the Queen of her woes.

When Queen Victoria learned of Sarah's illness, she wrote in her diary: "Grieved & shocked to hear that poor Sally, Mrs. Davies, was hopelessly ill at Madeira."

But in Funchal, at the Weissen Clinic, Sarah wrote in her own diary:

...You are young, Victoria, and may not grasp or comprehend it all. But one day when you read these words and try to understand and unravel your mother's complicated life and choices, you will come to realize that sometimes you don't know what your purpose is as life unfolds, and that is okay.

But in the end, I was one of the lucky ones. For as it turns out, my purpose found me. I am a teacher, and there is no telling the number of minds I have developed in that capacity.

This...has been my truth.

Sarah laid down her pen and looked at the silver inkwell. Her wedding gift from Sir Roger now long dead. She looked at all her books James had brought to the hospital, and she smiled at her husband who was there holding her hand with two of their children Arthur and Stella.

Her life had not been an easy one, but it had been good, she thought. She lived it well, her way, and influenced others. Now it was alright for her to join her parents and siblings, her dearest friends Kua, Princess Alice, Winston Benjamin, Sir Roger Carlyle...

...And the circle of ancients—which she did fourteen days later.

In August 1880 seventeen-year-old Victoria Matilda Davies was traveling by coach from London to stay with the Royal family. Queen Victoria had been given a note and sadly had to tell her goddaughter that her mother, Sarah Forbes Bonetta Davies died in Funchal, Madeira from Tuberculosis. Both women tearfully held each other.

The Queen later wrote: *"Saw poor Victoria Davies, my black godchild, who learnt this morning of the death of her dear mother."*

James had held his wife's hand as she passed from this life to the ancients. He buried her near the Anglican Holy Trinity Church in Funchal but could not afford a headstone at the time. After mourning Sarah for a year, he finally returned to Lagos, West Africa where eventually he started a cocoa farm and became successful again. In Lagos, James erected a granite, obelisk-shaped monument more than eight feet high in memory of his beloved late wife, with an inscription that read:

IN MEMORY OF
PRINCESS SARAH FORBES BONETTA
WIFE OF THE HON J.P.L. DAVIES
WHO DEPARTED THIS LIFE AT MADEIRA
AUGUST 15TH, 1880

James Davies remarried and had other children. But he never recovered from the death of his beloved Sarah.

Four years after Sarah's death, Prince Leopold died of Hemophilia at age 30. He bled to death from a simple scraped knee. His three children were all carriers of the disease. Princess Alice and her sister Princess Vicky were also carriers. Thus the "royal disease" was transmitted from Queen Victoria to most of the Royal families in Europe.

The source of Victoria's Hemophilia or whether she was the legitimate Sovereign of England remains shrouded in mystery. She and her mother destroyed all contrary evidence before her mother's death.

As for the whereabouts of Sarah's diaries, they are unknown, and Victoria Matilda Davies never saw them. It was rumored that James buried them, Winston's mawa, and Sir Roger's silver inkpot and blue silk scarf with his wife's body to conceal the knowledge that, although she had learned to love him, he was not the primary object of his wife's deepest affections.

Queen Victoria died on 22 January 1901 at age 81 of an intracerebral hemorrhage. She had served as Britain's Queen for almost sixty-four years, and at the time was the longest reigning sovereign in British history—a record not to be broken until the reign of her 6th great granddaughter Queen Elizabeth II surpassed it in 2015.

Like James Davies, Victoria never fully recovered from the death of her spouse—her beloved Prince Albert.

But true to her promise to Sarah, she sponsored Sarah's daughter Victoria Matilda until the end of her life and long reign.

Victoria Matilda Davies, Sarah Forbes Bonetta Davies'
daughter, and her two children (Sarah's grandchildren).
The girl is named Beatrice after Queen Victoria's youngest
daughter Beatrice who was the girl's godmother.

Author's Notes and Acknowledgements

I first heard of Sarah Forbes Bonetta when a friend gave me a copy of Walter Dean Myers wonderful book on her. My Sally Hemings/Thomas Jefferson miniseries for CBS had aired to much success the year before and I was anxious to do another historical drama. But I was shocked that so little information existed about Miss Bonetta—even within Queen Victoria biographies that contained the Queen's diaries which, in fact, featured Sarah in many entries. It was as though no one wanted it known that the Queen of England had adopted an African girl and provided for her. This, of course, meant I had to research for myself and the fragments of that research, particularly in the UK, led me to a story. It would be a journey lasting another ten years before I had enough bits and pieces to string together into a narrative, and two years of writing.

Although *Princess Sarah: Queen Victoria's African Goddaughter* incorporates the real-life story of Sarah Forbes Bonetta, Queen Victoria and the Queen's family, it is none the less a work of fiction and a product of my imagination. However, there are actual places, facts, events, people, and images in this book which required research and verification. I am deeply indebted to: The Malibu Press for their unwavering trust in my work; my agent BJ Robbins who so skillfully handled the material; my researcher Joanne "JM" Morris whose mammoth contribution of time and energy cannot be calculated; and to my genius editor Becky Rich, who helped me shape the work and kept me chronologically on track.

Many, many thanks are also extended to the archivists at Windsor Castle and Buckingham Palace for their efforts in helping me sort out Queen Victoria's diary entries regarding Sarah and daily activities at the palaces. Additionally, grateful acknowledgement is made to the following "angels" without whose help this book would not have been possible: George Alexander, Peter Bevan, Stanley Bennett Clay, Gerren Crochet, Eleanor Earl, Treva Etienne, Denise Gillman, Camille Gillman, Todd Grodnick, Todd Harris, Dave Ingland, Sharon Johnson, Mondella Jones, Karen Jordan, Wendy Kram, Lin McEwan, Marion Ramsey, Duncan Reid, Darryl Ross, Peter Touché, Erik Washington, Matthew Wolf…and the support of my family. All images in this novel are in the public domain and can be found online.

Most importantly, there were several source references and documents used in conjunction with this novel that were essential. They are not responsible for any interpretations, errors, omissions, or misrepresentations I may have made, but grateful acknowledgement must be made to the following selected authors and their scholarly works:

BOOKS:

Davidson, Basil. *The African Slave Trade*. New York. Back Bay Books, 1980

Elebute, Adeyemo. *The Life of James Pinson Labulo Davies: A Colossus of Victorian Lagos*. Nigeria. Kachifo Limited, 2013

Forbes, Frederick E. *Dahomey and the Dahomans, Vol. 2: Being the Journals of Two Missions to the King of Dahomey, and Residence at His Capital, in the Years 1849 and 1850,* London. Longman, Brown, Green and Longmans, 1851 (Reprinted by Forgotten Books, London, 2007)

Hedley, Olwen. *Windsor Castle*. London, Robert Hale Limited, 1967

Hibbert, Christopher. *Queen Victoria: A Personal History*. New York. Basic Books, 2000

Jones, Steve. *In the Blood: God, Genes and Destiny*. London. Flamingo, 1996

Longford, Elizabeth. *Queen Victoria: Born to Succeed*. New York. Harper & Row, 1964

Mackworth-Young, Robin. *The History & Treasures of Windsor Castle*. London. Pitken Pictorials, 1991

Myers, Walter Dean. *At Her Majesty's Request: An African Princess in Victorian England*. New York. Scholastic Press, 1999

Packard, Jerrold M. *Victoria's Daughters*. Gloucestershire. Sutton Publishing Limited, 1999

Potts, D.M, & Potts, W.T. *Queen Victoria's Gene*. Gloucestershire. Sutton Publishing Limited, 1995

Rappaport, Helen. *Queen Victoria: A Biographical Companion*. Santa Barbara. ABC-CLIO, Inc. 2003

Ridley, Jane. *The Heir Apparent: A Life of Edward VII, the Playboy Prince*. New York. Random House, 2013

Shaw, Karl. *Royal Babylon. The Alarming History of European Royalty*. New York. Broadway Books, 1999

Sherwood, Marika. *After Abolition Britain and the Slave Trade Since 1807*. London. I.B. Tauris & Co. Ltd. 2007

Ward, Yvonne M. *Censoring Queen Victoria: How Two Gentlemen Edited a Queen and Created an Icon*. London. One World Publications, 2013

Williams, Kate. *Becoming Queen Victoria, The Tragic Death of Princess Charlotte and the Unexpected Rise of Britain's Greatest Monarch*, New York. Ballantine Books, 2008

Wilson, A.N. *The Victorians*. New York. W.W. Norton & Co., 2003

ONLINE SOURCES:

Black History Month – *The African Princess: Sarah Forbes Bonetta* - http://www.blackhistorymonth.org.uk/article/section/real-stories/the-african-princess-sarah-forbes-bonetta/

New African Woman – *Sarah Forbes Bonetta: The Yoruba Princess Who Captured Queen Victoria's Heart* -

http://nawmagazine.com/sarah-forbes-bonetta-the-yoruba-princess-who-captured-Queen-victorias-heart/

BlackPast.org - *Sarah Forbes Bonetta 1843–1880* - http://www.blackpast.org/aah/bonetta-sarah-forbes-1843-1880

Franklin, Ronald E. - *"Queen Victoria's Black Princess"* -https://owlcation.com/humanities/Queen-Victorias-Black-Princess

Chandler, Emily - *The Stolen African Slave Who Became Queen Victoria's Goddaughter* –

http://www.messynessychic.com/2017/05/16/the-stolen-african-slave-who-became-Queen-victorias-goddaughter/

*Queen Victoria in her later years, after the deaths
of Prince Albert and Sarah Forbes Bonetta.
She wore black for the rest of her life.*

About the Author

TINA ANDREWS is the international award-winning author, screenwriter and playwright who won the Writers Guild of America Award, an NAACP Image Award, and the MIB Prism Award for her 4-hour megahit CBS miniseries, *Sally Hemings An American Scandal*. She also won an NAACP Image Award, and the Memphis Writers Conference Award for her bestselling nonfiction book, *Sally Hemings An American Scandal: The Struggle To Tell The Controversial True Story*. She is also author of the controversial novel *Charlotte Sophia: Myth, Madness and the Moor* about England's first black Queen.

She has written the plays *The Mistress of Monticello, Buckingham, and Coretta* as well as screenplays for the Warner Bros. film *Why Do Fools Fall In Love*, the CBS miniseries *"Jacqueline Bouvier Kennedy Onassis,"* and the Showtime animated series *"Sistas 'n the City."* Her next book is on Dr. Martin Luther King, Jr.

Miss Andrews divides her time between New York City and Los Angeles.

Sarah Forbes Bonetta and husband
James Pinchon LabuloDavies
on their wedding day, 1862

Printed in Great Britain
by Amazon